Buncololi

Illustration by Kantoku

2

Sasaki and Peeps

While I Was Dominating Modern Psychic Battles
with Spells from Another World, a Magical Girl
Picked a Fight with Me
~You Mean I Have to Participate in a Death Game, Too?~

"...Officer, do you know this psychic?"

⟨ Magical Girl ⟩

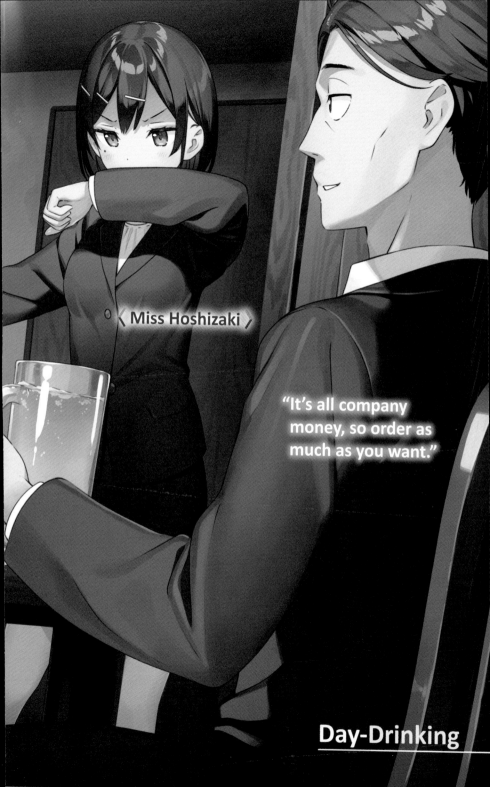

⟨ Lady Elsa ⟩

07/22/20xx
Ranran @natori980102

Good morning.

08/03/20xx
Ranran @natori980102

It's hot today.

08/08/20xx
Sasa Tree @wiQ2fK9p2xHgi4J

Went to the zoo.
Really got rid of my frustration.
Bought a yearly pass since it was cheap.

 3

Ranran @natori980102
Replying to @wiQ2fK9p2xHgi4J
Wait, did you get a girlfriend?

Sasa Tree @wiQ2fK9p2xHgi4J
Replying to @wiQ2fK9p2xHgi4J
I'm embarrassed to say,
but I went on my own...

Ranran @natori980102
Replying to @wiQ2fK9p2xHgi4J
Oh. Sorry, I guess.

08/11/20xx
Ranran @natori980102

It suddenly started raining.

08/17/20xx
Ranran @natori980102

Good morning.

Sasaki and Peeps

While I Was Dominating Modern Psychic Battles with Spells from

Another World, a Magical Girl Picked a Fight with Me

~You Mean I Have to Participate in a Death Game, Too?~

2

Buncololi

Illustration by **Kantoku**

YEN ON

New York

Sasaki and Peeps

2

Buncololi

Illustration by **Kantoku**

Translation by Alice Prowse
Cover art by Kantoku

SASAKITOPICHAN Vol.2 ISEKAI NO MAHO DE GENDAI NO INO BATTLE O MUSOSHITEITARA, MAHOSHOJO NI KENKA O URAREMASHITA ~MASAKA DEATH GAME NIMO SANSENSURUNODESUKA?~
©Buncololi 2021
First published in Japan in 2021 by KADOKAWA CORPORATION, Tokyo.
English translation rights arranged with KADOKAWA CORPORATION, Tokyo through TUTTLE-MORI AGENCY, INC., Tokyo.

English translation © 2022 by Yen Press, LLC

Yen On
150 West 30th Street,
19th Floor
New York, NY 10001

Visit us at yenpress.com
facebook.com/yenpress
twitter.com/yenpress
yenpress.tumblr.com
instagram.com/yenpress

First Yen On Edition:
September 2022
Edited by Yen On Editorial:
Emma McClain, Rachel Mimms
Designed by Yen Press
Design: Andy Swist

Yen On is an imprint of
Yen Press, LLC.

The Yen On name and logo are
trademarks of Yen Press, LLC.

The publisher is not
responsible for websites
(or their content) that are
not owned by the publisher.

Library of Congress Cataloging-in-Publication Data
Names: Buncololi, author. | Kantoku, illustrator. | Prowse, Alice, translator.
Title: Sasaki & Peeps / Buncololi ; illustration by Kantoku ; translation by Alice Prowse.
Other titles: Sasakitopichan. English
Description: First Yen On edition. | New York, NY : Yen On, 2022. | Contents: v. 2. While I was dominating modern psychic battles with spells from another world, a magical girl picked a fight with me -you mean I have to participate in a death game, too?-
Identifiers: LCCN 2022005660 | ISBN 9781975343521 (v. 1 ; trade paperback) | 9781975343545 (v. 2 ; trade paperback)
Subjects: LCGFT: Fantasy fiction. | Humorous fiction. | Light novels.
Classification: LCC PL846.U63 S3713 2022 | DDC 895.6/36—dc23/eng/20220203
LC record available at https://lccn.loc.gov/2022005660

ISBNs: 978-1-9753-4354-5 (paperback)
978-1-9753-4355-2 (ebook)

10 9 8 7 6 5 4 3 2 1

LSC-C

Printed in the United States of America

contents

Frontispiece, Book Illustrations
Kantoku

<The Daily Life of a Middle School Student>

(The Neighbor's POV)

Recently, I've been spending my days without meeting the older man next door.

The reason isn't clear to me; maybe his regular schedule has changed—or the way he does his work. But he's definitely been away from his apartment much more frequently. Maybe he was laid off and has begun working late-night shifts at a construction site.

I don't know. I don't know at all.

But whatever is going on in his world, my life continues without change. I have to go to school at the same time every weekday—in order to eat the school-provided lunch.

"Now, this equation's least common multiple is six, so we can multiply both sides by six to eliminate the denominators. Then we can simplify the left side of the equation by bringing over 'x'…"

But maybe if I was to stay at my front door from morning until evening, I'd be blessed with a chance to see him at least once. Once I start thinking about that, it becomes impossible to concentrate on schoolwork. Whether I like it or not, my attention drifts to the classroom window and beyond, to my building, and finally to the apartment next door to mine.

It doesn't matter very much what I learn anyway. To me, lunch is the only important part of school.

"...Mister..."

Maybe once I'm done eating, I'll fake being sick before lunch ends and head back to my front door, I think, letting the teacher's words pass in one ear and out the other.

Standing at the lectern is a male teacher who must be about forty. He isn't ugly-looking, but he isn't overly attractive, either. I suppose the only thing that pops out about him is the fact that he wears a suit and tie every day. He holds a textbook in one hand while he writes rows of equations on the blackboard with the other.

"Now we'll solve some word problems. The most important thing about word problems is to figure out what is constant. This word problem is asking for how long it will take for the brother to catch up to the sister. The constant here is the distance the siblings have walked, so..."

He's the same gender and age as the man next door. The suit and tie kind of remind me of him, too.

But I don't feel anything for him, further convincing me that *he* is special.

Class passes like that, and eventually, the bell rings to signal the end of fourth period.

The boys who had been fidgeting throughout class raise their voices in excitement, and the classroom comes to life. The students whose turn it is to fetch the food for lunch put on their white aprons and head off to the service room. The others all race to move their desks around, creating islands for our little preset groups.

Lunchtime looks the same today as it does every other day. I follow the other students' lead, pushing my desk up to my neighbors'.

Today's school lunch includes creamed stew and a steamed vegetable salad, with chilled mandarin slices for dessert.

Every day at lunch, the boys practically fall over each other racing for seconds, and the food always runs out. For some reason, though, when a meal includes slices of bread or rolls, there are always leftovers. I don't know how it is at other schools, but in mine, this phenomenon occurs in every grade. Many female students return their trays having eaten only one of their two bread slices and leaving behind the crusts.

And today, our lunch includes bread slices. Seeing it piled on our trays lifts my spirits a little; after all, any leftovers are going to be mine.

About twenty minutes later, the other students finish up their meals, saying good-bye and scattering off into the hallways. Those on meal duty clean up the trays and utensils, then head to the service room with the empty cart to put it away.

During lunchtime, most of my classmates play in the courtyard or gymnasium, while some stay at their seats and chat with friends. Occasionally, one or two read a book on their own.

"……"

Slipping out amid the crowd of rowdy students, I head for the service room, where I would find the returned meal carts.

My school runs its own cafeteria inside the building, and there is a small elevator inside the service room for ferrying the carts from the cafeteria to the other floors.

This process, however, creates a short period of time between when the students return the carts and when the cooks take them back.

For me, that tiny gap is vital for procuring food.

"……"

Making sure nobody else is watching, I sneak into the service room. Seeing all the carts from each classroom inside, I pick one and rush over to it. My aim, naturally, is any serving tray with bread in it. I sift through the plastic wrapping and find what I'm after.

"…Nice."

The bread slices look the same as when I had last seen them, stacked together in a neat pile, untouched. Occasionally, I'd find other food mixed in with them, and it made me want to kill the students on delivery duty. Today, though, they haven't been contaminated as far as I can tell, and there are quite a few pieces left—pristine, lined up nice and neat.

With this, I should be able to get by without my stomach growling for a day or two. I chuckle to myself. This is something I've been doing ever since moving up to middle school whenever there's bread on the menu. I reach for the plastic bag in my skirt pocket and hunch down as I peer into the carts.

At the same time, the door to the service room clatters open.

Startled, I pull my hand back out of my pocket and straighten up. My eyes shift immediately to the source of the sound. My mind starts working at a blinding pace, trying to figure out how to deal with whatever happens next.

I can't let them catch me stealing school meals. I could deal with awkward stares from my classmates, but if they decide to lock the service room from now on, that would be terrible. I intend to keep relying on the school's resources like this until I graduate.

"Kurosu? What are you doing in here?"

"……"

Satou, a boy from my class, appears in the doorway.

He stands out a lot in the classroom and is always the center of attention. Every day, our classmates crowd around him, chatting and having fun. His good looks mean he's popular with the girls, too, not only the boys. For obvious reasons, I've never interacted with him. What's a kid like him doing here?

He's not after my bread, is he?

"Were you looking for something?" he asks.

"…Yes, something like that."

"Oh, then I'll help you out! What are we looking for?"

"……"

Great, I think. *Shouldn't have said that.* I'm looking for leftover bread.

My position in our class hierarchy is pretty low—exemplified by how hard I am trying just to secure food. I don't have any friends I get along with, either. I never have the time—or the money—to go out and do things with people.

Even just talking to classmates who are all about fashion or entertainment is a real struggle. TV shows and online videos are all completely out of reach for me. My only exposure to media is when I read books in the library.

No one wants to talk to someone as boring as I am. In fact, in elementary school, I got bullied over everything I did. And besides, after school, I always spend my time waiting in front of my apartment for the man next door.

"I left my hair clip on my tray, and…"

"I see!"

For a lie I pulled out of thin air, that wasn't bad. I had just said the first thing that came out of my mouth.

The boy comes up and starts fishing through the cart right in front of me. He lifts the dirty silverware and tightly packed trays to check in between them. It seems like he really believes me.

"……"

I have to get rid of him and grab the bread. If we waste too much time, they'll take the carts away. We won't have bread again at lunch for another few days.

I couldn't rely on *him* forever, so I want to get at least three pieces—no, at least five. I had also spotted a few extra milk cartons left by another class that I *really* wanted to get my hands on.

"I noticed you're always by yourself, Kurosu."

"...Is that bad?"

"Oh no—I didn't mean it that way!"

We still have a few minutes until the older ladies in charge of our meals arrive. I have to send him back to the classroom before then.

"I just meant I want to be friends, if that's all right with you," he says.

"You have lots of other friends, don't you? You don't have to bother with me."

"What do you usually do at home? Do you have any hobbies?"

"......"

Satou is talking an awful lot.

He's popular with the girls from every class, not just ours. If anyone sees someone like him talking with a bottom-feeder like me, just the two of us, everyone will hate me. I'd already overheard a few female students talking about girls from other classes behind their backs because of him.

That's yet another reason it's dangerous to be chatting with him now. I would really have preferred not to.

But alas—in the meantime, the door to the service room opens again.

A middle-aged woman in a white apron and a mask comes inside. I've seen her before—she's the cart collector.

Normally, once I'd obtained what I was after, I would watch from a safe distance as she entered the room. I'd certainly never had a conversation with her. Undoubtedly, in her eyes, I'm just one of the many students here. She's probably never thought any more about me.

"Oh? What are the two of you doing in here?"

"I'm sorry," says Satou. "Her hair clip might be lost in here somewhere."

"Oh no. Is that right?"

"Could you let us look for it?"

"Well, I suppose I can bring the others away in the meantime..."

"Thank you!"

Satou does all the talking for me. I'm glad for the extra credibility it gives my lie.

Still, with him right in front of me, I can't reach for the bread. There's no other choice now.

"Satou, could you go check inside my desk in the classroom?" I ask.

"Huh?"

"I think I might have left it in there."

"I mean, I'm not sure I should look in a girl's desk without..."

There isn't really anything in there. Just my school-provided textbooks—and a notebook and some pens and pencils *he'd* given to me. I don't have many personal possessions at home, either. How would he react if I told him I'd never picked up a wallet before? Naturally, there is nothing I wouldn't want him seeing.

If anything, the problem is others seeing Satou fishing around in my desk. If some girl with a crush on him spots it, they'll probably come to me demanding answers.

Still, I can usually just bow my head and apologize to settle things. Since such girls are usually acting on emotion, saying sorry right away would defuse them. As long as I don't say anything sassy, it won't escalate into bullying. At worst, I could always grovel.

The most important thing is the bread. The weather would be turning colder in the coming days; I had to build up some fat.

"...It's okay. Can you do it?"

"Um, sure."

With a meek expression, Satou nods and leaves the service room.

After making sure he's gone, I turn back to the cart. The cart collector is in front of the room's small elevator, pressing its buttons. Since she can only ferry one cart at a time, I have a few minutes before she gets to the last one. That interval is my last chance.

I squat behind the cart to hide my hands from her sight. Taking the plastic bag out of my skirt pocket, I quickly stuff five pieces of bread into it, as planned. This plastic bag is from the man next door—he had once used it to give me some sweet bread. It's opaque, making it perfect for hiding the contents from others. Finally, I use my hands to press down on the top and decrease the volume of the bread.

I appreciate how you can flatten bread to half or less of its original size if you squeeze it. It doesn't taste as good afterward, but it's just as nutritional, so I don't worry about it too much. In fact, it seems to fill me up a little better, since the texture is firmer.

"……"

Everything up until now has been the easy part. Normally, I wouldn't even need a few minutes.

The issue now is bringing the filled plastic bag back into the classroom and getting it into my school bag. Before, there had never been anyone around to notice the plastic bag or ask about it. My skirt pockets could become pretty stuffed, too, and nobody would ever question it. Maintaining that environment is another reason I keep to myself at school.

But Satou is here today, and he has a persistent streak. He'll definitely question me.

I hadn't had a plastic bag at all until a few moments ago; it would stand out. I try putting it in my pocket as a test, but even though I've squeezed the bread down, the five pieces make a very obvious lump. Anyone would be able to tell I'd taken something from the service room.

And if my bread theft is exposed, they'll lock up the room from now on. It would be a disaster for me.

"……"

My mind spins frantically. I still have the woman collecting the carts to worry about. She is making steady progress sending the carts downstairs to the cafeteria, and now she is closing in on the one I am hiding behind. She seems unusually efficient. She barely even glances at the elevator buttons as she pushes them. She must have been working here a long time.

Grabbing the milk cartons from the next class's cart is a hopeless endeavor. I have no choice; I have to give up on it. But I want, at least, to secure the bread.

As I'm rushing through possible solutions in my head, my eyes happen to drift to the window facing outside. Past the glass is a balcony. All the classrooms on this floor are connected by a balcony, and students use it to travel around. The service room is no exception.

And then it hits me. I could hide the plastic bag outside for a little while, then collect it from the balcony.

Aha! A divine revelation!

"…It'll work."

I head over to the window. Best to strike while the iron is hot.

When she hears the clack of the sliding window's crescent lock opening, the lady taking the carts away looks over, but she doesn't say anything to me. If she were a male staff member, she'd have been all over me. I hide the plastic bag with my body, so I'm in the clear.

I stick my head out the window and quickly check for any witnesses.

Good. Nobody's out there. Probably because it has gotten chilly lately. That is great from a food sanitation perspective, too. I lower my haul down from the window. With a rustling sound, the bread-filled bag drops to the corner of the balcony.

I peer down; it just looks like some garbage, blown there by the wind. Nobody would want to investigate it; if I left it, it would probably stay there for months. Wonderful. I doubt I'll have to worry even if someone sees it.

"What's wrong? Looking out the window at something?"

"Ah yes…"

"Did you find what you were looking for? I'd like to send the cart down now."

"Yes, I found it. Thank you."

"Oh? Well, I'm glad."

After mustering the best fake smile I can, I leave the service room behind.

✱

(The Neighbor's POV)

That day, having safely retrieved the bread slices, I start on the road home, feeling satisfied.

I'd managed to get out of afternoon classes by pretending to be sick, so I head straight for my apartment without making any detours. On foot, it's pretty far away—when I first started middle school, it was a bit of a struggle. But after making this commute for several months, I've gotten used to the walk.

Silently, I travel down roads few cars drive on—the sort only locals would know the names of.

I can feel the eyes of people glancing at me as I pass them. I'm a uniformed student, out and about, with the sun still high in the sky. And since this neighborhood is residential, most of them are pensioners or older housewives.

" ...... "

It feels *fresh*, being out like this when I'd normally be at school. It feels liberating. My spirits soar even higher when I think about how I'll sit and wait for the man next door to return, and my steps naturally quicken.

As I approach the halfway point of my commute, something happens. From out of nowhere, someone appears on the road several meters ahead of me.

They hadn't come from behind a building, or fallen out of the sky, or anything like that. The person is literally just *here* all of a sudden. There wasn't even a hint of movement—they showed up just like teleportation.

Also, for some reason, they are lying faceup on the road.

Naturally, at first, I think I'm seeing things. But that doubt vanishes a moment later, when I get a better look at the figure.

Their gut is split wide open, and their ribs are jutting out, as if they'd been pulled apart.

I can't see any organs from the gaping hole in their stomach. I mean, I see *something* in there, but it's very badly damaged. It's like they got mauled and devoured by a wild animal. I can also make out damage to their clothes, like they'd been ripped away.

They seem to be already dead; they aren't moving an inch.

From the neck up is another terrible sight. The whole head is completely misshapen, like someone has taken a chainsaw to it. All that's left is pulp. Still, I can tell from the barely remaining hair and the skirt on the lower body that the remains belong to a woman.

When I see all this, my spirited pace comes to a hard stop. I immediately want to scream, but all I can manage is a squeak. I desperately fight back the heat rising from my stomach to my throat. I can't let my lunch go to waste like that.

A moment later, an older lady near me on the road lets out a shriek. She'd been walking in my direction from the other side of the dead body. Judging by the white plastic bag in her hand and the green onions sticking out of it, she'd been on her way home from the supermarket.

The police arrive soon after that. I don't know who notified them.

Meanwhile, I try to get away as quickly as I can. If some ferocious beast has broken out of a zoo, it'll be too dangerous to stick around. That's certainly what looks like happened to that body. But then the woman who had screamed starts talking to me, and I lose my chance.

It's an ordinary residential street corner.

Patrol cars drive up in swarms, and onlookers begin to gather nearby. The police lay a vinyl sheet over the corpse and string up yellow tape that says KEEP OUT.

A police officer questions me at the scene. Not only do they want to know about the sudden appearance of the body—but they, frowning, also ask why a student like me is walking around during school hours. Once I give them the whole spiel about not feeling well and having been on my way home, however, their attitudes soften.

Because of this, they let me go a little earlier than the woman who had been screaming. She had been declared the first one to discover the body and excitedly explains the whole thing from beginning to end.

Freed from the questioning, I get right back on the road home.

Right before my eyes was an unsolved case, the investigation just getting underway. It's possible the criminal is somewhere nearby. The best course of action for me is to get away from here, fast. The police had told me to go straight home as well.

But just as I'm leaving, I notice something. There are some people moving around the scene in plainclothes, in the midst of all the uniformed officers.

"Another one of these sudden deaths…"

"Same psychic as the last one, you think?"

"Yeah. Not much doubt about that."

Are they detectives? I can't really tell. But I remember reading in a book from the school library once that police officers with certain duties don't wear uniforms on the job. Two of them are now talking in low tones to each other over the corpse.

Both are men who look to be in their twenties. Compared to the rest of the people busily moving around them, they seem extremely young. But every single police officer, without exception, treats the two of them with respect, raising their arms to their heads in stiff salutes and the like. *They must be really important people.*

"We'll probably need to get Miss Hoshizaki out for this one."

"She's so young, but she kind of scares me."

"Hasn't she started teaming up with that Sasaki guy lately?"

"Yeah, he's basically just her water source. I feel bad for him."

"Wait, water source?"

"He can apparently make pretty big icicles."

"Well. That *does* make me feel bad for him..."

I have no idea what they are talking about. But my ears do perk up at one part of their conversation.

Now that I think about it, isn't *Sasaki* the name of the man next door?

Hmm. I'm probably overthinking it. Apparently, *Sasaki* is the most common three-character surname in Japan. Or at least, I remember my social studies teacher saying something like that in class once. And the person they are talking about must have been a fellow police officer. There is no way it could be him.

"......"

I don't want to end up getting scolded by them for eavesdropping, so I do as I've been told and set off again toward home. This is none of my business.

At the time, I couldn't have known that in the very near future, I, too, would become entangled in this string of events.

\<Recruitment, Part One\>

The war between the Kingdom of Herz and the Ohgen Empire had let up for the time being. After spending some leisure time in the other-world, I returned to modern Japan with the help of Peeps's magic. As usual, we ended up in my cheap studio apartment.

Right after hopping across worlds, I got the feeling something was wrong. I had initially planned to spend time in the otherworld equivalent to one or two days here, and as far as I knew, that was what I had done. But when I immediately went to check the time on my laptop, I saw that I was meant to return to the office *the very next day*.

It was always possible our calculations had been off, but time had passed over twice as fast as we had predicted.

"Peeps, what do you think happened?"

"*Hmm...*"

The two of us stared at the clock in the corner of the screen, racking our brains.

I double-checked the time zone, verified that it was connected to the NTP server, and confirmed a few other things, but the display time remained unchanged.

I was struck by the same feeling I got when my alarm clock didn't go off, and I realized, still in bed, that I was already late for work. And on days like that, there was always an important meeting first thing in the morning. That said, it looked like I'd just barely made it this time. I still had one day left. I hadn't gotten any calls from the section chief or other bureau employees, either.

"*It would seem the temporal distortion between worlds is variable.*"

"Should we be glad we noticed this now, rather than later?"

"Yes. If possible, I want to see if there's a pattern."

"I agree."

"I wonder what could be affecting it..."

Starting from now, I'd have to spend some time diligently collecting data when crossing over. A one- or two-day difference was tolerable. But if it was a matter of months or even worse, years, that would be a problem. If it got to the point that time started varying on the geologic scale, the environment could change so drastically I might die the moment I crossed back.

It would be no joke if I returned to find the earth itself on its last legs.

"We should make that our top priority."

"I think we should get a device to keep track of things."

The flow of time between the two worlds probably wasn't fixed—like how days got longer or shorter in the summer or winter. And considering how *incredibly* complex it was to tell time by the movement of the stars, even just approximating the pattern would likely be a huge job. We couldn't afford to do all the work by hand every single time.

"Do you intend to procure one of these laptops?"

"I'll go buy a small one with good battery life."

"If you can find one that can withstand impacts, it would put my mind at ease."

"Yeah, you're definitely right about that."

"It is a wonderful tool. I'm very excited."

The way he spoke while bouncing his body up and down was really cute. It was so sparrow-like it made my heart clench.

Though he could be really adorable, he was also shockingly clever. He already understood the usefulness of computers and the internet after only a few weeks of using them. If he kept adapting to modern life like this, it might not be long before he started programming. In that light, he was a little terrifying.

"I have work starting tomorrow, so I could go right now if you don't mind."

"Yes. Please be careful."

"Thanks, Peeps."

"I'd like the best one you can afford."

"I gotcha."

"*And I hear the ones with a lot of 'memory' are most friendly to use.*"

"No worries. I'll be sure to get one with plenty of memory."

"*And apparently it's best when the, er, see-pee-you is faster, and—*"

"It'll be fine, Peeps. I'll buy a fast, user-friendly one."

"*...Thank you.*"

He *really* looked like he wanted to come with me. Unfortunately, I couldn't bring him. *Sorry, Peeps.*

With the day's plans decided, I headed over to the Akihabara neighborhood to buy a machine for use in the otherworld. I didn't want the extra trouble of hopping worlds every time the charge ran out, so I figured I would buy a big mobile battery along with a solar energy panel.

For the time being, I intended to set it up in that high-class inn and use it as our workstation.

✳

A day after returning to modern Japan, this new government employee returned to the office after a nice, long break.

As for the machine I'd purchased the day before in the city's electronics hub, Peeps and I planned to bring it to the otherworld this very evening. Setting up all the software had taken the better part of the previous evening, so we hadn't yet had the chance to move it.

Come to think of it, the last time I'd installed MATLAB on a computer had been in college. I'd added a bunch of other things as well, so I was sure Peeps would be happy.

They didn't have the internet over there, so installations had to happen in my apartment. Even the great Lord Starsage had said that creating a cross-world access point for the internet was beyond his abilities.

At any rate, I headed into the office—only for Section Chief Akutsu to immediately summon Miss Hoshizaki and me to the conference room.

The room itself was pretty cramped, with only a table surrounded by six chairs. The chief sat on one side, and Miss Hoshizaki and I were on the other, like some kind of three-person interview. He had a laptop on the table in front of him, and its screen was being outputted to a wall-mounted display. On it were several photographs that seemed to have been taken secretly.

The subject was a young man in his teens.

To the side of the photographs was text with various information about him. He was, apparently, a high school student who lived in Saitama prefecture—and quite a few supernatural phenomena had occurred near him, thought to be caused by psychic powers.

After investigating, they'd confirmed he was, in fact, a psychic. At the same time, he seemed to have little to no affiliation with other psychics. The bureau had labeled him a stray and set about taking him into custody.

"So he can create fire? Sounds pretty dangerous," I commented briefly.

"According to our intel, his output is about the same as a miniature flamethrower," the chief replied plainly. "I'd say it's a good match for our water manipulator, Miss Hoshizaki. If she was to make a shield using the water you supplied, that should easily block him."

Miss Hoshizaki responded as if this was a familiar exchange for her. "Yes, it would seem I'm the woman for the job."

"Then get on out there and recruit him."

She always seemed to be raring for a fight. As her partner—all but locked in as her water source at this point—I had a few reservations. Wouldn't it be, you know, better to wait until the safety had been properly assessed? If this kid had the firepower of a flamethrower, he must be incredibly dangerous.

"You sure make it sound easy, don't you, Chief?"

"Did you have a question, Sasaki?"

Section Chief Akutsu had mentioned to me before that we would be recruiting new psychics. Apparently, our first mission involved this pyro kid up on the display. In terms of power matchups, I had no objection to him choosing Miss Hoshizaki. But still, I felt uneasy.

"I was just wondering if we should maybe investigate a little more thoroughly first."

"According to our investigation, he's not a very high-ranking psychic."

"That may be true, but Miss Hoshizaki here is a young woman, remember? What if she was to get burns on her face? Oh, and I've been wondering about this for a while now, but are there any psychic powers that can heal wounds?"

According to the display, the boy's psychic rank was E—the same as mine. Apparently, just being able to produce flames didn't make you a powerful psychic. If that was the case, then why was that little girl in the kimono we ran into on-site last week ranked A? She had some impressive physical abilities, but I didn't think that warranted such a high level of concern. Personally, I thought the hurricane user was way more of a threat.

"Yes, there are powers that can heal physical wounds. That said, they're extremely sought-after. In terms of rank, most of those with practical abilities are at least a B. And I appreciate your concern for Miss Hoshizaki, but if she stays behind, then you will have to go alone."

"You're right, Chief—the strength of us bureau employees is our teamwork."

I felt Miss Hoshizaki's gaze from beside me. "You always seem so serious, Sasaki, but you can be pretty careless, too, huh?"

She'd been raring to go from the very beginning. But she only had her gaze on her intimidated junior for a moment before turning it back to the display and rereading the intel. She was probably confident she could take this guy down, even in a fair fight.

She had such a strong will for a high school girl. And her suit and makeup gave her at least 30 percent more dignity.

"Worst case, I can settle it with a handgun. This won't be that big a job."

"What? Wait, do you mean, er…?"

"I'm leaving the on-site decision-making to Hoshizaki. I want you to support her, Sasaki."

"…Understood."

"Then let's get going, Sasaki!"

With the chief having given his go-ahead, Miss Hoshizaki bolted out of her seat like it was some kind of race. Following her lead, I, too, left the conference room behind.

*

Once we'd left the bureau, we boarded a domestic black sedan, and then it was off to the site. According to the driver, we'd arrive in about an hour and a half.

Aside from the man at the steering wheel, it was just Miss Hoshizaki and me in the car. We were both sitting in the back seat. Given that I was about twenty years her senior, I had a hard time thinking of shared topics of conversation. What naturally came to mind were psychics and their powers.

And now that I had the chance, I decided to ask a bunch of questions that had been bothering me.

"Miss Hoshizaki, could I ask you something about the previous case?"

"What?"

"Do you remember the girl in the kimono?"

"Yeah, what about her?"

"Well, I heard she's pretty famous in the psychic community..."

"Oh, right. We never actually told you about her, did we?"

She seemed to realize what I was trying to ask and launched into a quick, fluid explanation. Apparently, the little girl possessed an extremely powerful psychic ability for one-on-one fights. And despite her young appearance, her actual age was in the triple digits.

Her power, which I'd been wondering about, allowed her to drain energy. She was able to drain something akin to life force from any opponents she touched and make it into her own. Her strikingly youthful appearance and her superhuman physical abilities were both derived from that energy.

Still, she was near the bottom of rank A, very close to B. In which case, how insanely strong were the ones who were in the middle of rank A or even higher? It was frightening to think about.

Adding to that, the leader of the group that the kimono girl and the hurricane guy belonged to was a *real*, genuine rank-A psychic. However, the bureau didn't have any detailed information on their ability yet, and they remained shrouded in mystery.

"There sure are a lot of different types of psychics, aren't there?"

"It's a literal miracle we managed to survive her targeting us and getting close."

"I see."

So that was why she had been smirking back then, I thought, remembering the little girl arrogantly folding her arms across her chest.

"But in group-versus-group situations, things change. In that situation, for example, the telekinetic psychic with her was way more threatening. That's why she waited until things settled down before revealing herself, only showing up after our numbers had thinned. Make sense?"

"It did seem like she took a while to show up."

"The big restriction on her power is that she needs to touch her target directly."

"Don't you have the same restriction, Miss Hoshizaki?"

"I target water, so it doesn't actually make things that difficult."

"I suppose not."

"The reason she's treated as a rank-A psychic is actually because of how long she's lived and how much knowledge, experience, and mental fortitude she has—not her ability. I imagine the best role for her is really as a secret agent or an assassin."

"Can't say I like the sound of that…"

"Actually, she's often cited in connection with such incidents."

"……"

Now that I'd heard what Miss Hoshizaki had to say, I keenly understood that my decision at the time had been the best one possible. The ideal tactic for dealing with the little girl was to shoot her down before she got too close. That made my lightning magic the perfect countermeasure. She'd probably realized that, too, and decided to back off.

"I have no idea why they'd just leave like that, though," she mused.

"Maybe their goal was to put a dent in our combat forces?"

"Doesn't make sense to let me live, then."

"Well, I wouldn't be surprised if they had some kind of reason to keep the bureau around—some kind of ulterior motive. Or perhaps they wanted us to serve as messengers."

"…Yeah."

I didn't want to talk about what happened at the bowling alley any more than this. I was scared of accidentally letting something slip if I did. Miss Hoshizaki was not a very expressive woman, and whenever she stared at me from up close, it felt like she was seeing straight through to my innermost thoughts, and it made me want to tell her everything. Along with the thick makeup she used to conceal her age, I found it kind of eerie.

And so I steered the conversation in another direction. "By the way, it's a weekday. What about school?"

"The bureau is in contact with my school, so taking days off isn't a problem. My plan is to stay employed with them after graduating anyway, and the chief told me they'd let me graduate as long as I still went to school on days I don't have to work."

"I see."

"He also told me they'd get me into a university if I wanted to go that route."

A backdoor school admission? With government support, that was probably an easy task. Maybe the bureau we belonged to had even greater power than I'd assumed. Thinking about that sent a chill down my spine.

"I'm a little surprised at how much they're willing to give," I said.

"If they didn't, they wouldn't be able to secure psychics. It's not just the irregular psychic groups they're contending with. The employment of psychics is a total seller's market, both in Japan and abroad, so if the bureau acted like it didn't care, they'd all get snatched up by some other country."

"Wait, really?"

"It happens even at our bureau. Every year, a few people get pulled away overseas."

"…I didn't know that."

Even in the normal, non-psychic marketplace, and especially when it came to "human resources," Japan lagged behind the rest of the world. *We're probably on the defense constantly when it comes to psychics, too*, I thought.

And that got me thinking. For example, it was possible—likely, even— that the irregular group we'd encountered was backed by a nation antagonistic toward Japan. If so, then it cast their refusal in a different light. We may treat them as irregular, but they were likely a legal organization as far as the other country was concerned.

And wouldn't everyone rather work at a job with better conditions and benefits?

"Getting greedy, are we?"

"No, no. Not at all."

"Well, unlike in other areas, Japan takes great care of its psychics. The chief and the old-timers at the bureau do a lot for us; we get treated just as well as we would in other countries, at least. That's why I can be so positive about my work."

"I see."

Good thing I didn't do anything rash.

∗

After passing the time talking about psychics and their powers, we arrived at our destination. By finding a common topic, I had managed to keep things from getting awkward between this active-duty high school girl and me—that, at least, was something to be happy about. Before getting in the car, I'd been pretty worried about what I'd do with myself during the journey.

"That took longer than I thought," said Miss Hoshizaki.

"That's traffic for you," replied the driver.

According to the materials we'd been provided, this was somewhere in Iruma, in Saitama prefecture. Right after getting out of the car, we heard the roar of an airplane flying overhead. It had probably taken off from the JASDF base here. When I looked up into the bright blue sky to check, I found the plane was quite a bit bigger than I'd expected.

This was my first time visiting the area, so I was shocked to see one flying so low to the ground.

"What's wrong?"

"Nothing. Just surprised the plane was so close to us."

"Right…" Miss Hoshizaki nodded, looking skyward as well.

It was a little before noon, and the sun was high in the sky with not a cloud to be seen. It felt pretty darn good. There were fewer tall buildings than in the middle of Tokyo, too, so you could really get a sense of how huge the sky was. If not for work, this would have been an amazing change of pace for me.

"Let's get moving," prompted Miss Hoshizaki.

"Lead the way."

My senior had showed no reaction to the airplane. Seeing her already moving away, I followed along in her footsteps.

We were headed for the high school right in front of us, across the street. The bureau had sent word of our arrival, and when we got onto the campus, a man calling himself the vice-principal quickly came out to meet us. Our pretext was that we had been dispatched from the central government to observe the educational situation in the suburbs.

Because of that, the man's attitude was incredibly respectful. "I sincerely thank you for coming all the way here," he said. "We, here at this school, put a lot of effort into ensuring student autonomy and have a unique tradition of academic freedom. Giving our students a relaxed environment allows them to…"

High school vice-principals were more or less equivalent to section chiefs in sizable companies. In smaller ones, I supposed they'd be even higher up, like department heads. Having one of them bow so reverently to us... The Cabinet Office title was really something special.

I know it's rude to think this, but man, it feels so good. I'd always wanted to be fawned over like this, just once in my life. All hail state power.

Myself aside—I was almost forty—Miss Hoshizaki was very young. Going on-site together must have made us look like a man who had diligently climbed the ranks through hard work and the young ace who had come in above him. This probably made our story even more persuasive. Her decision to remove her uniform and replace it with a suit had been the right one. And in fact, Miss Hoshizaki had started out as a detective (in name, at least), so this fit her to a tee.

"...and so we put effort into our extracurricular activities as well. In that building over there are the clubrooms, not only for athletics but for the liberal arts. Our goal is to achieve good results at competitions and tournaments, so we encourage all our students to take part in..."

With the vice-principal there to guide us, we looked around the school. Classes were in session, so the halls were quiet and deserted. From time to time, we'd hear students' voices from the sports fields, taking me back over twenty years. I could still remember those days vividly.

What must Miss Hoshizaki have felt like, coming to a place like this? She was a current high schooler.

"...and last year, our school band won the prefectural tournament. And then there's our drama club and computer club. They are creating work incorporating top-of-the-line computers and were able to take the grand prize in one of our local competitions..."

But boy, did this vice-principal ever *talk*. He could probably keep rattling off facts until the sun went down. I had a good mental map of the school's layout by now, so at this point, I wanted to get on with our investigation and secure the psychic.

I gave Miss Hoshizaki a glance, to which she returned a small nod. With my senior's permission, I interrupted the vice-principal's speech. "Thank you for the thorough explanation. We were actually planning to look around the school by ourselves for a while—with your permission, of course. If we were to stay with you, the students and even the faculty may get nervous."

"Huh? Oh, yes, of course. Please, have a look around at your leisure..."

Perhaps because of our government authority, he acceded without complaint. *Time to take him up on his offer and do what we need to do.*

"If you need anything," he continued, "anything at all, please tell me. I'll be in the faculty room, so if you pay me a visit, I will respond immediately. If I'm not there, just call on one of the staff members. I've explained the situation to them."

"Thank you for your kindness."

"Please, it's no trouble at all. Now, if you'll excuse me," he said, giving a respectful bow and disappearing down the hallway.

After watching him go, it was time to start our on-site investigation. First, I confirmed the plan with Miss Hoshizaki—we both wanted to get this job over with and head back to the office before sunset.

"How should we handle this?" I asked.

"Let's look around the school a bit more."

"Did something catch your eye?"

"Just preparing—in case a fight breaks out."

"Understood."

She was being surprisingly proactive. I thought for sure she'd dive right at the kid and bring him in by force. Especially since he was both lower rank and at an elemental disadvantage.

"...And why are you giving me *that* look?" she asked suspiciously.

"No reason. Just thinking that you're a dependable colleague."

"Sasaki, are you making fun of me?"

"Of course not."

After this short back-and-forth, we set off walking through the school.

A little while later, we heard what sounded like students' voices. We'd left the school building by that time and were checking around the campus. After the bell rang to signal the end of classes, we started seeing more students around—to avoid being seen, we'd gone around to the rear of the building.

"The hell is this? Why do you only have five thousand yen?"

"I'm s-sorry..."

The rear of the building housed a few special classrooms, such as the science labs and the home ec rooms. And there, we found several students surrounding another student. The location got little sunlight, and nobody was around—the perfect spot for those up to no good. Fortunately, they didn't seem to have noticed us.

"You're sorry? You totally screwed up our plans."

"B-but I don't get any more allowance than this…"

"Then get it out of your dad's wallet!"

The scene was very easy to understand. It seemed we'd come across bullying in action.

The one being bullied was a timid-looking male student wearing glasses. Around him were the types you'd expect—hair dyed brown, uniforms worn improperly.

These bad boys, and a few girls, were likely high in the school hierarchy. The boy who looked the most prone to nasty behavior was in the process of threatening the kid in glasses. The others watched, smirks on their faces. The boy didn't seem to have any allies.

But if that was all this was about, we wouldn't have paid attention to it. Student issues were the school's problem, and the school's issues were the teachers' problem. Outsiders would do better to keep quiet, and besides, if things went south, it could cause trouble for the section chief.

However, this time we couldn't just let it slip, because the student being bullied was our target—the rank-E psychic who had the power to produce flames.

"Sasaki, let's go."

"No, let's stay back for now."

As we were peeking out from around the corner of the school building, my hot-blooded senior tried to jump right at them. I grabbed her shoulder and advised against it. When I did, she turned around to face me with a slightly frightened expression.

"Why?"

"According to the chief's report, no instances of spontaneous fire have occurred at school. The only confirmed uses of psychic power by the target have been near his house—and always in secret."

"And?"

"Judging from the current monetary transaction, this bullying has almost certainly been a long-term issue for him. It didn't just start in the last few days."

The five-thousand-yen bill passed from the glasses kid's hand to the leader of the delinquent group. The leader snatched it away as though stealing it, then stuffed it into his pants pocket. Despite his complaints, he'd still gotten his hands on the cash.

"If there haven't been any instances of his power going off at school during that time," I continued, "that means the boy has been enduring the bullying for a long while. And if that's the case, I can't recommend intervening now."

"…I get it."

"I suggest that we contact the target when he's alone."

"Gotcha. We'll use your plan, Sasaki."

"Thank you."

Still, I was more than a little worried about what we'd have to do if those kids got violent on our watch. And it was always possible that on this very day, at this very moment, he would make his psychic power high school debut. But once the delinquents got what they had come for, they quickly left the area behind the building.

"Actually," remarked Miss Hoshizaki, "I have a plan of my own."

"What's that?"

"I want you to leave contacting the target and all the negotiations to me."

"…Are you sure?"

"If you're right about this, the negotiations won't be hard. In fact, it would better if someone close in age was to approach him, without an adult along—that should lower his resistance."

"Yes, I believe you're right."

"Once we've finished watching over him, I'll head to the hotel the bureau booked for us. After that, I'll make contact with the target. In the meantime, Sasaki, I want you to put in a report to the chief about the bullying. It wasn't in any of the intel they gave us."

"Sounds good to me."

The delinquent group was walking in the opposite direction from us, so we didn't need to hurry and could watch until the end. Only the boy in glasses remained, looking down at his feet, fists clenched.

The scene was painful to watch.

That was why I wanted to avoid any situations that would damage his pride or self-esteem. Nobody, whether young or old, man or woman, wanted someone else to see them in such a miserable state.

Especially not if he might end up a workplace colleague in the future.

*

After making sure the glasses kid had gone back to his classroom, we withdrew from his school and headed straight for the hotel arranged by the bureau. It had been reserved for lodging in case our job wasn't finished within the day—or for use as a base of operations.

Naturally, it was a reservation for two rooms, one for each of us. Miss Hoshizaki had said she'd be making preparations right here for recruiting the glasses kid into the bureau and to contact her by phone if anything happened. With that, we began our separate operations.

It didn't take long for me to write up the report, so I soon had some free time. Miss Hoshizaki had said I could do whatever I wanted, as long as it was in the neighborhood, until she called me. What a considerate workplace senior! She'd actually said, and I quote, *You can go to a pachinko parlor, a brothel, whatever you want*—a statement that gave me the impression she had a rather difficult home life. I got the feeling I now understood how she viewed middle-aged men.

At any rate, I had a whole lot of free time on my hands.

"…Now what?" I murmured, sitting on the bed in my hotel room without anything to do. If Peeps had been here, we'd have had plenty of options: We could chat, I could help him with a bath, or we could even hop over to the otherworld for a quick visit. But I wasn't able to take him around on the job. Going on an official trip with a birdcage would be suspicious by anyone's standards.

"……"

With nothing else to do, I spaced out for a while.

Having no work in the middle of the day while my coworkers were all doing their own jobs made me helplessly restless. Especially when my partner was a younger woman. Still, I didn't feel right doing as Miss Hoshizaki said and going out to enjoy myself.

After a little while of thinking about it, I eventually decided to go buy Peeps a souvenir. That way, I wouldn't feel guilty about slacking off. My relationship with Peeps deeply influenced the work I did for the bureau. Keeping things happy and pleasant with him was an important part of improving my work performance.

With that array of excuses firmly tucked into my back pocket, I headed out. I ended up wandering to the supermarket near our lodgings. Suburban areas had much bigger stores than those in the middle of the city, and I was excited to visit one. Passing through the enormous parking lot and entering, I walked around the store—lively and filled with people— and found that even without anyone next to me, I was still having fun.

One head of cabbage for ninety-eight yen. Very cheap.

A tomato for sixty-nine yen. That was insanely good.

One bundle of green onions for one hundred yen. I wanted to bring some home with me.

After I glanced around the produce section close to the entrance, I headed up to the second floor.

That was where the home goods, sundries, and toys were sold. Bedding lined one aisle, then in another there were sparkling-new cooking utensils—taking in the rows of products was endlessly entertaining. I imagined myself moving to a new home—and what my life would be like there.

Getting out of my current studio with a kitchen—and the cheap lifestyle that went with it—was like a distant fairy tale before. But now that I'd gained the title of *government employee*, even that seemed within reach. *I bet I could even take out a pretty hefty loan.*

Considering my blessed lifestyle in the otherworld, maybe there was no reason to try to improve my situation here. My profits from the interworld trade were astronomical. Meanwhile, with no way of converting valuables from the otherworld into yen, the cost effectiveness of trying to improve my life here was abysmal.

Still, since I'd been born a Japanese man, I wanted to have my own house here anyway. I wanted to be the king of my very own castle. I'd have a big, detached house and live there with a super-friendly golden retriever. That was my dream.

"……"

After walking around the second floor for a while, I spotted a video arcade. Since it was after school, I saw a lot of kids in there. Most of them were in elementary or middle school. A few women were among them—probably housewives—and some older folks who were likely retirees sat dotted sparsely around the medal game area.

It was the perfect spot for killing time. *How long has it been since I've gone to an arcade?* I thought, drifting over. I didn't have any video games at home, either, so it had been quite a while since I'd had any contact with gaming culture. I stopped at the newest version of a machine that had been getting updates ever since I was a kid. Sitting down, I searched around for my wallet.

As I did that, someone familiar popped up in the corner of my eye.

"Oh..."

It was the flame psychic—the very same one Miss Hoshizaki and I had seen at the high school this afternoon. His bowl cut and black-rimmed glasses were still fresh in my memory. And given he was wearing the school's uniform, there was very little doubt it was him.

A female student, in a uniform from another school, was next to him. Her hairstyle stood out—two braids hanging behind her. She wore glasses like the boy did, hers big and round, which made her come across as rather plain. Her bag was hanging from her hand—they must have been on their way home from school together.

"......"

Was she the glasses kid's girlfriend? Were they on a date in the supermarket arcade?

They seemed so young to me as they walked side by side; the very sight caused this middle-aged man some psychic damage. Naturally, I averted my gaze—or almost did but changed my mind. I couldn't afford to take my eyes off him.

Suppressing the urge to flee the arcade, I focused on the target's movements. Miss Hoshizaki had told me to leave this to her, but where was she, and what was she doing? Was she observing from afar, just like I was?

Yeah, that's a good possibility.

Right then and there, I decided I would track the target as well. *Depending on how the situation plays out, I may even be able to lend her a hand.*

*

After playing a few games in the arcade, the two of them headed up to the food court on the floor above. Now they were gathered around a table eating some delicious-looking crepes.

"......"

Watching them from afar, I treated myself to a parfait.

With plenty of strawberries and chocolate in it, it *should* have been tasty and sweet, but for some reason, I could barely taste it. *I wish Peeps were here at least*, I thought, lonely. I'd nearly bought two out of pure habit.

"...It's...probably, because...that's..."

"...Because of that? ...Right?"

"Yeah... I guess not... Maybe..."

I was observing them, but at a distance, so I couldn't hear most of what they were saying. A lot of other patrons were nearby, too, so things were pretty noisy. The white noise masked their conversation, making it impossible to discern. It had been the same in the arcade.

The boy's face, however, had a smile that just wouldn't go away. And it didn't seem like he was faking it, either. It was a very honest, straightforward expression. So from the corner of my vision, it appeared he was enjoying the exchange.

But his female companion's reactions bothered me.

In contrast to the boy's unending grin, she had a somewhat stern expression. It didn't seem like she disliked what was happening, but I could make out a bit of tension in her expression. Was she nervous about going on a date with him?

"......"

After thinking all this, I began to feel a little miserable. Whether this was part of my job or not, it was pathetic. An old man snooping on two kids on a date? Not a great setup.

They weren't going to wait for me, either. Upon finishing their crepes, they left their seats and walked off, even though the old man stalking them was only halfway through his parfait! So long and farewell to all those strawberries I'd been saving for last.

With an almost panicked haste, I put the half-eaten parfait in the tray return area. Then I trotted after the girl and boy.

They were headed for the front entrance of the store on the ground floor. It seemed their after-school date would be moving from the supermarket to somewhere else.

I'd wanted to buy Peeps a gift from the food area if I could, but this was no time to complain. With reluctance, I followed them out the door.

Still... I must look like total stranger danger from afar right now.

Only the police badge in my inside pocket gave me any comfort.

I recalled the map we'd seen in the car ride to the site from the bureau, then matched it up with where they were headed. I was pretty sure there were a few parks around here. They were probably headed for a park bench, a staple of budget student dates.

If they were going to a hotel, on the other hand, I'd probably break down in tears. Praying it was anything but that, I continued to tail the target.

After a little while, some kids wearing the same school uniform as the boy approached from the opposite direction.

It was the group of delinquents who had been bullying the target at school today. The whole pack of them, too, walking down the street all buddy-buddy. Upon spotting the familiar boy along their path, they started getting rowdier.

I got the feeling the glasses kid was in for some more trouble.

The delinquents immediately walked over to him, crowding around him until they had him surrounded. It wasn't hard to guess what would happen next, judging by the smirks on their faces.

How could I not feel bad for the kid?

"Hey, now, wait up. What's this? You got a girl or something?"

The one who looked like their leader, the same one who had taken that five-thousand-yen bill after all the threats at school, looked absolutely elated as he spoke to the boy with glasses. His eyes went back and forth between the object of his bullying and the girl with the braids standing next to him.

"Actually, she's kinda cute, huh? A little plain, but still."

"......"

He knew what he was talking about. Yes, the girl in glasses was plain, but she was nonetheless cute. Her makeup had that natural look to it; you could barely detect it, but what she did have on really made her features pop. Still, thanks to the bland hairstyle and frumpy glasses, she wouldn't stand out too much at a glance.

Completely the opposite of Miss Hoshizaki, who really piled on the foundation. She always had those long fake eyelashes on, too, and her eyeliner was pretty conspicuous.

"You wanna hang with us, girl? We're in that kid's class, you know. We were gonna go sing some karaoke—I guarantee it'll be a time to remember. Actually, what school's that uniform from? Don't think I've seen it around here. It's real cute, though."

The delinquent leader's attention had shifted from the boy with glasses to the high school girl with braids. The rest of the group did the same.

"See, we've got some girls with us, too, so you'll be fine. How about it?"

The leader's arm reached out for the high school girl with braids.

Right before his fingertips touched the girl's shoulder, the boy with glasses raised his voice and shouted.

"D-don't do that!"

I heard it clearly where I was, hidden behind the corner of a building.

"What? What're you yelling about? You freaked me out."

"She told me she doesn't like that, so I just…"

Visibly trembling, the boy with glasses tried to be assertive.

It was kind of a cool scene for him, actually.

As I was peeking out at their exchange from the shadows, I had to admit, objectively, I felt pretty lame. I was literally just a creeper, wasn't I? I could make all kinds of excuses for it, like this being my job, but it was still painful nonetheless.

It made me want to contact the police, report the bullying, and turn right around and leave.

"There's a place we always go to. Want to come?"

The delinquent leader ignored the glasses boy and took the girl's hand.

A moment later, the girl's other arm had moved.

There was a hollow *clap*, which reverberated all the way to where I stood.

"Ugh…"

"I'd appreciate you not touching me without permission."

The high school girl's palm had connected with the delinquent leader's face.

Everyone else stared at her in shock. Apparently, they hadn't thought she would resort to violence. Still, that surprise was only temporary— the leader wasted no time taking action.

"What the hell was that for, woman?!"

He certainly appeared to have a penchant for domestic violence. He raised his right arm, ready to punch the girl.

When it came to high school students, there was a big physical difference between boys and girls. Plus, his fist was aimed right at her face. She wouldn't be walking away from this unharmed if she took the brunt of all that momentum. The strike could break a tooth or even her nose.

This wasn't good. Even for the middle-aged spy hiding in the shadows, the moment was tense.

But the kid never went through with the punch.

"Stop...stop it!" yelled the glasses kid.

Just then, my psychic power alert went off.

A ball of flames had appeared in front of the boy.

He was most likely trying to protect the girl. *Another scene where he gets to look cool*, I thought. Even after they stole his money and shattered his pride, he hadn't resisted—but now, in order to protect someone, he would use his power. Hot stuff!

Still, that *would* put those from a certain organization that devised countermeasures for supernatural phenomena in a tough spot.

I barely stopped myself from shouting.

With a grunt, the delinquent leader retracted his fist, panicking, then leaned back and out of the way.

Actually, maybe that was a misleading way to describe it. The fireball had been fired upward from down low, scorching past the leader's torso. The kid in the glasses probably didn't intend for the fire to hit him. Even if he hadn't reacted, the brilliantly blazing orb of flames wouldn't have burned anyone.

Being a member of the bureau, though, I sadly had to do something more than just stand around and watch. My most important job was to keep these psychic powers a secret from the public. If I neglected that job now, the chief would be furious.

But I wasn't sure what, exactly, to do. Possibilities flashed through my mind at a dizzying speed.

My worries, however, were only the beginning of the catastrophe that was to follow.

The fireball the boy had shot passed by the delinquent leader's side and rocketed into the air. It was gaining altitude. In a blink, it was dozens of meters up—then hundreds, until it became nothing more than a twinkling pinprick in the sky. If only it had eventually disappeared from sight, lost to who knew where, how wonderful that would have been.

But in a very unfortunate stroke of bad luck, it hit a passing airplane in the sky.

A loud *boom* reverberated down to us, rattling our surroundings—the sound of the fireball blowing one of the plane's wings clean off.

"You're kidding..."

Whose cry that was, I would never know.

The cargo plane, just having taken off from the SDF's base in Iruma, had been shot down by the glasses kid's fireball. Everyone's eyes boggled at the sight of the huge machine rapidly plummeting toward the ground, pumping smoke into the air as it fell.

And if it kept moving along its current course, I got the terrible feeling it was going to fall right where the glasses kid and everyone else were standing. I was well within the impact zone, too, only a dozen or so meters away, peeking out from around a street corner. The shrapnel would be flying straight at me!

This scene of a plane speeding toward the ground spurting fire from its ignited fuel chambers was something I'd seen many times on TV. Now I knew exactly what it felt like to be at ground zero.

Running away was the proper choice in this situation.

I was never here.

If I insisted on that, it would solve everything. The whole incident could be pinned on a stray psychic going out of control.

But that wouldn't work if I, a member of the bureau, had seen it happen. Why hadn't I been able to stop it? Had there been a mistake in the investigation? All sorts of troublesome questions would crop up—and I'd be pressed for answers, most likely.

I couldn't have that happen. It would be a huge blunder that could cost me my position. Because, in concrete terms, a plane like the one hurtling down now cost billions of yen.

If I gave up on the lives of the glasses kid and his schoolmates, I could avoid such a blunder. I could casually go right back to the food court in the supermarket, order another parfait to replace the one I didn't finish, and go back to the hotel at my leisure.

With the target's death, my job would end. Psychic powers would have never been revealed to the public. It was possible to play this crash off as a mechanical failure or something like that. At the very least, that would be what the bureau would do. I'd just have to make my report say whatever the higher-ups wanted it to say.

It was a tempting scenario. If Section Chief Akutsu had been here, he'd probably order me to do just that.

"......"

But I hesitated.

Would I be able to go home after that and face Peeps in the same way? Would I be able to give him a souvenir from my business trip guilt-free and go on a short trip to the otherworld like we always did?

"......"

That would be...difficult.

This middle-aged man wasn't built that tough.

More importantly, if I nurtured my personality in that direction, I'd be ill-suited for the Lord Starsage's partner.

Thank you, Peeps.

It's because of you that I can live proudly from now on.

"Sorry, Peeps. Looks like we'll be spending most of our time in the otherworld for a while."

Good-bye, my life in society. Hello, my life in another world.

"Dammit!" I shouted, bursting into a run.

The next thing I knew, the plummeting plane was right in front of me. Facing it squarely, this newbie magician cast his barrier magic. With the boys and girls trembling in fear behind me, I deployed my honest-to-goodness intermediate spell. After this string of bad luck, at least my incantation had made it in time.

But would this be able to block the whole thing? I was very anxious about that. I longed for someone to cling to.

In spite of myself, I thought of what had happened just a few days ago in the otherworld. I recalled Peeps fighting a person with purple skin, a member of the highly advanced demonfolk race. Seeing it in my mind's eye gave me the willpower to dig in, so as not to lose out to him.

I focused completely on my magic, putting all my determination behind it.

A moment later, a flash of light blinded me.

Then a massive *thud.*

The barrier had gone up in a dome shape around not only me but everyone else present as well. The plane must have crashed into one side of it. The flaming cockpit flew right up to me. The pilot had evidently ejected from the plane, since it was empty.

Counting that as a blessing, I took the collision head-on.

As I did, a blast wind ripped through, blowing flames everywhere.

The blindingly bright flash and the impact that hit at the same time whipped up the entire area around us like a dust storm. I couldn't help but flinch at the grating, roaring noises. I immediately shut my eyes and tensed.

Even so, nothing came flying in—no shrapnel or flames.

It looked like my intermediate magic had pulled through.

For a few seconds, my eyes stayed closed out of sheer terror.

Then, opening them again, I glanced around frantically.

What I saw was the plane, engulfed in flames and crashed into the ground, and us, standing in the middle of it, perfectly safe. My Peeps-certified barrier spell had absorbed both the hit from the crashing plane and the explosion that followed, and it managed to save everyone inside it.

However, everything outside the barrier was on fire. The plane hadn't been in the air very long after taking off, so it was still loaded to the brim with fuel. It was bursting all around us, creating incredible firestorms.

"Sa...Sasaki?!"

And then, suddenly and unexpectedly, my name was called. It was a pretty common last name, so I thought at first they were calling someone else.

But I also recognized the voice.

"...Is that you, Miss Hoshizaki?"

"What the hell are you doing here, Sasaki?!"

The voice was coming from the high school girl with the braids.

She'd been the one on the date with the glasses kid up until now, although she'd used a gentler, more refined tone of voice with him. And her conversation with the boy had been just what I'd expect from a high school girl. The kind of voice I would expect, for example, from a girl who always had her nose in a book.

Now, for some reason, her eyebrows were raised, and she was calling a middle-aged man by his last name with no *Mr.*

That was probably the reason I was able to tell right away that this high school girl in front of me was, in fact, Miss Hoshizaki.

"Isn't that my line?" I muttered.

"And what is all this...?"

She was gazing at the invisible wall covering all of us.

It was my intermediate spell. It had isolated us from the burning plane as it crashed. Otherwise, we would all be flat as pancakes from the impact by now. And with the raging flames crackling just outside, we would have been burned to a crisp as well.

The wrecked airplane and its surroundings were still fiercely ablaze. But we were nonetheless unharmed, thanks to the bowl-shaped barrier creating a safe zone. The invisible wall was blocking all the flames from getting in, as if we had been carefully cut out from the rest of the scene.

"...Is this your power, Sasaki?"

"I, uh, no, I have no idea..."

How do I answer this? I can't think of a good response. I'll just pretend to be surprised for now.

Naturally, Miss Hoshizaki's gaze was suspicious.

"......"

I had no way of knowing my workplace senior would get dressed up in her uniform and pretend to be a high school girl to get close to our target. Or maybe that wasn't the most apt description—she *was* currently a high school girl. Still, she looked completely different right now, and I wasn't sure what to say—she just seemed so convincingly normal. The power of makeup was truly terrifying.

"You ordered me to stand by, but I was observing him, too. Eventually, I saw him use his power and shoot down the plane. I couldn't exactly leave you all here, so I rushed in, and... Well, this happened."

"You were tailing us?"

"I suppose that's how it's turned out. But I had no idea the student with him was you, Miss Hoshizaki. I know you said you had a plan, but I had no idea you'd put on such a cute disguise..."

"O-oh, shut up. I thought this would work for sure!"

What now? How do I tell her? The secret of this translucent bowl enclosing us... *And when it comes down to it, I'm still scared of losing my life in society, Peeps.*

"Well, whatever. For now, we should concentrate on covering all this up."

"Covering it up? How will we do that?"

Right next to us sat the glasses kid and all the bullies, collapsed to

the ground in terror. We couldn't exactly make it so a massive disaster like this never happened. And the boy was the one at the center of it all.

"Give me some water. As much as you can."

"All right."

I produced some icicles. At this point, it might have been faster just to use my hose magic for the water. But I held off on that, instead supplying her with icicles like last time. There was still a possibility, however slim, of placing the blame for the barrier spell on another psychic.

I created several human-size icicles and lined them up in front of her. Miss Hoshizaki touched them, converting them into liquid.

"You're not thinking of trying to extinguish the flames, are you? It's jet fuel—"

"Didn't I just say we were covering this up?"

The mass of water floated into the air, reaching out like tentacles, heading for the boys and girls there with us. And then, in a surprising twist, it engulfed their bodies. Naturally, they couldn't breathe in there. Though they desperately writhed and struggled, they couldn't get out.

After a minute or two, everyone, the glasses kid included, passed out.

"...That should about do it," murmured Miss Hoshizaki, pulling the water away from the children's bodies. They all crumpled to the ground, unconscious and still.

She'd done it all without even batting an eye. What a frightful high school girl. *They weren't going to die from that, were they?* Wait, no. If their respiratory tracts were freed after passing out, maybe they'd be all right. Still, that was a rather reckless way of handling the situation. One false step, and who knows what would have happened?

"You seem pretty used to this," I commented.

"Got a problem with it?"

"No, no, not at all..."

"By the way, it doesn't seem like anyone's approaching, does it?"

"...What do you mean?"

"This barrier thing—if it's the power of another psychic, I would have expected them to approach us by now. With a power that can create a shield this strong, they'd probably be at least rank C."

"When you say it like that, it sounds like maybe you know of someone, Miss Hoshizaki...," I started, trying to misdirect her at all costs. I needed to save what I could of my social life.

But not far into my excuse, she interrupted me.

"Sasaki, you're not...a magical girl, are you?"

"Excuse me?"

I wasn't even sure how to begin with that one. Why in the heck would she think I was a magical girl? Did she forget about the second word in that term being *girl*? I was a washed-up middle-aged man, no matter what angle you looked at me from. I never thought the day would come when my very identity would be questioned like this.

If she'd demanded if I was a magical middle-aged man, my heart would have skipped a beat. Because that couldn't have been more correct. In fact, my magical sparrow was waiting for me at home.

"Miss Hoshizaki, you're not suffering from oxygen deprivation, are you?"

"But every single one of the magical girls known throughout the world has been a girl..."

"......"

Well, yeah. If that wasn't the case, we'd have a problem.

Maybe it referred to a specific power within the psychic framework that existed in this world. For example, maybe there was a power known as "magical girl." In which case, I guess I could understand her remark. Sort of.

And now I am, once again, the only one out of the loop. I needed to verify this—in order to lie about the barrier magic, too.

"Miss Hoshizaki, would you mind explaining magical girls to me?"

"You *really* don't know what they are?" she asked, eyeing me closely.

She wasn't wearing much in the way of foundation or powder right now, in a complete reversal from her usual thick makeup. As a result, she actually looked like a teenage girl for once. Subjected to this level of attention from a completely alien age group, I naturally tensed up.

When a young girl looks at me like that, this old man's heart can't help racing.

"Is it like those cartoons meant for children?"

"...All right." After we stared at each other for a while, she nodded. Had I convinced her? I couldn't tell.

Whatever the case, we didn't have time for a lengthy lecture. The flames were still bright and burning all around us. And we were starting to hear emergency vehicle sirens in the distance. I needed to do something about the flames right away, then clean up the barrier spell.

The pedestrians who had scattered away from the explosion when it had occurred were steadily coming back to rubberneck. Judging from what I could see through the flames, they were a few dozen meters away, many with their phone cameras out.

Beyond the simple fact of distance, we were surrounded by plane wreckage, flames, and smoke, so I doubted we would show up in any pictures or videos. At least, that's what I wanted to think. That was why we had to get out of here as soon as we could and hide ourselves.

"There are seven magical girls in the world—children who have acquired strange magical powers. They can cause inexplicable phenomena, too, but are bound by a different logic than psychics. One of them is Japanese, and she's been going around killing psychics."

"Huh…?"

Yet another incredible story. I found myself as curious about her backstory as I had been about Peeps.

"I'm sure you have plenty of questions, but can they wait until after this? For now, we have to do something about this barrier. If pictures or videos go up on the internet, things will get dicey. I want to avoid a pay cut at all costs."

"I see." A respectable viewpoint, indeed. If my bonus ever got lowered, my motivation to work would plummet with it.

But how could I resolve this? Letting down the barrier spell without a plan would mean certain doom for us. Plus, we had unconscious children right next to us to consider. I doubted we'd be able to carry them out without drawing attention.

But then, as I was thinking, something happened.

All of a sudden, the entire area was engulfed in a brilliant light.

I could see the atmosphere outside the barrier shaking. It felt like the spell Peeps had fired in the otherworld a few days before—the one that had sent the entire Ohgen Empire contingent to its grave in one shot.

"It couldn't be… The magical girl?!"

"Huh?"

Miss Hoshizaki had said *magical girl* again. Together, we strained desperately to see what was happening.

A few seconds later, our surroundings began to change.

As the roaring died down, the light outside the barrier faded. The flames that had been burning just seconds before had been quelled, blown out by the beam-like light. Plus, the airplane wreckage was totally gone as well, vanished into thin air.

The only ones around were those of us still protected by the barrier spell.

"Ugh, I knew it...," said Miss Hoshizaki bitterly.

She was gazing out at a single figure—someone, as it happened, I was familiar with.

"You're..."

Her clothes looked like cosplay, with plenty of cute frills. But they were covered in stains and tears, with some places unraveling. Holding together her pink hair, slicked with grease, were a pair of rabbit-shaped hair clips.

In one hand, she had a white plastic bag she'd gotten from somewhere, bursting at the seams. It looked like there was quite a bit in there. I caught a glimpse from its opening... What was that? A yam? *Yams grated over rice is simply delicious.*

In other words, her appearance was extremely distinctive.

So there was no doubting what my eyes told me. She was the homeless kid who called herself a magical girl. And with her staff in one hand, she was looking at me.

"Miss Hoshizaki, wait, you mean to say that she's a magical girl—?"

"Sasaki, we need to run."

"Huh?"

"Magical girls are powerful. We'd need several rank-B psychics to take her down—or the assistance of an A rank. Even with your support, I can't hold a candle to her as I am now. Lasting even a minute or two would be a miracle."

"But wait..."

She was going on and on, rattling off her words. Her expression as she did so was unusually serious. It reminded me of what I'd glimpsed from her last week at the bowling alley.

As a result, I realized that this young homeless girl I'd encountered in my neighborhood wasn't dressed like that for show. I didn't have a clue about the particulars, but it seemed magical girls actually existed, just like psychics.

"...Officer?" she murmured—she seemed to have noticed me, too.

"Sasaki, wait, do you know her?"

"I ran into her fishing around for scraps of food near my apartment and chatted. I had no idea she was related to psychics at the time, so I showed her my police badge and asked if she wanted to go to a police box."

"Then maybe this Magical Barrier was to save you, Sasaki."

"When you say *Magical Barrier*..."

"It's one of a magical girl's abilities. They fly with Magical Flight, shoot rays of light with Magical Beam, and put up shields with Magical Barrier. Your average psychic can't do a thing about them—magical girls are superior in both offense and defense."

"I see."

How many times had Miss Hoshizaki just said *magical*? It was all so very magical.

Maybe the magic that had driven off the flames just now had been Magical Beam, then. If that was true, then the girl had attacked us with the clear intent to kill. Miss Hoshizaki was misreading the situation, but thinking about it that way, it was pretty frightening.

"Each of the seven magical girls also has their own unique power. It differentiates them from one another and has been deemed dangerous enough to require the mobilization of rank-A psychics."

"Are they different from psychics?"

"Yes, they are. Magical girls are supernatural existences with a different set of rules than the ones psychics use. Although psychics have existed for some time, magical girls have only started appearing recently."

"I think I get it."

Another world, psychics, and magical girls... There was a lot more variety in the universe than I had thought. I felt like my worldview had rapidly expanded after I quit my job as a corporate drone. I was a little afraid even more things might emerge if I took the time to look.

"The magical girl active in Japan is always hidden inside her Magical Field, so we can't lay a hand on her. She, on the other hand, shows up wherever she wants and wreaks havoc. She hates psychics and goes around hunting them."

"You did mention that before. Sounds awfully unpleasant."

"I don't know how it is in other countries, but Japan's magical girl is the enemy of all psychics."

"Is that right?"

"Yes. As soon as she finds one, she'll attack without question—"

Meanwhile, as Miss Hoshizaki was speaking, the girl moved.

Her body floated up into the air and approached us.

It didn't seem much different from the flight magic I'd learned from Peeps. I wondered how fast she could move around in the air. Now wasn't the time for that, though. According to Miss Hoshizaki, she was an extremely capable killer of psychics.

"Officer, are you a psychic?" she asked, looking into my eyes, her face like an emotionless mask. Those cute features definitely belonged to the girl I'd run into near my apartment.

But what would be the best thing to say here? As before, the barrier magic was still up. Since it had turned the magical girl's beam away, she probably thought it was some sort of psychic power. Meanwhile, Miss Hoshizaki seemed to think she'd been protecting me with it.

In the distance, I could see rubberneckers, too, so we had to be careful with all this psychic power, magical girl stuff. Which made this a very difficult situation to act in. Still, thanks to her Magical Beam, the existence of my barrier magic remained hidden from the public for now.

This barrier spell was colorless and transparent. Without the flames licking around it, it would be tough to notice it at all. Now that the plane's wreckage and the smoke were gone, nobody would spot it from a distance. Considering that, her attack had been a stroke of unexpected luck. It meant, at least, that Chief Akutsu would have one less thing to scold us about.

After steeling my nerves, I decided to talk to her. "Um, what are you doing here—?"

"I saw a ball of fire in the sky," the girl interrupted.

"Ball of fire? Are you sure you weren't just seeing things?"

Miss Hoshizaki was terrified, so I would have to handle this. If I left it to someone like her, we'd most likely end up fighting it out.

"You blocked my beam. There must be at least two psychics here."

"Psychics...? What do you have to do with them?"

"I will kill all psychics. I won't let them escape."

"......"

My senior was right. She'd actually come for our heads, hadn't she? Seeing such a young girl speak so dispassionately felt like something out of a horror film. If my barrier spell hadn't blocked that beam earlier, what would have happened?

"Do you live around here?"

"There's a big store nearby. They throw away a lot of food, so I come here sometimes. But today, when I was looking for food, I saw flames shoot into the sky and hit a plane."

"I see."

It seemed this neighborhood was her territory. Going by what Miss Hoshizaki had said, she was usually inside a strange space called a Magical Field. The people from the bureau probably couldn't get a handle on where she was or what she was doing. She could have been going to every shopping market and convenience store in the country for all we knew. Were the other six magical girls like her?

"Officer, are you a psychic?"

"......"

It was that same question again, from the psychic murder machine.

If I said yes, she'd fire another Magical Beam at us. She hadn't hesitated with the first one. I didn't know why she was after psychics, but her intent to kill them was palpable.

And even more worryingly, she didn't seem to care who saw her.

"You gave me cake. Was it to trick me?"

"No, I'd never do something like that."

"Then what are you doing here, Officer?" she asked, her magic stick at the ready. At a glance, the thing looked like something you'd find in a toy store. It was pretty well-made, and you could see work put into the details, too. It was both cute and cool at the same time. That said, like her clothes, it was dirty in a few places.

And the magic that came out of it was devastatingly lethal. That much we understood properly.

If I was to face her head-on, what would happen?

I could deal with her Magical Flight with the flight magic I'd learned the other day. My barrier had stopped her Magical Beam. Her Magical Barrier was still an unknown, though; it would probably force me to respond with lightning magic.

If my attack could pierce her barrier, that would decide the match. If it didn't, we'd be at a standstill—neither of us able to deal the finishing blow. On the other hand, if she ramped up her Magical Beam's output, and it cracked through my barrier spell, I'd lose for certain.

I really didn't want to have to dodge her Magical Beams with flight magic. Flying always gave me horrible motion sickness. Virtual reality headsets couldn't hold a candle to the real thing.

Considering what Count Müller and Prince Adonis had thought of me, this girl had the specs to be considered a talented magician even in the otherworld. Miss Hoshizaki was right to be so scared of these magical girls.

Plus, the girl had one extra unique Magical ability that we still hadn't seen yet. That lined up with her being equal to a rank-A psychic rather than a rank B. I really wished someone had told me about this during training.

"Officer?"

"It's an officer's duty to come running when there's trouble."

"Officer, do you know what psychics are?"

She *really* didn't want to let the subject of psychics go. Her repeated questions made that clear enough.

If I answered honestly, the glasses kid and Miss Hoshizaki were probably doomed. They wouldn't stand a chance against this girl. Once she knew their faces and affiliation, she'd soon ambush them from within her Magical Field and take them out with her Magical Beam.

Thinking about it like that made these magical girls all the more horrifying. Despite her adorable face, she was an assassin, a killer— she had a penchant for the underhanded and immoral. Which was why I wanted to keep the situation from worsening at all costs.

"Psychics? I heard you say that before, but…"

I was keeping my responses vague, stalling for time while I thought about what to do. If I could manage to get this girl alone, away from the glasses kid and Miss Hoshizaki, I might have a chance.

But just as I began to take action, something happened.

"My, what is this? A magical girl has come out to play?"

From behind the magical girl came a voice addressing us.

Clacking footsteps approached—it was a figure I recognized.

"……"

The first thing I saw was the kimono, made of a deep-purple cloth. With her sleek, waist-length black hair swaying, she continued to walk, *geta* clapping along on the ground. Her imposing mannerisms were no different than when I'd met her at the bowling alley in the suburbs.

The kimono girl. What was her name, again?

As I was wondering this, Miss Hoshizaki cried out, "Futarishizuka!"

Apparently, her name was Futarishizuka. Probably.

She was the rank-A psychic belonging to that group of irregulars. Miss Hoshizaki had explained to me that she could drain some sort of energy from anyone she touched and make it her own. Despite having the appearance of an elementary schooler, she had superhuman physical abilities.

"Her name is Futarishizuka?" I asked.

"Yes, that's right," responded Miss Hoshizaki.

"Another odd name…"

"It's not her real name."

"Oh?"

"We call her that because of the color of kimono she likes to wear."

"I see."

Apparently, the name came from her choice of clothes; *futarishizuka* referred both to a flower and a deep shade of purple—the same purple as her kimono. I wondered—if she had preferred to wear a purplish-pink kimono the color of the *hagi* flower, would she have been called Haggy or something? Being called by an alias on the field felt so…*psychic*. I found it a little thrilling.

If I tried hard enough at my job, would I get a nickname, too? *Makes me want to get some nice clothing in a cool-sounding color for if and when that happens.*

"Having trouble?" she asked. "I could help, you know."

But she wasn't looking at Miss Hoshizaki—she was looking at me. She posed her question to me directly, with an evil smirk on her face.

I suspected her remark had something to do with the lightning spell I'd revealed the last time we met. Normally, psychics could only use one power. And Miss Hoshizaki's eyes were on me as a member of the bureau. It was probably this situation she was alluding to.

This girl named Futarishizuka had realized I was hiding something, something that I didn't want Miss Hoshizaki or anyone from the bureau to know about. That was why she was grinning; I was sure of it—and why she had made such an offer.

But why would she be offering to *help*?

"...Are you a psychic?" asked the homeless magical girl in the meantime, her reaction evident. She had spun away from Miss Hoshizaki and me and pointed her staff at the girl in the kimono.

"If I said yes, what would you do, child?"

"Kill you."

The magical girl moved immediately. She held her staff aloft and fired her Magical Beam, showing no hesitation.

As we looked on, a burst of light engulfed the kimono girl. The attack shook the very air around us.

Due to the plane crash, no one remained in the affected area—they were all watching from afar. As a result, no bystanders were caught up in the blast. That is, except the kimono girl, who had been swallowed up in the light.

My heart was pounding as I watched it happen.

The Magical Beam roared for a few seconds, then quickly faded.

"......"

Now there was no one standing before the magical girl. Only a stretch of asphalt remained. No cars were coming, either; they were probably being directed elsewhere.

But then, from right next to me, I heard a voice.

"Hnggohh..."

"?!"

I quickly looked over to see the kimono girl.

She seemed to have crashed into the invisible wall created by my barrier spell; her hands were over her face as she rolled on the ground. Apparently, she'd zoomed right toward us with her incredible physical abilities to avoid the Magical Beam.

But she didn't seem to have completely avoided it, and part of the hem of her kimono had been scorched.

"What...is this?" she muttered. "Something's here."

"Ugh..."

At the kimono girl's unexpected approach, Miss Hoshizaki made a move. She ran toward Futarishizuka, and using the water she'd knocked the kids out with, she created several sharp icicles. To her, both the homeless magical girl and the girl in the kimono were equally hostile.

And while the barrier prevented anything from getting inside, you could simply walk out of it. Without giving me a chance to stop her, Miss Hoshizaki darted toward the kimono girl and closed in on her outside the barrier.

"Coming all the way out here? You're making this easy for me."

Miss Hoshizaki grunted as the icicles she fired went straight into Futarishizuka's gut. Her opponent, however, approached without stopping—a choice probably made with her incredible regenerative power in mind.

"Why, you…"

Miss Hoshizaki, meanwhile, began spitting. She hurled her saliva, and in the blink of an eye, froze it and shoved it through the girl's eyeball from point-blank range.

"Guhhh…"

"Sasaki, get out of here—"

In a rare streak of maternal instinct, Hoshizaki ordered me, her junior, to withdraw.

A moment later, Futarishizuka's fingertips touched her forehead.

This was probably her energy-draining technique. No sooner had Miss Hoshizaki said my name than she was crumpling to the ground. I'd witnessed the same sight last time. The effect happened so quickly I couldn't help but feel uneasy.

"Miss Hoshizaki!"

The high school girl fell to the asphalt with a dull *plop*. After sparing a glance at her face, the kimono girl said in a detached voice, "Do not worry. She has only lost consciousness."

Upon closer inspection, I could see her chest moving up and down. She was breathing.

"Otherwise, you'd be in trouble, right?"

"…I see."

It seemed she'd done this out of consideration for my position—to help me avoid the eyes of the bureau, that is. I hadn't expected her to go to such trouble to set me up.

"Why do all this?" I asked.

"I had a favor to ask of you, actually."

"A favor?"

"That is correct."

"…Were you watching us?"

"I was, indeed."

"......"

That was another surprise. I hadn't noticed her at all.

This girl seemed just as much an assassin as the magical girl did. How long had she been watching us? If she'd witnessed anything going on in my apartment, she could have even learned about Peeps.

Meanwhile, the homeless magical girl was reacting to our conversation. With her magic stick still at the ready, she spun back to face me. Her expression seemed just a bit tenser than before.

"...Officer, do you know this psychic?" she asked, giving me a pointed glare. She must have deemed me an enemy.

At this point, I had no time to talk to Futarishizuka. The request she mentioned made me curious, but I had to focus on surviving first. If I wanted to live to see another day, if I wanted to save Miss Hoshizaki and the glasses kid, I had only one choice.

"Understood. For now, let's work together."

"Well received," responded Futarishizuka simply, a smile crossing her face.

A moment later, a Magical Beam struck.

By some unknown logic, she had narrowed the beam as she aimed at us. Apparently, its thickness could be freely manipulated. Perhaps it was a feature used to avoid collateral damage. If I could only learn more about her background, I might have a better idea. I might even find out the reason she was fishing around for yams in supermarket dumpsters.

"I'll support you and act as a decoy. Find a blind spot and try to close in."

"Indeed. Leave it to me."

I wasn't too keen on my role, but considering our powers, this was the best formation. I wasn't sure if my lightning magic would be effective, so it seemed a safer bet to rely instead on someone who could win simply by touching her opponent.

And besides, my attack was pretty gruesome.

If possible, I really didn't want to end up seeing a little girl with part of her body gouged out. We'd only exchanged words a few times, but she was an acquaintance now, which made it even worse.

"However, I would like you to refrain from killing her."

"Oh, are you familiar with this magical girl, child?"

Futarishizuka was using the term *magical girl* casually, too. Apparently, it was pretty common knowledge among psychics. They must be natural enemies—like a cat or a weasel is to a mouse.

"Something like that."

"...Hmm. Well, I suppose I don't mind."

With a brief nod, she kicked off the ground and dashed away.

After she was gone, I set my own plan into motion. I rose into the air with a flight spell. However, with so many people watching, I kept my altitude to just a few centimeters. Then, almost as though I was running along the ground, I moved my whole body toward my opponent. If someone had been watching from closer up, it would have looked very silly.

"Tck..."

The magical girl's eyes widened as she noticed my unexpected approach. From the tip of the staff in her hand, she unleashed a Magical Beam.

In response, this magical middle-aged man cast his barrier spell.

Even with one successful defense under my belt, I couldn't help swerving out of the way. It was still freaking scary. When I did, the beam struck the edge of my barrier and fizzled out. Seemed like that wouldn't be a problem.

On the other hand, if not for the flight and barrier magic, her attack would have killed me instantly. How terrifying. My decision to prioritize these two spells had really saved me.

Thanks, Peeps. I'll bring you a whole lot of delicious meat as a souvenir when I come home.

"So you were a psychic after all, huh, Officer?"

"No, I'm not."

"Then what was that?"

"It was magic."

"...Magic?"

"Like you, I'm a magical gi—a magical middle-aged man."

I genuinely did not want to fight. The term *magical middle-aged man* didn't exactly roll off the tongue, but that was offset by the sincerity behind it. *That's how I choose to think about it, at least.*

"......"

Still, it kind of stung how she clammed up like that. Really hit me right in the heart.

I was glad I was wearing a suit. I felt fortunate that I had my tie on properly, thankful that I'd worn my leather shoes. If I'd been in some jeans, a collarless shirt, and sneakers, this scene would have been too painful to watch.

But because I was wearing a suit, I could just barely work up the guts to call myself a magical middle-aged man.

Or maybe I was wrong, and this had all backfired.

But the girl's reaction was far bigger than I had predicted. I readied myself for another Magical Beam any moment, but the homeless magical girl just stood there, shocked, and repeated the awkward phrasing I'd just given her: "Magical...middle-aged man?"

"Psychics can only use one power. If you can fly, that's all you can do. If you can make an invisible wall, that's it. But magical middle-aged men are different. We're the same as magical girls. We can cause all sorts of strange things to happen, just like you."

"......"

This was such a terrible conversation. I actively felt like I was plotting to kidnap a child.

But I wasn't lying at all. It *was* magical power that Peeps had given me. It *was* magic that he'd taught me. There was some question as to the various sources of our powers, but Peeps had explained that the mysterious spells I could cast were magic. So I wasn't lying.

I found her next response a little odd.

"Then did the fairies ask for your help, too—?"

"Got you!"

A moment later, Futarishizuka was behind the magical girl. She reached out to touch the girl's skin. The energy drain was coming—and she was so close now that the girl couldn't possibly dodge it.

"Go away."

"Urgh..."

But she couldn't land a decisive blow. A moment before touching the magical girl, Futarishizuka was repelled by something invisible—probably the Magical Barrier that Miss Hoshizaki had mentioned. The kimono girl even went in a second time, aiming for the face, and was knocked to the ground.

They called her a rank-A psychic, but looking at her like this, she was kind of cute. Having to touch her target directly must be a huge nuisance when they had barrier magic or anything similar.

To be specific, she had gotten a massive nosebleed. Her cute face was bright red, and the color was staining her kimono, too.

Which meant it was time to pull out the lightning magic, but I hesitated to fire a spell at the girl that would unquestionably rip her body to shreds. I'd seen what it could do back at the bowling alley. If I could get by without using it, I would rather not.

That was why I had put my hope in Futarishizuka.

"Officer, why are you with these psychics?"

"Well, now that's a good question…"

The magical girl's interest had turned to me. That was a good sign. The best solution would be to resolve this through negotiation.

In the meantime, Ms. Futarishizuka was still going at it against the Magical Barrier surrounding the girl; it looked like she was doing pantomime. She tried punching it, scraping against it… *Ah, that'll never work.*

This was a huge shift from her previous attitude. Now she was a sorry sight, and it was adorable. She had seemed so incredible in our last encounter that she appeared even clumsier now, in comparison.

"……"

The magical girl kept staring at me, waiting for me to continue.

I, the magical middle-aged man, watched her in turn. Then something occurred to me—the curious phrase that had fallen from her lips.

Then did the fairies ask for your help, too—?

The two especially important words there were *fairies* and *help*. This seemed like information that would aid my understanding of what magical girls were. It seemed certain, at least, that some sort of creature calling itself a *fairy* was backing her, like a sponsor. Just a month before, I would have laughed at how ridiculous that sounded.

"Where is the fairy who spoke to you?" I asked.

"They're not around anymore."

"Did they go home to the fairy kingdom?" I offered, making up a country I wasn't sure existed out of whole cloth.

Her answer was plain. "I killed them."

"Huh…?"

"I killed them. This is their fur," she said, pointing to the stole around her neck. At first glance, it looked like it had belonged to a weasel or something along those lines.

"......"

Wow, I thought. *That is some excellent tanning work for someone her age.*

At first, I'd planned to act like I understood her situation in order to get closer to her. But her answer was a little more violent than I'd been expecting. The scent of blood was thick on this girl—at least as much as on Miss Hoshizaki.

And as she held up the fur for me to see, I could tell that it, too, was covered in oil, dirt, and grime, just like her clothes; the hair itself was standing on end. It didn't come off so much as a fashionable feminine accessory as it did a handmade pelt worn by a hunter for protection.

In any case, it was definitely *handmade.*

"You...killed them? Why would you...?"

"I didn't want to become a magical girl."

"......"

"So I killed them."

"...I see."

A very logical statement. I could appreciate that, at least.

I had intended to lie and introduce Peeps as my fairy; that way, we'd have something in common. I was going to suggest we could work together as fellow magicians with fairy friends.

Unfortunately, she'd probably fire a Magical Beam at us then and there. Mainly at Peeps. In spite of myself, a scene flashed through my mind of him flapping, trying to get away, feathers flying everywhere.

I felt like negotiations between us had ground to a halt. I missed how easy it was with everyone in the otherworld. Memories of pleasant, warm conversations with Vice Manager Marc, Count Müller, and Prince Adonis came to mind—only for them to be swallowed up by the presence of this magical girl in front of me. I missed the amazing food Mr. French prepared for us.

Everyone here was terrifying, including Futarishizuka, who was still pounding away at the Magical Barrier. My senior, Miss Hoshizaki, was the intimidatingly flawless athletic type. With the homeless girl in the group, it was a lot to deal with.

"Did something happen after you became a magical girl?"

"……"

She fell silent at the question.

I was sure, then, that misfortune had struck her.

For example, maybe she was judged to be an irregular psychic and attacked by the bureau—that was easy to imagine. And if she really was the age she seemed, fighting off a bunch of adults attacking her with the power of an organization behind them would have been next to impossible.

My section chief, for example, was a brutal man who would plant hidden cameras in a new recruit's home. I'd been too scared to ask if Miss Hoshizaki's house was okay. Without Peeps, I would have been in for it.

Ultimately, her fairy had become a stole, and the magical girl herself had transformed into an obsessed psychic-killing machine.

"Do you talk to any other magical girls?"

Partly to stall for more time, I chose to continue the conversation as my fake alter ego, the magical middle-aged man.

To that question, she gave a distinct response.

"They contacted me once."

"Did you answer them?"

"I told them I was busy right now."

Apparently, there *was* a community of magical girls. And I wasn't about to ask what she was busy with.

If she was equivalent to a rank-A psychic on her own, then even if there were only seven others in the world, they'd constitute a pretty valuable network. No doubt they were each allied with various organizations as well. It would be ill-advised to make light of them.

Unfortunately, though, Japan's magical girl was totally alone.

"Didn't you ever ask them for help?"

"I can't trust anyone else."

"…Oh."

She talked like a forty-year-old woman with a bad dating history. Pathetically, I felt myself empathizing somewhat.

At this point, it seemed wise to assume that psychics and magical girls were different things, like Miss Hoshizaki had told me. They probably both existed as completely separate entities unto themselves. I could sense different worldviews and perspectives behind each group.

Which only made the term *fairy* all the more curious. Was it like what Peeps was for me? A hypothesis popped into my head: Maybe she'd gained magic powers through a world other than our own, too.

And it was an easy hypothesis to verify.

"By the way, I noticed you can use several kinds of magic without an incantation."

"...Incantation?"

"Am I mistaken?"

"What do you mean by that, Officer?"

"Well, you see, I have to chant magic words in order to use magic."

"Really?"

She gave me a blank look in response, then tilted her head to the side. It didn't look as though she was lying.

If she'd been a magician visiting from the same world as Peeps, she'd have needed to chant incantations to use magic. Even if she didn't now, she would have definitely needed to learn them at some point in the past.

Since she'd denied it, chances were that the otherworld and the fairy world were two different places.

As a result, this conversation had let both girls in on a little piece of my secret. But it was a reasonable trade for the information I'd gotten. Another world, psychic powers, and magical girls—the three of these existed independently of one another, each with their own ideas and concepts.

I'd gotten some proof to back up Miss Hoshizaki's explanations, including when it came to Peeps and the existence of the otherworld.

"Okay. You're a magical middle-aged man, Officer. I understand."

After my string of explanations, the magical homeless girl nodded. The fact that I'd used several different powers with little relation to one another had probably helped persuade her—but her expression as she looked at me was still severe.

"Thank you. I'm glad you understand."

"But why are you with these psychics?"

She turned to face Futarishizuka, who had now given up on trying to break down the other girl's Magical Barrier. She was just standing there and staring—apparently having run out of things to try—arms folded imposingly, as if to say, "Hmph, it's not like I lost or anything."

I could clearly see the effort she was putting in to save her dignity. It was pretty adorable.

"I just ran into her here by coincidence."

"Then I can kill her, right?"

Futarishizuka gave a visible start. Having seen firsthand how tough the Magical Barrier was, she must have understood that this girl was trouble. The fact that she needed to touch an opponent to use her power also put Futarishizuka at a disadvantage.

"...Why do you hate psychics, if you don't mind my asking?" I questioned tentatively to stall for time—and I'd been wondering about it.

"Psychics killed my family. And all my friends."

This was another really heavy story from the magical girl.

I'd wanted to avoid the question because I was worried about this kind of answer but felt I had to check—and now here we were. I wondered what kind of reaction Peeps would have had, had he been here. *Wow, I can't even imagine it.*

At that moment, the girl's stare suddenly shifted away.

I followed her gaze and saw someone unfamiliar staring at us from a dozen or so meters away. It was a little boy, probably in elementary school. Blood covered his face, dripping down his cheeks and falling to the ground.

In his hands, he held the handlebars of a bicycle. However, from about ten centimeters past the grips, the entire rest of the bike was missing.

The kid had come from around the corner, and now he was staring at us in a daze, saying nothing.

I was so distressed, looking at him, that I wanted to dial 911 that instant.

A moment later, the magical girl murmured, "...I'm going home for today."

"Huh...?" I turned around and saw her floating up into the air. With a staticky noise, a black rift in space opened up right next to her. I'd witnessed this a few times already.

This was probably her Magical Field.

"Where are you going?" I asked gently.

"......"

The girl didn't answer my question. Her young body disappeared into the tear, which wasn't that big to begin with.

Not that I had wanted a reply, exactly. But it was difficult to watch, being unable to do anything as she vanished. Through our conversation, I'd understood that this magical girl had a lot of troubles of her own. And that made me wonder.

Why had she left of her own accord? Had it been the injured boy or her inability to break through the magical middle-aged man's barrier—or both? I couldn't tell. Either way, she had already disappeared into subspace—or whatever her Magical Field was.

If there was one thing I did understand, it was that Futarishizuka—who had been desperately beating away at the girl's Magical Barrier—had exerted no influence whatsoever on her withdrawal. The magical girl was at least powerful enough to overcome psychics of rank B and below.

Just as Miss Hoshizaki had said, to take down a magical girl, you would need several rank-B psychics or the help of an A rank. And depending on their compatibility—see Futarishizuka—even numbers wouldn't necessarily mean victory.

"We need to take the girl and get out of here," said Futarishizuka, her eyes on Miss Hoshizaki.

"You're right." Nothing good would come of staying here. I needed to focus on recovering our psychic and making my report to the higher-ups. I was sure our section chief was the type to want reports prioritized even more in cases like these. He might have already heard about the airplane coming down.

*

After fleeing the scene of the crash, we headed for our hotel room. For some reason, Futarishizuka helped me carry Miss Hoshizaki and the glasses kid. Of the unconscious pair, she took the girl, and I took the boy, carrying them on our shoulders as we retreated.

Miss Hoshizaki was the main reason I hadn't found a different hotel. If she woke up, and we were checked in somewhere else, despite the hotel the bureau had booked being located right nearby, she'd definitely start getting suspicious about all kinds of things.

"Is your employer covering this? My, it must be nice to work in an organization that uses taxpayer money," said Futarishizuka, surveying the hotel room.

Despite her implication, this was a business hotel without anything especially unique about it. It hadn't exactly been an economic boom lately, so one night here probably wouldn't even cost ten thousand yen. And if I was allowed to give my modest opinion, I just *hated* how the bathtubs and toilets were in the same little area.

"What, is your organization low on income?"

"Oh? Oh, no, that was just sales talk. I'm staying somewhere much nicer."

"…I see." And now I felt like a loser. *I wished she'd kept up the lie.*

Despite my disappointment, I had work to do. I laid the glasses kid and Miss Hoshizaki on the bed next to each other. Because of how the layout worked, I had to put them both on the semi-full-size mattress, which was a little smaller than a full-size one. They were basically sharing the bed. At a brief glance, they would have looked like a couple of corpses—they were still out cold, after all. My conversation with Futarishizuka was happening right next to them.

"In any event," she said slowly, in the manner of a much older woman, "are you willing to hear me out now?"

"I don't mind listening, but I can't make any promises."

"Is that right?"

"I do feel bad telling you this after letting you help with everything. However, you must understand I do not call the shots. I've only joined the organization recently. As such, my options are severely limited."

Even with my new job, I was still a rank-and-file employee—albeit for the government this time, I supposed. My status hadn't really changed at all. Naturally, I wouldn't have any of the rights of an administrator. That meant I couldn't use a single yen of taxpayer money on my own. If I was going to do something that involved business expenses, I'd need to clear that with a section chief or department head.

I wasn't particularly dissatisfied with that reality, but it made negotiations like this a pain. It bore a close resemblance to those unexpected deals that had to be made with a client without any managers present. Of course, when someone with decision-making power *was* present, the discussion might abruptly turn into agreements and contracts, which was its own kind of trouble. Foreign companies especially tended to give whoever they put on-site a *lot* of money and discretion. But since I was low on the corporate ladder and didn't have any such authority, I had to use every means at my disposal to stall for time.

I wondered if Miss Hoshizaki would have more discretionary power than I did in a situation like this. *I'm pretty sure the section chief told me in the meeting this morning to leave on-site decisions to her anyway.*

"Oh, but you're being so stiff and formal about it," responded Futar-ishizuka, assuming an air of dignity.

I couldn't even begin to guess what she wanted. Why had she broken into our fight to begin with? She supported *our* position, even to the point of fighting a magical girl—the mortal enemy of psychics.

"With that out of the way," I continued, "I'd like to ask what it is you're after."

"Oh, nothing much. I was just wondering if I could switch sides and join you, that's all."

"……"

Oh wow. Yet another sudden request.

<Recruitment, Part Two>

The girl I'd risked life and limb to fight just the week before had come to me with an unexpected request for a job transfer. Color me shocked.

I didn't even know how to answer until a moment later.

"When you say *switch sides*, do you mean you have an interest in the bureau I work for?"

"Yes, that's right," she replied. "I happened to remember your remarks when last we fought. And now I, too, desire to 'stick with the biggest player' after so long."

"......"

Of course I couldn't simply consent, so I hesitated to respond.

Several terms such as *trap* and *fraud* and *blackmail* started whirling around in my mind. If I accepted her request, would scary-looking yakuza guys suddenly burst through the door and ask me what the hell was going on?

I'd worked so hard to live quietly up until now, too. I'd heard the damages for impropriety normally ran in the millions of yen.

"I apologize, but I don't have the authority to make a decision one way or another."

"Then would you mind talking to your superiors about it?"

"......"

Well, I thought. *What now?* Considering our relationship thus far, the proposal had more drawbacks than benefits. Most of all, I couldn't imagine what kind of situation would make her capitulate like this.

"Your bureau lost personnel in the previous incident," she said. "From their perspective, the prospect of gaining a powerful psychic would be too tasty a morsel to pass up, surely? And you say you lack the authority, but wouldn't you be rewarded if our discussion led to successfully acquiring such a psychic?"

"It doesn't matter how strong the psychic is—if they're not trustworthy, there's no point in recruiting them."

"I am *quite* strong, you know."

"Yes, and that power is exactly what took so many bureau lives."

"Hmm. I suppose that does make it difficult..."

I had some experience helping with employee recruitment interviews from my last job—the kind of first-round interviews given by nonadministrative employees. While managers—section chiefs and above—would evaluate the candidate's personality and character, they'd rope *me* into appraising their actual abilities.

But this was my first time meeting an applicant with such high attack power. If I asked her about her strengths, her reply would probably involve a pretty brutal display.

If I was unlucky, I might end up dead. Frankly, even just talking to her like this had me on edge. A single touch, and her power would suck out my life energy or whatever. It was no exaggeration to say she had a genuine insta-kill ability.

Oh, what are your strengths? I'd ask, and she'd reply: *Draining energy.*

Personally, she was a talent I wanted to immediately recruit and then drop in the section chief's lap. I really wanted to see that stupidly attractive middle-aged face of his twisting into shock.

"I promise I won't harm you," she said. "Can I ask you to do this for me?"

"Well..."

The interviewee's resolution was firm. She was basically telling me to hire her by fair means or foul. I wondered if the group she belonged to was not actually paying her that much. Then again, she *did* just say their choice of on-site accommodations was far more luxurious than the bureau's. And last time she'd invited *me* to go with *them*, hadn't she? What was this all about?

"May I ask your reason?"

"You fascinate me."

Yikes, what a curveball. Trying to attract the recruiter's interest, eh? Someone sure knows their way around an interview.

All that stuff about her actual age being in the triple digits seemed to check out. I began to consider that, with how straightforward she was being, it might actually be best just to hire her already. She'd be a valuable combat resource, usable immediately—that much was for sure.

Viewing it in the long run, though, left me uneasy.

"What interest could you have in a person like me? I'm just your average middle-aged man."

"You jest. It has been a *very* long time since someone has overwhelmed me to that extent."

"Has it?"

She had to be referring to the incident at the bowling alley. Apparently, she had found what transpired there a lot more stimulating than I'd assumed. As a higher-ranked psychic, maybe she was holding a grudge over her defeat. Thinking about it like that, I should probably keep my distance. What if she killed me in my sleep or something? Scary stuff!

"Could it be," she remarked, "that you're hiding your power from the bureau?"

"……"

Now what? She hit me right where it hurts.

She was correct. I was sure *she* was sure, despite her prefacing her comment with *could it be*. And that was why she'd come to the negotiating table in the first place.

"Why do you think that?"

"They wouldn't have assigned you to support another psychic otherwise."

I considered Futarishizuka's background; Miss Hoshizaki had told me about it on the way here. In addition to her psychic power, she also possessed the experience and knowledge that came from a longer than average life span. That history was why she'd been assigned rank A. And now that I was speaking to her face-to-face, it all made sense.

"In addition to your ability to create icicles, you can unleash lightning and even float into the air. I cannot even begin to imagine what sort of psychic power would give rise to all that. And the power that stopped the magical girl's Magical Beam—did that not belong to you as well?"

"Hmm. Who knows."

Suddenly, hearing fanciful terms like *Magical Beam* in the middle of a relatively serious conversation was throwing off my rhythm. It made a certain magical homeless child seem a lot more irregular—for a variety of reasons. It was so out of left field, I wondered for a moment if this was all just a prank.

"If you introduce me to your superiors, I will remain silent about it."

"Is that a threat?"

"Do you think I would threaten you after saving your companions?"

"……"

That's some pretty obvious blackmail.

But it did have me on the defense. If not for Futarishizuka's intervention, Miss Hoshizaki would have found out about all those things. She'd already done plenty for me—if talking to the section chief was all she wanted in return, it was a good deal. In fact, that was probably part of why she'd intervened.

I was glad I'd been confining my interactions with Peeps to my apartment as much as possible. I felt a belated sense of relief at the fact that I had done so much on my own, such as buying the laptop for use in the otherworld. I was all but certain she'd been observing the apartment for the last few days.

"Before I take this to my superior, there is one thing I'd like to confirm."

"And what is that?"

"Why do you wish to leave your current job?"

"Are you curious?"

"Well, naturally."

"…It isn't a good work environment."

"And by that, you mean…?"

"That, and well, I was being bullied, too, a little."

"…I see."

"Though, I suppose it started all at once after that last incident with you."

"……"

Her position in her organization must have plummeted after the previous week's disaster. When I thought back, compared to the one making all the hurricanes, she hadn't actually done that much. At the same time, she had come out basically unscathed, while he had lost the whole lower half of his body.

"About the man using telekinesis back then…"

"Thanks to you, he'll be attending classes in a wheelchair for the time being. Everyone in the group is working around the clock to procure a high-ranking healing psychic to get him back in action. I'm sure they aren't happy with me going about as I please."

"I see."

"And well, even before, in the past, we have had several...differences of opinion."

Futarishizuka's story was about what I had expected. It seemed she wanted to quit her current job because her position had worsened. A pretty common motive for a career change.

"And that is why...I would be very happy if you were to accept me as one of your own."

"Again, I don't have that kind of authority."

"If you would allow me, I could do so much for you. Do you dislike young bodies, I wonder? My small size makes me perfect for *squeezing*. No matter how puny your manhood, it will be squeezed tight. Yes—very tight."

"......"

Another stimulating proposition. However, it would take more than that to make a clever amateur virgin waver. Virgins are made of different stuff, you know? And in Futarishizuka's case, I bet I'd catch some awful disease anyway.

"Again, I don't have that kind of authority."

"Well, I did say I would find it acceptable if only you would introduce me to your superiors, remember?"

She was being aggressive about this. Since she had a firm grip on my weakness, I supposed it was reasonable. What response would be best in this situation? Thinking from the perspective of a working member of society...

Once I started mulling it over, I came to a conclusion pretty quickly.

"All right, I understand. I'll talk to my superior about it."

"Truly?"

It was time to apply the protocol of "report, communicate, and consult." This was a rank-and-file employee's greatest weapon for dropping all responsibility in the lap of another. In some cases, that other person would immediately throw it back; I wondered how Chief Akutsu would react. This was the perfect opportunity to gauge his disposition as a boss.

I flipped open the phone he had given me and called his number. The address book had few contacts; other than his, the only numbers were for the bureau's front office and Miss Hoshizaki. I stopped and looked at her name in the list for a moment, struck by how surreal it felt to have exchanged contact info with a high school girl. By just pressing a button, I could talk to her without even paying! This seemed just as crazy to me as the existence of the otherworld and psychic powers.

My call was answered immediately, interrupting my idiot train of thought.

"What is it, Sasaki?"

"Chief, would you happen to have a few moments?"

"Yeah, no problem."

His normal, plain way of speaking was comforting. I wasn't very skilled at conversation, so his businesslike personality made talking to him feel relatively easy. Still, I would have liked to see a more human side to him once in a while.

"I've received an employment request from an irregular psychic, unrelated to the young man in question."

"Oh! That's excellent. What sort of psychic are they?"

"Her name is Futarishizuka. Do you know of her?"

"Ah yes, I— What?"

"Are you not familiar with her?"

"......"

I could practically hear him shudder over the phone. He swallowed whatever it was he was about to say.

The chief always acted like a real put-together guy, so his surprise was a new, fresh reaction for me. I called to mind his suit and shoes, his watch, and even his tiepin, all brand-name from head to toe. Imagining a person like that at a loss for words was a rare kind of entertainment, even if it was only over the phone.

Sorry, Chief, but your honest reaction has brought me true delight.

"What do you think?"

"Uh, right, well..."

It was pretty cute, listening to him struggle for a response. Maybe he was feeling the same surprise I had just a while ago. *I totally understand his shock,* I thought, beginning to feel some kinship with him.

"By Futarishizuka, you mean the psychic with the energy-draining

ability? I remember you saying that she appeared on-site where I dispatched you last time. She looks like an elementary school student—at a glance, you would think she was a little girl."

I could tell he was desperately trying to buy himself time. *Yes!* I thought. *I managed to bounce my on-site dilemma right back into the administration's face.*

"Yes, that would be her."

"I thought she was a member of an anti-government organization..."

"Forgive my bluntness, but may I take her back to the bureau with us?"

"......"

"Chief?"

"I'm interested in her motive for applying. Has she told you anything?"

"She says she wants to stick with the biggest player."

"......"

Even the chief would never expect that she was standing right next to me. This was getting more and more fun.

"Since you are familiar with her, you must know there isn't much I can do here. With her background, I believe it would be best to respect her decision as much as possible. Would you at least be able to prepare a place for an interview?"

I couldn't have him thinking we were conspiring behind the scenes, so I made sure to imply that we weren't. I wanted him to know that I was nothing but the messenger here. I was just the lowly little subordinate, but what did *he* want to do? He was going to be the one accountable here, and I had said as much between the lines.

Immediately, he fell silent. His capture during the bowling alley incident was taking its toll, no doubt.

"......"

"...Chief?"

The last operation had been a failure for the chief, so his mind was probably boiling with conflict right now. Any other person would have wanted to keep a low profile for the time being, slowly but surely building up a list of contributions. I bet he hadn't emerged unscathed, even if he *was* a section chief. Nothing had been made public, but he was most likely being forced to take responsibility in some form.

"Is she...friendly toward you?"

"Well..."

That was one point in particular I hadn't determined yet.

According to Miss Hoshizaki, this girl had been alive since before World War II. She had several times the amount of life experience I did. While I could understand the story she'd given me, to an extent, I still didn't have a clue what she was really thinking. She was still leading us around by the nose.

"I can't be certain, but I know she is interested in us. And the fact remains that we need more people at the bureau. If we can secure her cooperation, I believe it would allow us to expand our operations."

"......"

If I fooled around too much, my work assessment would suffer. I couldn't have my bonus decreasing. Now it was time to make it seem like I was somewhat competent—but only somewhat.

"If you'd allow me to make a proposal—how about conducting the interview via video conference? It's only natural you'd be apprehensive at the idea of meeting her face-to-face. But I believe, considering the nature of her power, keeping your distance should alleviate those concerns."

"Does that work for her?"

"I can't have her bothering you, Chief, so I can try negotiating with her myself," I offered, shooting a glance at our prospective applicant.

When I did, Futarishizuka gave a small nod.

Apparently, she wouldn't have a problem with a video chat. In fact, if I believed what she said about only wanting to be put in touch with my superiors, an objection would have roused my suspicion. Her answer here made sense, and I had expected it when I made the suggestion.

"...Hmm."

"Would that work?"

"I'd like to hear Hoshizaki's opinion as well. Is she there right now?"

"She was injured in an encounter with the magical girl. She's unconscious at the moment."

I heard him suck in air from over the phone. *Oh right*, I thought. *I didn't tell him about us running into the magical girl.* Poor Akutsu was getting hit by one surprise after another.

"Ms. Futarishizuka provided some assistance at the time."

"...I see. So that's how it is."

"What do you think?"

"All right. I'll get back to you with a specific date, then."

"Understood."

Great, I managed to get him to promise an interview.

He didn't make any reference to the plane crash. The information probably hadn't reached him yet. It hadn't even been an hour since it happened, and the chain of intel was held up somewhere. As a result, I'd been able to swing the conversation to my advantage.

"How is Hoshizaki looking?"

"No obvious external wounds. I believe she'll wake up by herself before long."

"In that case, good. I'd like you to get a report together later."

"I'll have it for you by the end of the day."

"Thank you."

"Now, if you'll excuse me, I have some things to deal with on-site."

"Right."

With the chief having agreed, I lowered the phone from my ear and hung up.

He'd probably call me back before long. Planes weren't cheap. I wasn't looking forward to that conversation.

And that was why I wished Miss Hoshizaki would hurry and wake up. Then the responsibility of reporting to the section chief would naturally fall to her. I looked over to the bed where she lay next to the boy with glasses. She was still unconscious, and though I watched for a short time, she didn't show any response. They looked like siblings, lying next to each other on the semi-full-size bed.

After a cursory glance, I continued my conversation with Futarishizuka. "Was that to your liking?" I asked, putting the phone back into my pocket.

"Yes. Thank you," she replied, sounding satisfied.

The way she smiled like that was cute. Looking at her now, she was just a little girl—a scary thought. It was hard to imagine those small hands having killed dozens, if not hundreds of people. I mean, it was so easy to picture her, an elementary schooler's hard leather backpack over her shoulders.

"Now, there's no guarantee you'll be hired," I said.

"No, my thanks were to you, for connecting me with your place of work."

"Ah."

In that case, maybe I could ask her for a small favor, too. I just didn't have enough information—especially when it came to magical girls.

"By the way, there was something I wanted to ask."

"What is it? Feeling in the mood now?"

"I was wondering if you could tell me what you know about magical girls. I hear that you've lived much, much longer than I have. If you have any knowledge about magical girls in general from your past experience, could you share that with me?"

"Oh, so cold."

"Please?"

Futarishizuka, still sitting on the chair at the hotel room's desk, was acting coquettish. I was lightly sitting on the edge of the bed that contained Miss Hoshizaki and the glasses boy. A good position—just in case.

"After all that about being a...what was it? A magical middle-aged man? You're asking me now?"

"That was more of a figure of speech to protect myself..."

Actually, I had another reason for asking her about magical girls. The person in front of me probably saw me as a psychic with unknown powers. At the same time, she was also likely suspicious of the possibility that I was a magical girl—well, magical middle-aged man.

In the future, then, just in case she did learn of Peeps's existence, and I could no longer pretend to be a fellow psychic, I wanted to lay the groundwork for my position as a "magical middle-aged man." In order to do that, I had to heavily imply that I didn't know the first thing about magical girls. I suspected Futarishizuka would read into this in just the way I wanted.

"You *are* a member of the bureau. I'm sure your superiors have told you all about them."

"As I said previously, I am a rookie who just recently completed his job training; they haven't given me much in the way of information. They might tell me if I asked, but I want to gather as much intel as I can as soon as possible."

"A tenacious one, you are..."

"Will you?"

"Well, I suppose I can tell you what I know."

"Really? I appreciate it."

She assented more easily than I had imagined.

For some time after that, as we sat in the hotel room, Futarishizuka gave me a lecture on magical girls. To cut to the chase, she was able to provide more than what we'd seen at the airplane crash site. She said she'd spoken with other magical girls outside of Japan before, and as a result, she had quite a bit of information.

It seemed as though this "fairy world" existed separately from our own. Messengers called fairies would leave their world and come here, then use their powers to transfigure certain individuals, who then became magical girls.

Worldwide, seven magical girls had been confirmed. This I'd heard from Miss Hoshizaki as well. However, Futarishizuka said it was believed more existed who hid their identities. Their areas of activity, aside from Japan, included the US, China, Russia, Germany, and France. The last of the seven didn't confine herself to a specific place.

Futarishizuka didn't seem to know very much about the fairy world. According to her fragmentary knowledge, magical girls worked with the fairies to do some specific sort of work in this world. She didn't know any more than that.

In addition, most magical girls were at least in contact with public agencies in each country, if they did not belong to them outright. After our confrontation with the homeless magical girl, I understood why those in power would prefer such an arrangement. One of the few exceptions to this was Japan's magical girl, who had personally explained her reasoning to us already.

"I see; so that's how it is," I mused.

"Yes, it is quite troubling how hostile Japan's magical girl is toward psychics."

"What about other countries?"

"I've never heard of one going around killing psychics, at least."

I'd learned more about magical girls than I had expected. With the information from Futarishizuka, I'd be able to make advance preparations to communicate with the girl as a magical middle-aged man the next time we encountered her.

My chance meeting with this young-looking psychic hadn't been without its merits.

"Better to stay away from children with a few screws loose, like her," she finished.

"I don't think she's a bad kid by any means; it's just…"

"She'd fire lethal magic at us as soon as she saw us, you know."

"When you put it like that, it's a bit hard to deny."

Just then, the phone in my pocket started vibrating. I checked the screen; it showed the section chief's name. After excusing myself from Futarishizuka, I picked up.

"Hello, this is Sasaki speaking."

"It's Akutsu. I just wanted to know what you two have been doing."

Unlike last time, I could sense a bit of anger in his tone. It was only natural, of course. He'd probably just received word of the airplane coming down. Though I didn't know whether we'd been confirmed on the scene, given the overlap between our trip's destination and the crash site, anyone would have their suspicions. The glasses kid's fireball had been fairly conspicuous, too.

How would I report this to him, then? If I explained honestly, he'd give us a good scolding for certain. We'd been unable to stop a stray psychic from going out of control, and we'd let a machine that was worth billions of yen come down right in front of us. A demotion or reduction in pay would be unavoidable. *I wouldn't be surprised if we got fired, either.*

As obsessed with her pay as Miss Hoshizaki was, she would probably lose her mind—and the kid with glasses would face trouble with the bureau in the future. Considering all that, there was only one choice.

"As I explained before, we had a battle with the magical girl on-site."

"Then the cargo plane from the Iruma base crashed because..."

"It was hit by the girl's Magical Beam and destroyed. She hesitated due to the presence of civilians at the scene, and we managed to flee."

I hadn't told any lies.

The direct cause of the crash had been the glasses kid, but the magical girl *had* shot the cargo plane. I probably couldn't cover up the fireball. Naturally, it would be quickly revealed that it had originated from the kid.

But I figured if I could establish that the root cause was *actually* our encounter with the magical girl, the harm might be reduced somewhat. It was well-known that the girl was going around hunting psychics for an unrelated reason.

With that, we could distance ourselves somewhat from responsibility. Essentially, it had been a natural disaster.

"Apparently, a fireball was seen at the time of the crash."

"Is the use of psychic powers not permitted while fighting a magical girl?"

Thanks to Futarishizuka's explanation, I had a good grasp on how magical girls affected the world of psychics. It pained me to use her as a scapegoat, but she'd already picked a fight with the bureau—just one plane could be swept under the rug. That's how I'd spin it.

It was our miss as bureau personnel, but I hoped to draw him into a compromise—we were up against a magical girl and forced to act. If I came out and said the glasses kid did it, the bureau would fall under some pretty heavy external criticism.

After a heavy sigh, he agreed. *"...All right. That does work out better for us as well,"* he said plainly.

"Thank you for your understanding." The chief appeared to agree with my opinion. "By the way, Chief, I had a question for you."

"And what might that be?"

"How does compensation work when it comes to psychic-related accidents? I doubt an insurance contract would include this kind of thing. This time, the loss was sustained by a government facility, but if it had been a private airline, would that put us in danger of bankruptcy?"

Leased vehicles had been on the rise recently—including aircraft. Even a single one going down could be a big deal. And that didn't just apply to the air transport industry.

"We're provided a special budget, under our bureau's control, for compensating incidents or accidents caused by psychics—though it's not public information. We'll probably end up using those funds for this mess as well."

"I see." Apparently, even Japan had under-the-table accounts. Hearing it made my heart race, even though I was the one who asked. I wondered how the funds were allocated. As someone responsible working on-site, the idea of vast amounts of money suddenly showing up from who knows where was enough to send a chill down my spine.

"Is that all?"

"Yes. Thank you for getting in touch."

"All right, then, if you'll excuse me."

Without getting too deep into the weeds, I ended my call with the boss. He'd seemed sour the whole time. He was more the type to weigh all his options with indifference, rather than angrily raise his voice, so it left me uneasy. Couldn't do much about that, though. If things didn't work out, I'd just flee to the otherworld like I had initially planned.

"Is it not going well with your boss?" asked Futarishizuka.

"No, it's fine."

"If I am allowed to defect, then he will be my boss as well, yes? Perhaps it is for the best to get a read on his character before interviewing with him. How about it? In exchange for my information on magical girls, could you tell me about him?"

"Yes, I wouldn't mind that."

Preparing for interviews was absolutely critical. The best method was to use industry news or social media to gauge someone's personality, but that wouldn't work when it came to our bureau. I'd actually searched Mr. Akutsu's name at home and gotten zero results. Considering he was a section chief in the Cabinet Office, not seeing *anything* about him was pretty impressive.

On a hunch, I'd searched my own name, too—and found the results I was used to seeing had all been deleted at some point. I was still able to find the cached pages, but I was sure those would soon be gone as well.

"That said, I've only known him for about a month, so please keep that in mind…"

And so I told Futarishizuka what I knew about the section chief—that he was young for his position, that he was good-looking, that he cared about how he looked, and that his personality was chilly and detached.

Putting it into words like this made me realize that, yeah, I only knew about surface elements. *I wonder if Miss Hoshizaki would know more about him*, I thought. *Maybe I should ask her later.*

"Oh, and one other important bit of info."

"What is it?"

"This is only for if you get hired, though. The chief will arrange for hidden cameras to be set up in your home or your base of operations— whatever you put as your address. I know it's creepy, but you'll want to choose a time to 'find' and destroy them."

"Ah, so bureau employees have that sort of thing as well, do they?"

"They've had several spies in the past, so they're probably on edge. It's against the rules for me to tell you like this, but I'm pretty sure they'll consider you a spy for now anyway, so I thought I'd inform you while I had the chance."

"I am quite used to such tests; I doubt I would have had much of a problem even if you hadn't mentioned it. And to be quite honest, all organizations do something similar. But I do thank you, sincerely, for telling me in advance like this."

If the person in front of me went on a rampage, even I'd be in danger, despite my steady acquisition of intermediate spells. I couldn't exactly have my barrier magic up twenty-four seven. The bureau's caution toward Futarishizuka was incredibly well-placed, so I didn't want to do anything that would unnecessarily set her off.

"Did you have any questions?" I asked, now that I'd told her roughly what I knew.

But as soon as I spoke, it happened.

"…Sasaki, was all that true?"

"Huh?"

The question had come from right behind me.

I turned around in surprise to see Miss Hoshizaki looking at me, her eyes wide. She was still lying on the bed, only moving her eyes.

It seemed like she was merely pretending to be asleep. How long had she been awake for?

"…Good morning, Miss Hoshizaki."

"Sasaki, was what you just said true?"

"What part of what I just said?"

She got up slowly, perhaps out of consideration for the glasses kid. Then, despite being in her school uniform, she assumed a cross-legged position on the bedsheet.

Her expression was the same as always—a flat countenance, absent of any emotion. That said, she wasn't wearing her usual thick makeup this time, making her expressions easier to read. I noticed my senior's cheeks were flushed slightly red.

"About the chief setting up surveillance cameras in bureau employees' apartments."

"……"

At those words, I became sure of it. *Yep—it's gotta be that, right? The chief's home must be chock-full of erotic videos featuring high school girls.*

"Sasaki, answer me right now. Is it true that the section chief puts hidden cameras in bureau employees' apartments? It isn't that you're an exception? Everyone gets that treatment?"

"He did say they didn't discriminate..."

"Ugh..."

Miss Hoshizaki's expression changed. Her eyes widened, and she fell silent.

From that reaction, it was certain that she hadn't realized until just now. She had said before that she lived a normal life at her parents' house, going to work and school from there.

Of course, she would have been doing all the things a regular high school girl did there without a care in the world—changing clothes, studying, hanging out with friends, and depending on the situation, inviting a boyfriend over to try to fulfill more sexual needs.

And the chief had his hands on all of it.

If she'd been treated anything like I had, she was being secretly filmed by multiple cameras from a variety of angles. They had audio recording devices on them, too. Plus, unlike the nine-to-fiver who had just joined the bureau recently, she'd been working with them for quite some time.

Untold hours of footage—this was a *miniseries*.

"Miss Hoshizaki, I don't believe the chief puts them there for any shameful reasons."

"We've retrieved the target. Let's head back to the bureau."

"Um, if possible, I'd like to buy a few souvenirs for the bureau and friends of mine..."

"Souvenirs?" she repeated, turning to glare at me.

"...Understood."

The section chief probably had his hands full dealing with the airplane crash, but this looked to be even worse. All I could do was watch from a distance. I definitely could not let her find out I was a little excited about the whole thing.

Sorry, Peeps. Doesn't look like I'll be able to get you a gift from Iruma. And here I'd heard of a new brand of meat, Saiboku, which is supposed to be delicious. Was looking forward to it, too...

*

Before the day ended, we returned to the bureau with the glasses boy. We had parted ways with Futarishizuka back in Iruma; we couldn't exactly bring *her* back with us. Instead, we exchanged contact information.

Though we'd used a car on the way here, we took a taxi on the return route. Miss Hoshizaki told me we could put it down as a business expense later. That allowed both of us to relax, despite the long distance. It was a stark contrast to my old job, where they'd refuse to pay the difference if I had to take a train that wasn't on my designated route to visit a client. Kudos to the Cabinet Office's Paranormal Phenomena Countermeasure Bureau.

Still, the entire trip back was awkward. At least she hadn't heard any of that magical middle-aged man stuff. When I'd asked, she'd told me that right after waking up, she'd been hit with the news about the hidden cameras. I was very pleased the damage caused by her feigned sleep was limited to the section chief.

In terms of where everyone sat, I was in the back seat with the unconscious glasses kid, while Miss Hoshizaki was riding shotgun. The boy had remained asleep the entire time, so I'd needed to carry him around while we moved.

After a stretch on the Tokyo Expressway, we arrived back at our base of operations in Tokyo. Miss Hoshizaki got out of the car first, breaking into a run as soon as her feet hit the ground. She was headed for our department with a ghastly expression.

I wasn't confident I could carry the boy all the way by myself, so I had the taxi driver wait there. Even just bringing him from the hotel room to the taxi had really done a number on my hips. If I didn't have healing magic, it would have been outright impossible.

Once we returned to the bureau and talked to the department in charge of taking in psychics, our mission would be over. They knew we'd been out recruiting, so it wasn't hard to coordinate with them.

And so after a hasty back-and-forth...

I finished everything up and returned to my own desk to take a nice, comfortable break—which only lasted a moment before a murderous-looking Miss Hoshizaki called for me. She led me to the adjacent conference room; there, the section chief was waiting for us.

The sun had already set, and it was long past time to head home. Our boss, however, was still working at his desk like it was the most natural thing in the world. *How very like a government employee,* I thought. *I really wish he'd gone home, if only just this once.*

"What's this sudden thing you wanted to talk about, Hoshizaki?" he asked.

"I had something I needed to confirm with you, Chief."

"I don't mind. I had things to ask you as well."

While Miss Hoshizaki was huffing and puffing like she'd just run a marathon, the chief also seemed to have something he needed from us. I could hazard a guess as to what that was—it probably had something to do with taking in Futarishizuka. He had promised to set up a meeting with her in the near future.

"Is it all right that Sasaki is here, too?"

"He's the one who told me," said Miss Hoshizaki, not even trying to hide how irritated she was. I wished she wouldn't get her junior employee involved with workplace quarrels. "He said you dump a bunch of hidden cameras in bureau employees' homes!"

"Oh, yes. What about it?"

That took her aback; the section chief didn't even bat an eye as he answered. Like it was a matter of course, as far as he was concerned. Personally, I kind of thought he'd react like that, so I wasn't exactly surprised.

The same didn't go for the high school girl sitting next to me, though. "D-do you honestly believe that sort of thing is allowed?!"

"Yes, it's allowed. I have that authority."

"What...?"

His tone was indifferent, as always. He probably wouldn't change it even if Miss Hoshizaki was kicking and screaming. Futarishizuka had informed me they did similar things in many places, so I sort of figured we couldn't do anything about it. I'd avoided any personal damage, thanks to Peeps, so this matter was completely unrelated to me.

"Please, don't worry. I would never leak it to anyone else."

"That's not the problem here!"

"Then what *is* the problem?"

"So are you into that kind of thing, Chief?!"

"Oh, that's what you meant."

"Of course it was!" shouted Miss Hoshizaki, pounding on the conference table and rising from her seat. If I didn't know any better, I'd say she was about to use her power.

The chief was totally unfazed, however. Her repeated questioning hadn't bothered him a bit. He had likely foreseen all this in advance. Maybe it had even happened before.

With her being a psychic—and one with offensive capabilities, at that—she might as well have been holding a gun up to his forehead. And yet I couldn't even see the slightest break in his flat expression.

That only made remembering his reaction when I'd brought up Futarishizuka even more thrilling, though it was only over the phone. How would he act during their interview? If at all possible, I wanted to stand in as an observer.

"This is sexual harassment!" yelled Miss Hoshizaki in utter rage.

The chief's response was very businesslike. "You don't need to worry about that. I'm gay. I have no interest in women."

"Huh…?"

The chief chose that exact moment to come out to us, of all things. Miss Hoshizaki's eyes were wide with shock.

"I'm far more excited by men my own age in suits and ties than high school girls in student uniforms."

"……"

The wrath on her face vanished in an instant. As it did, she stole a glance at me. I sensed by the suspicion in her eyes that this had created something of a misunderstanding.

Wait. What if it *wasn't* a misunderstanding?

I suddenly felt like the fire in Miss Hoshizaki's yard had hopped the fence into mine.

The clamorous conference room fell quiet—Miss Hoshizaki had stopped her questions. Now she was looking back and forth between the two of us. This was so incredibly uncomfortable. It made me want to bolt right out the door and flee.

But wait. I have to clear up the misunderstanding.

"Chief, putting it that way will cause confusion."

"Why is that?"

"Because I'm the one who told her about this."

What a candidly indifferent reaction for someone spying on a minor's private life. He really didn't seem to think it was problematic. Maybe those who had fought hard to move up the ladder really were different from the rest of us.

I didn't want this to complicate my relationship with my coworkers

later on down the line. I wanted to clear this up while Miss Hoshizaki
was here to see it. I had to make it clear to everyone present that there
was nothing going on, gay or otherwise, involving me.

"Is that so?" he replied.

"Yes, it is."

"In that case, you don't have to worry about what you're thinking."

"Are you certain?"

"Yes, positively."

"Wonderful. Glad to hear it."

"You're not my type anyway."

"......"

*Your subordinate is desperately racking his brain, trying to clear this
up, and what kind of reaction is that? I didn't even confess, and yet it
feels like I just got one-sidedly rejected.*

Was this his way of asserting dominance? I mean, I understood.
Considering my looks, this attractive middle-aged man in front of me
would be a prize well beyond my reach. *Then be a little more considerate here! Now the peanut gallery is just gonna feel sorry for me.*

"What's the matter?" he asked.

"Nothing. Nothing at all."

I didn't have a shred of interest in him, but I couldn't help suddenly
wondering about stuff like plastic surgery and weight training—probably because I was, from head to toe, very weak when it came to
romance. People only toughened up when others desired them.

The absolute *nerve* of him asking *What's the matter?* after telling me
I wasn't his type spoke volumes about the strength of his mindset.
You're wounding your poor subordinate, here. But given my complex
feelings on the matter, I wasn't going to voice any complaints.

"As you can see, I am not foolish enough to start a relationship with
someone in the bureau, Miss Hoshizaki."

"Even so, hiding surveillance cameras is..."

"I've rooted out a significant number of spies with those surveillance cameras. Have you considered that aspect? This bureau isn't like
other ministries and agencies. If anything, we're closer to being a public security organization."

"......"

The chief's admission had taken most of the sting out of Miss
Hoshizaki's attitude. For someone with his title, the facts he'd just laid

out were reasonable. Still, considering the context, the words *public security* rang extremely dubiously in my ears. Like something an FBI agent would say in a B movie.

"Do you have a question, Miss Hoshizaki?"

As always, the chief spoke smoothly and with a high-handed tone. His expression hadn't changed one bit.

Staring at him, Miss Hoshizaki replied, "I believe the bureau has already gotten enough information regarding my identity. If you *really* don't get off to voyeuristic recordings of women, Chief, then could you have the hidden cameras removed from my home by the end of the day?"

"All right. I'll arrange it immediately."

The chief easily agreed to Miss Hoshizaki's request.

I happened to glance at her face just then. Under the table, her fists were clenched. I was pretty sure her anger hadn't subsided at all. *Maybe I should be extra considerate toward her for a while.*

"Also, Sasaki, regarding a schedule for the interview..."

"Oh, right."

This was one exploitative company. I wanted to hurry home and talk to Peeps this very instant. My weary heart longed for some communication with my pet bird. I wanted to have fun surfing the internet together.

At the same time, though, considering how desperately Miss Hoshizaki was trying to hold everything in, it seemed likely there was a bonus in our future. I felt pathetic getting excited about it.

It was tough to be poor.

∗

Once our meeting with the boss that day was finished, we left. I wouldn't be coming back into the office until the next day.

The boss had arranged an interview with Futarishizuka first thing in the morning, before anyone showed up in the office. I contacted her again by phone, and she jumped at the offer. She said she'd already left her old workplace, so she was just kicking around without any plans for the time being.

At last, this public servant was heading home.

Or at least he *tried* to.

"You're late," came the drawl. "Overtime?"

"......"

The kimono girl was standing in the road in front of my apartment.

The sun had set, and she was hidden in the shadow of a building on the dark road. Her old-fashioned outfit made her look like a ghost, and her extremely cute appearance only reinforced the illusion.

She had some kind of travel bag in her hand.

"Something the matter? You look quite weary."

"I, uh, just didn't think we'd run into each other in a place like this."

The whole way back home, I'd been thinking about soothing my mind, rattled from work, by chatting with Peeps. And now, right in front of my apartment, this was happening. In my hand was a bag with meat I'd bought at a local butcher, to replace the souvenir I wasn't able to buy during the business trip.

Since they'd given me a travel allowance, I got a little excited and bought one hundred grams for 1,500 yen.

"I *did* say I've been monitoring you."

"Yes, well, I remember that, but..."

It was just that I didn't think she'd come to me *now*.

I'd just contacted her a couple hours before regarding the time for her interview with the section chief, and I planned to see her the next day, too. She should have known I wasn't going to fly the coop. But in that case, why would she barge in here and risk upsetting us?

"Did you need something from me?" I asked.

"Ah, that. It isn't much, really."

"What is it, then? I'd really like to hear it."

"While monitoring you, I saw something odd through the window."

"......"

Wait. What? I always drew the curtains before going anywhere.

After all, on weekdays, Peeps perused the internet in the apartment. He'd sit down right in front of the laptop and use his magical golem creature to surf the web just like a human would.

Naturally, we couldn't afford for anyone to see that. Whenever I checked to make sure the gas was off every day, I checked the curtains, too. I'd told Peeps about this, and he understood. He was far wiser than I, so it was unlikely he'd forgotten.

"Did someone suspicious break in?" I asked flatly, resisting the immediate urge to look over to my apartment.

The girl took an object out of her kimono. It looked like a combination between a listening device and a small audio amp. The rectangular, metal case had several handles on it, and it was connected via a cable to a tool that looked like a bug.

It had to be one of those microphones that could pick up sound through walls.

"Any idea what this is, hmm?"

"...Not really. What is it?"

People from detective agencies used them for investigating illicit relationships. They could pick up sound even from the other side of a thick metal door or reinforced concrete walls. I had heard there were certain conditions where they couldn't be used—but as for my apartment, a layperson like me had no way to know.

Of course, I'd proceed on the assumption she was bluffing. Even if she had picked up on Peeps's voice, I could just tell her a friend had come over to visit. I could pass off any conversations related to magic or whatever as being about an anime or a video game, and she'd have no way of establishing the truth.

"In simple terms, it's a listening device."

"Then if you were listening in on my apartment, did you find anything?"

"No—this tool alone was insufficient."

Then she opened up the travel bag she was carrying and plucked out an object from within. At a glance, it looked like a video camera, though the manufacturer's label on its side didn't match any of the well-known makers.

It wasn't a video camera she'd just taken out—it was a thermal imaging camera.

This device could create a picture by detecting infrared light, then building a heat map that showed temperature differences in the space imaged. The manufacturer's label on the body of the camera belonged to a company that made equipment like this; they were known worldwide. I knew this because I had experience handling some of their products for work.

Thermal imaging cameras were astronomically more expensive than video cameras. The one Futarishizuka was holding was an industrial model, too—it must have cost three or four hundred thousand yen. Even then, they usually only had VGA levels of resolution. The ones with high-definition cost close to a million.

"A video camera? It's pretty big, though," I said, playing dumb for now. So what if she had a thermal camera?

"You must have heard of thermal imaging cameras, right? They show up on TV quite often. This particular one is surprisingly simple to use. Depending on the sensitivity of the device, it can safely be used from farther away than normal surveillance cameras."

"All right, then what about it?"

"Using the camera and the microphone together, I have discovered something."

"...What?"

"You seem to quite enjoy conversing with someone—a bird, it would appear."

"Are you sure you're not mistaken?"

"Oh?"

"That voice might have been from the next apartment over. Audio collected by a microphone can be affected by pipes, among other things, and I hear it's common for sounds from other rooms to get mixed in. In an apartment complex, it's easy to confuse sounds from your own place and your neighbor's, don't you think?"

"I saw and heard it all in broad daylight. All your neighbors, in every direction, were absent at the time. And I notice you're not denying that you own a pet bird. It left its cage all on its own and seemed to be doing as it pleased on your desk. The room isn't full of bird droppings, is it?"

Wait. That didn't make any sense.

No matter how pricey that thermal camera had been, she wouldn't be able to observe the inside of the room through the windowpane. Neither the heat from the laptop nor Peeps's body heat would have made it to the lens she was showing me now.

"I wasn't aware you could observe infrared light from a living creature across glass."

Most windowpanes would block the amount of infrared light given off by a human body. If you absolutely had to detect that kind of temperature change, you would need to target some pretty small wavelengths. To do so would naturally require a higher target temperature.

If Peeps's temperature was four hundred degrees Celsius, it would certainly be possible.

But then he'd be yakitori.

"...Oh, come on."

Hold on. Was she asking leading questions? But then how did she know so much about Peeps's behavior? He did get on the desk to surf the internet, after all.

"I had wanted to show a little tact, but now I seem to have put you on your guard."

"......"

Either way, Futarishizuka definitely seemed to know about Peeps. But then, what had she come here looking for? It she intended to harm us, I might have to settle things before the next day's interview.

At this distance, I could potentially ward her off with my magic and join forces with the Lord Starsage. If we captured her and banished her to the otherworld, our secret would be safe.

"I apologize, but I let myself into your apartment the other day."

"...And?"

"The camera I placed there was fairly clear about what it showed."

"......"

Well, crap. Now I can't laugh at Miss Hoshizaki. This middle-aged man had just been expertly caught on a hidden camera.

It was true that several days had passed since meeting Futarishizuka at the bowling alley. During that time, Peeps and I had been out of the house for a significant amount of time, including both outings here in Japan and our activities in the otherworld.

I couldn't deny the possibility that she had waited for an opportunity and sneaked inside.

Actually, if she was visiting me like this, she *must* have.

Deep in my heart, I prayed she hadn't captured anything indecent.

"What have you come here for, Futarishizuka?"

"Would you mind it at all if I stayed with you for the night?"

"......"

And to make things worse, she had yet another troubling proposition for me.

She seemed embarrassed—but it had to be an act. Her psychic power could instantly kill an opponent just by touching them. Naturally, I

had to be wary around her, but so did Peeps. In the unlikely event that anything happened to him, I wouldn't be able to keep my cool. That was another reason I hesitated to let her into my apartment.

It's an owner's responsibility to protect his pet bird.

"Based on what you told me this afternoon, your lodgings are more luxurious than the bureau's, right? Why come stay at a cramped old apartment, then? I promise I'll get in touch with you for the interview, so…"

"That bird who speaks to itself in front of your laptop is quite the curiosity."

"……"

When I tried to convince her to turn back, I was met with a terrible smirk. She seemed set on entering my home, whether I liked it or not. Was she after Peeps? Or was it something else?

This was not acceptable. "What are you getting at, exactly?"

"Should you flat out refuse, I might have a word with your boss."

"In that case, you may have to wait a while for an interview."

"I jest. But don't you feel your guard is somewhat lax?"

Did she come all this way just to tell me that?

Taken with everything that had happened in the past, I couldn't seem to get a handle on this girl. Honestly, I was ready to give up. They said she'd lived much, much longer than I had. I'd never had an eye for people, really—how was I supposed to figure out what someone like her was up to?

That was why I'd tried to pass the buck to the section chief…and now this.

"It's a rare opportunity to be personally targeted by a rank-A psychic," I said.

"For this, it wouldn't have mattered if I was a psychic or not. Isn't it your side that's more adept at covert operations? Your bureau's generous non-psychic support staff is its strong point, I should think."

Even I grasped what Futarishizuka was implying. My boss *had*, in fact, planted surveillance cameras once already.

Unfortunately, I couldn't just move without the money to do so. I'd considered relocating to a house with more security several times since meeting Peeps. I wanted a big living room and a big dog to play with.

But considering the bureau's power, I'd need more than a run-of-the-mill property.

The boss would *definitely* take advantage of his government-backed authority to boldly waltz straight into his subordinate's house in broad daylight. Unless I had guards standing watch at all hours of the day, there wouldn't be much point. And if I went *that* far, it would stand out too much—he'd wonder, "Who the hell is this guy?"

In that light, I was content to live with the status quo.

But considering the existence of irregular psychics, the girl's point stood. Here I was, being threatened by one right now. If I'd been living in a high-class estate with surveillance cameras on the property, maybe this situation could have been avoided.

"It would pose an issue if your magical girl status was to be revealed to the bureau, would it not? Messengers from the fairy world visit this one by possessing the flesh of beasts. The bird I witnessed talking in your apartment must be such a messenger from the fairy world—and your partner, no?"

And then, unexpectedly, the term *magical girl* was on her tongue. I was grateful for the misinterpretation. It seemed she believed my bizarre "magical middle-aged man" spiel.

No, it would be more accurate to say she was hoping to add a side dish to this magical girl—a fairy world collaborator. As I'd imagined, pretending Peeps was a fairy messenger was a very convenient way to hide his true identity. I was glad I'd set this up beforehand.

I thought for *sure* she'd figured out about the existence of the otherworld.

At the same time, I felt like I understood why Futarishizuka had come here, even if it meant revealing the hidden camera. Assuming she really did want to gain employment with the bureau, she must have been trying to take the initiative by seizing upon this weakness.

There was no doubt she was interested in the fairy world and the powers magical girls wielded, too. This unabashed forwardness was just like her.

"To tell the truth, I, too, would like to pay a visit to the fairy world."

"……"

Based on the content of my conversations with Peeps in the apartment, I calculated that Futarishizuka must have planted the camera during all that noble title nonsense. Otherwise, she would have easily figured out that Peeps's original world existed separately from the fairy world.

And it had been the day before when I returned to Japan. This morning, I'd been flustered by the acceleration in the passage of time and had ended up going straight into the office. In the meantime, the only thing I'd done was go out alone to buy a laptop for use in the otherworld. I'd been hard at work that night setting it up, so I barely talked to Peeps at all.

We did mention the time difference between worlds, but from this girl's point of view, that must have been irrefutable proof of the fairy world being real. Even Futarishizuka didn't seem to have extrapolated the existence of a third world apart from that one and the one we inhabited.

Though things might have been different if she'd taken a little more time to observe.

"So what will it be? I would appreciate a reaction, at least."

In that case, our stance on the matter was decided. For the time being, when in front of her, I'd insist on being a magical middle-aged man.

"Japan's psychics don't look favorably upon magical girls," she went on. "You may feel safe as a bureau employee, but I should think you'd be well served to tighten your own defenses a little more, at the very least."

"You didn't come all the way here just to tell me that, though."

"No, I was being truthful when I said I'd like lodging for the night."

"Tell me why," I asked, readying myself.

The answer came more easily than I had expected. "I am being targeted by my former organization. I would like to count you as an ally."

"Ah."

Her prior organization's mindset must have been along the lines of "If the cuckoo does not sing, kill it." A surprisingly bloodthirsty culture, given its generous company benefits. The bureau definitely had a leg up on them in that regard. Maybe that was part of why she was looking to change jobs.

"If I'm with someone from the bureau, they will find it more difficult to act."

"I understand. But if I accept, I'll be exposing myself to unnecessary risk. Why did you think I'd agree? Did you not consider the opposite possibility?"

"Oh, that's quite simple. I was counting on your dependability and resourcefulness as a man."

"Are you threatening me?"

"Please. You haven't understood a single joke all night."

Futarishizuka may have looked like a little girl, but her chuckling was strangely philosophical, creating an unbalanced impression—only made keener by her history of manipulating me.

"I may not look it, but I am a woman of great means. I have accumulated much, having lived so long. Perhaps with some of it, we can strike a bargain? Regardless of how well paid the bureau's employees are, you must seldom have the opportunity to earn lump sums. And it is clean money, perfectly usable right away, of course."

"……"

Futarishizuka's offer was very enticing.

With the deals I'd been making in the otherworld, my own financial situation was far from healthy. Even the reserve funds I'd received upon entering the bureau had begun to run out with all the stocking up I'd been doing lately. My first paycheck wouldn't arrive for a while yet, so things were pretty tight at the moment.

Maybe it would be a good idea to discuss the amount with Peeps. He was now a modern-day bird, chock-full of knowledge he'd gained from the internet. In all likelihood, he'd been learning quite a bit about the worth of goods and services in this world. He would doubtless prove helpful when negotiating the price.

"…I would be willing to accept, depending on the amount."

"Truly?"

"But I can't make this decision alone. I'd like some time to discuss it."

"A reasonable request."

Plus, whether I let her in or not, I didn't like that she knew about Peeps, but he didn't know about her. I would have to introduce her to him. If she ever turned against us in the future for some reason, it would be vital for him to have met her beforehand.

"I'll introduce you to my partner. Will you come with me?"

"Of course. That is what I'm here for."

"And I would like you to dispose of the camera you planted in my room immediately, please."

"Oh, aren't you a shy one?"

And so we headed to my apartment together.

*

It was important to get my story straight with Peeps before letting Futarishizuka in. Now that I'd explained him as a messenger from the fairy world, if something *was* to happen, and that strange and fantastic otherworld's existence was exposed, I'd have no idea how to proceed.

To solve the problem, we left her just outside the front door and jumped from our apartment to the otherworld.

Before doing so, I remembered to mention the words *Magical Field* and act like I really was a magical middle-aged man for the benefit of the surveillance camera, its location still unknown. Peeps, clever as always, picked up on the odd way I was speaking and used his magic without needing an explanation.

The special effects were a little different from our supposed brethren, but that was inevitable, given the situation.

Like always, we jumped to the cheap lodging we'd reserved for this very purpose. Then, making use of how time passed differently here, I reported Futarishizuka's presence to Peeps.

Despite the changes to the flow of time in the past few days, a few minutes in the otherworld would still be just an instant back home. We could relax, take a seat, and have a talk—without any fear of being caught on hidden cameras.

There was so much to share: Futarishizuka and her powers, the existence of magical girls, fairies, and the fairy world. I had a lot of new info for Peeps, so explaining it took a decent chunk of time.

"*Ah, I see. So that's the gist of what's going on.*"

"If this goes well, we might be able to make our monthly chateaubriand a *weekly* chateaubriand."

"*...Really, now?*" replied Peeps, his tone changing. A serious look had crossed the sparrow's face.

Just how much does he love meat?

"Yeah. But I'll need to secure the best conditions to guarantee it."

"*Then I'll put my all into it as well.*"

"Great."

His considerable enthusiasm inspired a sense of dependability. His neck seemed a little more upright than usual, and his back was a little straighter.

After much discussion, and a very optimistic approval from my partner, we returned to our cheap apartment. We checked the clock; as we'd predicted, it hadn't even been a few minutes yet.

She couldn't have made any serious moves in such a short time. Even if she had used her hidden camera to see us vanish and reappear, we could mention the Magical Field and easily convince her.

"I think we'll be fine, Peeps, but don't let her touch you, no matter what."

"*I am familiar with those who use such magic. It will be no issue.*"

"Wait, really?"

"*Indeed. In your wor— Oh, but I promised not to say any more about it.*"

"Sorry about that, but we're dealing with someone who has no problem spying."

"*Given your position as a government worker, I can understand her thought process.*"

"Yeah?"

"*There is always the possibility of you selling her out to this 'bureau' or what have you. She must want greatly to protect herself.*"

"I see."

Peeps didn't seem fazed in the least by Futarishizuka's tactics, either. *What an understanding sparrow!*

Having completed our calculations and estimations, we went to the front door together. Peeps took up his usual position on my shoulder. Ever since we'd met, the feeling of his claws through the fabric of my shirt relieved me. It really helped me get myself together. *I wonder why—we've only been together a few weeks, even including our time in the otherworld.* Was this what it meant to raise a pet?

After moving from the living space to the front of the apartment, I pushed open the metal door; it wasn't very thick. Futarishizuka was standing in the passage outside the apartment, staring up at us with a travel bag in one hand, exactly as I'd left her.

"That was very fast," she commented.

"There wasn't all that much to talk about."

"Is that being with you the messenger from the fairy world, then?" she asked, her eyes flitting to Peeps on my shoulder. No matter how you looked at him, he was just a Java sparrow. Nobody would ever think he could speak like a human.

"*Indeed, that is correct. My name is Piercarlo.*"

"I'm Futarishizuka."

The two exchanged greetings.

Watching this was making me sweat. But I figured if she intended to do anything to us, she'd have already done it the day before. The true worth of Futarishizuka's power lay in the efficiency of her surprise attacks. She'd never walk straight up to someone first.

"*I understand you wish to stay here for a time?*"

"That's right."

"*How much would you be willing to pay in exchange?*"

Peeps took the lead, asking her the questions—probably because his meat was riding on this.

As far as I could tell, he already had a grasp of the value of goods in this world—in Japanese yen, at the very least. This was a good chance for him to strut his stuff. *Maybe I can leave this to him—just like he leaves everything in the otherworld to me.*

"I'll be straight. How much would you like?"

"*I can't ask for what you don't have. It depends on how much you can pay.*"

"It seems you're taking my request into consideration. I'm very pleased."

We couldn't just stand out here in front of the apartment forever, though. It would be disastrous if anyone saw us while Peeps was talking.

If he'd decided to negotiate, we'd have to move. Even if she did sleep over, my apartment was only a six-tatami room—I'd be up all night. It was just too small. We'd have to live out of a hotel room somewhere for the time being.

After all, she wasn't looking for a place to stay, but for an employee of the bureau to stay with.

"Well, we don't have to stand around here. Now that we've had our introductions, let's move somewhere else. I obviously can't let you into my apartment. As you can see, it's very cramped, with only one bed and no accommodations for a visitor."

"I wouldn't have minded lying on the floor."

"I would have."

"Very well, then. Shall we find lodgings in the neighborhood?"

"But before that, please do remove the camera."

"You can't let me keep it there for just a little while longer?"

"Why would I? If you refuse to remove it, or leave part of it behind, then assume we will become your enemy, just like the magical girl we encountered earlier."

"Such a difficult world we live in…"

Um, actually, I think I'm being perfectly reasonable! I would have to have an expert double-check sometime soon.

✳

After leaving the apartment, we ended up at a high-class hotel in the city.

The guest rooms included not only a bedroom but a living room and reception area as well, plus access to a personal butler. It was the very lap of luxury. The difference between this and the business hotels the bureau booked was like night and day. I was too scared to ask how much it cost.

I thought it would be impossible to get a same-day reservation, but Futarishizuka got it done snappily with a single phone call. She was handling all the expenses, including for Peeps and me.

The implication seemed to be this: Now that she'd insisted on staying somewhere with better security, she was showing us an example. And she was right—most burglars wouldn't bother with a room high up in a hotel, dozens of meters off the ground.

Finally, we came to the living space. After settling down on the sofas, we faced each other over a low table. Peeps was perched on my shoulder. I casually glanced at him and saw that he was staring hard at Futarishizuka. The sparrow's face in profile was awe-inspiring; it made me want to snap a picture.

"If you don't mind," she began, "I would like to discuss compensation."

"Before that, I have a question for you."

"What is it?"

"How would you feel about a form of payment other than money?"

Peeps spoke as though he'd just thought of something. This wasn't part of the discussion we'd had earlier; I found myself turning to look at him in spite of myself. "Peeps?"

"The fact that you have amassed a fortune must mean you have the

connections with which to buy and sell things of great value. We have very few such worldly connections at present. As compensation, would you consider sharing some of those with us?"

"......"

"We've been graced with a golden opportunity. It would be a waste for our relationship to end after this."

Bringing up such a deal at the last moment to someone we weren't sure if we could trust took nerves of steel—as expected of the Lord Starsage. He was so cool. You could really tell how much of his past had been spent dealing with crafty court nobility on equal footing.

"I wouldn't mind that, I suppose, but what about *him*?"

"Do you mind this arrangement?"

I'd be lying if I said I didn't have apprehensions. According to the chief, Futarishizuka was a psychic belonging to an anti-governmental organization. I couldn't imagine the connections such a person would have involved anything legal. For comparison, she was far more frightening than the yakuza.

The only reason we were able to have a relationship at all was because I had permission from the chief. Otherwise, I couldn't even be seen with her. If I screwed this up, I could be arrested the very next day.

But if this was what Peeps wanted, then I would do my best to make it happen—just as he'd given me the freedom to choose in the otherworld.

"Your proposal has me very interested, Peeps."

"Truly?"

"But I would like to avoid anyone at work getting angry with me..."

"I plan to discuss that, too, during these talks."

"Ah, I see." Futarishizuka looked convinced by what Peeps had said. She seemed interested as well; she had a hand to her cheek as she appeared to think it over. "That would mean you have something to sell, would it not?"

"That is correct."

"Items from the fairy world, perhaps?"

"Are you interested in valuables and treasures from another world?"

He had to speak vaguely, but this was the issue that had been plaguing us until this very day—how to convert valuables from the otherworld into yen. If we could leverage Futarishizuka's connections to do that, I'd be excited, too.

It was always best to ask a pro, it seemed.

If possible, to reinforce my lie that I was a magical girl, I wanted to disguise the items as being from the fairy world. However, there would be no proof that the items we brought over existed in the fairy world at all. To me, the safest option would be to sneakily avoid telling her where they came from for the time being.

"Well then, I suppose I should venture the question. What do you plan on bringing?"

"For now, we have our sights set on precious metals."

"Of the sort that exist in our world, hmm?"

"Would you prefer types that didn't?"

"There's no telling what could happen were you to bring me something ill-advised. That would be most unfortunate."

Peeps seemed to understand that much as well. He continued, speaking plainly.

"I see."

"Still, that idea does certainly whet the appetite...," added Futarishizuka.

"Ms. Futarishizuka, we have no issue making a deal with you, but we will not act outside the bounds of Japan's rules and regulations. I hope you can understand that point. In the worst case, we would have to throw you to the wolves."

I didn't know how effective it would be, but I warned her regardless. If any problems were to occur as part of my relationship with Futarishizuka, considering Mr. Akutsu's personality, it was easy to imagine a future where he cut us both off. That was why I hoped making myself clear right from the start would prove meaningful.

For the time being, I wanted to lead a lazy, idle life as a phony government employee.

I had never imagined that being someone who didn't have to go to work every day at the same time could be this wonderful. I could avoid being packed like a sardine on the train, and I didn't even have to wait until I learned teleportation magic. That alone felt like it put me in a special class of person in modern Japan.

At the same time, this was an important matter that would directly impact Peeps's chateaubriand lifestyle.

"It isn't as though I'm pawning off suspicious drugs, all right?" she said.

"It will depend on the item, but there are many ways to handle such things. It is difficult to move large amounts of money, but it shouldn't be an issue at all to move our living headquarters to this hotel."

"...I see."

"Still, I must say, you are quite a straightforward person."

"I just couldn't think of a better threat, that's all."

She then gave me a concrete number, which shocked me. It was way, *way* higher an amount than anything I'd been expecting. I had thought if I could secure about as much as the reserve funds provided by the bureau, I'd be over the moon. But her proposal was two, if not three digits more than that; I could hear my heart almost explode.

No matter how you looked at it, this hotel was in the hundred-thousand-yen range. The person in front of me seemed to be much richer than I'd imagined. How much had she managed to stow away?

At a glance, she was just a small child. This enormous gap in perception made the whole conversation very weird.

"Either way," she continued, "I cannot make any promises before confirming the goods."

"We will prepare them for you in the near future."

"I cannot wait. It is making me more excited than one my age has any right to be."

And thus, Peeps and Futarishizuka came to an agreement.

I'd be lying if I said I didn't have any concerns. There was always the possibility she'd betray us and tell the section chief everything. But now that she already knew about my position as a magical middle-aged man, there wasn't any point in hesitating to strike a deal with her.

And, I thought as I watched Peeps chattering enthusiastically, *once his beloved pet bird has made a decision, isn't it the pet owner's duty to show his magnanimity and accept it?*

✳

The next day, Futarishizuka and I were in the hotel's living room, facing a laptop computer. We sat on the sofas, both looking at the device on the low table in front of us. Only Futarishizuka was reflected on the screen, though. I was sitting on the opposite sofa, watching her. Peeps was on my shoulder.

We'd brought another monitor, separate from the laptop, and placed it on the table. The image, connected via an external output, was positioned so I could see it, too, from my spot on the other side of the laptop. All this had been provided by the hotel.

On the screen was Section Chief Akutsu's face. Good-looking as always. One of those attractive middle-aged men. The suit and watch he had on looked expensive, too.

Behind him was most likely a conference room in the bureau offices. He sat in a chair, facing his own device's camera. No other bureau employees were visible, but it was always possible others were positioned just out of sight.

"Thank you for making the time for me today. I know you must be busy."

"I'm going to be direct with you. Do you truly wish for a transfer into the bureau?"

Though Futarishizuka had started off with a formal greeting, the chief simply questioned her without emotion. He watched her closely and carefully.

"Yes, I do."

"You were an executive member of an organization hostile to us, correct? It's hard for me to believe you now wish to transfer. Do you have the grounds to convince me? If not, then I won't be able to accept your proposal."

"What you say is reasonable."

This was turning into a stressful interview—probably because Futarishizuka was the interviewee. As a psychic, she excelled in harming others. If she got into the bureau, then betrayed us, the losses would be massive. No matter how short on hands we were, even I felt strongly that the risks here were too great to justify the returns.

"Still, you are a very talented psychic. Of that there is no doubt."

"Will you consider my request, then?"

"At the present time, it won't be possible for us to accept you as an official bureau employee. However, I can think about giving you tasks as a part-timer. Depending on how well you work, I could conceivably think about bringing you on full-time in the future."

"Hmm, I see."

This was about how I'd expected it would go.

If we didn't take her under our wing, she would end up with some other group. If that other group was friendly toward our bureau, there would be no problem. But if a hostile organization took her in, and if her volition to change jobs was sincere, that would become its own problem.

And for that reason, we'd never actually had the option of turning her down.

"The bureau cannot yield any more than that."

"In that case, I would be grateful if you allowed me to help with your work."

She'd probably requested the interview after considering all that as well. It hadn't taken long for her to answer the question.

As she answered with a glittering smile, she appeared closer to her physical age—that of a little girl. If we hadn't met at the bowling alley, she probably would have fooled me with that smile and taken advantage of me.

Come to think of it, the neighbor was about this girl's size when I first met her, too.

"...All right."

With her consent, the section chief nodded and agreed in his detached way.

It looked like she'd be working as a part-timer or a temp worker. Given how rich she was, it wouldn't cause her any financial issues. Which meant it all came down to how good she could make the bureau look to the public.

As for that, though, we wouldn't know until we saw her in action.

"So then, what will become of my status? I have no particular preferences for part-time or contract work as long as I can do that work under the bureau's name, but it may not appear so to others."

"Right. Regarding that, I'd like to leave it up to Sasaki to look after you."

I sighed. *What's he saying now?* I wondered. *He can't be serious, can he?* "Chief, hold on a moment."

Before I knew it, I had cut into the conversation.

The camera wasn't facing me, so I wasn't visible in the video. But he'd still be able to hear me through the microphone. I had no intention of letting what he just said go by unnoticed.

"Have you been listening? Well, you heard me—please do your best."

"Have you forgotten I'm a new employee who just joined the bureau?"

"Of course not. And you are an extremely talented member of our team—your superiors think highly of you."

"I still have concerns about this decision."

My policy is to emphasize those who stand out, regardless of how long they've been employed.

What I'd *wanted* to do was throw the entire Futarishizuka matter in the section chief's lap and revel in his reactions. I never thought it would come bouncing right back to me. He had just placed a rank-A psychic in the care of a newbie who had only gone on-site twice. Would the rest of the bureau even accept that?

"Keep in mind I have no authority. If something was to happen, my response may be delayed."

"That's very true. I haven't given you much authority, have I?"

"Then—"

"In that case, I'll give you the same level of authority as Hoshizaki."

"What?"

"I'll send over a sheet listing all your official powers later today; use that as reference."

"Chief, isn't authority something that comes along with a managerial position or compensation of some kind?"

"I don't think I need to tell you this, but human affairs here at the bureau are different from those at the Cabinet Office. I'm entrusted with the whole kit and caboodle. Isn't this a good thing, Sasaki? You've been promoted twice only a couple weeks after being hired. It's virtually unprecedented."

"Still, Chief, I—"

"And she's someone you invited in, right? You'll take responsibility until the end, I'm sure. Acting like this is only going to cause her trouble. We await your work for the betterment of the bureau, Sasaki. I want you to give this your absolute best."

He knew exactly how to get to me. But even so, I was troubled.

I didn't have the time to worry about it much, though. *"That's all for the interview. She's in your hands, Sasaki."*

"No, hold on a second. I mean—"

"I'll contact you again with our schedule. For today, I want you to deepen your familiarity with your new subordinate. This will be included in the list of official powers I'll send later, but your entertainment allowance will be expensed up to one million yen. This is as a capital investment for us, after all. So make sure to always keep your receipts."

"Chief, ah, er, when you say capital investment—"

But before I could continue, the phone conference ended. The video cut off, and the screen faded to nothing.

There were *so* many things I wanted to say to him about all this.

And now it was awkward in the living room. With the conversation over, the space had fallen silent. The sound of the laptop's fan spinning was oddly loud. No matter how long I waited, the chief's handsome face would not grace the screen again.

For a while, there was quiet.

Eventually, Futarishizuka turned to me and said, "Is looking after me truly so unpleasant for you?"

"……"

Her eyes, turned up to look at me, were frighteningly cute. She certainly seemed a far cry from a woman of character who had lived since before the war.

She was definitely faking it.

"…As a fellow new hire, I hope we can get along," I said.

"Indeed. I may cause problems here and there, but I look forward to working with you."

Now I was one win and one loss against the chief. *Next time, I'm going to fluster him for sure*, I thought, determined.

✱

After escaping office life, working in the public sector was so freeing.

The sun was still shining, and the boss had ordered me to take the rest of the day off—*and* to get a daytime drink. *And* he said the company would pay the entire bill. Essentially, there was no limit; no normal *izakaya* would ever get close to the amount he had given.

"Nothing beats paying for drinks with taxpayer money while the sun is still high in the sky," she drawled.

"Yeah."

The beer was delicious. Even the foam.

Whoever first thought up that slogan must have been an absolute genius.

"Ah, but does this not want to make you call for women as well?"

"Oh, no, I could never."

"I could put you in touch. It would all fall under the business expenses."

"No, I couldn't do something like that in front of someone as pretty as you, Ms. Futarishizuka."

"Oh, really? Your objection fills me with anticipation."

I would be lying if I said I wasn't happy.

I was *really* happy.

Day-drinking on someone else's dime was the *best*.

We were in a private room, in an *izakaya* downtown near our hotel, having a drink together. More and more places like this were serving alcohol in the daytime—just to get people in for a drink or two, that kind of thing.

Of course, when we first entered the shop, they'd refused Futarishizuka's order because of her appearance.

She had then shown them her driver's license. What stood out to me was that it was up for renewal next year. The clerk figured it was a forgery, but after she showed them her passport, too, he took her order without any further issue.

I only heard later that both of them *were* forgeries. She'd already lost her real passport; she told me it was no longer extant—or something. I bet it was filled with stamps from countries that didn't exist anymore.

"May I order the fried chicken and potato salad?" asked Futarishizuka, her tone languid as always.

"I'm surprised you seem to prefer common food."

"Alcohol hits you hard on an empty stomach. I'd rather eat a bit first."

"In that case, is it all right if I get this assorted sashimi platter?"

"Oh! Yes, please do."

"It's all company money, so order as much as you want."

"My, how generous. In that case..."

We're going to eat and drink until the cows come home.

If there was one thing that bothered me, it was Peeps's absence. I couldn't exactly bring the birdcage into the *izakaya* and then let him out to peck away at some food. Lately, even places like these had started putting up surveillance cameras.

So during outings, I'd taken to making excuses, like wanting to dip out early so I could do some drinking back at my hotel. The Lord Starsage had accepted this, thankfully, in exchange for me bringing him Kobe beef chateaubriand as a gift.

I planned to take advantage of the occasion and make my own dent in the entertainment expenses for Futarishizuka.

Normally, taxes were only something I had to pay. The idea that I might be able to take some of that money back via *izakaya* and grocery bills was driving me to eat and drink until my stomach couldn't fit any more. *In fact, why don't I go and buy chateaubriand by the kilogram as a souvenir?*

"By the way," said Futarishizuka, "your boss seems to trust you quite a lot."

"Oh, no, that's really not the case at all."

"Isn't it?"

"He believes in meritocracy, so this is probably because you're here."

"Ah, I see. So our destinies are linked."

"Even if you stumble, I plan to do my best."

"Oh? How cocky you are—especially when I'm right here."

"It'd make me nervous if I didn't say anything. No need to tease me."

"People who talk like that are the biggest schemers."

As we chatted, I took care to keep the conversation light and entertaining. But if I was able to unearth even a scrap of her true intent, I would be more than satisfied.

We continued to enjoy our drinks and talk about nothing important until, a while later, when we'd both finished off our third mug, the door to our private room suddenly swung open. I couldn't remember making any orders. Naturally, our attention snapped to the hallway.

And there we saw Miss Hoshizaki.

"Sasaki! I've been looking all over for you."

"Fancy seeing you in a place like this, Miss Hoshizaki."

We hadn't seen each other since parting ways at the bureau the day before. As always, she was armed with her suit and a lot of makeup—that thick lipstick was wonderful.

"I used your device's location info to track you down."

"Ah, I see."

Come to think of it, I did carry a device like that around, didn't I? My thoughts turned to my pants pocket.

Still, why *had* she come all the way here anyway? If she needed something, she could have just called. We weren't that far from the bureau, but she would still have needed a taxi to get here. If she'd come by train, all the transfers would have been a real hassle.

"Did you need something from us?"

"I heard from the chief. He put you in charge of Futarishizuka, huh?" she said, looking at the girl in the kimono sitting opposite me.

Her expression appeared stiff and tense. She normally looked sullen, but this time she was significantly more on edge.

"Do you understand how terrifying she is?"

"Yes. I believe you were the one who explained it to me."

"And yet here you are, drinking the day away with her like none of that matters…"

Wait, did she come here because she was worried? In that case, what about letting her join us? She couldn't drink since she was in high school, but I doubted it would be an issue for her to eat something. For a shop we went into out of pure momentum and zero research, it was surprisingly delicious and satisfying.

The horse mackerel sashimi was especially incredible. Anywhere that had good horse mackerel was a trustworthy place, in my book.

"Would you like to join us, Miss Hoshizaki?"

"What kind of idiotic nonsense is that?"

"I don't know what to tell you. The chief ordered us to do this."

"Yeah, I kind of doubt even the chief would have thought you two would be drinking the day away like dumbasses. When I checked your location, it showed you parked at an *izakaya*! That's why I came all the way here to check up on you. Couldn't you have figured that out on your own?"

Wait. What? He was joking?

The list of official powers he'd sent me earlier had included the social expenses amount he had indicated. That was why we'd started day-drinking without asking questions. From our conversation so far, Futarishizuka didn't seem dissatisfied with the arrangement, either.

"…Oh. I see."

That section chief! His jokes are too hard to understand.

The giant octopus sashimi that came out in a little boat was out of this *world*. The wasabi soy sauce just kept on flowing. In my opinion, when it was served on those big leaves, you knew it was quality.

"Old men really *do* talk business while drinking, huh?"

"That wasn't exactly what we were going for here…"

Once Miss Hoshizaki entered the room, the complaints started flying.

"I remember you, child. The bureau's water-manipulating psychic, hmm?" said Futarishizuka, unable to sit by and watch the two of us.

"And what if I am?"

"Then we shall have to get you set up with a drink! Go ahead and order something."

With a grin, Futarishizuka held out the remote control used to send our orders. Then she breathed out, and the stench of alcohol made Miss Hoshizaki's face scrunch up into a scowl. Her expression said *Don't talk to me anymore.* She really was just a high school girl caught up with a couple drunks, but one of them looked like a little girl, which made everything weirder.

Since Futarishizuka had started it, I decided to hop on the bandwagon. "Have you eaten yet, Miss Hoshizaki? If you haven't, why not eat with us? We spoke with the chief, and he approved of us eating here as a business expense."

At the same time, I didn't forget to mention the entertainment budget to my coworker. A corporate drone's worst nightmare was finding out that a meal wouldn't be covered by the company, after all. I remembered every receipt that I wasn't able to turn in.

"Wait. Are you drunk right now?"

"I can't deny the possibility."

"……"

I didn't think I'd be drunk after three glasses, but with an upstanding high school girl in front of me, I didn't want to act careless, so I replied honestly. I was keenly aware of how dangerous the person in front of me was. My intent had always been to drink in moderation, without forgetting the presence of my important guest. *I'd imagine it's the same for Futarishizuka, too.* That was why she had ordered side dishes like fried chicken and potato salad.

"All right, fine."

Then, for reasons I didn't understand, Miss Hoshizaki took a seat next to me. She'd taken an empty space on one side of the four-person table.

"Miss Hoshizaki?" I ventured.

"You invited me, remember? I don't have a problem eating here."

"I see. Well, thank you."

"You know," said Futarishizuka, "you're more reasonable than I'd assumed."

Normally, the high school girl's tone was conspicuously brusque, but maybe her true personality was more caring. Or was she just worried about her good-for-nothing junior? Either way, I was more than happy to accept the generosity.

✳

It happened at the *izakaya* when I got up to go to the bathroom. As I was walking down the hallway, someone called my name from behind.

"Sasaki, could I talk to you about something real quick?"

"What is it?"

Miss Hoshizaki trotted over to catch up to me.

I figured she was hesitant to be alone in the private room with Futarishizuka. I couldn't say I didn't understand; I wanted to put as much distance as possible between her and me, too. Being here without Peeps was forcing me to put in the effort whether I liked it or not.

"Yesterday was so busy I didn't have a chance to thank you, so…"

"Thank me?"

"I lost consciousness partway through when Futarishizuka drained my energy. But you stayed on-site until it was over and retrieved the target and me. I never thanked you for it."

Come to think of it, I remembered her inviting me out for lunch as thanks after that bowling alley incident, too. I wouldn't have thought she cared about such things, but her personality was surprisingly conscientious. The gap between that and the suicidal mindset she got into on the battlefield was staggering.

"You don't need to. We were on the job as a team, so I only did what I was supposed to."

"Still, you saved me back there. I had no idea you'd end up asking Futarishizuka for help in that situation and then driving off the magical girl. The airplane crash was my fault, too, for not stopping the target. It's only because you interceded that I'm still even able to work."

"Did the chief get on your case about this?"

"He just told me to appreciate you more."

"I see."

What I did back then was more for my sake than hers. But if acting that way saved someone else on the side, there was no point in being unhappy about it. Especially if it was my work partner, the other half of my team.

"Still, everything that happened was the product of coincidence, so I don't think you need to be so formal."

"Really?"

"Yes, really."

"Well, even if it was a coincidence, you still saved me. That's a fact."

I was glad to hear her thank me, but I was scared I might expose something if we talked about it any more than this. Though I felt bad for wrenching the conversation in another direction, I did what I had to. "By the way, I had something to ask you."

"What might that be?"

"I've already heard that your power is to control liquid, but does that not include the body fluids inside a living human? Like, if you could touch someone's skin and manipulate their blood, that might be on par with Futarishizuka's ability."

"If the blood is outside the body first, I can control it."

"But not if it's still underneath the skin, then?"

If that was possible, it would be an effective deterrent against Futarishizuka. Since the girl could only use her power when she was touching her opponent's body, too, Miss Hoshizaki would at least be able to go down with her. I doubted Futarishizuka would go that far to take down Miss Hoshizaki, so her safety would have been guaranteed at the very least. But alas.

"I've tried doing stuff like that a bunch of times, but it's never worked out. The same goes for liquid that's been partly absorbed into the ground—and water vapor. I can't control those, either."

"I see." Guess it really was impossible. Though I supposed it would be pretty scary if she *could* do it.

"Still, I'd like to get to that point one day."

"That's possible?"

"Who knows? Sometimes a psychic's power grows as they use it."

"Now that I think about it, I do remember learning that during training."

Although psychics couldn't awaken to new powers, they could cultivate the one they already possessed. However, doing so necessitated an uncommon level of effort or a deep understanding of the power itself; the explanation had made it sound really tiring.

And this was battle-crazy Hoshizaki, here—she probably trained every single day.

"I'm sorry, but could you let me go to the bathroom now…?"

"Huh? Oh, right, sure. Sorry for stopping you."

"Don't worry about it."

After cutting the conversation short at an appropriate point, this lying bastard dashed into the bathroom.

✳

Later, after wrapping up our day-drinking, we parted ways with Miss Hoshizaki and returned to the hotel Futarishizuka had booked for us. Miss Hoshizaki, upon confirming the situation, had finished her *izakaya* lunch and returned to the bureau. That was a stroke of luck, since Peeps was with us in the hotel. As his owner, watching him stick to his sparrow act in her presence would have been painful to watch.

The last remaining issue was the matter of our short stays in the otherworld.

Futarishizuka's interview with the chief had gone mostly as anticipated, so I wanted to return straight home after reuniting with Peeps. The girl would be able to start her work as part of the bureau now, which should lower the chances of former colleagues attacking her.

"I think I'll be going now," I said to her, holding Peeps's cage in one hand.

However, in response, she asked us to wait. "Leaving already, are we?"

"It may only be part-time, but a new hire is a new hire. Go ahead and file for your transfer in triumph."

"Personally, I'm in the mood to spread some more lascivious rumors, perhaps about some romantic relationships between bureau employees."

That would end up harming me as well, wouldn't it? I thought. *Definitely out of the question.*

Still, considering my future plans to sell valuables from the otherworld, I'd have to actively help her in some way and gain her trust. You couldn't foster a friendly relationship when you always wanted the other person to do things for you.

If we were going to stick together for a long period of time, I'd have to demonstrate that she would benefit, too. And in gambles like these, the opponent was at an extreme advantage. The older, the wiser, so the saying went. *Better to be sincere than try to use poorly thought-out schemes*, I thought as I watched the girl grinning greedily.

"Do you know about the Magical Field used by magical girls?"

"I do. A strange magic that allows one to move anywhere they wish, yes?"

"If anything happens, I'll come straight to this hotel."

"You would do that?"

"Yes. I promise," I said, shooting a glance over at Peeps and seeing him give a little nod.

He, too, could probably see the chateaubriand sizzling before his eyes even now, with our goal of interworld trade dangling right before us. The chunk of meat I'd bought as a gift on the way home from the *izakaya* was doing the trick in all its two-kilogram glory—and it was a particularly exclusive cut.

It was amazing, having the right to decide when and how I'd eat and drink. And it was all being financed with taxes. I felt like I'd gotten every bit of my residents' tax and income tax return from the previous year. *So this is why dirty jobs never disappear from the world.*

"For a member of the bureau, you are surprisingly caring."

"Is that right? Well anyway, I'm going to get going for the day."

"Yes. I look forward to working with you from now on."

After returning her smile with a slight bow, I left the hotel with Peeps.

(The Neighbor's POV)

During lunchtime, I decided to read a book in the library. Since today's main course was rice, I didn't need to devote any time to securing food. All I did was secure about three extra helpings of the green onion miso salad, since it was so unpopular. The dish was rich in flavor and filling. Plus, wonderfully, there was always so much of it left over.

"……"

In sharp contrast to the lively classroom, the library is very quiet. With the librarian keeping watch, you never hear students raise their voices. I come here a lot, since I have a hard time with loud places.

And for someone who can't even watch TV or read newspapers or magazines at home, the school library is also a vital place for me to get information on what is happening in the world. With how many different kinds of magazines this library has, it is even more valuable a resource than the lectures we get in the classroom.

Just like every other day, I have a stack of newly published informational magazines on the table. When I flip through the articles, I never bother thinking too hard about the contents. It all just flows into my head; I accept it all as simple information and never really scrutinize any of it. You never know what kind of knowledge may come in handy in any particular situation.

Most importantly, some of it might help me talk to the man next door.

I spend a while like this in peace and quiet.

Then I hear voices from another table close by.

"Did you hear about the murder that happened the other day near the school?"

"Wait, you mean the one at the intersection on Second Street?"

"Yeah, that one!"

Judging by the color of their slippers, the two girls are in their second year, one grade higher than I am. The two of them are sitting side by side at their table, chatting away. They're not speaking loudly or anything. At their volume, the librarian wouldn't start nagging them to shut up, as long as it didn't last too long. But since no other students are making any noise, I can hear them all the way over at my table.

"Apparently, stuff like that is happening all over the country."

"Wait, really?"

"My dad was talking about it this morning. He's a police officer."

They are talking about the incident I had run into the other day. My attention naturally shifts away from the magazine in my hands to the girls' conversation.

"But you know how it's not really on the news much?"

"They have a—um. Muzzling order? That's why they're not talking about it."

"Muzzling order? You mean a gag order?"

"Yeah, that's the one! I think."

"Wait, for real? That's like the stuff you see in TV dramas."

After all, I'm curious about it, too.

A person has died—and in a way that would have made headlines everywhere. It is strange that it isn't being talked about on the news. Even the magazines I'd been reading today hadn't mentioned it once.

Plus, they haven't caught the culprit yet. At least, nobody is reporting that they have. The criminal could even be hiding out somewhere nearby.

"It's true! My dad was really annoyed about it."

"I bet it's making his job pretty hard."

"No, not that. Apparently, he hates it when big shots from the government come to talk to them."

"Wait, what? I don't get it."

Does that mean they had a conference on how to respond to the incident?

If that is the case, the information about the gag order seems a little more trustworthy. A local police officer complaining to his family about government interference—that kind of makes sense.

As I stare at the magazine in my hands, my imagination starts running wild. They are right—this *is* like something from a TV drama. I'd never seen one, but I can hazard a guess. It seems like they're about things like this.

I only get to listen to their conversation for a few moments, though, since the bell rings, marking five minutes until the end of lunchtime and the start of fifth period.

The two girls who had been talking get up and leave the library. I watch them out of the corner of my eye as I rise from my own chair. After returning the stack of magazines to their places, I hurry out of the library.

Just student rumors. Probably nothing to worry about.

Getting a chance to talk to the man next door is far more important to me anyway.

<The Otherworld and Psychic Powers>

After returning to our apartment, Peeps and I decided to head for the otherworld right away. We hadn't been able to do so the previous night because we were at the hotel with Futarishizuka, and while the time difference may have changed since our last trip, we could be sure that about a month had passed. Partly because of that, I was nervous during our journey.

As always, we arrived in the cheap inn room in town we had reserved for this purpose. After that, I relied on Peeps's teleportation spell to get to Count Müller's castle. If we wanted information in this world, there was nobody more reliable. We urgently needed to learn how things were going here after the incident with the Empire.

The guard standing watch at the castle's entrance was a familiar face I'd already encountered several times on my way in and out. When he saw us approach, he gave a reverent bow and said, "Ah, Sir Sasaki—w-welcome back!"

"Huh? We've...met before, haven't we?"

Last time we spoke, I remembered him being a little friendlier. He'd say things like, "Hey! Welcome back!" or "Just stay put for a second," and announce us to Count Müller.

"Sir, I, er, deeply apologize for any rudeness I may have displayed in the past!"

"Wait, what are you talking—?"

"You are a *noble*, Sir Sasaki!"

Oh, right. Now that he mentioned it, something like that *had* happened, huh? If I was remembering correctly, I'd received the rank of knight. Everything that had happened back in modern Japan had been so shocking I'd forgotten all about matters in this world. That said, knights were the lowest rank of nobility according to the count. If a guard was having to humble himself to this degree... Well, social status in the Kingdom of Herz was certainly nothing to shake a stick at. No matter what I said to the guard after that, he retained an air of profound respect.

Eventually, we ended up in the reception room in Count Müller's residence.

"Thank you for coming, Sir Sasaki. Lord Starsage, I am honored by your presence."

"I'm sorry for barging in all of a sudden. You must be busy."

"My apologies for not contacting you in advance, Julius."

"Please, no apologies necessary. I have plenty to discuss with you both as well."

"In that case, why don't we get right down to business?"

The only ones in the room were Peeps, the count, and me—two men and one bird. Count Müller and I sat on the sofas as we spoke. The table between us was set up with tea and several sweets brought in by a maid just a moment ago.

She'd also placed a wonderful perching tree next to the tea set, along with more finely cut pieces of candy that now sat in a shallow dish in front of it. There was also a small teacup about as deep as the bird's beak was long—these would make it easier for Peeps to peck away at everything. The whole set must have been custom ordered. Every part of it spoke to the depth of respect the person in front of us had for the Lord Starsage. I glanced at the bird on my shoulder, and he fluttered down to the tree on the table.

The corners of Count Müller's mouth turned up in a slight smile. The sight of them both brought a smile to my heart, as well. I began to wonder if it might even be better to leave Peeps in his hands for a while during our stay here.

"Sir Sasaki, would you mind terribly if I shared my news first?"

"Please do, my lord."

"I apologize for the rush, but there is something I very much need to inform you both of."

Hearing Count Müller say this with such an air of formality was

kind of scary. Despite myself, I tensed up in preparation. "What would that be, my lord?"

"The invasion by the Ohgen Empire into the Kingdom of Herz has set unprecedented events into motion within our nation. These events concern certain privileged classes—the royalty and nobility, specifically, and I want to make sure you're aware of them, Sir Sasaki."

"I would be more than happy to listen. We had been hoping to ask about current events, ourselves."

Peeps and I both turned to focus on what Count Müller had to say.

And what we heard struck me as very uncharacteristic of the Kingdom of Herz. The source of this disturbance had been none other than the king—the very one I'd previously been bestowed an audience with. He had made a shocking proclamation addressed to all Herzian nobility.

In his words: *Our nation will implement various measures to regain our past prosperity*, and so on. One particular part of this speech, according to Count Müller, caused a stir throughout the kingdom's nobility, from the highest to the lowest in rank.

As for what part was so provocative... Well, to summarize, it's quite simple.

The current king had several children, and he intended to have each play an equal part in the politics of the nation. After five years, he would unconditionally cede the throne of the kingdom to whoever achieved the most remarkable feats.

It seemed His Majesty was truly concerned about the direction this country was taking.

Left desperate in the face of invasion, then blessed with a windfall recovery, he had found himself ready to welcome revolutionary reform. I didn't know how it was for nobles, but once a nation was defeated and occupied by another, the death of its royal family was a foregone conclusion. Such things had happened repeatedly in my own world.

"I see, my lord. So that's what's been happening..."

"His Majesty had a lot to think about, no doubt."

"Come to think of it, how was the war's outcome explained publicly? As you know, the enemy's combat strength up and vanished. I figured Herz might have some difficulties explaining it."

"Both nations are reporting that they were caught up in a battle between two great war criminals. Traces of great magic, or magic even higher than that, have been confirmed at the site. The Ohgen Empire probably doesn't think the Kingdom of Herz is responsible, either."

Count Müller's eyes darted briefly to Peeps. The sparrow wasn't fooling him.

I naturally recalled the purple-skinned woman he'd engaged in aerial combat for such a long time. She had a frightening nickname—the Blood Witch, if I remembered correctly. According to Count Müller's words at the time, she was one of the seven great war criminals.

I wasn't sure what kind of people these "great war criminals" were, but based on what I was hearing now, they sounded similar to Peeps: remarkably talented and, from the perspective of the rest of us ordinary people, more akin to a natural disaster than anything else.

"I feel bad for involving you in all this trouble, Sir Sasaki. You received your title by the will of the second prince's mother, and everyone believes this latest development is going to lead to a struggle between the first and second princes."

"It isn't something you need to apologize for, Count Müller."

"No, I *am* responsible for involving you both."

Noble affairs here in Herz would probably be absolute chaos for the time being. And with Count Müller being closely allied with the second prince, I doubted he'd be able to remain uninvolved. His promotion to count, still recent news, wouldn't make anything easier for him, either. From what I'd heard in the past, the first prince had appeared recently and shown great talent—and was now rumored to be next in line for the throne—but before that, the second prince was far and away the favorite. There was little doubt the forces assembled around the second prince were still significant.

"Count Müller, I personally hold Prince Adonis's love for his country in high esteem as well."

"If the prince heard me say this, he would probably be angry, but there is really no need for you to be concerned with us. I think I have a good understanding of your position, Sir Sasaki. That was why I wanted to tell you about this as soon as I could."

"Thank you, my lord. Still, to think that things had turned out that way..."

After saving Prince Adonis's life on the battlefield, Count Müller had ascended to the rank of count and become very close friends with the second prince. He was his confidant now, and that seemed to place him right in the middle of the vortex—the struggle for power that had begun swirling in the court and was just now picking up even more speed.

I'd seen it many times before: a newly appointed section chief being overloaded with work from other departments. That work would inevitably trickle down to his subordinates. It made me think about what a company was really supposed to be—what the term *management* really meant. In that sense, my position wasn't altogether safe.

"I also wanted to discuss something with you, Sir Sasaki."

"What is it, my lord?"

"You should leave the country as soon as you can and head for the Republic of Lunge."

"Count Müller, I don't think—"

"I am confident you will be wildly successful there."

I've never had a single section chief say something like that to me, I thought. In fact, I'd only ever heard the opposite. As a result, Count Müller's proposition stirred my heart. I got butterflies in my stomach, despite my age.

"Lunge is famous as a country where goods flow and business transactions are made," he continued. "And I have a few connections there myself. I can set things up to send you to them. What do you say to using this opportunity to travel the continent, experience the cultures in other cities, and broaden your knowledge?"

"……"

How could I simply agree after all that? I wanted to keep playing this game of being a corporate drone under a really good boss.

Naturally, my mind shifted to the bag resting on the floor next to my sofa. Then my eyes drifted over to Peeps, who was perched on the tree set up on the low table in front of me. I would ask the great Lord Starsage for his opinion.

The answer came right away. The sparrow gave a slight nod. What an adorably cool and sophisticated bird.

"I understand your proposal, Count Müller, but we would still prefer to stay in this town for a while longer to do business. If it's all right, would you look through the products we've brought? I stocked some extra transceivers, too."

"B-but, Sir Sasaki, that's—"

"Can we interest you in this purchase?" I asked the count, staring straight at his attractive face.

Then his expression broke into a bashful smile, and he nodded. Normally, Count Müller was able to exude an air of authority without much change in his features, so whenever he showed real human emotion like that, it was always clear and bright.

"...I'm sorry. You don't know how much I appreciate your thoughtfulness."

I was beginning to understand why Peeps had so much concern for this man.

✳

After we'd confirmed the state of affairs in the otherworld, and the count had confirmed our products, our business was settled for the moment. No problems came up during the exchange, as the items I'd brought this time were all ones I'd sold before. Since I'd had to deal with Futarishizuka, I hadn't had time to pick out anything new.

The final purchase amount was more modest than on previous occasions, too, at a few hundred gold pieces.

And with that, our business talk wrapped up for the time being. The next topic to come up was Mr. Marc, vice manager of the Hermann Trading Company.

"While I'm thinking of it," said the count, "I had something to ask you about, Sir Sasaki."

"What would that be, my lord?"

"Have you seen Mr. Marc of the Hermann Trading Company recently?"

"No, it's been some time since I've seen him."

"...I see."

"Has something happened?"

"I have several things to discuss with him, so I figured I would wait until the next time he visited the estate. However, I haven't seen him since the week before last. He pays the estate a visit every week, so I'm a little concerned."

I hadn't met up with the vice manager since our previous short stay in this world, so I doubted I could be much help to Count Müller. "I'm sorry, I haven't seen him since last month."

"No, don't worry about it. I'll send a messenger to his store—as soon as tomorrow, perhaps."

This was only conjecture, but I imagined the man was very busy with what Count Müller had explained earlier. Mr. Marc had not only heard about the count rescuing the second prince but also had information from me, too, so I figured he was making every possible effort to profit from it.

After a little less than an hour of talking about this and that, there suddenly came a knock at the door. It was a knight—and one, it appeared, who personally guarded the count on a regular basis. I'd seen several knights on guard duty in the estate in the past. Of them, it seemed one of them was always waiting just outside the reception room.

No sooner had the man been admitted into the room than he began speaking, almost in a shout. "Count Müller, we've received an urgent message from the Hermann Trading Company!"

"An urgent message, you say?"

"Shall I convey it to you now, my lord?" the knight asked, glancing in my direction.

It must have been pretty vital information. Count Müller, however, nodded without hesitation. At this point, he saw us as participants in the trading company. As an outsider starved for information, I was extremely grateful.

"Yes, please do. Here will be fine."

"Mr. Marc, the vice manager of the company, has been arrested for the crime of disrespecting the nobility."

Another piece of sensational news—apparently, the man had offended a noble somehow. From the knight's tense expression, I'd guessed it wasn't good news beforehand. But I never imagined that a friend of mine had been placed under arrest.

However, disrespecting nobility seemed very uncharacteristic for the vice manager. I hadn't known him for *that* long, but I couldn't even imagine him defying someone of the upper classes. He was always such a humble, unassuming person.

"Is that true?" asked Count Müller, his eyes wide in surprise as well. He seemed to be thinking, *No, that's impossible*—just the same as I was.

"Shall I send a messenger to the store, my lord?" said the knight.

"Yes, please do."

"Understood, my lord."

I had a feeling more trouble awaited us.

*

The messenger from the Hermann Trading Company told us the details in Count Müller's reception room. It seemed there had been some internal trouble at the company. The issue was more involved than I'd thought.

Apparently, the manager was the one behind the vice manager's fall.

The manager was striving to set up a new storefront in the capital in order to move their main functions there. In contrast, the vice manager had been working in the store here—right in Count Müller's lap. It was inevitable that the two would come to a disagreement on something. However, this was a little abrupt even then, wasn't it?

When I asked a question along those lines, the messenger replied that the vice manager's actions had been the cause.

Having obtained early insider information that the war, driven by the Ohgen Empire's invasion of Herz, would be ending, he had profited handsomely, involving his clients and customers as well. According to the messenger, the amount he had made easily exceeded the Hermann Trading Company's usual yearly sales.

There was little doubt that the manager, wary of his subordinate's success, had struck first out of fear he'd be overthrown. When I asked how they could be so sure of it, the man serving as messenger said he'd been at the scene of the crime.

He explained the incident in detail, but essentially, the offended noble had faked an accident. He had claimed to have been hit by a carriage, and the vice manager had been arrested. This truly was another world—the position of the victim and suspect were totally reversed from what I was used to in Japan.

We pressed for further information and were told the noble who had accused the vice manager of the crime had a long-standing grudge against Count Müller. Considering the manager's wish to move company headquarters to the capital, this must have seemed the easiest option to ruin the vice manager.

The manager's ideas and those of a noble burning with opposition toward Count Müller must have intersected and led to the plot. And so the vice manager had been dumped into prison on bogus charges.

Once we'd seen the messenger out of the reception room, the count bowed to me. "Sir Sasaki, I feel I must apologize yet again. This trouble, too, is my responsibility."

"No, don't apologize. None of this is your fault, Count Müller."

The king's proclamation about the conditions to inherit the throne almost certainly had something to do with all this, too. The noble accident-faker in question was apparently part of the first prince's faction. That was motive enough to attack Count Müller, who was friends with the second prince, even disregarding the Hermann Trading Company's internal affairs.

Herzian noble society was quite the hornet's nest.

"I'd like to pay a visit to the noble in question as soon as possible."

"In that case, I believe I'll go and see Mr. Marc, my lord."

"That will ease my mind. Thank you."

I couldn't exactly enjoy my easygoing life in another world in *this* situation. In any case, I would be too anxious to eat until I made sure the vice manager was safe. I also trusted Peeps would understand.

"Sir Sasaki, I want you to hold on to this."

The count held something out to me from across the low table.

It was a sheathed dagger.

Beautifully ornamented, it must have had more worth as a work of art than as a weapon.

"My lord?"

"If you show someone this dagger and give them my name, your commands will be regarded as my own. I want you to use this power to vouch for Mr. Marc. Since he isn't a noble, he will be treated very badly in prison. Many who have been accused of disrespecting the nobility end up dying before their sentence is passed."

"I understand, my lord."

Wow. This is a huge responsibility, I thought. If I had been alone, I doubted the count would have trusted me with such an important task. Peeps definitely played a role in his decision. That meant I needed to give this my all, so as not to harm Peeps's reputation.

No, that's not right. The vice manager's mental and physical health were more important than anything else. He was a good person, and I'd rescue him by fair means or foul.

*

We took a carriage to get to the prison where the vice manager was being held. Count Müller had arranged for it, along with everything else, ensuring that we arrived safely at our destination without losing our way. Peeps may have been knowledgeable, but he probably didn't know where the prison was in every single provincial city.

Once there, the dagger loaned to me by the count had its chance to shine. I showed it to a man who appeared to oversee the prison, and I received the red carpet treatment as I was guided in.

That said, while the facility itself was located in the town Count Müller governed, the vice manager had been arrested for offending a noble of at least the count's rank. Because of that, it didn't look like we'd be able to do whatever we wanted with the accused.

In the prison, we saw a knight keeping watch, apparently under Count Dietrich's name. This was the result of Herz's aristocratic system. It would appear that the authority and jurisdiction to make legal judgments—as it was called in my world—weren't necessarily tied to the lord of the land.

If I used the magic Peeps had taught me, I could have driven off the guard and broken the vice manager out. That, however, would cause a huge problem for Count Müller, so it had to be a last resort.

The prison overseer under Count Müller and the knight on guard left here by Count Dietrich accompanied me through the prison. After a short walk, we came to the end of one of the facility's underground passages.

Through the bars, we could see the vice manager. His hands were bound in chains and his feet in shackles.

"M-Mr. Sasaki, what are you doing here?"

"I apologize for how long it took me to get to you."

The underground prison was dark with few light sources, so I used an illumination spell to brighten Mr. Marc's cell. When I did, I saw large bruises on his cheeks. Probably the result of scuffles with knights or military policemen at the time of his arrest.

I hastily used my healing magic. When I cast it, the knight with us readied himself for a fight, but when he saw that my goal was to heal the man's wounds, he put down the hand reaching for his sword. The vice manager's bruises healed without a trace within a few seconds.

"Thank you so much for doing this for me—I'm hardly worthy of it."

"I heard what happened from the company. Count Müller is making preparations on his own end regarding this incident. It won't be long before he proves your innocence, Mr. Marc."

"Wait, but…but that would be so much trouble for you and the count, and…"

Mr. Marc's gaze drifted to the knight standing next to me. When I saw that, I suddenly remembered that I'd heard Count Dietrich's name before. He'd allied himself with Count Müller's butler Sebastian in the past; he was the top of the faction trying to bring down House Müller. He had previously shown up only in name, however. Apparently, he and Count Müller had a long history of discord.

"You don't have to worry; just wait for him. He's sure to get you out of here."

"Mr. Sasaki…"

Count Müller said he'd do it, so everything should be fine. If, even then, things didn't work out—and I didn't want to think about this— I'd blow up the prison and flee somewhere with Mr. Marc. We could head for the Republic of Lunge, though that wasn't part of the count's plan. And I was sure Peeps would help if it was to save Mr. Marc.

"Also," I said to the knight, "I had something to talk about with you."

"…What is it?"

"I have a message I'd like you to convey to Count Dietrich."

"Speak."

"It appears as though he has allied himself with the manager of the Hermann Trading Company, but when it comes to business talent, none can rival Mr. Marc. I would humbly advise him to think wisely, with a view to the long run, about which side he should really take."

"Doesn't the dagger at your hip mark you as a member of House Müller?"

"I would also suggest, sir, that he look into how much of a profit Mr. Marc made after the recent dispute with the Ohgen Empire. I think that will make it clear whom he should be sheltering."

"That's pure nonsense."

"Perhaps. But shouldn't Count Dietrich be the one to decide that?"

"Ugh…"

Right now, I wanted to focus on keeping Mr. Marc safe. And no matter how the cookie crumbled, I was confident Mr. Marc would ally himself with Count Müller anyway. For that reason, I decided the correct move would be to buy some time, even if it meant pretending I was cheating on a certain noble. Otherwise, I doubted the prison would alter their treatment of the vice manager.

"...Fine. I'll tell him for you."

"Thank you, sir."

"But I wonder what would happen if others were to find out that a foreign merchant turned noble, who happens to be in the second prince's favor, has been fawning on those of us supporting the first prince. Between your facial features and skin tone, you're the talk of the court. You are this Sasaki person, yes?"

The knight watched me and spoke with a smirk. It seemed like he was trying to assert his dominance. Considering Mr. Marc's position, I couldn't let him pin me down like that. Even if I had to act a bit arrogant, I decided my best move was to be assertive myself.

"To me, this man here is more important than the second prince."

"What?! Are you mad?!"

"S-Sir Sasaki..."

"So I'd very much like you to convey my message to Count Dietrich."

"You would offend nobility! Your lord, who you should revere!"

"If you're dissatisfied, you can go ahead and inform Prince Adonis himself."

"Wha—?"

"In fact, I can go and tell him right now—*personally.*"

It would have been simple if I had discussed all this in advance, but even if Prince Adonis was to hear of it, I could easily explain the situation to him. I was confident I could count on Count Müller's understanding as well—though this was all a product of the Lord Starsage's influence, of course.

"Don't...don't think I'm going to bail you out if you regret this!"

"I wouldn't expect you to. But I do promise not to bring any sort of harm to Count Dietrich."

"Ugh...!"

Even the knight looked shocked at that.

Whatever happens, it looks like I managed to buy us some time.

✳

After our discussion in the prison regarding the Hermann Trading Company's vice manager, we next set off straight for the Republic of

Lunge. To get us there, Peeps kindly provided his teleportation magic. It would have taken way too long to get there on foot, so while I felt bad for asking for the bird's help, I had little choice.

His spell brought us there instantly—and we were met with the lively city streets we'd once visited to procure supplies for Count Müller. This place was so bustling and crowded, it surpassed not only our home base of Baytrium, but Herz's capital Allestos.

"I simply doubt there will be anything here that will help that man."

"I think it's worth a shot, Peeps."

"Really?"

"That said, it will take some work to reach our goal..."

As I chatted with my beloved pet bird, I gazed out at the people going back and forth on the main road. Mr. Marc's social position was on the line this time, so I wanted to do everything I possibly could. Thankfully, I had over a hundred thousand gold coins on hand—more than enough to go for the only opportunity I could think of. I knew the finances belonged to both me *and* Peeps, but I really wanted this chance.

"I know I'm dragging you around, but will you let me give this a try?"

"Well, the man has been a great help to us many times in the past..."

Peeps had no objections—he was probably remembering the stupendous meat dishes we'd tasted in Mr. French's restaurant. He was indeed a very human sparrow—which only served to make him all the more adorable.

"Thanks so much, Peeps. That makes me really happy."

"But if you're doing this, you need to make sure you win."

"Of course! Mr. Marc's future is riding on it, after all."

"His loss would be very painful for us."

If Count Müller heard that, I thought, *he'd probably be jealous. He might even get competitive, seeking the same praise from Peeps.*

I walked through town for a while with the ever-popular bird on my shoulder. Eventually, we reached the Kepler Trading Company, where we'd come looking for a business deal in the past. Once there, we asked for Mr. Joseph, who was in charge of foodstuffs—the one we had dealt with last year, too.

It was surprisingly easy to secure a meeting with him. Before we could even get a word in, we were shown to the reception room. A familiar face was already sitting there on the sofa waiting for us.

"It's been so long, Mr. Sasaki."

"Yes, it has, Mr. Joseph."

He encouraged us to sit, so I settled onto the sofa across from him. Peeps stayed put on my shoulder, pretending to be a familiar and watching Mr. Joseph through his cute, round eyes.

"I really appreciate you making time for us. You must be busy."

"Not at all—I've actually been curious about you as well."

"...You have?"

Mr. Joseph smiled as he spoke. His casual attitude was no different from last time. "I've been in charge of this store for a long time, and it's very rare that someone is able to fool me so thoroughly. It made me very interested in who you are. To think you weren't from the Ohgen Empire at all—but from the Kingdom of Herz!"

His eyes, however, stared at me so fixedly it was like he had forgotten to blink.

It had been over a month since the Herz–Ohgen disturbance. They'd probably gotten plenty of news about it here in the Republic of Lunge as well. Naturally, they'd been looking into the merchant they had made such an investment in.

"You said previously that you were in charge of foodstuffs..."

"To be more accurate, I am *also* in charge of foodstuffs."

"...I see."

Apparently, this man was much more important than I'd initially assumed. It seemed like his position was closer to store manager. If that was the case, maybe my buy-and-run tactic had been a little shortsighted. Still, considering the personal interest he now had in me, I felt like my decision had worked out in our favor.

"Thanks to you," I said, "we should be able to maintain peaceful relations with the Ohgen Empire for the time being. From our perspective, the reprieve seems like the perfect chance to do even more lucrative business with you. That is my reason for coming today."

"May I ask the specifics?"

"I'll be up front with you. We're thinking of opening a trading company in this city. We came here to discuss whether Kepler would be willing to invest in it and provide support. After all, this is a different country, and it has its own rules and customs."

"You don't actually believe we'd consider something like that, do you?"

Though the Kingdom of Herz had repelled the Ohgen Empire, it was only a temporary reprieve. In truth, Peeps's magic had handled everything; naturally, other nations wouldn't be changing their opinion. Herz was still experiencing terrible deterioration, making any investment a big risk. Even so, in this case, I intended to keep pushing. Thankfully, we had with us a whole array of rule-breaking items to trade.

"Consider this a request from me personally, not from the Kingdom of Herz."

"...Oh?" Mr. Joseph's expression shifted slightly.

Poor Herz, I thought. *He's less averse to personal business with me.*

"I believe that you will, in fact, accept this proposition, Mr. Joseph."

"Then by all means, please, show me the basis for your confidence."

"The goods we deal in are of a rather unusual variety..."

Before coming here, we borrowed several of the items Count Müller had purchased from us from the estate. Specifically, calculators and other mechanical goods the likes of which would be difficult for this world to develop and manufacture. I showed these to Mr. Joseph.

"...What are these?"

"Allow me to explain."

I had two broad reasons for coming to the Republic of Lunge.

The first was that I figured it would be hard to do very much in the Kingdom of Herz in the future due to the discord between Mr. Marc and the manager of the Hermann Trading Company. I didn't know how any of that would shake out, but it wasn't hard to envision roadblocks in our future.

The second was that asking for an investment within Herz seemed like a lot of trouble. It was way too scary to think about borrowing money within the kingdom. The nobles and rich people who supported them were already on edge because of the feud over the royal inheritance.

And so I gave Mr. Joseph a rundown of the products we'd brought with us. We started with the calculator, then moved on to the transceiver and the motion sensor camera that ran on dry-cell batteries.

This time, we'd also brought with us a Breathalyzer that had been sleeping in a closet in my apartment, along with a toy camera and a battery-less film-developing device. I'd always figured I'd use them at some point; never thought it would be like this, though.

As I explained, Mr. Joseph's expression turned serious. That smile from before disappeared without a trace.

"We plan to deal in products such as these at the company we'd like to establish," I said.

"Mr. Sasaki, before we talk about that, can I ask a question?"

"What is it?"

"Why us? Sure, the Republic of Lunge is fairly well off, and we're proud of it. But if you were merely looking at scale, surely there were many other contenders?"

He stared at me, his expression dead serious. It didn't seem to be a good time to joke around with him.

"It goes without saying that the Kepler Trading Company's capital strength is significant. But you also have excellent financial muscle, and we've already made a successful business transaction in the past. For these reasons, we would like to explore the possibility of forming a long-term relationship. To be perfectly frank, I wouldn't balk at approaching other trading companies as well to accomplish my objective."

I decided to casually drop some flattery in my answer. It was a common tactic used when dealing with start-up companies that were doing well but still had an inferiority complex toward bigger corporations. I didn't know exactly how large the Kepler Trading Company's operations were, but if other large trading companies did exist, I doubted that would pose an issue.

"Well, I'm honored to hear that."

"First, I would like you to understand that I have already done business in these goods with the Hermann Trading Company in the Kingdom of Herz. However, I would personally prefer to limit my wholesale to a single client and develop something like a brand awareness."

"......"

"That said, I would also like to stay on good terms with the employees at the Hermann Trading Company. Unfortunately, it seems there are hardheaded people everywhere you go, and it's become more difficult to keep things friendly and profitable."

"...I see. So that's what's going on."

And most importantly, Peeps had introduced me to this place. He was staying perched on my shoulder again this time, watching closely, not moving very much. Throughout the conversation just now, he hadn't seemed to react at all. I assumed that meant he was fine with all my propositions thus far.

"What do you think?"

"I understand what you're saying, Mr. Sasaki."

"I appreciate it."

"However, this deal would present a significant risk to us as well. I know it's rude of me, but you *are* from the Kingdom of Herz. Considering the situation with the Ohgen Empire, we can't be sure of what lies ahead."

"I think it's natural for you to be concerned about that."

"Though we made a deal in the past, it was a one-time affair. On that point, Mr. Sasaki, would you be able to prove to me that you are a man worthy of our trust? I'm hesitant precisely because the goods you deal in are so attractive."

From his point of view, that was a perfectly reasonable reaction.

Any observer would have seen a merchant from a defeated nation who had come crying and begging. Both Ohgen's defeat on the battlefield and Herz's extended lease on life were, to the public, merely the result of getting wrapped up in a fight between dangerous war criminals; it was a temporary windfall—and nothing more.

Everyone probably believed the two countries would clash in the near future. Or maybe another nation would attack Herz instead. The kingdom had mobilized a significant number of troops during the war effort; it wouldn't be strange at all if war profiteers picked this time to swoop in and reap the benefits. That was precisely why the king of Herz had issued so many new measures. Even I, an outsider, had no trouble imagining the worst.

"In that case, I have a proposal for you," I offered.

"I'd very much like to hear it."

"The next time I come here, I will sell my products to the Kepler Trading Company in bulk. However, we'll divide the payment for those goods, setting some of it aside for after our company is established, which you can keep as collateral."

"I see..."

Unfortunately, we didn't have anything to offer them other than our goods. If he said no to this, we'd end up leaving quietly and visiting other trading companies. And come to think of it, if a merchant from one country made profits somewhere else, how would taxes work? I'd have to check with Peeps later.

"Will we be able to discuss the numbers on each individual product you plan to sell, then?"

"Yes, of course."

"In that case, then yes, we would be happy to cooperate with you."

"Thank you very much."

Mr. Joseph broke out in a smile. It seemed he would approach this with an open mind. It would have been a pain to visit other trading companies at this hour, so I was glad we got Kepler to accept. Having to explain all that again from the start would have been really annoying.

I also wanted to keep my presence here as quiet as possible. If I went around asking other companies, rumors about me would spread in the blink of an eye. That would be about as troublesome as having someone run away with the goods I had left as collateral.

"I'd like to ask a little more about your circumstances," said Mr. Joseph. "Do you plan to serve as representative of this new trading company?"

"No, there's someone else who's better suited for it."

"I see. I'd like to meet them soon, if possible."

"I'll do my best."

"In that case, let's begin the negotiations for management rights based on the amount of investment, as well as profitability."

"I appreciate it. Let's get right down to the details..."

If this conversation went smoothly, I could potentially secure a place for Mr. Marc as a merchant, should he be left with no alternatives. Considering Mr. Joseph's reaction, it didn't seem impossible for him to carry over his personal relationships, either.

After that, we fell deep into conversation for about half a day. We were able to discuss most of the practical details of setting up a trading company.

"Oh, but first," I began, "as for the name of this new company, I'd like to call it the Marc Trading Company."

"Is that the name of the person who will be its representative?"

"Yes, it is."

"I understand. I'm looking forward to the day I get to meet him."

Finally, after communicating our desired name for the business, Peeps and I left the reception room behind us.

*

Our negotiations with the Kepler Trading Company had gone smoothly. After leaving, we took a stroll around Newsonia, the Lunge

Republic's capital city, looking at all the trading companies along the road, as well as at the ubiquitous open-air shops.

The reason for doing this was to hunt around for otherworldly valuables we could use in our dealings with Futarishizuka in the modern world. I was determined to find something as cheap as possible to buy that would fetch the highest price possible.

"The Kepler Trading Company was in a pretty clean and neat area, but downtown is kind of chaotic, huh? Everything's all jumbled together—honestly, I can't tell what's what here."

"*Personally, I feel a certain charm from the sheer variety of shops all standing side by side.*"

"Yeah, I think I can understand that."

It reminded me of other places I knew that had little shops all mashed together, like Akihabara's electric town or Shinjuku's golden town. If I called this a fantasy version of those, it would be all the more fascinating for a modern person who grew up with a passion for certain media.

"Just walking around looking at everything is surprisingly satisfying."

"*Oh? You understand its charm, then?*"

"I don't know if I have the same impression of it as you, Peeps, but… Hmm. For a person from our world, it's the kind of place you grew up knowing in your heart, always wishing to visit but were never able to."

"*What an odd perspective.*"

"You might understand once you get more used to our world."

"*Hmm. That does certainly whet my curiosity.*"

If he turned his passion for the internet away from electronic dictionaries and academic sites and toward manga and anime, the day might come when he felt the same. But no, maybe that was hoping for too much.

"Oh, would you mind discussing what we plan to stock?"

"*Hmm? What is it?*"

"I can't help but think gold would be good."

"*Any grounds for that?*"

"In our world, gold always goes up in price whenever there's a war or an economic crisis—any big problems that come up. Since it's not feasible to synthesize gold, there's only ever a fixed amount of it."

"*So even in a society as advanced as yours, humans still seek value in gold?*"

"Maybe it's because nothing can replace it..."

My world had seen many new items and mechanisms crop up, such as bonds and Bitcoin, meant to preserve value. However, gold was always king whenever something happened. Platinum and palladium were relatively expensive, but gold had a far better conversion rate.

"*Wouldn't more valuable metals like orichalc or mythril work?*"

"Peeps, we don't have stuff like that."

"*You don't? I see it mentioned on the internet every once in a while.*"

"I think you were looking at fiction."

"*Hrm. So that was it...*"

These subtle differences in perspective really marked him as a bona fide otherworlder. It was possible he'd gotten some mistaken information, too. Maybe it was best to broaden the range of our topics when we chatted to compare and reconcile information. It was a little scary to think some minor misunderstanding might lead to a fatal mistake.

"So you're not sure about gold?"

"*No, in that case, let's start off with gold. This is just based on what I've seen on the internet, but the amount of gold flowing in your world is, as far as I can tell, far less than in this world. In that sense, it would be a good decision.*"

"Really?"

"*Yes. I'd already been considering it as a candidate, in fact.*"

I remembered seeing an article on the internet that the total amount of gold in the modern world, including what was saved in storehouses, was about two hundred thousand tons. It seemed as though this number might fluctuate based on advancements in mining technology, but for now, the article said that was basically everything.

The possibility of gold losing its value in the future due to humans learning to synthesize it like pearls or diamonds, or as the result of some revolutionary new mining technology, wasn't zero. However, at the present moment, it was still an extremely reliable investment.

"*If we bring it into your world as coinage, we might end up being tracked in the future, so we should melt it down into ingots. Oh, and we'll need to raise the purity as well. The internet said most gold circulating in your world has very high purity.*"

"Then why don't we head back to Count Müller's town for now?"

"*Mm.*"

If this worked, there was no real need to stock up. We could use the gold coins we had on hand. I felt some hesitation toward melting down currency, but seeing as how Peeps didn't seem to care one bit, I supposed a little couldn't hurt.

The only other thing I supposed we would need was a box to hold the ingots.

*

Once we'd finished sightseeing in the Republic of Lunge, we returned to our home base—the town governed by Count Müller. From there, Peeps and I parted ways, each of us with our own job to do. After telling me he'd make the gold coins into ingots, he'd taken the box with the money in it and used teleportation magic, disappearing from sight. I, on the other hand, was off to procure a large wooden box to hold our stock going forward.

It didn't matter what world it was—we couldn't exactly carry gold with us where everyone else could see it. At the same time, after bringing the gold to Futarishizuka and exchanging it for money, we'd need the container for carrying stocked goods back in the otherworld. Hence the need to prepare a wooden box for transport.

The size of a small truck bed would be about perfect. That wasn't the kind of thing I'd be able to get all by myself in modern Japan. It would draw way too much attention. As a result, I would have to purchase one in this world. Peeps had already confirmed it wouldn't be a problem to take it along when we teleported.

I found what I was after and finished my task before Peeps, so I returned to the high-class inn to await the bird's return. The inn had been generous enough to store what I'd bought in the warehouse behind the building.

Soon enough, the maid assigned to our room paid a visit.

"You have a guest, sir. What shall I do with her?"

"Who is it?"

"It is the young lady of the Müller family."

I could only think of one person who fit that description—the girl with the memorable piled hairstyle. Her name was Elsa, if I recalled correctly. But why had she gone to the trouble to visit our room at the inn?

"Shall I show her in, sir?"

"Is Count Müller with her?"

"No, the lady is by herself."

I might have understood somewhat if her daddy was here with her. But it was strange for her to visit alone.

"She desires a meeting with you, sir. Should I show her in?"

"Yes, please. Thank you."

There was no way I could refuse. She was Count Müller's treasured daughter. She was extremely important if I was going to build a harmonious relationship with him. I'd rue the day I slipped up, refused, and invited her wrath.

"Understood, sir." With a reverent bow, the maid left the room.

After a few moments, the innkeeper led Count Müller's daughter into the living area of our room. She really was here alone; her father was nowhere to be seen. The only people with her were the knights assigned as her bodyguards, and she'd told them to wait outside in the hallway.

Naturally, the knights had balked at that. I'd have done the same if I'd been entrusted with the safety of the count's beloved daughter. But after the pile-hair princess personally and politely told them to leave, we were left alone in the room.

"Is it true the Hermann Trading Company's vice manager was thrown in prison?"

"Yes, it is, madam."

She looked taken aback. Apparently, she'd run all the way here because she'd been worried about Mr. Marc. When I gave her the plain truth, she clearly became frustrated. Here was a girl who wore her heart on her sleeve.

"Th-then are you—?"

"Yes, madam. Both your father and I are planning a rescue."

"...Really?"

"Naturally, madam. This town can't be without him."

"......"

Though I didn't know for sure, I imagined her visit had something to do with how Mr. Marc had sheltered her upon the news of Count

Müller's death. She couldn't let things stand as they were and had come to spur us into action.

As if reflecting her resolve, her hair was piled higher than ever. You could even see some accents here and there that implied pretty high attack power.

"I have already had words with a retainer employed by the mastermind—Count Dietrich, madam," I explained. "At the very least, he'll be treated properly as long as he is in prison. Your father is on his way to negotiate with the man himself as we speak."

"…Will Marc be able to come back safely?"

"Please, rest easy, madam. I promise we will take back both Mr. Marc and the Hermann Trading Company, so don't worry about a thing. I beg you to have faith in us. Everything will go back to the way it was."

"But Count Dietrich outranks my father."

"That doesn't mean our hands are tied."

"But…"

The pile-hair princess stared at the low table, her eyes uneasy.

Wait, I thought. *Could it be?* Could she have some kind of romantic interest in Mr. Marc? There was a big age gap, but he was handsome, with a kind of sophisticated charm; plus, she was about the age when girls started developing an interest in older members of the opposite sex. An image of her declaring her love for him and the vice manager panicking crossed my mind.

"…What's the matter? You're staring at me."

"Nothing, madam—only that you have proved to me once again how kind a person you are."

"Are…are you making fun of me?!"

"No, not at all. It was touching. Really."

"…Hmph," huffed the pile-hair princess, looking away.

At just that moment, a magic circle appeared in the room.

I'd seen that glow many times in the past. This was bad—but I had no way to stop it. Peeps had returned. My guest's attention was pulled toward the newly appeared magic circle.

In the blink of an eye, an adorable Java sparrow had materialized in the middle of it.

"I'm sorry for taking so long. I've—"

He had appeared right on the low table between the sofas, over which the pile-hair princess and I had been talking. In fact, since I'd seated her in the place of honor farthest into the room, Peeps ended up staring right into her face.

And then there was the stack of gold ingots right next to him.

"Huh…?"

The uneasiness in her eyes was replaced with shock.

And in response, our great Lord Starsage began to tweet and chirp as loudly as he could.

"*Tweet! Tweeeet! Tweeeet! Tweeeet!*"

"……"

This was some *awful* timing on the bird's part. What was running through that wise old brain of his as he tweeted away? *I feel like I've been seeing these pretend chirping scenes a lot more often, Peeps.*

"He, um, just talked, right?"

"*Tweet! Tweet! Tweet!*"

"You can't fool me! You *definitely* spoke!"

"*Tweet! Tweet! Twit, tweeeet!*"

It was the Lord Starsage versus the pile-hair princess.

If Count Müller had been here to see this, he would have gone blue in the face. Peeps was so cute when he got desperate. I guessed about half of those chirps were blaming me for letting her into the room; he kept glancing my way, after all.

Yes, I really should have reserved a separate room for meetings—and I had, in fact. But I never expected Peeps to come back while the inn's employees were still setting it up.

At this point, there was no way I could pretend Peeps hadn't spoken. But depending on how we explained it, we could probably keep damage to a minimum. Thankfully, magic in this world was astoundingly versatile.

Familiars who could speak seemed to be exceptional here, but Lady Elsa was a noble without much knowledge of magic. Considering her dad had introduced me as a magician-cum-merchant, it shouldn't be impossible to convince her.

"Lady Elsa, may I have a moment?"

"Wh-what?"

"My familiar is somewhat special, you see. He's able to speak and use high-level magic. That makes him quite rare—and thus a ripe target for others. I would like to ask you to please never speak of what you just witnessed to anyone."

"…Are you being honest?"

"I am, madam."

I was by no means lying to her. He *was* the greatest sage in the land.

"But just now, he showed up out of nowhere, didn't he?"

"He is equipped with such a spell, madam."

"……"

My different skin color and facial construction was handy in situations like this. Even she could tell that I was from a foreign country. She also understood that we were on friendly terms with her dad. As a daddy's girl, she was sure to hesitate before pressing any further.

"If the public learns of this, madam, we will need to leave this town. You can ask Count Müller as well, if you wish. He is aware of our circumstances. If you wish to know more about our situation, please feel free to ask."

She seemed taken aback. I felt bad for phrasing it like a threat, but I really couldn't have her blabbing about my lovely sparrow's secret. If, somehow, the public *did* learn about the Starsage being alive, things would get very problematic. The slow life he desired would forever remain a dream.

"A-all right, fine. I won't tell anyone!"

"Thank you very much, madam."

Lady Elsa gave a small nod; she must have understood my feelings on the matter. I was relived the pile-hair princess had such a straightforward personality.

In response, Peeps took a step toward her and introduced himself.

"I go by Sta—Peeps. Please call me Peeps."

"That's a really cute name. My name's Elsa."

The sparrow stood there, his tiny body atop the low table. At a glance, he was totally birdlike, so no one would suspect he could talk. Even I'd been flabbergasted when he first introduced himself to me. It was ridiculously cute how his mouth popped open and shut when he used his voice.

Still gazing at the bird, the pile-hair princess continued. "I'm really sorry for hurting you last time."

"I am fine. There is nothing to worry about."

She was referring to the time at Mr. French's restaurant when we ate together. Her fingertip, which she'd been using to pet Peeps, had accidentally hit him in his big, cute eyeball. At the time, the shock had made him cry out in his real voice.

Would the day ever come when he could call himself Piercarlo in front of others? I wondered casually, seeing the bird come so dangerously close to slipping up.

✻

Peeps and I had been treated to an unexpected visit from Count Müller's daughter at our base of operations in the high-class inn. But after explaining to her that we were busy with our own work, she obediently headed out. Despite her formidable manner, she was considerate about such things.

With that, we were able to get to work right away. As for the nature of our task—we were devising a way to transport gold from this world back to my own.

"*That should just about do it.*"

"Yes, I think so."

We'd borrowed the inn's courtyard to prepare our cargo. Since we'd requested that they keep people away, nobody was here except Peeps and me. As guests who stayed in these pricey rooms for multiple days in a row, we were apparently considered VIPs; when we asked an employee about it, he immediately provided us a workspace.

In one corner of the courtyard sat the large wooden box I'd procured.

Just in case, we'd lined the inside of the box with some dried grass I'd also purchased, then placed the gold ingots provided by Peeps into the middle, hiding them from sight. At a glance, it looked like feed for livestock.

The idea of bringing dried plant material over from this world was, to my way of thinking, pretty scary in a number of respects. We still had some pretty terrifying diseases in my world, like swine fever and foot-and-mouth disease. Because of that, once the transfer of the ingots was finished, we'd want to burn all the grass as soon as possible.

When I'd purchased it, I was told it had already been smoked to kill any insects so that it could be used as bedding. But there was no harm in being extra careful. If the worst was to happen, we wouldn't be able to stop an invasion of otherworld insects in Japan.

"Shall we head to that world, then?"

"Oh, hold on just a second. I haven't nailed it shut yet."

"You are being quite strict about this, aren't you?"

"We really have to cover all our bases here."

It might have been unlikely that the box would tip over, spilling out the contents midtransport. However, I still wanted to limit the possibility of someone inadvertently seeing our goods as much as possible. That was why I'd gotten enough nails, plus a hammer, while out buying the wooden box.

As I was working, I suddenly heard someone call my name.

"Sir Sasaki, I'm terribly sorry for interrupting you."

"Oh, yes, what is it?"

It was the maid who had announced Lady Elsa's visit earlier. She was standing in the covered passageway facing the courtyard. In this world's time, she'd been with us for several months now, more or less. We'd had nothing to do with each other aside from short work-related conversations, but she was starting to become familiar to me.

"You have a guest, sir. What shall I do?"

"Who is it?"

"A Mr. French."

Whoops, it's the chef. He'd probably heard about Mr. Marc's imprisonment just like the pile-hair princess had and come to visit us about it. In which case, I would have to explain the situation. He and Mr. Marc were probably both involved in management of the restaurant. Normally, I should have been the one to contact him.

"Would you mind bringing us to him?"

"Of course not, sir." The maid nodded with an air of reverence.

We followed her, leaving the courtyard behind us.

*

As I'd expected, Mr. French's business with us had to do with Mr. Marc. Apparently, he'd heard from some of his regulars that the man had been thrown in prison, and unable to sit still, he came to me.

I gave him the same rundown we gave the pile-hair princess.

Several times, he asked if there was anything he could do. Unfortunately, there was nothing in particular he could help with. In fact, he might cause more problems if he tried to accomplish anything recklessly. After promising him we would rescue Mr. Marc, we sent him back to the restaurant. I did feel a little bad about it, but this was one thing I couldn't do much about.

Still, the meeting showed me that he and Mr. Marc were on good terms. I felt assured that leaving the restaurant in their hands was a good decision. Thinking of it that way, things weren't all bad. I decided to try to be positive about our current situation.

After parting ways with Mr. French, we returned to the inn's courtyard, and I hastily finished putting the nails in the wooden box's lid. Then, as originally planned, we used Peeps's teleportation magic to switch worlds.

The destination for our shipment was one of many wharfs dotting Tokyo's coastline. We brought the cargo into a very large warehouse, which was packed in among lots of other very large warehouses.

We had contacted Futarishizuka as soon as we arrived, and she had immediately responded that she would receive the goods this very day. She seemed to have a lot more free time than I had thought—quitting her previous job had probably helped.

Peeps and I transported the cargo together, using Peeps's magic. Because Futarishizuka had prepared a destination away from prying eyes, we were able to carry it inside much more easily than initially anticipated.

Since I'd introduced the teleportation magic as a Magical Field, I didn't have any hesitation using it in front of Futarishizuka. In fact, if she'd gotten a rental truck or something, the chances of the section chief noticing it would drastically increase.

"The souvenirs from the fairy world are in there?"

"Souvenirs? No, these are just extra things I had lying around."

"And yet you've brought so much of it," she said, looking at the wooden box we'd brought into a corner of the warehouse.

Nobody else was around, and the warehouse was quiet. Our voices traveled well. It certainly seemed like the perfect location for illicit dealings. I started to feel like I was a character in a yakuza movie, trading recreational drugs or prohibited weapons. The sunlight shining through the high windows was the only source of light in the dark interior.

"Most of it is packaging."

"Packaging?"

"I didn't want others seeing it on the way here."

"Ah, I see."

It was possible that, depending on the circumstances, I might have been questioned by the police. Their white motorcycle headlights gleamed all throughout the Tokyo metro area. I figured I'd be fine even if they confronted me since I had my own police badge, but just in case, I'd been extra careful about setting all this up. I was most frightened of my own boss—ironic, but I couldn't bring myself to laugh.

"Go ahead and remove the lid."

"All right."

As we looked on, Futarishizuka went over to the box. She grabbed the lid, which I'd nailed down, with both hands—then tore it right off. Despite her young body, she possessed physical abilities beyond the understanding of humans. Even an adult like me would have had a difficult time handling the lid, but she easily plucked it away.

The *craaaack* it made reverberated around the inside of the warehouse.

And then, a moment later, we saw the figure of a person reflected in our eyes. Someone was curled up inside the wooden box, surrounded by all the dried grass.

"Oh! Even I hadn't expected you to bring something…*perishable* like this," said Futarishizuka, gazing at the person.

My eyes met those of the girl lying down in the bed of grass, hugging her legs to her body. I keenly felt Peeps give a start on my shoulder.

"…Lady Elsa, what on earth are you doing in there?"

"I…I was just curious about what you were doing! So…"

Oh. Oh no.

I never expected the pile-hair princess to stow away in the wooden box. I thought for sure she'd gone home to her estate without a second thought. Her piles of hair were tangled in the dried grass, a total mess.

Naturally, our attention shifted to Futarishizuka, who was staring at the unforeseen stowaway. What did she think of the girl covered in plant matter? Would she believe that this was a cute messenger girl who came from the faraway land of the fairies?

No. That would be *far* too convenient for us.

"Excuse me," I said to Futarishizuka, "but is it all right if she and I had a word in private?"

"Oh, but I'd very much like to hear what *she* has to say."

"It is going to be a pretty complicated discussion."

"I've never heard of a human living in the fairy world before."

It seemed humans didn't live in the fairy world. Another piece of trivia regarding magical girls, in the bag. Personally, I hadn't the slightest intention of pretending the products we wanted to sell to Futarishizuka were from the fairy world—in the first place, we had absolutely no idea what kind of goods they'd even have in a world inhabited by fairies.

"This girl is the daughter of a friend of mine..."

"Why has the daughter of a friend of yours sneaked into your cargo? The wooden box was shut nice and tightly with nails. Don't tell me you have one of those perverted fetishes where you find pleasure in locking young children up in enclosed spaces."

"She probably slipped inside when we weren't paying attention during the loading."

In fact, I bet it had happened while we were talking to Mr. French. We'd finished loading the box up by then, but we'd only hammered in the nails afterward. It was highly probable she'd sneaked in while we were distracted.

"My, look at those outlandish clothes. If this is your idea of role-playing, it is sophisticated, indeed. Those metal accessories she wears—could they be genuine articles? Their colors have an oddly beautiful sheen to them."

"......"

The way she was threatening me, it was clear she wasn't backing off anytime soon. I hated the way she was smirking at me like that.

At this point, it seemed like it would be very difficult to deceive her. I had no way to guess how much she had figured out or what she was thinking. If my intuition was wrong, and I judged poorly, it would come back to bite me in the butt—especially up against a wily old girl like her.

Seems like I'll need to change up my strategy, I thought, throwing a glance toward my shoulder.

Peeps nodded to me.

Given how Mr. Marc's life was on the line, we could *not* afford to botch this up. I had to go for a bit of a power play here. Normally, I was a good little yes-man, a devoted corporate drone—but I could, at least, tell when I'd need to take risks.

I'd bring Futarishizuka to the otherworld with me and make her an accomplice.

If she betrayed me now, the drawbacks would be massive; however, significant gains were possible, too, considering the deals we could make in the future. Since she had no way of crossing between worlds, we also had the option of casually abandoning her on the other side and going about our business, if it came to that.

And who knows? She might actually prefer living there.

I'd considered doing so already if she ever tried to blackmail us over our business dealings. It would be a huge hassle if the section chief was to find out about these valuables of unknown origin. In that case, it was better to let her in on our profits.

"Lady Elsa, would you mind explaining yourself?"

"…All right… Fine."

I shifted my gaze from Futarishizuka's smirk to the downcast eyes of the pile-hair princess. She had left the box and now stood right in front of us. Under the stares of everyone present, she sighed in resignation and began to mumble out her explanation.

It wasn't all that complicated.

If her words were to be believed, she actually did plan on returning home at first. But then she changed her mind, thinking that maybe there was something she could help us with, after all. And so she'd slipped past the watchful eyes of her bodyguards and headed back to where we were, only to find us in the courtyard.

Naturally, the big wooden box we'd put in the yard had drawn her interest. After seeing us stuffing gold ingots into it, she'd grown suspicious that Peeps and I might be involved in Mr. Marc's imprisonment.

Come to think of it, considering our conversation immediately prior, anyone might have found our actions suspicious—it would seem as though we were preparing to fly the coop, only saying we intended to help.

In short, the pile-hair princess had thought we'd gotten all that money from selling out Mr. Marc to Count Dietrich—and that now we were trying to flee from Count Müller.

In that case, though, she'd been inside the box the entire time Futarishizuka and I had been negotiating since we'd returned to Japan. That was no short length of time. Her eyes were drooping slightly, and they were red—she'd probably been crying, unbeknownst to anyone.

She was so scared of us finding her that she couldn't call out for help; she had just quietly stayed hidden. I was sure she'd been sobbing in there, all alone. And finally, she'd brilliantly exposed what we were doing. Belatedly, I felt like I understood her fiery admiration for her dad.

"I suppose I can't blame you for looking at it that way, madam."

"…Was I wrong?"

"You were, madam."

"But then where is this?" she asked, looking across the dimly lit warehouse.

All around us were dozens of huge metal containers. Each one of them was designed to be exactly the same, and given their awesome size, it looked kind of spooky. It was probably overwhelming the pile-hair princess, too.

"This is something we need to do to save him."

"Wha—? How is that?!"

"The gold we packed in this wooden box is the money we'd saved doing business in your father's town, madam. We were going to use it to make a deal with this girl here, then use our profits to buy back Mr. Marc's former position."

"…Is that true?"

Without any real evidence, it was only natural she'd still be suspicious.

Which meant I just had to deal with her faithfully and honestly. "Unfortunately, now that you've appeared, madam, we risk the deal falling through. If you think anything of Mr. Marc at all, I hope you'll remain quiet and do as I say. Otherwise, you may come to regret it very much in the near future."

"Ugh…"

When I spoke a little more forcefully, her expression changed. Hesitation spread across her lovely face. It looked like my lecture had worked. Innocent kids like her were easy prey for no-good, deceiving adults. If only Futarishizuka had been this straightforward—it would have been a lot easier to deal with her, too.

"Please don't worry, Lady Elsa. I am an ally of your father's—of Count Müller's. No matter what happens, I will never do anything to betray his trust. Mr. Marc is an important friend of his, too, and I am not about to abandon him."

"Sasaki, can I truly…believe what you're saying?"

"I'd like to be friends with Count Müller and his family for a very long time."

"...I see," answered Lady Elsa.

I'd answered Elsa with complete sincerity—given it my all. I'd put my whole heart into it. Apparently, my zeal had affected her. Though she still looked reluctant, she seemed to understand and accept what I'd said. I figured we'd at least escape any situations where attack magic would start flying.

Unfortunately, she only had a moment to pull herself together— because then Futarishizuka did something unexpected.

She kicked off the ground and leaped forward, reaching a hand out for the pile-hair princess.

This was bad.

"You've given yourself away, girl."

Instantly, Peeps fired a spell. Completely smooth, with no incantation.

"Ugh...!"

Invisible objects slipped through the air and severed all four of Futarishizuka's limbs from her body.

Blood spurted out, dying the surroundings red with its spatter. A few of the drops struck Lady Elsa, causing her face to convulse in terror.

Without anything to support her, Futarishizuka fell to the warehouse floor with a *thump*. The sight of it reminded me of that day at the bowling alley. No, this was even more gruesome. Peeps's attack had been particularly vicious, perhaps because I'd warned him about Futarishizuka's physical abilities.

"You were going to lay a hand on her. What for?"

"Urgh... What was that? I didn't see anything..."

Peeps spoke with composure. Seriously, what a dignified sparrow.

The fluffiness around his belly seemed 30 percent plumper than before. As he looked down at Futarishizuka on the floor of the warehouse, his gaze was like that of a soaring eagle that had just spotted its prey. Wait, no, that wasn't right. Look at those cute round eyes. What a lovely little sparrow.

"S-Sasaki! What was this girl trying to—?"

"I'd like to ask the same question."

At Lady Elsa's prompting, I addressed the girl in the kimono.

She definitely just tried to use energy drain on Lady Elsa. Oh, Futarishizuka, you just had to cross the line, didn't you?

"What exactly *were* you attempting, Ms. Futarishizuka?"

"There was an insect on her shoulder. Where is that little thing? Don't you worry, child, I'll take care of—"

"*I wouldn't mind finishing you off right now.*"

When Peeps said that, her shoulders jerked.

"Ugh..."

Her arms and legs were already starting to heal—I could hear the flesh hissing. However, it seemed like regeneration would take some time, and she wouldn't be able to fully recover instantaneously. She'd need some more time before she could start moving around to her satisfaction.

"*I am now going to place a curse on you.*"

"A curse? What does that mean...?"

"*Upon receiving this curse, you will become obedient to us. It is very inhumane. What was it you called it in this world—human rights? It rejects them utterly. It will be lethal and humiliating. Now prepare yourself to receive it.*"

"O-oh, well, that does sound scary. Could you possibly show a teensy bit of mercy?"

Seeing Futarishizuka so visibly ruffled was a new experience.

Still, I'd never heard of curses before, either, so I was just as frantic as she was. Wondering how cruel it would be, I turned toward the bird on my shoulder in spite of myself. Futarishizuka had been the one to betray us, but I was still hesitant about anything too intense happening right before my eyes.

Incidentally, Peeps had probably learned the term *human rights* from using the internet in my apartment. He was putting new terms to immediate practical use—how adaptive! It made me want to teach him all sorts of words.

"Peeps, hang on—"

His cute little beak was muttering some kind of incantation.

In response to the chant, a magic circle formed on the warehouse floor beneath Futarishizuka. It seemed strangely bright in the darkness, casting the girl in a fantastical, glittering, bloodred light.

"W-wait!" she cried in protest as Peeps stared at her. "That was just a little joke; I—"

But he paid her no mind.

A few moments later, the light shone even brighter, illuminating the whole inside of the warehouse. It was so bright I reflexively looked away.

"Ugh..."

No flames raged, and no gusts blew. We only heard Futarishizuka softly groaning from the other side of the light. Compared to the grand magic I'd witnessed on the Herz–Ohgen battlefield, this seemed rather plain.

Eventually, when the light dissipated, we saw her limp on the floor, her arms and legs regrown.

"...What did you do to me?"

"Take a look at the back of your right hand."

"......"

Futarishizuka did as she was told and looked down at her hand. From where I was, I could see some sort of emblem—like she'd just been tattooed.

"What is this?"

"That crest will rapidly eat away at your body in response to any hostility or malice you may harbor toward us. Right now, it is only on the back of your hand. However, it will eventually proliferate over your entire body—quickly—at which point you will meet your end as a misshapen lump of flesh."

"What—?"

"No matter how excellent a regenerative ability you have obtained, it will not save you from the bodily collapse brought on by this curse. If you dread an eternal life with nothing but your thoughts to keep you company, then do your best not to harbor any negative emotions toward us."

Another really brutal spell, I thought. But that also made it seem like the perfect restraint against Futarishizuka, since we could never tell what she was thinking. Peeps's overflowing practicality and decisiveness made him seem so dependable.

"Urgh...!"

No sooner had he finished speaking than Futarishizuka moved—dashing toward us.

In an instant, she had her small fist up, clenched, right before my nose. However, Peeps used a barrier spell to block it, so it never reached its target. Interrupted by something invisible, her hand stopped a few dozen centimeters in front of us.

Not having to chant seemed really useful. I wanted to be able to pull that off one day, too.

The pattern emblazoned on the back of her tightly clenched fist began to change before our eyes. It writhed like a living creature, increasing in complexity. The sight of the tattoo's organic movements made me feel a little sick.

Overall, it seemed to have grown a little larger. While before it had been limited to the back of her hand, now it was like a bracelet, wrapping around her wrist as well.

The design itself was actually pretty cool—at a glance, you'd think it was a trendy tattoo. It might bar entry to public bathhouses, but I doubted it would garner any criticism.

"...It seems you were telling the truth."

"*And you seem to have a very decisive personality,*" responded Peeps in admiration. Apparently, what she'd done had rated highly with the sparrow.

"If you had been lying, I would have strangled you."

"*If you had killed me, the crest that appeared on the back of your hand would have spread to your entire body, transforming you into a lump of flesh. If you desire a long life, then you should cooperate with us for the time being.*"

"I see..."

"By the way," I cut in, "why *did* you try to go for the girl?"

"I told you already. There was a bug on her shoul—"

"*You do know that the crest will grow if you don't answer truthfully, right?*"

"Urgh..."

At Peeps's words, Futarishizuka reluctantly began to explain.

If she was to be believed, she'd been searching for my weakness. At first, she'd looked for family members or lovers—anyone close to me. Unfortunately, this lonesome middle-aged man flying solo through life had left zero openings for her to exploit. No matter how hard she searched, she couldn't find any candidates. Apparently, the camera she'd put in my apartment was part of this endeavor.

Her goal had been to force this magical middle-aged man under her control. And just now, when she had seen Lady Elsa, who we clearly seemed close with, she resolved to use her. To borrow Peeps's words, she certainly wasted no time making decisions.

In reality, if Peeps hadn't been with me, she would have succeeded. She had only lost because she wasn't able to predict how ridiculously strong the Starsage was. Who would imagine this adorable little Java sparrow had lived so long, leading tens, if not hundreds of thousands of citizens as a political leader—and had sent even more to their graves as a great magician? Even I sometimes had a hard time remembering.

"Sasaki, I—I think I want an explanation…"

"Ah yes, madam."

The pile-hair princess, still with us, was frightened. She'd been looking at us aghast after seeing Peeps use his magic followed by Futarishizuka's counterattack. She must also have realized that she was the trigger for all this.

But ultimately, we'd gotten a step ahead of Futarishizuka, so I wanted to thank her. Even so, asking her to go back to the otherworld posthaste seemed the best option.

"Peeps, can I ask you to do something?"

"Yes. I was thinking the same thing."

It made me happy to feel like we really understood each other.

We exchanged brief nods, then turned back to face the pile-hair princess.

"Lady Elsa, we will be sending you back home now."

"Wait one moment, Sasaki!"

"What is it?"

"I…I still have all kinds of things I need to ask you!"

"In that case, we will visit you again upon our return."

"…I want to know now," she muttered, staring at us. Her expression was serious. "I didn't think there were any buildings this big in town—or anywhere nearby."

Given that this warehouse was meant for storing cargo coming in from ships, it was extremely expansive. In terms of floor space, it probably rivaled Count Müller's estate. The ceiling was incredibly high as well, enough to leave a deep impression on someone unaccustomed to it.

"Where are we, exactly?"

"……"

Now, then. How to go about answering *that* little question?

Peeps's offensive spell had also served to put the pile-hair princess on her guard. She must have had a lot of doubts concerning her visit to this world, as well. It was very possible that her back-and-forth with Futarishizuka had only expanded those doubts.

Our relationship with her would greatly affect our relationship with the count. If you wish to kill the general, first shoot his horse—so the saying went. Though, in this case, the horse we were supposed to be shooting had just bucked against us.

It happened all the time—your relationship with someone going south because you ended up on bad terms with their family.

Which was why I decided to be earnest in the matter.

"What can we do to convince you?"

"......"

Now that Futarishizuka was no longer a threat, we turned to face Lady Elsa.

When we did, she questioned us openly. "Where are we? Who are all of you? I want an explanation."

"Well..."

The one thing I couldn't afford to reveal was the existence of the Starsage. It was also his wish to remain unknown, so I would do my best to guard his identity, even when it came to Count Müller's daughter. One always had to be careful when handling others' personal information.

Then what about the existence of modern Japan in relation to the otherworld? Even if I were to explain that to her, nobody from the otherworld without a means of crossing over would be able to confirm it. Even if we were to put Japanese goods right in front of them as hard evidence, they'd never be able to interfere.

It wasn't really that different from my claim that I'd come to the Kingdom of Herz from another continent. I would have liked to have kept it a secret, but even if I admitted it, this fact was of no importance when compared with the existence of the Starsage.

"All right, Lady Elsa. Allow me to show you my homeland—where I was born."

"...Really?"

"Really."

A few minutes walking around the inner city would be more than enough to convince her of how different this place was from the world she lived in. Getting questioned by police would be an annoyance, but with the badge in my pocket and a police station business card, I could easily deal with that.

If there was any problem, it would be Section Chief Akutsu discovering her existence. Given the strength of his governmental authority, if I tried to claim she was a relative, it would be easy for him to investigate and disprove in the blink of an eye. That meant if I needed an excuse, I'd have to search for it somewhere beyond his influence.

As for Lady Elsa, I'd just be an acquaintance of Futarishizuka's. Considering what had happened, she was unlikely to protest. Still, I was pretty sure her impression of me was in the gutter at the moment; in consideration of those feelings, I intended to bring her into the loop about the otherworld. Personally, I hoped to establish friendly relations with her going forward.

"First, a few things about this world…"

As Futarishizuka looked on, I explained the situation to Lady Elsa. I told her that this was a different world from hers—that no matter how far she walked from her world, no matter how many oceans she crossed, she'd never be able to get here. I explained that I was a visitor from this place to their world, and that once I'd arrived, I'd met Count Müller and started a business.

Explaining all this without revealing the Starsage's presence was taxing, to say the least. I felt bad for him, but with Futarishizuka watching, I had to lie and say that the spell to cross between the two worlds came from my powers as a magical middle-aged man.

"Is that all true? It's so unbelievable."

"I knew you'd say that, madam."

"Then—"

"Why don't we do a little sightseeing after this?"

"Sightseeing?"

"I believe you'll understand once you see it for yourself."

"……"

From the architectural styles to how the people lived their lives, our culture and civilization were completely different from theirs. Getting her to grasp what I was saying seemed an easy task. In fact, the bigger problem would be what to do when we were finished.

"Ah," said Futarishizuka. "You know, I do have something to ask you."

"And what would that be?"

Now that I'd wrapped up my explanation to the pile-hair princess, Futarishizuka piped up. Was she going to complain again? I hoped she wouldn't rile up my Peeps too much.

"How is it that you are able to communicate with this girl?"

"What?"

Even after receiving a painful present from Peeps, the way she talked, it was like nothing had happened. It made me keenly aware that her long life wasn't just for show. Still, I had no idea what she was asking.

"I'm not sure what you mean."

"Well, it certainly doesn't seem to me as though you and the girl are having a conversation."

Her expression was honest, with her head tipped to the side—I doubted she was lying. That was the attitude of someone who was legitimately confused. Which meant that I, in turn, found her words incomprehensible.

Fortunately, the answer came quickly—from the bird perched on my shoulder.

"*She does not comprehend the language of our world.*"

"Peeps?"

"*You receive the benefits of my magic because we are connected by a path. It is for that reason that you have no trouble conversing across worlds. She, however, is another story. She can't understand the language the girl is using.*"

"But she understands what I'm saying to Lady Elsa, doesn't she?"

Otherwise, even Futarishizuka would never have made a break for the girl. She'd attacked because she kept hearing my words of concern.

"*Your words are uttered in your native tongue, but through my magic, those from the otherworld understand you as well. However, this child speaks in the language of my world. Naturally, those here cannot understand her.*"

"Oh. So that's how it works."

In other words, Futarishizuka heard the voice of this magical middle-aged man in Japanese and the voice of the pile-hair princess in the otherworld's language. I didn't blame her for being dubious— Lady Elsa and I had basically been speaking different languages to each other.

Well, wasn't that a wonderful miscalculation? That meant if Lady

Elsa was to accidentally say something about the otherworld to Futar-ishizuka, we'd still be safe. I could keep everything about my position and relationships in the otherworld a secret.

That said, she probably knew quite a bit just from what I'd mentioned previously.

"Hmm," mused Futarishizuka. "I suppose I understand."

"As long as you understand what Peeps and I are saying, to continue from before, we'd like to show her around the city for a while. I was hoping you would accept these goods and deal with them as necessary."

"In that case, perhaps I will come along."

"...Why?"

"What do you mean, *why*? That sparrow on your shoulder has my life in its hands. Ah, what a terrifying bird. I suppose I must serve my master loyally and honestly. You may use me as you will, whether that be as a pack mule or anything else."

"What will we do about the goods we brought?"

"I can make a few calls. That shouldn't pose a problem, should it?"

"...I suppose I don't mind."

It was like the lethal curse wasn't even a big deal to her. I didn't know what she really thought about it, but the aloof, unconcerned way with which she spoke was just the same as it always had been. Her psychic power was impressive, but the strength of her mental fortitude frankly alarmed me.

Plus, she looked like a little girl. The gap was mind-boggling.

"If that is settled, then what are you waiting for? Introduce the girl to me."

"Understood."

And so Peeps and I headed into the city with the two of them in tow.

*

After departing from the warehouse on the shore, we headed to Shiodome. Out of all the places we could get to via taxi, I had chosen the sights that would contrast most with those I'd seen in the other-world. I expected the Shiodome Sio-Site area would really resonate with Lady Elsa.

Ever since its reconstruction in the mid-Heisei era, the Sio-Site had featured tall buildings packed into every street corner. It had been some time since their construction, but every single one was quite the sight to behold. Not a bad choice, in my opinion, if you wanted to give someone a basic impression of Tokyo. Plus, unlike Roppongi, Shibuya, or Shinjuku, there were, conveniently, fewer people around. Looking back, I could remember being overwhelmed by this place when I'd first arrived in the city.

And just as I'd planned, the cityscape had easily captured Lady Elsa's heart.

"Your explanation was correct, Sasaki. I am certain there is nowhere like this anywhere in the Kingdom of Herz, nor in any nearby nations. And the people roaming the streets look like you: a slightly deeper skin tone and less defined facial features."

"Do you understand now, madam?"

"...This truly is your homeland, isn't it?"

Thankfully, since it was a weekday, most of the people quickly criss-crossing the streets were wearing suits. Still, I did spot a few people in more casual clothing, who looked like they were here to sightsee, same as us.

This area was filled with high-class condominiums geared toward the overseas employees of foreign companies. You could see a lot of pale-skinned families in the nearby supermarket, too. And now that more and more people were visiting from overseas on vacation, Lady Elsa's blond hair and blue eyes didn't seem to stand out at all.

Of course, we'd already found her some clothing more suitable for this world. We had her change up her hairstyle to something simpler as well. Finally, we had her raise the hood on her sweatshirt, making her extremely inconspicuous.

Incidentally, I'd given her a brief rundown of our relationship with Futarishizuka before setting off. I'd said she was my business partner at the moment. Lady Elsa probably wouldn't have any chances to meet her after this, so our explanation wasn't that important.

"These *auto-mobiles* surprised me, but the buildings along the street are even more shocking."

"Does it make you more inclined to believe me?"

We found a pedestrian walkway connecting one cluster of buildings to another and looked out across the city. Through the clear enclosure, you could see the flow of traffic on the road below us. Up above, you could see quite a few high-rise buildings, too.

How long had it been since I'd visited this area anyway?

"I... Yes, I believe you, okay? I mean, after all this, I'd have to..."

"I'm grateful that you understand, madam."

For our outing, I'd placed Peeps in his carrying cage. We'd gone to grab it from the apartment using his teleportation magic.

"But then, why did you visit our world, Sasaki?"

"...What do you mean?"

"What would someone from such a prosperous nation want from a world like ours?"

"Ah. Well..."

I hesitated at the pile-hair princess's insight. It didn't feel right to say I'd gone there to do business as a side gig. Her and our respective... motives, if you want to call them that, were of two entirely different orders of magnitude.

A corporate drone, tired of serving his organization, had paired up with a Java sparrow—their goal being to seek out delicious food and a tranquil life. This girl, though, was worried about the fate of her home nation. I was sure she was considering what would happen if we were to invade them.

"I suppose you could say it's to ensure our worlds have a positive relationship."

"Hmm. Really?"

"Yes, really, madam." I hadn't *lied*, per se. But I didn't want to stay on this topic. "By the way, would you mind if we asked a question as well?"

"What is it?"

"Only you know about what I've told you. And we won't tell anyone other than you, Lady Elsa. If anyone in your world, aside from us, was to learn of it, assume that it will mark the end of our relationship with Count Müller and his family."

"What about that black-haired girl?" asked the pile-hair princess, looking over at Futarishizuka.

She was right—she *had* been around for that conversation. "She lacks the means to travel between worlds. And we won't ever be taking her there, either. Hence, should what we talked about cross the barrier between worlds, we will determine that it was something done at your behest."

"Mgh... Yes, I understand." The pile-hair princess nodded with an audible gulp.

I felt bad about phrasing it like a threat. But being so firm with my request would ensure her silence for the time being. And even if she did spill the beans, it would probably only be to Count Müller. And we'd told *him* about the Starsage and everything, so we wouldn't have any issues there.

"Ah, hello? I would like to join this conversation as well..."

Futarishizuka, unable to comprehend Lady Elsa's words, was requesting a translation. Elsa and I were walking side by side, while Futarishizuka always trailed a few steps behind.

"She was just talking about how wonderful the kimono you're wearing is."

"Hrm?! Is that true?"

"Yes. She says the color is splendid."

"Oh well. That does make a lady happy."

I just flattered her randomly, and now she's squealing with joy like a little girl.

The pile-hair princess shot me a suspicious glance but didn't say anything in particular about it. I'd already explained to her that while she and Futarishizuka couldn't understand each other, my words were intelligible to them both. She seemed to realize what I was getting at.

Exactly the social acumen you'd expect from a young noble like her.

"In that case, does the child wish for me to pick out a kimono for her as well?"

"Oh, no, we can't exactly do that..."

Futarishizuka was getting ahead of herself, rattling off suggestions that would do more harm than good.

It was right about then that it happened.

We had just turned a bend when we ran across a group of people making a lot of noise in front of the Yurikamome waterfront line's Shiodome Station, across the corner from a convenience store. A few of them were holding up big industrial cameras and directional microphones. It looked like they were in the middle of a photo shoot.

Past the cameras was a woman dressed in gorgeous clothing.

"The Tokyo Waterfront New Transit Waterfront Line—more commonly known as the Yurikamome. Did you all know each station on this particular line uses a different voice actress for its announcements? Today I'm here with our group members in front of Shiodome Station..."

We stopped walking and tried to listen in. It seemed like they were recording some kind of program. Apparently, a member of a newly formed idol group was in charge of the announcements at the Yurika-mome Station in Shiodome, and this group was on the scene reporting about it.

"Sasaki, it looks awfully lively over there."

"It does, doesn't it?"

The best option would be to take a detour.

Unfortunately, something happened just as I had decided that. One of the people in the group making all the noise seemed to notice us and started gesturing. The woman on camera responded to this and started walking our way.

"My, what adorable guests! Where are you all off to today?"

We had no chance to escape. A moment later, the cameras were on us. Talk about awful timing. Shibuya or Ikebukuro would have been one thing, but I hadn't expected to run into a film crew like this in the Shiodome area.

"Sasaki, what is this person saying?"

"Is this one of those live-streaming events?"

Ignoring the pile-hair princess's question, I asked the most important thing first. My response would vary greatly based on the answer. If they were just recording, then I could have the bureau use its authority to confiscate the data without question. That was what I had assumed when I asked the question.

However, my shallow hopes were quickly crushed.

"That's right! We're live on the air!" came the overly energetic response.

I felt my stomach drop.

Immediately, I took a step forward, putting myself in a position to hide Lady Elsa's face. At the same time, I exchanged a look with Futa-rishizuka, willing her to do something to handle the situation. As for the one in the cage—well, he was probably fine. Peeps had been studying on the internet; he could mind his manners without issue.

"I'm sorry, but could I ask you to point the camera elsewhere?" I told the woman plainly.

The crucial thing here was to not make the situation any worse. This person was an idol, apparently, and such people always had some number of zealous fans attached to them. I didn't want to imagine what might happen if we somehow earned their ire. If they whipped up an internet frenzy, things would not be easy. Scandals involving government employees *already* stood out.

But if I could deal with the situation calmly, we would be all right.

The name of the idol group they mentioned was one I hadn't heard of. They probably weren't in the major leagues, as it were. There was a low probability this was being broadcast on cable. If this was an internet stream, they wouldn't have that many viewers watching in real time.

Later on, if the bureau went behind the scenes and took control of the upload site, the information wouldn't spread very far. I was glad Futarishizuka was here. If I requested a takedown using a rank-A psychic's presence as the reason, it should be possible to gain approval.

I was seriously glad I had approved her request to come along with us on this little outing.

"Please, ma'am?"

"O-oh, yes! I'm very sorry for suddenly stopping you!"

She seemed to be experienced at this as well; she immediately averted the camera to the side. She'd turned its lens toward the ticket booths and the train platform. Probably a conscious choice, given that their other option was an unattractive convenience store. The woman doing the reporting then quickly placed herself back in front of the camera.

Naturally, our attention was drawn in that direction.

And then, as everyone was watching, an accident happened.

A mother and her child were just about to come down the staircase.

"Mama! TV! There's TV people here!" shouted the young boy as soon as he saw the big cameras. Then he took off running. And of course, he slipped impressively and took a dive—and from pretty high up. He was headed toward the base of the stairs with considerable momentum.

He lost his balance, and his body tipped forward and down. There were over ten stairs between him and the ground. Depending on where he landed, it could be a disaster.

"Ack...!"

The first person to move was the pile-hair princess.

Taking a step forward, she raised her voice in a shout.

"Levitation!"

Hearing her treble voice, I could definitely imagine it lifting something into the air.

And then the boy's body literally started to float.

I remembered this spell—I had learned it from Peeps not long after I'd first visited the otherworld—it temporarily made the target float. It wasn't difficult to learn, and many people could use it without an incantation.

Its effective duration was extremely short, however. Apparently, it was used as a part of daily life, such as when moving furniture or for construction work. If the target was able to use magic, it could also be easily blocked.

And it was exactly this spell that gently caught the falling boy. His small body floated through the air, drifting, until he landed at the bottom of the stairs. It had taken only a few seconds. The entire event happened very quickly. However, the camera lens had been pointed straight at it the entire time.

"That could have been dangerous," said the pile-hair princess, exhaling, as though she'd just finished up a good day's work.

The filming crew, on the other hand, was frozen in shock. Somehow, we'd landed in even more trouble.

"My, you're in for it now, aren't you?" came Futarishizuka's mean-spirited voice from behind me.

She was right, though. This was it. At this point, I could only throw up my hands. Lady Elsa's magic had been livestreamed to the entire world. She may not have personally been in the shot, but you could definitely hear her spirited shout of "Levitation!" and see the boy float safely to the ground.

Oh, but wait—she was speaking the otherworld's language, so maybe everything's fine... Was everything fine?

"What's the matter with you? Why do you look so surprised?"

"Well, Lady Elsa, that was..."

"Spit it out! Do you have some complaint about my magic?"

"......"

The pile-hair princess spoke coolly, as though she'd only done what anyone else would have.

This time, however, her utterly straightforward personality had put us in a tough spot. Her pure heart, immediately willing to jump in to save someone, had done massive damage to our social lives.

No, that was wrong. This was all my fault. I couldn't blame her for anything. I'd never told her what "magic" meant in this society. For her, and others from her world, magic was a normal, omnipresent phenomenon.

There were so many other things I had needed to tell her that I'd forgotten that simple fact. Or perhaps I, too, had been infected by the otherworld's magical culture. All I'd had to tell her was to please not use magic in this world.

More than that, I hadn't even expected her to be able to use magic. She'd told me herself that she had no talent for it, so it had slipped my mind. She might not have had talent for it, but that didn't necessarily mean she *couldn't* use it.

At the same time, considering her disposition, I knew she probably would have used magic even if I had warned her. She had saved the boy without even thinking. It was probably like a conditioned reflex.

And right now wasn't the time to ponder all this. Whatever the case, I had to cover up the evidence.

She wasn't a psychic, but without knowing the context, it might as well have been the same thing. Intending to carry out my responsibilities as a member of the bureau, I very hastily slipped around behind the man holding the camera, who was currently engrossed with the confused boy standing at the bottom of the stairs.

"Ms. Futarishizuka!"

"You're a rough taskmaster…"

I'd learned during training how to respond to a situation like this. According to the manual, I was to "preemptively gain total control over the situation." The bureau would take care of the rest.

Just the other day, after the incident in Iruma, I had witnessed just how good they were at wiping their employees' asses. I imagined this must be what it felt like to use one of the latest bidet toilets. This was why employees on-site could make decisions with confidence.

"I cannot abide you taking videos without permission," said Futarishizuka, her hand touching the cameraman's back.

A moment later, the man's body collapsed, drained of its energy. It had happened so quickly he didn't even have time to cry out. I doubted there was a power as handy as her energy drain for reliably disabling living creatures.

As he fell, so, too, did the camera on his shoulder. It struck the paved concrete, smashing against it. The plastic cover came off, sending little fragments scattering in all directions.

Just to make absolutely sure, Futarishizuka stomped the camera underfoot. With her superhuman strength, she crushed the whole thing in one go.

"Hey!" the woman reporter cried out, almost screaming. The situation had shocked her, and her eyes kept darting between the fallen cameraman and the young girl who had crushed their footage. Her expression made it clear she had no idea why any of this was happening.

Futarishizuka wasted no time in making her next move. She dashed, closing the distance in an instant. And then, just like she'd done with the cameraman, she touched every single one of the film crew members present, starting with the girl dressed in idol clothing. As they were touched, they each fell unconscious.

I, on the other hand, pulled my phone from my pocket. Not the bureau-provided one but my personal one. They were always monitoring the location of the former, so I made a point to carry it as little as possible whenever I was doing anything with Peeps.

According to what I'd learned in training, if I dialed a specific extension from the center of the city, they'd have people here within twenty or thirty minutes. I'd tell them I encountered a stray psychic.

"Wait, Sasaki! What's the meaning of this?!"

"Lady Elsa, listen carefully," I said, keeping my voice down lest it be picked up by microphones on any surveillance cameras in the area.

"Wh-what…?"

"Magic doesn't exist in this world."

"What are you saying?! You use it, too, don't you?!"

"My magic is something I learned when I came to your world. To make a long story short, what you just did is as incredible as a sparrow speaking where you come from."

"…Wait, really?"

"She's doing this to deal with the situation."

"……"

Since we were near a train station, there were probably plenty of surveillance cameras in the vicinity. Someone from the bureau was sure to check them. Actually, there was a very good chance they'd all be confiscated. It wouldn't be easy to make it so Lady Elsa was never here.

I needed to avoid anything that might cause unwarranted suspicion from the section chief, while also sending Lady Elsa back to her world without making her unhappy. The mission in front of me was, it seemed, my most difficult one yet—it was like the kind of quest in a video game where you could only choose one objective to complete.

"High-ranking telekinetic psychics are extremely dangerous, you know," said Futarishizuka.

"I'm fully aware of that."

The full party wipe we'd experienced in the bowling alley due to the hurricane psychic was still fresh in my memory. In other words, a psychic with similar potential had been caught on camera.

The scary thing about psychic powers in this world was that even though you couldn't increase your options, you could increase your level of proficiency over time, strengthen your power, and broaden the situations in which you could put it to good use.

"The bureau is sure to keep that girl under close watch."

"Please help me so that doesn't happen."

"Getting needy now that you've put that curse on me, huh?"

"You're in the same boat as us. In exchange, I'll guarantee your safety."

"Really? Well, in that case, I suppose I shall cooperate."

At this point, we had no choice. For the time being, we'd need Futarishizuka's help to succeed.

My life was already so turbulent I could scarcely imagine what things would be like in half a year.

✳

Our tour of the city had transformed into a psychic mess.

Strictly speaking, the culprit was a magician from the otherworld, but we decided to pass it off publicly as the work of a psychic. If we hadn't done so, the bureau might end up digging into Peeps's and my secret.

As for the idol and film crew Futarishizuka had knocked out, bureau employees came running to the scene to retrieve them. Watching them show up in black vans and collect the unconscious was more than enough to make my hair stand on end.

They quickly found the streaming site with the recording and stopped the broadcast. Two or three thousand people had been watching the stream in real time. That was a lot of people, but not actually that much for this kind of program. After returning to the bureau, I heard from the department in charge that they'd probably have a relatively easy time with it.

Afterward, I headed to the bureau's conference room, where we had a meeting with Section Chief Akutsu.

"I didn't think I'd be seeing you again so soon like this," he said.

"You may not believe it," drawled Futarishizuka, "but I am simply overflowing with the desire to do good work. I thought I'd start right away."

The chief's attention was on Futarishizuka, likely because he feared her psychic power. He pretended to be calm and collected on the outside, but I could easily guess what was on his mind from how frequently he glanced at her. She and I stood side by side, with a table separating us from the chief, and even from my vantage point, it was plain as day.

The pile-hair princess stood to my other side. Lady Elsa had been clear to see in the recording. Futarishizuka and I were the only ones on-site. While Lady Elsa's Levitation chant had been in a foreign language to them, it was only natural the bureau would want to ask her about why the boy had suddenly floated into the air.

For that, I got Futarishizuka to help me introduce her as a psychic from a foreign country. I'd initially considered the plan of sending her back to the otherworld and pretending like I didn't know anything, but with the crucial moment recorded, carelessly trying to hide her could ruin my position within the bureau. Depending on how things shook out, the section chief might have started paying special attention to—or even tailing—me.

After thinking it through and talking it over with everyone, we ended up introducing her to the boss.

I'd had Peeps go back alone to Futarishizuka's hotel. I couldn't

exactly come into the office with a sparrow carrier, and with his teleportation spell, he could get in and out of the room without needing
a key.

"We at the bureau would much rather have less work to do, actually," said the section chief, his eyes moving from Futarishizuka to
Lady Elsa.

The girl, whose hair was a strikingly beautiful blond, also had very
fair skin and blue eyes. Though we'd had her change into modern
clothes from what she'd been wearing before, she certainly didn't look
Japanese. The section chief's eyes said it all: Who on earth was she,
and where did we find her?

"This psychic is an acquaintance of Futarishizuka's."

"Is this a result of your hard work, Sasaki?"

The work he was referring to was recruitment, which was my
assigned job for the time being—scouting new psychics.

"No, she was there by coincidence, and we had struck up a
conversation."

"I was under the impression that other countries handle their psychics much the same way we do."

He seemed to be criticizing Elsa's use of her power in public. We'd
involved the SDF in that little incident in Iruma only the day before—
the bureau was probably under heavy fire right now. Someone from
another organization had likely been made to take the fall already.

"Surely there was another way to handle this."

"She is a very kindhearted girl, Chief. And the stairs in that station
are particularly high. If she hadn't used her power, the boy would have
been injured—of that I have no doubt. He could have even been para-
lyzed, depending on how he landed."

I doubted I could get the chief's understanding with that alone. He
clearly considered maintaining the secrecy around psychic powers
more important than the future of some boy he didn't know. But I also
needed to back up the girl sitting beside me.

"If she is a friend of Futarishizuka's, does that mean she's an irregular psychic?"

"No. I don't know the details, either, but she said the girl is from
another country. Apparently, they got in contact again when Ms.
Futarishizuka defected to us. That's about all I know. I'll leave any
further investigation in your hands, Chief."

"...I see," he said, eyes flitting between the two girls.

Explaining it like this would probably keep him from pressing us with stinging questions. On top of that, making the girl out to be the friend of a rank-A psychic would be enough even to temper *his* persistence. I could tell he was hesitating over his next words.

I'd shared what I'd be saying with the girls beforehand. We couldn't afford for Lady Elsa to end up in the bureau's custody. That would make our relationship with Count Müller a lot worse. That, more than anything else, I wanted to avoid.

"If it's not too much trouble, I'd like to speak with you for a moment," said the section chief, looking at the pile-hair princess.

"......"

But she didn't answer him. Obviously not—she didn't speak any of this world's languages. The only reason I could talk with her normally, even in the otherworld, was because I was connected to Peeps via a magical path. Because Lady Elsa had no such connection, she wasn't able to understand what anyone in this world was saying. Having a conversation was totally out of the question.

"Have I said something to displease you?" the chief tried again.

"Sasaki, what is this person saying?"

Lady Elsa's brief question probably echoed in the chief's ears as a string of mysterious sounds. And that went both ways. Naturally, they both turned their gazes toward me.

"What did she just say? What language is that?"

"Sasaki, is he trying to talk to me?"

I didn't want to speak to Lady Elsa here. My words would be understood by all, whether they spoke Japanese or the otherworld's language. If the chief found out about that, I was sure he would have some questions for me. But I'd explained all that to Lady Elsa already.

"Oh, that's right. I shouldn't be talking," she said.

Ah, there we go. I was glad she remembered.

The chief was also quick to follow up. "Sasaki?"

"I hear she speaks a minority language as her mother tongue."

"...Ah, I see."

We'd discussed that answer ahead of time, too. It was the only excuse I could think of.

"She's friends with Futarishizuka, right? Could we have her interpret?"

"I'm sorry," I interrupted, "but could you ask that of her directly, Chief? I'm just accompanying Ms. Futarishizuka. I'm in no position to make requests. She's only here to begin with because of her goodwill."

"......" Chief Akutsu and Futarishizuka looked at each other.

In terms of social status, the chief had the clear upper hand—but Futarishizuka had a biological advantage. That, along with her long-standing participation in a certain illegal organization, made her a threat the chief couldn't ignore.

No matter how high a position or rank he held, he'd always be vulnerable to assassination at her hands.

"What's this? You have a job for a part-time psychic like me?"

"...I think I've grasped the situation regarding this new psychic."

"Is that so?"

Futarishizuka's expression was making it clear she wanted to be hired as a regular employee. And since this was the chief we were talking about, he was probably reading all kinds of things into her attitude—especially considering her very recent defection. According to my colleagues at the bureau, he was a graduate from a certain very high-ranking educational institution. His credentials were top class. I knew for certain his mind worked a whole hell of a lot faster than mine.

"Regarding your friend, I understand. I won't pry into it any further."

"I apologize for all the trouble recently," replied Futarishizuka.

Partly thanks to Futarishizuka's former employers, we were able to avoid any further questioning regarding Lady Elsa. I wasn't certain how far the chief's authority reached; still, matters extending to other nations must have been beyond him. After all, he had no way of knowing which countries, or what sort of organizations, were sponsoring her.

Also, I'm pretty sure Futarishizuka just took a dig at me.

"Moving right along," continued Mr. Akutsu in a more composed tone, "I have a commission for the bureau part-timer, as it happens."

"Please, ask whatever you like," she replied, as if she was above it all. "I will surely carry it out with flying colors."

"I understand that in your previous organization, there is a rank-B psychic with a telekinetic power able to be applied over a wide area. Along with you, he interfered with our operation only a week ago."

"Hmm, and what about him?"

"I want you to eliminate him."

The chief had given Futarishizuka a job request—her mission was to assassinate her former colleague. A bloodcurdling proposition, indeed.

"May I assume this is a test, and upon passing you will officially hire me?"

"You are free to assume that."

"Really, now?"

"Personally, I'm in favor of hiring you."

"Hmm."

This sort of thing was probably unavoidable. Considering who she was, they'd need a *very* good reason to admit Futarishizuka into the bureau. I'd guessed this would happen, but hearing it with my own ears still set me on edge.

"You'll do it, then?"

"I shall. It's natural the bureau would ask such a thing."

"For our part, I'll assign Sasaki to you as support."

"Huh...?" I said out of reflex. This was Futarishizuka's problem—they weren't trying to drag me in now, were they?

"His capabilities as a psychic may leave something to be desired, but he has all the proper authority as a member of the bureau. If you should need anything from us during the course of your mission, please go through him."

"My, how reassuring."

"Hold on a minute, Chief."

"You scouted her. She's your responsibility, isn't she?"

"But..."

"Just as Hoshizaki has taken responsibility for you. Or hasn't she?"

"......"

Miss Hoshizaki treated me more like her portable water supply. I was like a human-shaped flask to her. Well, maybe she had displayed *some* concern for my well-being. She hadn't abandoned me, at any rate.

When I thought about it that way, it was hard for me to refuse.

"I'm not setting a deadline, but please get it done as soon as possible."

"Yes, I understand fully. I will return in no time with his head in hand."

Futarishizuka had agreed—without even a hint of hesitation.

✳

Having survived our meeting with the section chief, we exited the bureau and headed for Futarishizuka's hotel room.

Once there, I had intended to rejoin Peeps and send Lady Elsa back to her world. We'd been able to pull the wool over everyone's eyes for now, but we didn't know what would happen next time. I felt bad, but we needed to send her home with a priority stamp on her head.

Unfortunately for us, the pile-hair princess had other plans.

"Sasaki, I'd like to learn more of this world."

"Why on earth is that, Madam?"

We were in the familiar living space of the hotel room. Lady Elsa's declaration had come as she rose from the sofa cushion right beside me. Opposite us across the low table sat Futarishizuka. And on the table itself there was a little tree—I had no idea where it came from— upon which Peeps was perched.

"My father has shown me the goods you've brought in the past."

"Ah." I could imagine what she'd say next.

"Those items were created in this world, weren't they?"

It was just as I'd guessed.

"Even if that was true, Lady Elsa, what is it you intend to do?"

"I'd want to learn all about this world! And then I'd bring the knowledge back to our world and share it with everyone else. If I did that, I'd be of some use to my father. I wouldn't have to marry into another house just to contribute to my family!"

As the local lord's daughter, she was extremely conscious of the world around her—it wasn't odd at all for this idea to occur to her. Unfortunately, this was a request I couldn't approve. If the section chief learned of Peeps or the existence of the otherworld, everything would become a lot more complicated.

I'd probably be buried in unfair work requests and demands. No matter how high-ranking my boss was, there were plenty of people even higher. I had zero faith I'd be able to skillfully work around all of them. The only future I could see in that direction was retirement in the otherworld.

The kind of magic over there, where you could perfectly cure some-one's wounds with a wave of your staff, was too much for those living in the modern world.

"I'm terribly sorry, but I cannot allow that."

"B-but why not?! I promise I'll keep this world and everything about you a secret!"

"I have been very careful not to tell anyone around me that I am able to travel between your world and this one, madam. If you were to cause a stir in my vicinity, it would render all that hard work meaningless."

"Oh, come now. It can't be that difficult to shelter one young girl."

"I beg to differ—it will be *very* difficult."

"Well, I'm not convinced."

"As you already know, Lady Elsa, this world is more advanced than yours in many respects. One of those respects is how we manage our people. Each one of us has an identification number issued by our government, allowing for absolute supervision."

"Is that even possible? Babies are born all the time. Wouldn't keeping track of every last one of them be too difficult? I can't even imagine how much money it must cost."

"When someone has a baby, they report it. The same thing happens when someone dies. It's each person's responsibility, and failing to comply is a crime. Leaving and entering this country is strictly con-trolled, and illegal immigration is treated very severely."

"...Then they...really do keep track of everyone?"

"If something happened, and a member of the military police was to question us, they would notice that you look foreign and realize you don't have one of our identification numbers. Without an explanation, we would be taken into custody and thrown in prison—that much is certain."

"......"

"To make matters worse, the man we just spoke with works for the government, and his job is to oversee people. In your world's terms, consider a head minister—then count down a few links in the chain of command. That's who he is. You can think of him as equivalent to a count—part of the nobility."

"He...he was that important?!"

"Yes, and he already has his eyes on you."

"What...?"

"It is paramount that we send you back home right away, in order to ensure your safety, Lady Elsa. If you stayed in this world, and something was to happen to you, I wouldn't be able to face Count Müller."

"......"

Bringing up Count Müller put even her at a loss for words. She was still a daddy's girl. Considering her father's character, I could totally see why she'd love him so much. Plus, he was tall and handsome, slim but muscular—not to mention a noble deeply trusted by his people. It was fundamentally unreasonable to expect anyone not to be fond of him.

That said, she only remained silent for a moment. Then she really let me have it.

"E-even so, here's what I think! If this world was to attack us right now, we would be unilaterally wiped out. Knowing that, for the sake of my world, I must boldly set foot in this one!"

"There is no such possibility, madam."

"How can you be so sure? *You've* visited already."

"...You're right."

She spoke with an uncharacteristically serious expression. But she *was* right, and I couldn't exactly argue. From her stubborn objections, I could sense how sharply she felt the danger.

"Lady Elsa, I don't believe your world is as weak as you think."

"How can you say that?"

"This world doesn't have magic. We don't have giant monsters like dragons, either. We may be winning in terms of civilization, but if we were to clash, bringing all our respective forces to bear at once, our world might be the one to lose unilaterally."

"*I agree on that point.*"

Oh, and it looked like Peeps would grace us with his viewpoint as well. I was curious what the Lord Starsage had to say.

"*The types of weapons that exist in this world mostly utilize heat or impact,*" he began. "*If you were able to defend yourselves with barriers in advance, they would have a hard time overrunning you. In addition, they require much time and money to use their weapons, which would work in our favor.*"

This knowledge seemed to be the result of his internet study sessions. How far had he taken his investigation, exactly?

"*Were you to employ monsters against whom physical impacts and heat were ineffective, such as wraiths, you would overwhelm them easily. And if our people came together and coordinated with powerful elementals, it would even be possible to bring this entire world under our control and use it as we see fit.*"

"I-is that right?"

"*Indeed, it is. Our world is rich in versatility.*"

Perhaps the citizens of earth should be concerned.

From Peeps's explanation, I saw that my own world's situation was considerably more precarious than I had thought. Now it was my mind spinning. All of the pile-hair princess's concerns had become mine.

I doubted Peeps would do anything like that. At this point, I fully trusted him. Still, I couldn't entirely deny the possibility that, ultimately, such a future might come to pass. A variety of delusions paraded through my mind before fading into the distance.

"Oh-ho? Is that fear I see on your face, Sasaki?"

"Well, this is my homeland, after all."

I may have been destined to die alone, but I still had a friend or two who would come if I invited them out for a drink. I had quite a few acquaintances from work, too, who had treated me well. The prospect of seeing all of them wiped out, no chance to resist, weighed heavy on my heart.

"Your expression is giving me the creeps," said Elsa.

"You jest, madam."

"Especially considering all you've done is lecture me since I got here."

"I sincerely apologize for that, but—"

"You know, you're the only person aside from my father who has ever lectured me so much."

Lady Elsa spoke cheerfully. That dubious sparkle in her eyes—I'd pretend I didn't notice that. The way she smirked made me very uneasy. I'd always wondered if the little lady had a sadistic streak to her.

"*Worry not. I would never do such a thing.*"

"Come on, Peeps. I trust you."

"*...So you do.*"

Just then, I heard a vibrating noise from somewhere—it sounded like a phone. I looked around for the source, and eventually my gaze

settled on Futarishizuka. It seemed the phone she had tucked in her kimono was receiving a call. She took out the device, checked the screen, and answered it in front of us.

Everyone watched and waited, mouths shut.

The call only consisted of a few words. After nodding a few times, Futarishizuka ended the conversation. A moment later, after returning it to her pocket, she said, "The merchandise you brought has been checked."

It seemed our goods had been appraised.

Since we had brought her gold ingots of unknown origin, Futarishizuka had requested earlier that she have someone confirm the authenticity and purity in advance of cutting a deal. She'd wanted to conduct tests using X-rays and ultrasound.

Apparently, the call was to inform her that it was finished. It looked like gold from the otherworld would pass as gold in this one, too.

"As for the price," she said, "I am fine with what we discussed earlier."

"Thank you very much. I'd like to leave it in your hands."

"How would you prefer the payment?"

"Actually, I wanted to discuss that with you."

"...Go ahead."

"If possible, could I receive a portion of the payment in specific items? I won't ask you to get anything difficult. I just don't want to make a huge, conspicuous shopping trip."

"Hmm..."

"Is that all right?"

"Will I receive pay for this labor, hmm?"

"Yes, of course."

"In that case, I suppose I can be somewhat flexible."

"That will be a big help. Thank you so much."

Continuing to make big purchases under my own name was sure to get me tracked. I could easily imagine the section chief, or someone along those lines, questioning me about it. I hoped Futarishizuka would be able to provide assistance on that front. This, along with purchasing the valuables, would prove an invaluable source of support.

As things stood now, it seemed we might regain custody of Mr. Marc very soon, indeed.

<Otherworld Business Negotiations, Part One>

Futarishizuka and I concluded our deal within the day. Since the items I was looking for were all commonplace goods in modern Japan, she was able to procure them without much trouble. In terms of volume, she quickly filled the wooden box I'd brought from the otherworld. The easy flow of commerce in modern times was a big help.

Our desired merchandise in hand, we left Japan and headed for the otherworld. Because of how much she already knew, we set off right in front of Futarishizuka from the warehouse she'd provided, taking the pile-hair princess and the wooden box along with us.

After that, we went our separate ways. Having deposited Lady Elsa back home, we headed for the Republic of Lunge to fulfill our promise and bring our goods to the Kepler Trading Company. We gave Mr. Joseph's name at the front of the building, and in no time we were shown to a storage room.

"Are you truly going to sell all of this?"

"Is the quantity insufficient, sir?"

"Not at all. It's just that we discussed collateral..."

"I should be able to bring a little bit more next time."

"...Is that right?"

Our goods were lined up in a corner of the storeroom. Though they had been stuffed haphazardly in the wooden box, now everything was laid out neatly on a pricey-looking sheet so the whole thing could be seen at a glance.

This had all been taken care of by the trading company, and it reminded me a little of police seizing evidence.

These were articles I'd sold to the Hermann Trading Company in the past. In addition to the calculators and binoculars, mechanical devices that didn't need a power source, we had also brought sugar and chocolate—relatively expensive luxuries in this world.

Most of the volume came from the latter. It had taken up 90 percent of the wooden box. According to Count Müller, there was considerable demand among the upper classes for our sugar. Mass manufacturing of pure-white sugar was something my world had only achieved after the industrial revolution, so any merchants who dealt with it in bulk were highly prized. In fact, half of the selling price was just the sugar.

But it was the small number of mechanical items that really stole the show. Even the calculators, of which we'd brought the most, only numbered two dozen. I'd bought each of them for 1,980 yen. Mr. Joseph couldn't keep his eyes off them.

"I would like to accept this deal."

"Thank you very much, Mr. Joseph."

It seemed we'd gotten him to accept without issue.

With this, there was no doubt we would be able to establish the Marc Trading Company in this country. Most of the credit went to Futarishizuka. Without her help, it would have been a lot more difficult to go all out and bring over so many goods.

The foodstuffs especially—everything we'd brought in the past combined didn't amount to even half of what we had with us this time. Comparatively, this deal was huge. You couldn't exactly purchase all this from a neighborhood supermarket.

"I believe we have fully understood your intent, Sir Sasaki."

"I'm pleased to hear you say that."

Stocking up hadn't required any exchange of currency this time. I'd left the remainder of the profits from the ingots—a considerable amount—under Futarishizuka's supervision. In the worst-case scenario, I knew she might run away with it. Even so, this was the best option for my personal safety. With this arrangement, it was unlikely even the section chief would uncover our dealings.

"Now," I said, "I'd like to send a message as soon as possible to the one in charge within the Kingdom of Herz."

"Your efforts are appreciated," returned Mr. Joseph.

"I can't promise a specific date, but we will advance matters as quickly as possible."

With Mr. Joseph's approval, our work in the Republic of Lunge was over for now. Since national borders were involved, it would probably take some time. But it was possible the situation would have progressed by the next time we visited.

"Actually, there is one thing I'd like to ask you, Mr. Sasaki."

"What might that be?"

"Why do you support the Kingdom of Herz?"

"...I'm not sure I understand."

"Forgive my rudeness, but you appear to be from another continent."

He was probably referring to my olive skin and flatter facial features. This question involved Peeps, so I didn't want to discuss it too much. But for now, the plan was to establish a good business relationship with this man. A poor lie could remove us from his good graces, and I wanted to avoid that. Especially after we'd already tricked him once.

"Certain interpersonal relationships have led me to give them my support."

"Would that happen to include others from your homeland?"

"No, I'm referring to those who have shown me kindness since I arrived here."

"Ah, I see."

"Is there something you were curious about?"

"I was wondering if there was a community on this continent, somewhere, of those who share your homeland—and if so, I wished to ask if you could introduce me."

"If that's what you meant, then I must confess I ended up here by pure accident. I have unfortunately lost contact with anyone outside this continent."

"I see. I apologize for prying."

I remembered giving Count Müller some story about a shipwreck and my drifting here. That conversation was in limbo already, now that he knew about Peeps, but I would probably be best served by sticking to my story.

I didn't want him asking any more questions, so it was about time for me to change the subject. "I actually wanted to discuss my next shipment," I said.

"If you're referring to the sugar and chocolate, then please do bring more of it for sale. Particularly, white sugar will be a strong seller; the upper classes tend to prefer vivid coloring in their sweets."

"I did wonder if a trading company in the Republic of Lunge might have other sources."

"You can't get sugar this white from very many places. Manufacturing methods are closely guarded secrets, preventing the industry from growing. And either the producers are controlling their outflow or they simply can't produce in large quantities—either way, the selling price remains high."

"Ah, I see."

"How much will you be able to sell us?"

"For the time being, I wanted to continue supplying at a fixed rate."

According to Futarishizuka, it was easiest if I ordered in bulk. In other words, I'd have to keep the MOQ—the minimum order quantity—at the front of my mind if I was going to continue stocking it in the future.

I'd probably have to involve Mr. Joseph in those negotiations, eventually.

"...Is that true, Mr. Sasaki?"

"It is. Please, leave it to me."

In addition, despite the recent fluctuations, one day in the modern world was still over ten in this world. If I missed even a single visit, a lot of time would pass here. I needed to bring in the products at least once every two or three days.

Thinking about this depressed me—it was like I'd gone right back to my days as a corporate drone.

"When can we expect another exchange?"

"I wanted to visit like this again within a month."

As for the all-important stocking price of sugar, one gold ingot would pay for enough to fill several of the containers we used for transport, including the labor fee. On the other end, the profits I made from selling that same amount of sugar to the Kepler Trading Company equated to *dozens* of ingots—I had calculated this value based on the number of gold coins Peeps had used to make the ingots. If all went well, then starting next time, a single round trip would produce profits in Japanese yen of anywhere from tens of millions to *hundreds* of millions, and it would all go into our pocket.

If I might be allowed to give my personal opinion, this amount of money was so surreal that it made my legs go wobbly. Was it all right to keep going like this? I already felt anxious. At some point, my armpits had started to sweat. A lot.

"Quite honestly, I hadn't expected so much."

"I could always bring a variety of other items, should you need any."

"That is reassuring. I'll avail myself of your offer when the time comes. About the sugar again—if it seems you'll be able to bring a larger amount, I'd appreciate it if you contacted me in advance. Like your more complicated goods, I believe the sugar alone could serve as a core item for your newly established trading company."

"Thank you for the advice. I'll be sure to look into it."

Unlike manufactured products, which were valued for their novelty and rarity, foodstuffs had the benefit of perpetual consumption. If I could leverage them to gain a foothold in this marketplace, the Marc Trading Company's finances would likely be assured.

The thought of conflict with other trading companies scared me, but we had the Kepler Trading Company's support, so I trusted it would mostly work out. If any truly precarious situations cropped up, I planned to go crying to the Lord Starsage.

I was sure he'd help me out—if it was for that Kobe beef chateaubriand.

*

After leaving the Kepler Trading Company, we set off from the Republic of Lunge with Peeps's teleportation magic, returning to Count Müller's town of Baytrium. Our first stop was the count's home.

I wanted to get a read on any new developments since my last visit. I'd probably also need to explain what had happened with the pile-hair princess.

The time difference between worlds meant that she'd been missing for several days. No matter how busy a man Count Müller was, not seeing his daughter for that long must have made him uneasy.

I'd brought her back to the estate beforehand, so she'd probably had a little father-daughter discussion with him about what had happened. We'd been pretty honest with Lady Elsa, so I wanted to believe that she would, to an extent, back us up on this one.

Whatever the reason, the fact remained that we'd kidnapped his daughter. Given that, I was tense about our visit.

However, the first thing he did upon meeting us at his estate was deeply bow his head.

"Sir Sasaki, I sincerely apologize for my daughter's behavior."

"Count Müller?"

I saw Lady Elsa waiting in the wings. We were in the same reception room as always. Ever since the Ohgen Empire's invasion, the lack of furnishings had been making the place a little lonely. I couldn't manage anything *too* expensive, but maybe I could buy some things at the neighborhood supermarket and bring them here at some point.

"She told me everything. I am truly sorry."

"But I should be the one apologizing, my lord."

We almost let his daughter get taken away. Had Futarishizuka not been there, the situation would have been very dicey.

"It is my fault for telling her so many things about you, Sir Sasaki. I think that's why Elsa became so curious. But please, could you find it in your heart to forgive her? I will endure any punishment you see fit."

I was a little put off by his attitude—this level of formality was simply uncalled for. The pile-hair princess at his side was also in a state of confusion.

"Um, it's really all right."

"But…"

Times like these called for a few words from the Lord Starsage. I shot a glance at the sparrow on my shoulder.

He immediately piped up, addressing Count Müller, "*Julius, there is no need for concern. We are the ones to blame for this.*"

"No, I heard everything from my daughter. This is, without a doubt, my own mistake."

"*They were the actions of a child. Smiling and forgiving such things shows the magnanimity of an adult.*"

"She may be a child in terms of her age, but she is still my daughter whom I have raised, and I believe I have taught her more than enough. However, it seems my teachings did not take. That is my failure—and no one else's."

Continuing to insist that *he* was the one in the wrong made Count Müller look even better. You could really feel how much he loved his daughter. Watching him, I had to admit the idea of getting married and starting a family might actually be nice. That said, the reality was that I was a withered old man, and the prospect was simply too far above my pay grade. For now, I wanted to focus on getting along with Peeps.

Now that I think of it, I wonder if he ever got married when he was human.

"Whatever the case may be, what's done is done. Don't worry about it too much."

"But I—"

"Your apologies are troubling him as well."

My distinguished Java sparrow shot me a quick glance. Birds generally didn't have any white in their eyes, so it was more like his neck had twitched in my direction. I'd remarked a few days ago how it felt like he was looking at me no matter what angle he was at, and ever since then, he'd been rotating his neck—what a kind bird. It made me want to pet him right on his adorable little head.

"Sir Sasaki, the Lord Starsage is—"

"I share his opinion, so please stop worrying about it, my lord."

While we were fussing over this, there was a terse *knock-knock-knock* at the reception room door. For now, we put our exchange aside as everyone's attention naturally shifted to whatever was outside the room. I wouldn't soon forget Count Müller's intensely apologetic expression. But now his voice grew firm as he called out, "We're in the middle of something. Is this urgent?"

In return came a rather exciting answer: "A-a representative of the Hermann Trading Company has arrived!"

"…What?" The count's expression froze.

I didn't blame him. This was the person who'd had Mr. Marc thrown in jail. The manager must have some idea about Count Müller and Vice Manager Marc's close friendship. Why would he spare the time to visit like this?

Even if the manager had his own relationship with Count Müller, he must have known the man was working to get Mr. Marc released. How bold of him to come waltzing right into the enemy's stronghold.

"All right. Show him in."

"Yes, my lord."

"Count Müller, should I—?"

"You're involved in this, Sir Sasaki. I'd like for you to remain, if it's all the same to you."

"Thank you for your consideration, my lord."

He probably wanted Peeps to be here as well.

Now that I thought about it, this would be our first time meeting the president of the Hermann Trading Company. We'd never had the chance before, since he'd been operating in the capital for so long. My heart started beating faster—what kind of person was he?

*

After a short wait in Count Müller's reception room, the man in question was led in by several guards—military police, dressed in showy outfits. Too much security for a meeting between a mere merchant and a local lord. I found myself on pins and needles thinking about the conversation to come.

"What brings you here today, Hermann?"

"I heard a rumor, my lord Count Müller—that you have been so kind as to show consideration with regard to an internal issue at our Hermann Trading Company, and so I have humbly come to pay you a visit. It has come to my attention that you have been showing a great deal of goodwill to one of our own."

"What about it?"

We'd changed up our positions in the reception room—now Count Müller and the Hermann Trading Company president were seated across from each other. I'd moved to a smaller sofa next to the count's. Peeps was perched on my shoulder.

The Hermann Trading Company's president looked to be in his midforties, of medium height and build. He had wisps of brown hair just barely covering his head, his hairline having receded toward the crown, and eyes of the same color. He was dressed in fairly expensive attire; if you'd told me he was a noble, I probably would have believed you.

Next to the slim, muscular, and tall Count Müller, he appeared a little flimsy—though I was in much the same boat. I briefly considered going to the gym next week, though by now I'd lost track of how many times I'd had that idea and failed.

"This is all an internal matter, my lord, and the purpose of my visit is to assure you that it is nothing that warrants your efforts. I am sure you are quite busy with your newfound peerage, my lord."

"I will be the one to decide that."

"……"

The manager spoke in a very humble way, but Count Müller was blunt. It was so familiar; I was reminded me of how he'd acted the first time I'd met him. While it had only been a few weeks in real time since that audience, strangely, it felt like much more time had passed.

However, the manager wasn't about to back down.

"Then allow me to be straightforward, my lord."

"What is it? Speak."

"The issue at hand, my lord, is a charge of disrespecting the nobility, brought by Count Dietrich. It is with him that the authority to pass judgment lies. This town may be your domain, Count Müller, but I pray that you understand this point."

"I see. So that's what it was."

"Yes, my lord."

The two of them stared at each other. Sparks were flying.

"If by any chance his location here should pose a problem of some kind regarding the offender, it will mean another discussion—and not with me, but with Count Dietrich. Please understand that the criminal has been transferred from the trading company to the count."

The manager, a commoner, was speaking politely out of respect for the count's position. His remarks themselves, however, revealed his hostility. Essentially, he was borrowing Count Dietrich's name to threaten Count Müller.

In a world where the divide between commoner and noble was inviolable, the way he was speaking to someone who held the power of life and death over him was incredible. He wasn't the head of a trading company for nothing; the man had nerves of steel.

But Count Müller wasn't budging, either. He listened to the manager's words with a calm detachment. He must have been used to conversations like these.

However, even his face turned at the man's next words.

"That said, my lord, this matter will not drag on for long. We plan on executing the offender within the month. Until then, I apologize for the trouble but ask that you lend us the space to hold him."

"……" The count's attractive eyebrow twitched.

Even I was surprised at that; I almost cried out in spite of myself. I would never have guessed they'd already scheduled an *execution* for the vice manager. I thought for sure they'd have, you know, some kind of trial first, even if it was just for show.

Actually, Count Müller himself had told me such a system existed.

"I have not yet prepared the criminal's judgment yet."

"Count Dietrich is in a hurry to return to his own domain, my lord. We have made an exception this time and dispensed with the formality. The incident with the Ohgen Empire has not spared him the time for disputes with commoners," the manager said, smirking. This last part was probably the whole reason he visited.

"...I see."

"Then if you'll excuse me, my lord, I will show myself out."

There was little doubt Hermann had switched sides: from Count Müller to Count Dietrich. I guessed that his plan was to bid farewell to this town forever once he'd moved the trading company's headquarters to the capital.

Considering the conflict with the Ohgen Empire, maybe our geographical proximity to the enemy had factored into the decision. In this world, where setting up shop required keeping an inventory, I could sort of understand his concern.

The Hermann Trading Company's manager left the reception room in high spirits with a wide grin.

As for those of us still left in the room—what now?

"Sir Sasaki, it would appear we must hurry."

"Yes, my lord, it would."

This was no time for messing around in the Republic of Lunge.

My deal with the Kepler Trading Company had been to save Mr. Marc's social position, since he had lost his base of support here. Now, however, it looked like his *actual* life might be ending before I could even think about his social life.

*

Once the Hermann Trading Company's manager had left, we burst into action. Count Müller was going to pay a visit to Count Dietrich. I, meanwhile, was going to go see Mr. Marc in prison a second time. Whatever happened next, we had to verify his safety.

My plan before all this had been to head straight there once I had finished my meeting with the count, so this wasn't really a change. That said, my mental state was considerably more strained than I had anticipated then. I took off by carriage, praying that he was all right.

Soon, we had arrived at the prison; the guard showed me to the cell I was after. Like before, Mr. Marc was inside. However, he'd gotten much thinner compared to when I had last seen him. The disheveled stubble probably didn't help matters, but his cheeks were clearly sunken. His clothes, too, were covered in grime and sweat, with conspicuous stains here and there.

"I'm sorry it took so long for me to come visit, Mr. Marc."

"Ah, Mr. Sasaki? You're back again..."

Upon seeing me, the vice manager smiled a little. I couldn't call him enthusiastic by any standard, but he was still showing consideration for us.

"How are you doing? You don't look so good."

"Thankfully, I wasn't tortured. Have you and Count Müller been pulling strings? They've allowed me to live with all my limbs attached, as you can see."

"Have they been giving you enough food?"

"I suppose..."

"Yes? You do look rather thin, though..."

"...They've mixed laxatives into the food a few times already," said the vice manager, face clouding. He seemed like he was at the end of his rope.

"That's awful. In that case, I will arrange for your food to be delivered from Mr. French's place from now on. He was very frustrated he couldn't do anything for you. I'm sure he'll help."

"No, I couldn't possibly put any more burden on—"

"Please, Mr. Marc, don't give up. We're all trying our hardest to save you. Just hold on a little longer. You *will* get out of here, regain your freedom, and go back to your days living as a merchant."

"Thank you for going through all this effort for someone like me."

"Don't worry about a thing. You've done more than this for me already."

"Mr. Sasaki..."

"If you'd like, I have something to eat."

I passed a wrapped gift I'd bought on the way here through the bars. The guard and a knight assigned to Count Dietrich had already checked it, so they didn't say anything. They merely stood beside me, listening in on our conversation.

Inside the package was food, drink, and a change of clothes.

"Thank you so much, Mr. Sasaki. Nothing could have made me happier."

"I'll be visiting again in the near future."

I wanted to talk with him a little longer, but we didn't have time right now. Leaving Mr. Marc, we hurried out of the prison as fast as we could.

*

Once we were out of the jail, we went straight to Mr. French's restaurant. There, we explained Mr. Marc's situation and asked if he could have some food delivered. He agreed to it without so much as a second thought. Clearly indignant that they would mix laxatives in with the man's food, he promised in a loud voice that he'd deliver his very best dishes.

That took care of the immediate problem of food, at least. I had been a little frightened by the sight of Mr. French, burning with rage and twisting up his face like a gangster.

Still, I hesitated to say the vice manager's situation was looking better. The real issue at hand was what Count Dietrich was trying to accomplish. One word from him, and Mr. Marc's head would go flying. Plus, the Hermann Trading Company's manager had been willing to challenge Count Müller. The man had been brimming with confidence; he and the other count must have had a rock-solid relationship.

What kind of deal had the two of them struck anyway?

"Can't sit around complaining. I'll do something about this."

As soon as we had left Mr. French's place, Peeps spoke.

Judging by his tone and based on prior experience, I could assume he meant he'd do something about Count Dietrich. But if he did that, everyone involved would find themselves in a bad position—Count Müller first and foremost.

It was our last resort—and one I wanted to avoid if possible.

"I may ask you to do it in the end, Peeps, but could you wait just a little longer for now? I think there's still a few things I can try."

"You have a plan?"

"For the time being, let's go see Count Dietrich."

"If you say so, then yes, I understand."

When Sebastian, the man who had been serving as Count Müller's butler, had betrayed his master, he had said Count Dietrich was the one backing him. I remembered the butler seizing the chance to request all sorts of modern goods from me.

That was what gave me hope, though it was faint.

Could I possibly negotiate with the man using the goods I had on hand?

That was my idea anyway, as I hastened toward Count Dietrich's lodgings.

✳

The inn where our man was staying was very respectable.

I'd figured that when nobles paid visits to other domains, they simply stayed at the estate of the local ruler. However, I was told that Count Dietrich had procured these lodgings himself because of his factional difference with Count Müller.

That much I'd confirmed with the count before my arrival.

After reaching our destination, we requested a meeting and waited approximately one hour.

Using the transceiver to ask for an introduction, I was shown to the reception room. I'd never been so thankful for my noble title as I was at this very moment. Though we'd been made to wait a pretty long time, we were still allowed to meet the count. If I'd been a commoner, he might have refused. Or he might have just confiscated my wares without meeting with me. Considering that, I had nothing but gratitude toward the second prince's mother.

"You're the one dealing in all those mysterious items, yes?"

"That is correct, Count Dietrich."

I sat on a sofa across from the man in question, a low table between us. This was Count Dietrich. At a glance, he looked to be in his mid-forties. His silvery hair was combed back, and his deep, pronounced facial features and blue eyes made him strikingly attractive. His face was good-looking from every angle. Along with his splendid beard, it combined to lend him a fearsome aura.

Count Müller was present as well. He'd come here after our meeting with the manager, and the two had likely been discussing things between themselves.

"Sir Sasaki, what brings you here?"

"I apologize for acting out of turn, my lord."

Count Müller was seated beside me—the two of us facing off against Count Dietrich. Peeps was, as usual, perched on my shoulder. I'd said he was a familiar, and they had let me into the reception room without any questions. That said, the knights on guard had still stared at me with suspicion.

"I would very much like to join your discussion with Count Dietrich, my lord."

"...I see. I apologize for disappointing you so."

"No, my lord, that isn't what this is about at all."

I felt awful for harming his reputation like this. But with Mr. Marc's life hanging in the balance, I hoped he'd forgive me. I had to avoid everything falling apart in my absence—the worst possible scenario.

"What are the two of you discussing?" demanded Count Dietrich. "Mind letting me in on it?"

"I'm terribly sorry, my lord," I said. "I neglected to contact him in advance."

"Well, fine then. More importantly, on to the matter of your wares."

I wasn't sure how his conversation with Count Müller had progressed. But if the other count's interest was now on my products, there was probably still room for discussion.

His curiosity seemed to be genuine.

"Might you require anything, my lord?"

"I have heard you have an item that enables conversations over long distances."

"Yes, I do indeed deal in such tools."

"And you have much more—devices to see long distances without using magic and items that do calculations quickly using digits from another country. I *also* hear they must consume a strange metal to work."

"All these are goods I have previously sold to the Hermann Trading Company in bulk."

"I'll be straight with you. From now on, sell them all to me."

"My lord?"

"Do so, and I will ensure that merchant lives."

"…I see, my lord."

That was the response I'd predicted. If it was enough to save Mr. Marc's life, I was more than willing to comply. I could simply break the promise the moment the vice manager's safety was guaranteed. He could criticize me all I wanted, but with Peeps's help, I could spurn him as necessary.

But I couldn't do that just yet.

I'd already made an exclusive deal with the Kepler Trading Company, so I couldn't afford to break it and make a deal with someone else. If Mr. Joseph happened to catch wind of it, it would shatter our relationship of trust. Everything we'd talked about might end up falling through.

"I apologize, my lord, but I would need a short amount of time to consider this."

"Is there anyone else in a higher position? I hear you are under Count Müller as part of the second prince's faction. If you wish to discuss matters, I wouldn't mind at all if you did so right now."

"Actually, my lord, there is someone other than Count Müller…"

"By the way, I hear you come from another continent. Is that true?"

Count Dietrich was posing rapid-fire questions at me, wasting no time in between. It must have been a ploy to prevent me from having time to think, though I also felt a more genuine, personal interest from him.

"It is as you say, Count Dietrich; I have come here from another continent."

"Is this person also from your continent, perhaps staying nearby?"

"No, my lord, they are from this continent as well. They have treated me kindly, so…"

"Hmm. I see…"

"I've heard, my lord, that you are quite a busy man. But we will require a bit of time to consider things, and while I know it is very rude of me to suggest this, I still ask you for just a little extra time."

"Fine, then. In that case, I will prolong my stay here by another month."

"Thank you, my lord. I very much appreciate that."

"I hope you will choose wisely."

"Thank you for your consideration, my lord."

I'd been able to get his approval more easily than I'd thought. It definitely seemed that Count Dietrich was essentially in control of the

Hermann Trading Company. Otherwise, it would have been difficult for him to make such a quick decision.

Thanks to that, we'd won a month's delay.

I could even go back to Japan, if only for a day.

The negotiations hadn't exactly succeeded, but we'd at least avoided Mr. Marc's scheduled execution at the end of the month. The Hermann Trading Company's manager would have to defer to Count Dietrich as well, so Mr. Marc should be safe.

*

I had managed to buy some additional time, but with that, my discussion with Count Dietrich came to an end. As for Count Müller's negotiations—those had been all but over by the time we arrived.

"It appears I was not up to the task, Sir Sasaki," said Count Müller, "Forgive me for having burdened you like this."

"No, my lord. I'm the one who should apologize—for sticking my nose into your negotiations."

We were currently in a carriage headed away from the inn and toward Count Müller's estate. With its clattering wheels as background noise, we discussed our strategy regarding Count Dietrich.

"But are you truly all right with this? If you go forward with this deal, he's only going to take advantage of you. You've brought all these wonderful items, but at this rate, you'll end up without any chance to show your talents."

"That's no reason to give up on Mr. Marc's life, my lord."

"I am truly sorry. If only I was more reliable..."

"Nothing is decided yet, my lord. I have some ideas in mind, and I intend to try everything I can to save Mr. Marc, right up to the last moment. All hope is not lost."

"Then you may use me however you see fit, if I can be of help. I'd very much like to join your efforts."

"Thank you for understanding, my lord."

"Would it not simply be best for me to deal with this?"

"That's our last resort, Peeps."

What a scary sparrow—when the time came, he wouldn't hesitate. And the Herzian court had even managed to assassinate *him*—terrifying. I hoped the second prince was doing all right.

"I've always felt that you are surprisingly unwilling to give up."

"Yeah, that's just how I am."

The Kingdom of Herz was already mired in underhanded political conflicts over the question of succession. Considering our position and that of Count Müller, I wanted to avoid starting something with a noble in the opposing faction as much as possible. Doing so would likely create even worse problems.

And well. You know. This was exactly the kind of time the boss was supposed to strut his stuff, right?

"Count Müller, I do actually have a proposal."

"Yes, please share it with me."

"What do you think of asking for Prince Adonis's help, my lord?"

"...What might that entail, exactly?"

Having someone you could go crying to was truly wonderful. This was the perfect chance to have him repay his debt to us. He was the leader of one of the conflicting factions, but he was still royalty, and he had a right to the succession. If he was to call upon Count Dietrich for a face-to-face discussion, that would shake even him up a little.

"I've been entrusted with Prince Adonis's personal finances. Let's say we were investing them in the goods we deal in—and that Mr. Marc was the one doing the practical work. By interfering with that, Count Dietrich would surely warrant a stern talking-to from the prince."

"Yes, that does make sense. Even the count wouldn't be able to ignore him."

"The question is whether Prince Adonis will agree to it..."

"You can leave that part to me. I'll head straight there to discuss it with him."

"Are you sure, my lord?"

"Yes. I'd like to leave for the capital right away. It looks like we'll be able to put that extra time you pried out of the count to good use immediately. With an extra month to spare, I can have the prince write a letter and then make the return trip."

"In that case, I will handle your outward journey."

"Are you sure?"

"You've done a lot for me, after all."

"I know it's presumptuous, but yes, I would appreciate it."

"Then you may leave it to me."

With that settled, it was time to head for Allestos, the capital of the Kingdom of Herz. We'd been given a month's delay, but that didn't mean Count Dietrich wouldn't change his mind. I couldn't help but envision the Hermann Trading Company manager going to him and filling his head with nonsense until he retracted his promise.

*

After arriving at Count Müller's estate, we moved straight to the capital. With Peeps's teleportation magic, it took but a moment. A handy spell, as always. I still had my sights set on learning it someday. I'd been so busy lately that I hadn't had much time to practice magic. I resolved to make some time for it once this whole kerfuffle died down.

After depositing the count at the palace and promising to see him again in a month, we headed off on our own.

We headed back to Baytrium, where we decided to spend the night before returning to Japan. As if the otherworld's problems weren't enough, now things were getting troublesome back home, too. I always left the phone the chief had provided behind in my world, so I figured I'd have to pop back home in order to check in on the situation.

From our transit base in Count Müller's town, we moved back to the apartment in Japan. We had only been gone about a day, and nothing in particular had changed. I looked out the window to see the dark of night.

I checked the clock; a few hours had passed. Again, the progression of time between worlds had changed. Previously, an entire day in the otherworld would have only been about one hour in this one.

"*What shall we do now?*"

"I'm going to get in touch with Ms. Futarishizuka and talk about how we want to proceed."

"*Hmm. I see.*"

"I also want to discreetly check on the Lady Elsa situation at the bureau—"

As I was speaking to Peeps, I heard a buzzing noise. It was coming from the bureau-supplied phone I'd left on my desk. Apparently, I was getting a call.

Who could it be, this late at night? If it was from the bureau, maybe I'd pretend to be asleep and ignore it.

As I was thinking about it, Peeps took off from my shoulder and drifted down onto the desk, peering at the vibrating phone's screen. The way he was so casually birdlike sent a pang to this pet owner's heart.

"*...It appears to be from that woman.*"

"Thanks, Peeps."

He was probably referring to Futarishizuka. Which meant I couldn't ignore it. It could have been a call for help, depending on the situation. Come to think of it, since she was contacting me so late, it seemed safe to assume something unanticipated had occurred.

I quickly picked up the phone and answered. "Hello, this is Sasaki."

"*Apologies. I would like some help.*"

"Are you at the hotel from before?"

"*Yes. And please bring the bird...*"

The call ended abruptly after only a few moments, with barely any words exchanged. I tried calling her a few more times, but she seemed to have disconnected her phone. I got the whole "the number you are trying to reach is unavailable" spiel.

"Peeps, can you bring us to the hotel from yesterday?"

"*A pressing matter?*"

"Looks like it."

"*Then let us hurry.*"

It was a good thing we had gotten some sleep in the otherworld before returning. Otherwise, I would have been hard at work for over twenty-four hours. Nevertheless, I couldn't deny that my lifestyle was growing irregular. After moving between worlds repeatedly in a short period of time, I'd completely lost my sense of day and night.

If I kept up at this rate, I was scared my body wouldn't hold out.

*

(The Neighbor's POV)

That night, I wake up to what sounds like a person's voice.

I live in a cramped studio apartment. My bed is in the corner, against the wall that separates this apartment from the one belonging to the man next door. I'm lying down on the bed, wrapped in a blanket. It used to keep me warm when I was smaller, but now that I've been growing, my hands and feet stick out, and I'm pretty cold.

My mother is tucked into a futon on the other side of the room, on the other side of the low, round dining table. I can tell she's fast asleep from how measured her breathing is.

"......"

If she's asleep, then the voice must be coming from outside the room. At the sudden realization, I press my ear to the wall in front of me.

When I do, I can hear someone's voice, just as I had thought. It's very quiet tonight, and the thin walls allow me to listen in on the conversation.

"*What shall we do now?*"

"I'm going to get in touch with Ms. Futarishizuka and talk about how we want to proceed."

"*Hmm. I see.*"

Two people are speaking in serious voices. One of them is the man—the room's tenant.

Who is the other one? I'm sure I've never heard this voice before.

A coworker? I suppose someone could have missed the last train and is staying over. As far back as I can remember, though, the man next door has *never* brought any friends home.

The person with him sounds very young. And androgynous, in fact—I can't tell if they're a man or a woman. But the man next door bringing a woman into his apartment is just unthinkable.

"Peeps, can you bring us to the hotel from yesterday?"

"*A pressing matter?*"

"Looks like it."

"*Then let us hurry.*"

He just called them Peeps. *They must be very close.*

I couldn't just let that slide. Careful not to wake up my mother, I tiptoe to the front door. I crack it open a little, then peek outside and steal a view of the next apartment over.

Who on earth is the man speaking to in such a friendly manner? I try sneaking a peek in the hopes of finding out.

But no matter how long I wait, I never see anyone leave the apartment.

Why? They were just talking as though they were leaving right this second.

"......"

I wait a few minutes before deciding to try to listen in again. I go back into the apartment and over to my bed and press my ear against the wall again.

Somehow, the voices I had heard just minutes ago have vanished. I hold my breath, pushing my head against the wall so hard it makes my ears hurt. But I don't hear a single word. In fact, I can't even hear anyone moving around.

Suspicious, I make the bold decision to check outside the apartment. I sneak out the front door and creep to the opposite side of the building. I want to try getting a look through the outward facing window.

"Huh...?"

I only manage a glance before I gasp in surprise.

The lights in the man's apartment are off.

It'd been hours since sunset. If any lights were on, I would have been able to tell, even if the curtains were drawn. But it's pitch-black. No matter how much I strain my eyes, I can't see even the faintest glow from within.

"......"

I push my ear up against the glass.

Like before, I can't hear anything. The outdoor unit of the air conditioner is off, too.

"But how...?"

How indeed? He'd left at some point. But I didn't even notice him opening and closing his front door.

I wouldn't need to have my ear against the wall to hear someone next door entering or leaving their apartment. And just now, I'd been looking right at his door. Yet before I knew it, the man had disappeared from his apartment.

Had he left through the very window I was currently touching?

"......"

I check the lock on the other side of the window; it's shut tight.

If he had left from here, the fasteners would have been open. Maybe it was possible to relock it from outside using thin strings or something. But that would probably make some noise, wouldn't it?

And why would he need to do something like that in the first place? He couldn't have noticed me spying on him.

I don't know. Ah, I just don't know!

Mister, all I want to do is talk to you.

Why won't you let me into your room? You let that Peeps person in, so why not me?

You can take me in whenever you want, however many times you want.

Mister... Mister... Why can't you just be honest with yourself?

\<Psychic Powers and Magical Girls\>

With the help of Peeps's teleportation magic, we left my apartment behind and appeared in the high-class hotel room where Futarishizuka was staying.

The sight that met our eyes upon arrival was completely different from before—it was a total disaster area. The sofas had been overturned, and the low table now hung halfway out the window, which was broken. Here and there, patches of wallpaper were torn or burnt.

Blood spatter was all over the room. It was alarming.

Frantic, I tried to cast my barrier spell, but Peeps, wasting no time, had already taken care of it. Instantly, I felt a thin film wrapping around us. I was deeply impressed by his speedy technique. I understood why Count Müller had been so charmed by him.

A moment later, we heard an awful sound. *Shh-tat-tat-tat.*

Checking my surroundings, I spied a machine gun barrel peeking out from around a corner in the hallway.

How terrifying. Was this really Japan? Maybe I should double-check.

The bullets all fell to the ground, blocked by Peeps's barrier.

"Thanks, Peeps. One wrong step, and I'd have been dead."

"I must apologize. I should have prepared in advance."

"Don't worry about it—nobody could have predicted we would immediately be shot at."

At this point, what worried me most was Futarishizuka's safety. I knew she wouldn't die from just a pistol shot, but if that machine gun had made her into Swiss cheese, even she might be done for. Quickly,

I surveyed the room. I spotted her outside the dining room, hiding in the back of the kitchen.

She was sitting on the floor, propped up against the wall. Turning our backs on the ceaseless machine gun fire, we hurried over.

"Ms. Futarishizuka, are you all right?"

"Ah. You really came."

"I promised I would."

She was looking at us with surprise.

She was in terrible shape. Her favorite kimono was red with blood. A closer look revealed several holes in the fabric, and the blood flowing out from them had formed small pools on the floor. It seemed like they'd really shot her up.

The very fact that she was still alive probably said a lot about how much power she had.

"Hold still a moment. I'll heal you right away."

"...Heal me?"

She already knew our secrets, including the existence of the other-world. And since we'd restricted her words and actions with a curse, there was no need to pretend. I'd just use the healing spell Peeps had taught me.

I chanted the spell, and with a single grunt, I blasted it at her. A magic circle emerged from the floor. Illuminated by its light, her skin began to regain its color.

"This... Now *this* is a power the bureau is likely to desire."

"If you tell anyone, I'll be very angry."

"Ooh, how scary. I wouldn't have done so, in any case."

"Well, you *do* have a record."

Even in a situation like this, she was able to joke around with me. It was kind of impressive, actually.

She must be used to this kind of thing, I thought. Both the one perched on my shoulder and she hadn't shown even a hint of agitation—one day, I wanted to be able to face down problems with their level of calm.

"You managed to stop me, so no hard feelings, right?"

"If I hadn't, you would definitely have told."

"That sounds like speculation..."

As she stood on her own, she rolled up one of her kimono sleeves to show the back of her hand. The curse mark was inscribed there, courtesy of Peeps, just the same as before. It hadn't changed since its last growth spurt immediately after we'd given it to her.

She truly didn't seem to be plotting anything untoward.

"Look. It hasn't changed since then—proof of my sincere, unwavering faithfulness."

"Well, that's good to know."

"I *am* sorry for calling you this late at night."

"I happened to be up, so it wasn't especially inconvenient. Thankfully, that meant we were able to come right here. Still, I would rather this didn't become an everyday occurrence."

"Mm, yes. I, too, wish to avoid that."

As we spoke, the machine gun continued firing without pause. A bunch of other stuff was flying by, too, like balls of fire—probably all the products of psychic powers. Even with barrier magic, I felt a chill run down my spine. I couldn't help wondering, *What if the barrier just smashes to pieces?*

"Silencing their own first, huh?"

"Something like that, yes."

It seemed that even her ability, which was incredibly powerful in one-on-one fights, couldn't be put to good use when outnumbered and in a floor layout this complex. To my annoyance, her troubled face as she spoke, combined with her youthful appearance, provoked my protective instincts.

Remember, she's an old lady inside.

Still, this served as confirmation of her defection.

That meant we'd come out of this situation with one piece of good news, at least.

"Is this enough to overwhelm even a rank-A psychic?"

"They brought several rank Bs along who hold a natural advantage over me."

"I see."

They seemed to be attacking in earnest. I had learned during bureau training that a handful of rank-B psychics made for a very powerful fighting force. The current situation only reaffirmed to me how much the little girl—a rank-A psychic, despite her appearance—was feared.

"*What will you do now, then?*"

"As it happens, our target is among them."

"The one with telekinesis from the bowling alley?"

"Indeed, that one."

"Wait, you want to go after him right now?"

"Desperate times call for desperate measures."

I could sort of understand why she'd make such a decision.

As old as she was, her abilities were nonetheless more than enough to designate her as a rank-A psychic. She had probably considered the possibility she'd scare off her target, causing him to flee. It was very difficult to find someone who wanted to stay hidden in this wide world of ours.

"It will probably be harder to chase him down if we miss this chance, huh?"

"Psychics with his rank are in great demand all over the world."

"In that case, we can't simply escape."

Promising words from my distinguished Java sparrow. He had been surprisingly belligerent lately.

My personal opinion was that we should finish up this business with Futarishizuka as quickly as possible, given how chaotic things were in the otherworld. If we took too long here, the days would fly by on the other side. We couldn't afford to be taken in by the bureau under any circumstances.

As we discussed the situation, furniture suddenly came flying into the room along with the bullets. A big-screen TV and a sofa shot from beyond the kitchen counter, making a quick midair turn and heading directly for where we hid behind an island-like counter. There was no doubt about it—this was the hurricane user's power.

We covered our heads on reflex, but the objects slammed into the barrier and fell to pieces in front of us. Futarishizuka was right—our target was here. The continued barrage of furniture and appliances made me certain he was among the enemy forces. Someone—a psychic, I assumed—jumped in alongside some of the home goods, but a light touch from Futarishizuka sent them collapsing to the ground. Somehow, I doubted the bureau had given a kill order for that one.

"Let's wrap this up, shall we?"

"Will you fare well against so many?"

"This world's magicians—nay, psychics, you called them? I have an interest in them. Depending on what happens, we may need to rethink our approach in the future."

"You know, I never did hear what your goals were."

"*We cannot say.*"

"Playing it close to the chest, eh...?"

This was the sparrow that wanted to eat high-quality beef chateaubriand for all three meals while surfing the internet from morning to night, acting all pompous and smug to Futarishizuka. He talked a big game, but without his "goals," he was just a deadbeat.

"Peeps, what are you going to do?"

"*Just leave everything to me.*"

"Wait, are you sure?"

He seemed even more confident than usual.

Maybe he was excited about his first away game—combat here in modern Japan. Normally, his attitude was more philosophical, but knowing he had this other side to him filled me with love and affection.

I found myself wishing I could take a picture of him in action. Thinking back, I couldn't remember ever taking a photograph of him. I felt a little sad, from a pet-owner standpoint.

"It's highly likely he's teamed up with a psychic who can block perception. We probably won't be able to spot him just by looking around. And if we allow ourselves to become preoccupied with the items whizzing around our heads, they may attack us from an unexpected position."

"*So there are psychics with that sort of power as well, are there?*"

"As an ally, they are quite dependable—but as an enemy, they are a force to be reckoned with."

"*Then I shall endeavor to disable that one first.*"

The perception-blocking psychic must have been that girl we'd encountered last time at the abandoned bowling alley. She'd appeared to be about middle school age and had been sticking right beside the hurricane user. Her elaborate Gothic Lolita clothing had stuck in my memory. From Futarishizuka's tone, it seemed they frequently worked as a pair. Like Miss Hoshizaki and me, perhaps.

"What will you do, then?" asked Futarishizuka.

"If possible," I cut in, "I don't want to let them see anything magical."

"*That does make things a bit more difficult.*"

There was no telling where the section chief had eyes. I'd expect him to have planted an informant somewhere among them, at least. We couldn't afford to let him find out just how incredibly cool Peeps was.

Just then, we heard a voice.

"Wait, you're still at it? Isn't this taking a little too long?"

It was an awfully tranquil voice, incongruous with the brutal scene in the hotel room, bullets and psychic powers flying. It sounded like someone chiding a friend for not being able to beat a video game with the difficulty set to "very easy."

At the same time, the enemy attacks abruptly ceased.

"Over here? Are you there, Shizu?"

A figure appeared in the living room, staring past the dining room and into the kitchen. A glance revealed a man of about twenty. He was probably Japanese. His long hair reached to about his shoulders, and he wore black-rimmed glasses. He was spindly and about as tall as I was. He wore old, faded jeans with an oversize checkered shirt, under which you could spot an anime T-shirt.

One of those *Akiba* types, in other words. He certainly fit the stereotype of an anime- and manga-obsessed nerd.

"Wha—?"

Futarishizuka's expression tensed as soon as she saw him. Following the path of her gaze made it obvious what had surprised her. She was staring at the nerd, eyes as wide as saucers. She always acted so nonchalant and detached—this was certainly a novel reaction.

"You know him?"

"He's the leader of our group."

"I see."

So he was a pretty big fish—rank A, from what I'd heard. And unlike Futarishizuka, he didn't require a lot of qualifiers and outside considerations—his rank was purely a product of the fear he inspired.

"This changes things. We need to withdraw."

"Is that man truly so troublesome?"

"We would never win in a fair fight."

"What sort of power does he use?"

"According to him, his power makes fantasies manifest. His abilities are so varied that even I, who was part of his team, don't know much about the limits of his powers."

I remembered getting a similar rundown at bureau training. Despite psychics above rank B being infamous, many of their abilities were unknown. They'd told me that if I ever met one, I should take the utmost caution. Now that the time had come, I wondered how, exactly, I was meant to do that.

"*Hmm...*"

Peeps seemed to be thinking about something.

In the meantime, our opponent started speaking.

"Rad! You're actually here. But wait, who's the old guy next to you?"

He placed his hand casually on the kitchen counter and peered down at us like he was gazing at some rare zoo animals through the bars of a cage. He was so close that it seemed like he could see us even as we huddled on the floor behind the center island.

"Wait, Shizu, don't tell me you let Daddy *live*."

"Regrettably, you all were rather rough with me. So yes, I let Daddy live."

"No way..."

The comedy routine continued. It appeared what she had said about this man being from her group was true. Still, regarding their dialogue, this "daddy," who was in no way, shape, or form an actual dad, had a few objections.

"That seriously makes me sad, y'know. I relied on you for so much, Shizu."

"That may be true of you, but not so for the others, eh?"

"I'm sure they were just jealous. You're stronger than all of them."

"Is that so?"

"Well, of course it is!"

This guy was really going hard. He was acting like a hawker in a red-light district. Maybe it was rude of me to think this way, but the gap between his behavior and his appearance was *really* throwing me off. *Preconceived biases can really do a number on you.*

"That makes this discussion more troubling, indeed," she mused.

"Let's talk about the future. I'll be straight—do you have any intention of returning?"

"Not if I was allowed to choose, no."

"Huh."

Futarishizuka's expression faltered as she answered. It was pretty clear she had trouble with this guy.

That made me curious about a few things, but it wasn't our place to butt into another organization's issues. Instead, Peeps and I just watched over the exchange in silence. If something happened, she'd probably ask for our help.

As I was lost in thought, something happened.

"Well, you'd be a formidable enemy, so I suppose it'd be easier to bid you farewell right here and now."

"Ack..."

With that, he moved.

There had been no hint of motion beforehand.

One moment, the man was speaking in that lighthearted tone of voice—and the next, Futarishizuka appeared in front of us.

It was like I was watching a scene from a video game or something. With a low *vrrrr*, a figure suddenly came into focus, out of nowhere, looking exactly like the girl crouched next to us. Even the clothes she wore had the same design.

"Good to see your power is as distasteful as ever," said the original Futarishizuka.

"Oh, but I need to fill the hole you'll leave, don't I?"

Apparently, this was the anime nerd's power as well. She'd said he could give form to fantasies, but there appeared to be surprisingly few restrictions. The copy of Futarishizuka, identical inside and out, couldn't possibly have all the same abilities, right?

One wrong move, and even Peeps might have trouble with this one.

"Ms. Futarishizuka," I said, "does she have—?"

"I hear he cannot give form to things he cannot fantasize—but as long as he can dream it up, he can give it form. Considering my ability is well-known among my former colleagues, there's a good chance she can use it."

As she spoke, she looked at her double with disgust.

Even the bird on my shoulder stared, on his guard. At this point, maybe we didn't have the luxury of worrying about keeping our secrets.

"Could I trouble you to help me?" she asked. "Opposing both my copy and that man would strain me beyond my limit. But with your help, we should be able to escape, at least."

"If we're fleeing," I replied, "that shouldn't take too long."

"Right?"

"*Are you sure?*"

"I'm sorry to impose, but yes, could you?"

"All right, then."

I wasn't sure why, exactly, but I got the feeling there would be another copy to replace every one we took down. In that case, the difficulty level of this particular stage would skyrocket, all thanks to Futarishizuka's brutal power. She could kill with a single touch—if we had to face several of her at once, we'd be helpless. If we didn't take the chance to run when we could, we'd regret it for sure. I'd had the same experience countless times when playing roguelikes.

"I've been curious for a while now," said the man, "but that bird on your shoulder sure talks a lot, doesn't it? Do you have a power that gives you a familiar—some kind of little friend you bonded with? Seems more like a power for a cute girl, though."

Yeah, I get what you're implying, here. In a magical girl sorta sense.

"Let's go."

Peeps ignored him. With a single shout from the bird, a magic circle emerged at our feet.

It was the Lord Starsage's teleportation magic. I didn't know where he intended to bring us, but it didn't matter, so long as it was away from these people. He could unleash all the fantasies he wanted, but he couldn't bring us back from parts unknown.

Otherwise, rather than attacking Futarishizuka at home like this, he would've just used his power to bring her to his location. This was just speculation, but maybe he was limited to materializing objects with a clear and concrete form.

"Farewell, then."

The very moment Futarishizuka bid her good-bye, our visions blacked out.

The surrounding scenery had changed in an instant.

We'd come to the storehouse on the wharf where I'd brought our shipment the other day. There were only so many locations the three of us all shared, so Peeps had naturally settled on this place. The lack of people around made it extremely convenient for us, too.

"Was this acceptable?"

"Y-yes. You saved me. This time, I truly feared for my life."

"I want to know what conditions that man must meet before he can materialize something."

"I'm hazy on the details myself. However, I have never heard of him manifesting a natural phenomenon."

"Hmm. I see."

Futarishizuka and Peeps must have been thinking the same thing as I was. I didn't really feel like checking my answers at this point, but I figured I wasn't too far off the mark. For now, we'd just have to stay vigilant as we continued about our daily lives.

"Well," Futarishizuka said, breathing out, "this *does* make the bureau's request exceptionally difficult."

"You still plan on trying?"

"Oh, well, naturally," said Futarishizuka like nothing had happened.

Fearless, as always. From her point of view, it must have been a narrow escape from the jaws of death, but she wasn't acting like it. Perhaps her senses had dulled with age. That was the only explanation I could come up with.

"As long as you stay cautious, I guess," I said.

"How cold of you. Is this not the scene where you extend your hand in aid?"

"Oh, I could never."

Futarishizuka's tone grew sly and a little playful, though I could sense an indescribable pressure behind her nonchalant behavior.

"Actually, I have a proposal for you two," she said.

"What is it?"

"Do you remember our previous conversation here?"

"I suppose I do. Why?"

"Were you to assist me in entering the bureau, I could work with you on future exchanges. I would stick my neck out for you, as well, to an extent. If needed, I could set up a base of operations for you outside the country, where I have many acquaintances. I wouldn't mind helping you with all that."

"Have you forgotten the curse engraved on the back of your hand?"

"Peeps, could you let me handle this one?"

She wasn't speaking arrogantly, but despite her appearances, I got the sense that she was a very proud woman. I could tell by the edge that had come into her voice under our current circumstances. She was panicked.

And that's what would give any promise we made here particular importance.

"You're so particular about such strange things."

"That's just how I am."

Maybe it would have been possible to make her obey us, using Peeps's curse as a shield. But the person in front of us would never forget it. She had been at fault on that occasion, but when it came to our future deals, we were on equal footing.

When I thought about it like that, it seemed crucial that we keep negotiations fair in order to maintain a smooth relationship with her.

Based on our time together, I could tell Peeps and I had totally different ways of doing things. And I suspected it was his rather aggressive personality that had earned the resentment of those around him and led to his assassination.

I felt bad for making him go along with my wishes like this, but I hoped he would leave things to me this time.

"What is it?" prodded Futarishizuka. "Interested in my proposal?"

"I think it's worth exploring. However, our lives are just as important to us as yours is to you."

"Of course."

"If you have some sort of plan, we might be willing to help. Though, that will depend on what it entails."

"...Hmm."

If her tactic put us in danger, I might feel bad, but I'd simply flee. Doing business with her was an attractive prospect, but we could always look for a replacement. And—in the absolute worst-case scenario—I could go crying to the bureau.

After a pause, Futarishizuka began to speak, her expression serious. "All right. In that case—"

But she never gave voice to the next words.

That very moment, in the corner of our vision, there was a change at one end of the warehouse.

Someone had broken through one of the high windows and come inside. At the loud crash of breaking glass, everyone's attention shifted to its source. Right before our eyes, the figure effortlessly dropped several meters to the ground to land softly on the floor of the warehouse.

"How...how did you...?!" shouted Futarishizuka in shock.

It was her boss.

The anime fan—the one we'd been talking to just a few minutes ago.

Right next to him stood the hurricane user. They must have chased us here using his telekinetic power. He'd been tossing around heavy building materials like they were nothing, so a human body was no challenge to him.

Location-wise, we were a dozen or so kilometers from the hotel when measured in a straight line. Soaring through the air would get you here in a few minutes.

If they had come straight here, I supposed I could understand the entrance. But how did they know about this place?

The distress was plain on our faces at the anime fan's sudden appearance.

Futarishizuka owned this warehouse, and she'd told me herself that the others from her organization didn't know about it. She was just as surprised as we were, so it certainly didn't seem like she'd been lying. Naturally, the rest of us were also struggling to decide our next move, clueless as to what was happening.

Then, as if in answer to that very question, the anime fan spoke. "A good friend tipped me off."

"This is the first I've heard of such a handy acquaintance."

"Well, of course it is. I never told you," he said, glancing over at us.

Why had he looked this way? Was this acquaintance someone we both knew?

No, there was nobody like that.

"……"

Wait a minute. There was *one* person who fit the bill.

Process of elimination left me with only one possibility. And it was someone fairly close to me, too. One I'd only recently become acquainted with—and someone whose private life was veiled in mystery.

But if that was true... Well, I couldn't think of anything more troublesome.

"Oh! Did you figure it out?" asked the man, taking notice of my change in expression. His words and actions held such a relaxed confidence.

"I would have never dreamed you were secretly communicating with the bureau."

I said that mostly to make sure I had the correct read of things.

But when I did, a little smile crossed the man's lips.

He didn't give me any concrete name in particular, but I had no doubt. That meant Futarishizuka wasn't the only one in trouble—I was, too. I felt a squeezing pain in my stomach, empty except for the acid welling up inside.

"You're…you're in league with the bureau?!" exclaimed Futarishizuka.

"Looks like you picked the wrong place to go job hunting, Shizu."

"Mgh…"

The anime fan continued to talk, smirking at Futarishizuka. She'd been completely and totally played. "And that's why I was aware of everything you two got up to."

"That still doesn't explain why you knew of *this* place," she replied.

"Thanks to all that state authority, I guess? I don't know the details myself, but they scraped the surveillance cameras and uncovered all your comings and goings. They're really nosing about in their subordinates' business, huh?"

"……"

I could definitely see Chief Akutsu doing that. And it was well within his means. These days, cameras were set up even in private homes and restaurants. He'd probably grabbed all the footage from the day we showed Lady Elsa around the city, working backward until he got to Shiodome Station.

But the fact that it was possible didn't mean it was *easy*. How many people had he mobilized for this purpose? The speed with which he'd uncovered this warehouse was terrifying.

When I'd first introduced Futarishizuka to the chief, he'd seemed honestly surprised about it. Had that been an act? Or had this anime fan only made contact with him afterward? I could imagine several possibilities.

But given the man's considerable self-respect, I felt the latter was more likely. That flabbergasted reaction of his had been my greatest achievement during the past few days.

At the same time, I wondered how closely involved these two parties were. Did their interests just happen to overlap this time, or was this a long-term arrangement? If they'd been like peas in a pod since before I joined the bureau, as his subordinate, I'd probably start to cry.

"*I apologize. I should have been paying more attention.*"

"No, no. There was nothing you could have done about this one."

Peeps was so cute, getting all apologetic on my shoulder like that.

No, this time, it had been my responsibility. As someone unfamiliar with the modern world, he couldn't have seen this coming.

"Peeps, let's go somewhere else qui—"

"Whoa, there. Come on, stick around a while."

I decided to request a second helping of teleportation magic from my pet bird. A magic circle appeared underfoot.

But the anime fan was already in motion, not waiting for the spell to go off. Quicker than we could disappear, he materialized something directly underneath us.

It was a pile of hand grenades. And the pins were all out. Several of them now lay at our feet.

"*Hrm? These are...*"

Even Peeps seemed to recognize their shape. A moment later, they exploded.

A series of *booms* rang in my ears. I hadn't even had enough time to kick *one* of them away from us.

I thought I was dead for sure.

But the shocks never hit me. Nor did my vision fill with smoke and fire. Almost as if the bursts had occurred in a very limited space—like toy firecrackers. Something invisible had closed them up, preventing the blasts from reaching us.

It seemed the grenades had been covered with barrier magic. That had to be Peeps's doing—such blinding speed.

"Thanks, Peeps. Once again, I thought I was dead."

"*Mm. It made me sweat a bit as well.*"

I could never have pulled off a stunt like that.

It was like he was teaching me that simply being able to use high-ranking magic didn't make you a great magician. It made me want to work hard and study everything he knew, regardless of whether I liked a spell or not. Incredible masters brought out their students' desire to learn.

"Hmm! You're not bad."

The man's voice came to us this time from atop some cargo stacked in the warehouse—I didn't catch him moving up there. He'd probably done so to escape the grenade blasts. The hurricane user must've moved him away from us with his powers.

"Peeps, you knew those rolling things were explosives?"

"The internet is wonderful, indeed. They are illegal in this country, yes?"

The way this sparrow spoke so indifferently about such things gave him an air of dependability. Right there, I swore in my heart that I'd protect my pet's exclusive internet connection even if it cost me my life.

"Would you like to go look at smartphones sometime?"

"A new one? Did you not just purchase a laptop a few days ago?"

"No, I meant one for you specifically, Peeps."

"...You would buy one for me?"

"As a present. Would you like one?"

"......" Peeps's tail feathers twitched.

I had *never* seen a reaction like that.

"I won't force it on you or anything, of course..."

"Then I would very much like you to bring me along when you go. Smartphones are those highly portable devices you always use outside, yes? I hear that with one, you can use the internet no matter your location. And there was actually one model in particular I was interested in."

"Sure. We can go to the store together."

Peeps, you're just so excitable. The way his beak was flapping open and shut was just too cute. I bet he'd found a product he was interested in but was stressing over it on his own, unable to tell me he wanted it. Imagining it made my heart flutter. I should have suggested it a long time ago.

I thought back to when I'd gotten my first cell phone. It had been a moving experience.

"But we'll have to do something about this first."

"Right you are."

The lovely sparrow nodded firmly, his gaze fixed on the man standing on the cargo.

At some point or another, the hurricane user had moved to stand beside him.

"Any objections to me dealing with that one?" Peeps asked Futarishizuka. I felt reassured by his tone—I had a feeling this sparrow was about to enter combat mode.

"I... Yes, if you can, but..."

"Why, Shizu, isn't that a little mean?"

"Mean? So says the one who came and attacked me."

"You two, stay here and watch."

The anime fan standing atop the cargo pile had the absolute calmest expression while he spoke. But Peeps was unfazed, instead declaring triumphantly he would handle it alone. It was looking like we wouldn't have much to do.

The lordly sparrow fluttered up and off my shoulder.

According to him, he couldn't use certain advanced magic when he was away from me. If he'd flown away, that meant he had plenty of confidence. The two of us, nothing but baggage at this point, looked on in silence.

"I see. A psychic who can use his familiar for both offense and defense."

"……"

Peeps watched his opponent as he hovered in midair, flapping his wings. He should have been able to fly even without beating them, using magic. I was sincerely grateful for him continuing his sparrow act, even in this mess.

And so in this warehouse procured by Futarishizuka, their battle began.

The anime fan was the first to make a move. He thrust out his palm in front of him and shouted, "Crimson hell flames burning eternal, incinerate all those who defy me!"

"Hmm…?"

What a strikingly fantastic line.

I suddenly had the feeling I'd heard those words somewhere before. Ah yes—the main character of a video game that had recently gotten popular said it when he used a certain spell. He shouted it out every time you chose to use it, so it had left an impression even on me.

The next thing I knew, a magic circle appeared at his feet. From it burst a round cluster of flames.

"Oh!" Futarishizuka breathed out. "What *is* that? It is almost like the magic you and the bird use."

"I thought you said he couldn't cause any natural phenomena."

"I didn't say he couldn't; I just said I'd never seen it. Either way, does that look like a natural phenomenon to you, hmm? Looks a bit more like it came from a fairy tale than something in nature."

"What are you getting at?"

"To be honest, it looks exactly like a spell from a game I played quite a bit of..."

"Oh, so you played that one, too, Ms. Futarishizuka?"

"Oh, you too?"

"I'd assumed he couldn't conjure up anything without a solid form. You were part of the same group as he was, so you wouldn't happen to have any info on that, would you?"

"I had assumed the same."

Perhaps he'd been purposely hiding it, even from his allies. And now that he was up against a powerful enemy like Peeps, he had to undo the seal, as it were. Or maybe he'd leveled up his psychic powers and recently gained the ability to give form to a broader range of things.

No, wait; hold on. If I remembered correctly, you could only use that spell when you had something equipped—more specifically, when you were wearing some kind of ring. If, hypothetically, that was true for him as well, then...

In great haste, I checked the anime fan's hands. And there it was—a ring of a peculiar design on his finger.

"I get it."

He must have given form to the ring he needed to use the magic, not the spell itself. But if he was able to do *that*, it meant he could pull off way more than we thought—he could even conjure items from fictional worlds.

"Ms. Futarishizuka, could it be that your former colleagues didn't trust you very much?"

"I... I'd appreciate it if you didn't put it that way!"

The ball of flames traveled straight for Peeps. Its exaggerated appearance bestowed an even greater sense of power to it.

The bird, however, accustomed to such phenomena, safely swept it aside. I didn't know what spell he'd used, but the flames dissipated with a flap of his wings. The swelling flames scattering in every direction reminded me of fireworks.

Peeps was being especially cool recently.

"Huh. That didn't surprise you?"

"What was there to be surprised about?"

But the anime fan hadn't given up just yet.

Once again, a ball of fire appeared in front of him. And this time, it was far, far larger. His last shot had been the size of a volleyball, but this one rivaled the containers in the warehouse. If that thing exploded, we wouldn't be making it out of here. Wouldn't that endanger the user, too?

"You two are dead…," said Futarishizuka, face visibly tense.

"Don't kill us off just yet, please," I replied.

Peeps was handling this one, so I had faith it would work out fine. But that didn't mean there was no danger. In that case, it was my turn to use the barrier spell—the one that had blocked the direct hit from the crashing airplane. That should help a bit, at least.

In a rush, I chanted the spell, and with a heave, an invisible barrier went up. I included Futarishizuka inside it as well.

"This is over."

At the same time, the anime fan had shot the fireball toward Peeps.

There wasn't much distance between the two of them. It approached in the blink of an eye—and hit Peeps head-on.

However, that fireball, too, vanished into thin air with a single flap of his wings—what had happened? The flames had been so violently ablaze, but it was like someone had sprayed a fire extinguisher over it; all at once, it was just gone. Not even an ember remained.

"Whoa, hold on. What's up with your familiar? This doesn't make sense."

Even the anime fan seemed shocked by this—he looked baffled.

Judging by what he'd been saying, familiars were a known psychic power in the modern world. They probably weren't the same as the ones in the otherworld, but I could probably use this fact to conceal Peeps's true identity. I'd have to investigate it more thoroughly when I had time.

Incidentally, the hurricane user who had been standing next to the anime fan just a moment ago was now totally gone. It seemed he, too, had been created by the anime fan's power—a product of fantasy. He must have used it as a means of movement.

"Creative application of a spatial power? No, wait, that can't be…"

"It's my turn to attack now."

"Ack…"

The little sparrow darted up high into the air.

The anime fan prepared for an attack.

Right then, there was a change at his hands.

Another ring joined the first on his finger.

A moment later, a fireball flew out from below the lovely sparrow. It had the same design as the anime fan's previous attack, but it was about a meter wide. *I'm a little worried about the heat, Peeps—we're inside a warehouse, after all.*

But right before it struck the bird, there was a dry, shrill noise—and it dissipated. It was as though it had bounced off an invisible barrier.

"Oh? It seems you can nullify my magic."

"See? I told you. How was it? Surprising, right?"

The cause was without doubt the additional ring. He'd given form to a fantasy excelling in defense, just like our barrier magic. I wasn't sure about the man's physical abilities, but if he could simply equip these strange items and use them immediately, he was a force to be reckoned with.

"It's that ring, isn't it?" mused Futarishizuka. "Even that is the same as the game."

"You noticed it, too?"

"If you knew, I wish you would have told me."

"Well, I assumed you'd already figured it out."

At this point, the possibilities for what he might use expanded to cover even fictional meta-items like bombs to destroy the world and swords that could cleave dimensions. It was terrifying. My feelings were complicated—on the one hand, I kind of wanted to see something like that; on the other, I most certainly did not.

"But you know," murmured the anime fan, moving again, "this isn't really the time to be watching and waiting."

The next change was more conspicuous.

This time, his hand gripped a bladed weapon. The blade itself was thirty or forty centimeters long, and its design was reminiscent of a large knife.

"Wait! Is that...?"

"Oh, you know it?"

Futarishizuka was the first to react, and she cried out as soon as she saw it. Having lived for so long, she probably had a wealth of knowledge in this field. How reliable. Since I was still hazy on the details of psychic powers, having someone beside me to explain really set my mind at ease.

"It's another item from a game I was obsessed with…"

Cancel that. Just another video game.

"I didn't know you liked playing games so much, Ms. Futarishizuka."

"It's one of my few hobbies."

"What sort of item would that be, then?"

"It erases anyone it cuts from existence."

"What do you mean by erases?"

"It's handy for taking down enemies with more armor. But you don't get experience points for it."

"I didn't mean how it works in the game…"

She did this sometimes—acting like she didn't know what I was talking about. Was she teasing me, or was she just getting on in years? I figured it was fine, but if it was the latter, I'd have to give some thought to the way we did things in the future.

"If you're hit by the blade, you vanish from existence."

"I still don't know what you mean by 'existence.'"

"That's what it said in the game's help window. And when you use it to attack, and it hits, then no matter how little damage it does, it defeats the enemy. It didn't work against boss monsters, though, and you didn't get experience points for it."

"…I see."

That actually put us in a pretty tight spot, though, didn't it? Even her energy drain paled in comparison to this. Seemed like even healing magic wouldn't be able to turn the tables. Great.

"Peeps, don't let that blade hit you!"

"What is it? Do you know something?"

"She says if it hits, you vanish from existence!"

"Vanish from existence? Hmm…"

Naturally, I had turned to my bird and called out to him. If possible, I wanted to flee with him.

But the anime fan was staring him down, ever vigilant; I was sure he'd react immediately no matter what we tried. Considering how varied his methods of attack were, we couldn't make any indiscreet movements. There was always the possibility he'd give form to some other fantasy with an insta-kill mechanic.

Peeps, please, come back to my shoulder.

"You're spoiling it for them, Shizu. Now it's boring."

"The game just came out, and you've already stolen the idea. It's your own fault."

"Guess I can't argue with that. I was never great at retro games anyway."

Now he was complaining to Futarishizuka.

I'd heard that some kids these days had a lot of trouble with pixel-art games. Since lifelike 3D was the norm now, they had grown unused to the rougher pixel designs. Personally, looking at pixel art calmed me down.

"I find myself more and more interested in these so-called psychic powers."

"I kinda hate that condescending attitude," responded the anime fan.

The hurricane user rematerialized to his side.

The next thing I knew, the blade had left his hand and was flying through the air. His goal was probably to use telekinetic power at the same time to drive it straight at Peeps. Each power was strong on its own, and he could combine them? Talk about unfair.

At a blinding speed, the blade's tip shot toward Peeps. But it didn't pierce him. Blocked by a barrier spell that had appeared around the bird, the blade froze in midair.

A moment later, someone appeared behind Peeps.

I recognized the outfit as belonging to the woman who could teleport. I'd met her at the bowling alley along with the hurricane user; about twenty years old and sporting a very sexy look. Considering the timing, she was probably one of the anime fan's fantasies. In her hand, she gripped the same sword that had been stopped by the barrier.

And this one, she drove straight through Peeps's wing.

"Hrgh..."

"There, there. That does it, hmm?" said the anime fan gleefully.

The one he'd hurled at the bird head-on had apparently been a decoy. The man's true aim was to use the teleportation psychic to quickly get into Peeps's blind spot. Considering Peeps didn't know about her to begin with, he was taken completely by surprise.

The scene was so shocking I couldn't help but cry out. "Peeps!"

"No need to panic. Just stay there and don't do anything."

"But…!"

How could he be so calm? *I'm beside myself with worry over here, Peeps. I'll give you all the chateaubriand you want once we get home— I'll get you an unlimited data plan for your smartphone, too—so please, don't vanish on me. I don't think I could go on.*

The cage he lived in, for example, would probably stick around forever, empty. It hadn't even been six months since we'd met.

But that pathetic pang in my chest was only momentary.

"Wait. What the heck?"

The anime fan let out a surprised exclamation.

His eyes were on the woman who had stabbed Peeps. Was it my imagination, or was her body fading as we spoke? I, too, was astonished. It was exactly what I would imagine if I heard the phrase "vanish from existence."

But somehow, it was happening not to my sparrow, but to *her.*

"It seems like my powers are effective even against these psychic abilities of yours."

"Hold on just one second. Why's *my* fantasy vanishing? You must have reflected it just now. How can something that can reflect *also* use teleportation? That doesn't have anything to do with manipulating space! That's against the rules!"

"Why indeed? That is for you to think about."

"Ugh…"

Come to think of it, I remembered Peeps telling me once that he had a defensive spell that could block every supernatural phenomenon under the sun, like magic or curses. That matched exactly with what I had just seen.

And now, the anime fan was the one on the defense. If he attacked thoughtlessly, he could easily be the next one to vanish. He didn't know that the cute little sparrow he'd just picked a fight with was a grand magician who could use as many spells as there were stars in the sky. His confidence quickly turned to anxiety.

"Several other options were available to me, but if that worked, then this will be simple."

Peeps, hovering in the air, moved forward a bit as he spoke.

The anime fan rushed backward atop the container.

"What the hell are you? This isn't right. I don't get it."

"*Neither do I. This world is filled with all manner of things I do not understand. Learning about each and every one of them is a joy unto itself. When man ceases to learn, when man forgets his desire to improve himself, what follows is a death of the mind. Eventually, a dead mind will kill even the body.*"

Peeps was so cool when he went into lecture mode like this.

In the meantime, the blade piercing his small body dissipated like cotton candy melting away in saliva. Blood had overflowed from the wound, but once he activated his healing magic, it was gone in the blink of an eye.

"W-wait, stop! If you want her that much, you can have her!"

"*Have her? Whatever do you mean?*"

"Shizu! Your bureau scouted her, right? Who cares about this crap?!"

The anime fan gave up on fighting—he seemed completely over it. The other blade hovering in front of Peeps dissipated as well. Finally, he turned on his heel to face away from us in a show of frustration.

I couldn't help but think he might still be plotting something. But considering what he stood to lose against his potential gain, the act seemed trustworthy enough.

"*Oh. You're giving up already?*"

"It's *so* not worth it. Risking my life? What do I look like, some kind of idiot?"

"*...I see.*"

Peeps seemed a little disappointed to me. I hoped it was just my imagination. It was great that he had an amazingly inquisitive mind, but as his owner, my pet's safety was my first priority.

I hoped he'd be more careful going forward.

*

The fight between Futarishizuka's boss and Peeps had ended in victory for the latter.

That made it all the more important we not let this chance slip by. We were up against the top of a large group of high-ranking psychics. Plus, if he had connections even to Section Chief Akutsu, I wanted to use this opportunity to get to know him a little better. In fact, if I didn't do so right now, my ties to the bureau would probably turn precarious later.

Peeps had worked hard to overpower the man, and now it was my turn. Thus determined, I addressed the anime fan.

"There is one thing we'd like to talk to you about."

I needed to do my best to protect my future life in society. It was necessary to achieve my ideal, relaxed life with my pet bird.

"...And what would that be? What could you possibly want from me other than Shizu's transfer?"

"It involves our future relationship with her."

The man stood atop the shipping container, looking down at us nervously. Maybe he was having trouble gauging the connection between Peeps and me. The hurricane user had disappeared at some point, so he was all alone now.

"If you're telling me to sell out my group, I can't do that."

"Strictly speaking, we don't want your head or those of your comrades. We need to provide the bureau with proof that she has left your group, and I was wondering if you might be able to help us with that."

"You want me to speak to your boss or something?"

"Essentially, yes."

"Sounds pointless to me."

"The person you spoke of is the very one who ordered us to deal with your group. I can't begin to guess his intentions, but is your relationship with him significant enough to put your group in danger?"

"What? Don't even joke about that. Our interests just happened to align."

Oh, good, I thought. *Looks like they're not on great terms, after all.*

That said, what *was* their relationship? It wasn't all that strange, I supposed, if you considered their similar positions—both of them headed an organization employing a large number of psychics. They'd probably come up against each other time and again. Naturally, exchanging blows wasn't the only way to handle conflict.

"If I may," I said, "have you known the section chief for very long?"

"Do you expect me to be honest about that?"

"Not at all. I just wanted to try asking you directly, since we're all here."

"Well, I did lose the fight… I guess I could give him a call, at least."

Now we just had to wait and see how Futarishizuka's employment exam turned out.

In the meantime, I couldn't forget about approaching the anime nerd.

"By the way, can I ask one more thing?"

"You're still not done?"

"We've been presented with a chance to get acquainted. I'd like to talk for a little while."

"…Are you trying to threaten me?"

"The bureau is home to a great variety of people, as you well know. For my part, given that your group is where Ms. Futarishizuka originally hails from, I'd like to establish a positive relationship. Not to mention I very much doubt the bureau poses a threat to you with its current forces."

"Uh-huh? What about that familiar of yours?"

"Like I said, this is my personal viewpoint."

"……"

The worst possible outcome would be for Section Chief Akutsu to team up with this man and attack us. I wanted to come to an agreement with the anime fan, right here, to prevent that from happening. Peeps had just overpowered him, so now it was my turn to strut my stuff.

The section chief was clearly fine with selling out his employee's movements for his own benefit, after all.

"I don't intend for this to be a one-way deal, of course. Perhaps we can make it a give-and-take situation? Obviously, we have some points on which we cannot yield, and I'm sure you are much the same. However, I think there is still room to compromise."

"And what would I be getting out of all this? I can't say it's particularly obvious."

"Thankfully, the abilities I've just shown you are not known to anyone from the bureau. If you stay silent, we won't have any reason to wield them against you. As a member of the bureau, I have my own hands full simply providing rear support."

"...Uh-huh?"

"How about it?"

I hastily attempted to secure his silence with an offer of friendship.

Any further exchange could be handled through Futarishizuka in the coming days as the situation demanded. If we sought too much from him, the man might try to take advantage of us. Contrary to his appearance, the anime fan had a pretty aggressive personality.

"Are you unhappy with the bureau, too, then?"

"No, nothing of the sort."

"Sure, that's what you *say*."

"Will you not regret losing your relationship with Ms. Futarishizuka? Her abilities as a psychic aside, her assets must be considerable even for your organization. There's no need to split up over this."

"......"

In reality, I didn't know how much she possessed. Still, I thought it would be best to butter her up here. If I got her involved, she could serve as my pipeline to this man in the future. That would bring us huge benefits.

I felt like if Peeps and I were to personally correspond with him, things could get a little dangerous.

At the same time, Futarishizuka, too, would no doubt prefer to maintain a cordial relationship with her old workplace.

"What do you think?"

"...Well, I don't really care, I guess," said the anime fan reluctantly, before nodding.

He didn't seem very pleased, but that was just as well. If we were able to provide him with some lucrative future deals, his attitude toward us would probably change. I hoped he'd consider the long run.

"I very much appreciate your wise decision."

"Yeah, right. Not like I had any choice."

"In the not too distant future, you will have cause to be thankful for all this."

"Really, now?"

We would align our own interests with those of the psychic world—I believed this was crucial, since we had so much to hide. That way, if something was to happen, or the chief was to abandon us, I'd still be able to cling to my position as a member of the bureau.

"Speaking of which, how is the man with telekinesis powers doing?"

"He's still in a wheelchair. What about it?"

"Not to change the subject, but if I used my abilities, I could restore all his limbs. Just the same as how *he* healed the cut from the blade earlier. He won't even need rehabilitation—he would be up and moving again the same day, like before he was injured."

I indicated to Peeps with my gaze as I spoke. There was still blood on him, but the actual wound was nowhere to be found.

"Are you seriously implying you'll just...*heal* him for us?"

"I believe it's necessary to prove my willingness to compromise."

"......"

"What do you think?"

The anime fan fell silent at my proposal. He seemed to be thinking about something—but not for long. "All right," he said, nodding. "I'll contact you through Shizu soon."

"Understood."

With that, it seemed I had received his acquiescence to our little partnership, as well as the group's approval of Futarishizuka's withdrawal. They probably wouldn't be attacking her lodgings and trying to kill her in her sleep anymore.

That only left Section Chief Akutsu, who I got the feeling would be the most annoying part of all.

*

After we exchanged a few words, the anime fan went on his way, leaving Peeps, Futarishizuka, and me. We were in the same place as before: a corner of the cargo warehouse set up on the wharf. We ended up putting our heads together and discussing our new position in light of what had just happened. My distinguished sparrow was in his usual location, too, his little feet perched upon my shoulder.

Before he had moved there, he'd produced hot water using magic and dumped it over his head to clean himself off. *I could not sully your clothing with blood,* he'd said considerately. The sight of him shaking off all the moisture clinging to his feathers was so charming.

"Thank you for everything. Without your help, I would have surely died."

"Peeps here was the star of the show."

"I simply obeyed this man's will. I have no reason to be thanked."

Futarishizuka bowed her head in gratitude. The solemnity of the action, when combined with her graceful kimono, made for quite the picture. Though as the one she was bowing *to*, I couldn't help but feel uncomfortable, since I'd relied on Peeps for pretty much everything.

"Not to mention, this incident has been quite stimulating."

"What do you mean?"

"That man would be considered quite powerful, even in my own world."

"Ah. I thought so, too."

"If I had been mistaken in my responses, I might have gotten in a lot more trouble."

"That's a little scary to think about…"

Hearing that from the Lord Starsage himself made me unconsciously stiffen up. But perhaps it was a good thing to confirm this fact at the earliest possible stage. It meant even psychics in this world, if they were rank A, could match top-class pros from the otherworld.

I wondered how the man compared to the purple-skinned person Peeps had fought in the sky. If worse came to worst, we might have to secure combat forces from the otherworld. For example, if that anime fan was to join up with another rank-A psychic.

"It isn't much by way of thanks," said Futarishizuka, "but I have a proposition."

"What is it?"

Was it time? Time for Futarishizuka to bestow upon us a reward? She was filthy rich, so my hopes were naturally high.

"As I said previously, I will fully assist you both going forward."

We'd made a verbal promise in the high-class hotel kitchen amid the barrage of bullets and psychic powers. She'd mentioned something about setting up a base of operations for us outside the country, too, if I was to help her handle the hurricane user as part of her employment exam.

It seemed her intentions had been pure—though, it couldn't have been a malicious lie anyway, given the curse.

"We should secure a base of operations separate from this warehouse with all haste," she suggested. "If you need anything, say the word, and I will bring it there. I promise to be as accommodating as possible. If you're stocking up on bulky goods like sugar, you'll need somewhere to store it as soon as possible, won't you?"

"That's an extremely welcome proposal."

"And a commendable attitude."

"You did save my life. I do, at least, pay my debts."

"Do you?"

"I can't afford to keep borrowing without paying back," she said with a chuckle. "Being in constant debt to people like you seems a fearsome prospect."

Her proposition seemed incredibly attractive, given how things had been for us lately. After all, if we were going to fill the Kepler Trading Company's requests, we'd need to bring in literally tons of product basically every day. Acquiring the space to do that and finding a stable way to procure the goods had been giving me headaches.

For the time being, we'd be able to rely on Futarishizuka, which had been my intention in the first place. But I'd been worried that if it continued for weeks, and then months, she would start to complain. That problem, however, had just been solved quite nicely.

"In that case, I'd like to procure three hundred tons of superfine sugar."

"My, don't we have a sweet tooth? What will you do with that much sugar?"

"Can you get it for me?"

"I'll have it for you by the end of the week. And you can pay me at a later date."

I'd meant that mostly as a joke, but she'd accepted the task, seeming pretty unfazed. Considering the sheer amount I wanted to stock, I'd really have to work at my business dealings, or I might not be able to pay her later. That said, for this sort of foodstuff—the kind that needed to be mass-produced in factories—you could sell however much you could bring, which put my mind at ease.

I'll be adding another digit to my stock for the Kepler Trading Company next time.

"That really does help, Ms. Futarishizuka."

"I thought you might ask, so I already have about fifty potato sacks' worth of it," she said, looking at the tall stack of pallets in another corner of the warehouse. The stuff may keep for a long time, but what would she have done if I hadn't wanted it? I couldn't imagine any businessperson wanting to buy a stock of sugar from an outlaw like her.

"Now," she continued, "this warehouse is useless to us for several reasons, so I'll want to clear out as early as tomorrow. If you have any requests as to the location or facilities, tell me now. It'll be much harder to work out later."

"You'd do that much for us?"

"Well, certainly! It seems that if I treat you well, I'll probably have plenty of lucrative opportunities of my own."

"I'll do my best to make sure you don't sustain any losses."

"What a vague response. Can't you be a little more enthused about it?"

"I would rather hold off and provide you with tangible results."

"Ah. I see. In that case, I will wait patiently."

At her grin, I felt a jolt to my pride. I recalled my feelings from back when I was a fresh recruit, straight out of college, about a certain superior I had respected. When my training period was over, he disappeared somewhere. Rumor had it he'd been demoted and sent away to an affiliated company.

Looking at the little lady in front of me, I felt the same as I did back then.

In the meantime, Peeps was harboring other emotions—mostly apprehensions.

"If you try to fool this good-natured fellow, the curse will progress."

"How insulting. I have no such ulterior motives."

She took the opportunity to expose the back of her hand. The curse's pattern was there, with no apparent change since the last time we'd seen it. According to Peeps, its surface area would increase if she harbored any hostile intentions toward us.

"Yes, it does appear so."

"Believe me now, do you? Rest assured—I am your loyal slave."

"When you put it like that, it actually worries me more."

"A rephrasing might be in order."

"Um. I would prefer to at least have the freedom to choose my own words…"

And so we continued to discuss our future plans with Futarishizuka.

*

After finishing up our discussions, I suddenly heard my phone begin to vibrate in my breast pocket. The rhythmic buzzing meant someone was trying to call me. This was my personal device, which I'd been carrying since before any of this happened. Whoever it was had probably called this number after not being able to reach me on the one the chief had provided, which I'd left back at the apartment.

"Sorry, could you excuse me for a second?" I said to Futarishizuka, taking out the phone.

The display showed a familiar name—Miss Hoshizaki. I'd add her to my contacts list just in case. And *not* because I wanted to gloat about having a high school girl's number in my address book.

"Hello, this is Sasaki…"

"Sasaki! Sorry for calling you so suddenly, but are you with Futarishizuka right now?!"

The voice on the other end sounded very harsh. That alone told me she must be in a pretty desperate situation.

"I am. What about it?"

"Again, sorry, but please bring her to the bureau right away!"

"Is this urgent?"

"We're under attack by the magical girl!"

One thing after another. According to my bureau training, magical girls were impossible to face unless you mobilized a whole handful of rank-B psychics. The people there currently must have been in the fight of their lives. Personally, though, I had a hard time working up the appropriate amount of fear when the subject had such a sweet-sounding name.

I mean. A *magical girl.*

"I thought the bureau employed a bunch of rank-B psychics."

"There are two magical girls here! One more than last time!"

"Oh wow…"

Apparently, the homeless girl had brought along another magical friend. That put the bureau in grave danger.

"There's a helicopter heading your way! Thanks, and see you soon!"

"Huh?"

This was my personal phone—and yet she'd gotten my location data anyway. I was shocked. She had probably gone through the same system used for reporting emergencies. That thing would pilfer your location data whether you liked it or not as soon as you picked up the call. I'd have to be more careful when responding in the future.

This time, I had an excuse—the matter involving Futarishizuka. But that wouldn't always be the case.

In the meantime, Miss Hoshizaki had ended the call. She was probably in a rush, her hands full with the situation at the bureau.

"What is it?" asked Futarishizuka. "That is quite the odd expression."

"The magical girl is attacking the bureau—with a friend."

"Oh! Looks like our little adventure isn't quite over, hmm?"

"There's a helicopter coming; she wants you to come along."

A taxi was one thing, but a *helicopter*? They sure had a lot of money to throw around. Or maybe that was just how desperate the situation was. I'd never ridden a helicopter in my life, though, so my heart was already pounding.

"Ah, more work, even though the bureau still hasn't approved my employment."

"And what shall I do?"

"I'm sorry, Peeps. Could you go back home ahead of me?"

"Will you manage on your own?"

"My barrier spell works against them, so I should at least be able to flee if needed."

"I see. Then I will await your return at the apartment."

The sparrow rose into the air. A moment later, a magic circle appeared underneath him—the teleportation magic I'd grown so familiar with over the last few days. The next instant, Peeps was gone. I admired the sight of it every time. It was the ultimate commute spell, and I yearned for the day that I, too, would be able to cast it.

"Then you are my only companion...," said Futarishizuka.

"What are you looking at me like that for?"

"Nothing. I just have a bad feeling about this."

"I'll be counting on you, Ms. Futarishizuka."

Once we'd seen Peeps off, we rushed outside. The helicopter probably wouldn't be able to spot us otherwise. As we exited the warehouse, the sky had begun to brighten. While we weren't paying attention, a new day had dawned.

"Wouldn't the preferable course of action be to place this curse on your boss as well?"

"If I kept doing stuff like that, eventually *nobody* would trust me."

"It seems I really drew the short end of the stick here..."

"You reap what you sow. No use being depressed about it."

A short while later, the helicopter arrived, propeller roaring. It made landfall in a storm of ferocious winds, whipping our clothing and hair. I felt my heart beating faster—the machine was more powerful than I'd expected.

According to Futarishizuka, a helicopter would be able to reach the bureau in just a few minutes.

*

After enjoying a quick jog through the sky, we alighted in a park near the bureau.

There were no pedestrians to be seen. No cars passing by on the roads, either. The police must have mobilized to keep people away from the area. Seeing only a few uniformed officers standing here and there was extremely unsettling. A lot of emergency response vehicles were standing by, too; it was a very impressive sight.

We ran straight through it all toward the bureau.

On the way, we'd questioned the helicopter's pilot; apparently, the incident was being reported to the public as a large-scale terrorist bombing. The same thing was being told to the police grunts directing pedestrian and vehicular traffic.

I asked about the media situation, too, and he told me the bureau had restricted all movement in and out of the area. No wonder the only thing we'd seen in the sky was our own helicopter. I felt like I'd gotten a glimpse of what this nation was capable of when it was serious.

Section Chief Akutsu was probably pretty desperate right now—his status within the bureau would be at stake.

"Oh? I can see them," remarked Futarishizuka.

"Yes, there they are."

We located our targets by the entrance, right in front of the bureau's building.

One was the magical street urchin—the one we'd met the other day.

She was filthy, as always. Even from afar, I could tell how disheveled her hair was. She appeared to be in even more dire straits than when I'd seen her last; she must have been homeless for a while. Seeing her like this, I couldn't help pitying the girl.

Next to her stood someone else—a girl who appeared to be a similar age. She, too, wore clothing with tons of frills on it. Her clothes, however, weren't dirty in the least. Her hair was smooth and neat as well. As I'd guessed, the former seemed to be an exception among her peers.

At a glance, this new magical girl didn't appear to be from Japan.

She was striking—her skin was very fair, her eyes were blue, and her hair was blond, reaching down to her waist. Her magical girl outfit differed somewhat in its base colors and design, as well.

The two girls stood with their backs to each other, faces serious as they confronted the bureau's psychics surrounding them.

Behind them, I could see part of the building's wall had crumbled, from the third floor to the fourth. From the cross section of reinforced concrete—it looked like something had taken a huge chunk out of it—I guessed it was probably the result of a magical beam passing through.

"We can't charge at her," noted Futarishizuka. "She won't even let us close with her Magical Barrier. It looks like the bureau's psychics' attacks aren't connecting, so they likely *already* have it up. We won't be able to scratch her like this. Well? Any clever plans?"

"Hmm..."

As she had said, all kinds of psychic powers were raining down on the two already, from flames to ice to weird-looking beams. Every last one of them, however, was being obstructed by something invisible. Whatever it was, it seemed to work on bullets as well, and the machine guns flanking the main force had already ceased firing.

In the past, even Futarishizuka had given up on trying to break through the Magical Barrier. The image of this little girl punching at the invisible wall was still fresh in my memory.

Had Peeps been here with us, I could have had him teleport Futarishizuka right beside them and settled things immediately.

No, I thought. *There's no point in wishing for something we don't have.*

Could I think of a good way through?

As I mulled it over, I hit upon something.

"What about attacking with water?"

"What do you mean?"

"Last time, we learned the Magical Barrier doesn't let human bodies through. I doubt water would get through, either. I was wondering if we could produce a large quantity of water inside the barrier, then have them cancel it momentarily to let it out."

"Can your powers create this water for us?"

"I'd need to get closer, but thankfully, they're close to the entrance—I should be able to make an attempt without showing myself. The problem would be the bureau members catching a glimpse, but if they do, I can tell them my power to create icicles has evolved."

When using the spell I learned from Peeps to create water, I could adjust how much magic power I used, increasing or decreasing the amount of water produced, just like a faucet. If I put every ounce of my strength into casting, I should be able to fill up even their somewhat large Magical Barrier within seconds.

If that succeeded in confusing them, it was highly likely they'd let the barrier down, if only for a moment.

"I've heard," said Futarishizuka, "that using powers inside a Magical Barrier is difficult."

"My powers aren't psychic, so I think it's worth trying."

"The barrier might not work the same when traveling outward from the inside. What will you do if the water won't stay in?"

"In that case, I'll create my own barrier and overlap it with theirs."

If I could produce water inside their barrier, I could probably use my barrier magic as well. Just like what Peeps had done against the grenades—creating a barrier that went around the boundary of their Magical Barrier would cause the water to accumulate.

I wasn't sure how far I could fool them with it. Still, if they let down their Magical Barrier for even a second, I could send in Futarishizuka. If even *that* didn't work, we'd have to think of something else.

The most important thing here was to create a way for Futarishizuka to strut her stuff in front of all the bureau members.

She seemed to grasp that as well and quickly agreed. "Yes. If that is what you're after, I will go along with your plan."

"But whatever you do, do *not* kill the girls. My hope is that you can disable the pink-haired magical girl, then force the other one to retreat using Magical Field."

"You just *love* ramping up the difficulty on me, don't you?"

"Can you do it?"

"Well, I *do* need to start winning some points."

"Then I'll be counting on you."

I wanted to settle everything in a single attempt—we'd only have the element of surprise once.

✳

Not long after separating from Futarishizuka and arriving at my position, I received her call. She was all set.

I couldn't see her from my vantage point, but she must have been standing by. Thanks to Peeps's curse, I didn't have to consider her betraying me at this crucial moment. I'd just do what I needed to do.

I was several meters from the target.

From my position behind a building wall, I directed my water-producing magic toward the magical girls and fired.

I heard a *glug-glug* sound from inside their Magical Barrier as a glob of water emerged midair, about as big as a size 7 basketball. A huge stream of water poured from it, as though someone had gouged a hole in the bottom of a giant water tank.

"There's…there's water coming in…"

"What is this?!"

The magical girls began to panic.

The bureau's psychics gathered in the area were similarly confused. They started raising their voices, wondering what had brought about all this unexpected water. Even their powers, which they'd been incessantly launching, abruptly stopped.

Meanwhile, the water continued to fill the inside of the Magical Barrier. In just a few seconds, it had reached the girls' waists. It was like looking at a fishbowl, the way the clear liquid filled the dome-shaped barrier. And because it was two young girls trapped inside, the sight was especially guilt-inducing.

Incidentally, hearing the magical girl newcomer cry out in Japanese piqued my curiosity.

"Sayoko, the Magical Barrier!" she exclaimed.

"But—"

"We'll drown!"

A few more seconds passed, and with the water all the way up to their chins, they finally acted.

The Magical Barrier was disengaged.

With loud splashes, all that water burst free of the sphere it had occupied. They'd only opened up very small parts of the barrier. Holes, about ten centimeters long, right at the bottom; the water drained out from there.

I hadn't needed to worry about drowning them—their barrier seemed pretty versatile. Theirs was also a barrier of sorts based on magic, but it seemed to work differently from the barrier spell Peeps had taught me.

Interesting. Could they make it into different shapes, or was it only spherical? *Wait, now's not the time to be thinking about that.*

Using more magical power than before, I increased the flow of water. It flowed in faster than the water could drain and began to fill the Magical Barrier again. I decided to create icicles as well and place them around the barrier to plug up the holes.

"No! It won't be enough!"

"But any more, and it'll..."

The magical girls had once again started to panic. The holes in their barrier grew.

Now it was time for Futarishizuka to take the stage.

She closed in on the girls, completely disregarding the flow of water rising to her knees. She probably had her superhuman physical abilities to thank for that. At a blinding pace, she crossed through the stream and ran toward the Magical Barrier.

All this occurred within a few seconds.

"Sayoko!"

"That's the psychic from—"

In the end, Futarishizuka overcame even the water bursting directly out of the Magical Barrier's drains and managed to get inside. At that point, things were easy. She reached out suddenly with her fingers and touched the foot of one of the girls—the panicking street urchin.

"Ah—"

The barrier had probably been hers, because a moment later, all the water in the dome rushed out in all directions. Waves of water crashed and flooded into the surrounding area.

At this, the bureau members beat a frantic retreat. Trying to avoid being swept away, they began practically climbing over each other to escape. A few even floated up into the air. As for myself, I got my feet up onto one of the building's window frames and waited out the flow of water passing underneath me.

Meanwhile, I used my magic to cancel the source of water hovering in the air. Without the barrier containing it, the water flowed out in a matter of seconds. All that remained were three soaking-wet girls.

One of the magical girls was unconscious, and the other one was holding her. Two or three meters in front of them stood Futarishizuka. This was the exact situation I'd asked her to create.

"Did you want to keep going?" asked Futarishizuka leisurely.

"Ugh..."

Incidentally, her soaked kimono was strangely erotic. The fabric stuck to her skin, bringing out the lines of her body in vivid relief. Though her chest was modest, her waist was pinched, and her rear and thighs were shapely. Combined with her long black hair, also soaked, she looked more mature.

"What did you do to her?"

"Oh, that? She'll wake up after a few days."

Apparently, the other magical girl didn't know who Futarishizuka was. She glared at the kimono-clad girl in irritation. "You'd better remember this, got it? Because I *won't* forgive you."

"I'm so happy to have made the acquaintance of a magical girl."

"Hmph!"

Futarishizuka's tone was detached.

The blond-haired magical girl continued to glare at her as she engaged a Magical Field. With a kind of sizzling crack, a pitch-black hole opened up right next to her. Just as I'd heard before, it seemed like all magical girls were able to use the same magical abilities.

Using Magical Flight, she—and the girl she'd called Sayoko—lifted off into the air and disappeared into the hole.

I hoped she'd have a nice nap.

*

In the end, our original plan had gone off without a hitch: Futarishizuka had used her energy-draining ability to force the two magical girls into a retreat. As I watched them go, I wondered what kind of world that pitch-black hole led to.

A moment later, the bureau members in the area began to move, crowding around Futarishizuka. Everyone wore a cautious expression as they prepared for a fight. I spotted a few here and there whose knees were shaking. Every one of them was white in the face. On a whim, I looked more closely at the group and saw the glasses boy Miss Hoshizaki had scouted in Iruma standing toward the rear. Like myself, he'd been thrown into actual combat immediately after entering the bureau.

"What?" drawled Futarishizuka. "Is that any way to greet the most meritorious among you?"

All the people surrounding her hadn't flustered her a bit. Perhaps this was the confidence of a rank-A psychic. As I watched her, I wondered why I always wanted to go crying to Peeps for everything. Since I knew she was an old lady, much older than I was, on the inside, I felt no reservation in wondering all sorts of things.

I couldn't exactly leave her be, so I ran out toward her.

Though she was considered a part-timer, and had officially joined the bureau, we hadn't been informed how they were handling the matter internally. Given Chief Akutsu's personality, it was possible he purposely hadn't told anyone. It would be miserable if we were attacked now.

"Please, wait! She bears you no ill will!" I insisted in a loud voice.

I'd only joined the bureau recently, but I was one of the few survivors from the front lines of the bowling alley incident. And given my role as Miss Hoshizaki's partner, I was in their good graces.

Confusion rippled through the bureau members as they studied my middle-aged face—like they were wondering what on earth I was doing here.

"She is currently working for the bureau part-time. She's not an enemy."

"What's this?" said Futarishizuka. "Your defense of me is quite spirited, hmm?"

"The chief did entrust me with your safety."

"Oh, I'm sure you're simply having lewd thoughts about me now that I'm dripping wet."

"It's true; I think you're far more attractive when soaked."

"Oh?"

"Yes, so if you ever want to pour water over yourself again, just let me know."

"You…really are a bore, you know that? One would think you could show me at least a *fraction* of the consideration you show that bird of yours. Why must you be so unsociable? Do you perhaps prefer the company of men?"

"Having a relationship with an acquaintance just seems like a lot of trouble, you know?"

"What was that now? Are you scared?"

"I am, indeed. And I can always go to a brothel if I need to."

"…You really are too mature for your own good."

If I wanted to feel the warmth of the opposite sex, I could pay for it, and if I felt the urge of the flesh, well, I could handle that on my own. Given Japan's cultural mechanisms, the cost effectiveness of a relationship was far too low for a middle-aged man without any physical or capital assets.

I'd rather leave all that to attractive young men. Women would probably be happier that way anyway. Instead, I wanted to funnel my efforts into future feasting with my pet bird.

"More importantly," I said, "I would prefer if you focused on your current predicament."

"I doubt this crowd will listen to anything I have to say," said Futarishizuka, looking out over the assembled bureau members.

Just then, we heard familiar voices.

"Sasaki! Was all that water just now your power?!"

"Sasaki, I would have preferred it if you'd *captured* the magical girls."

It was Miss Hoshizaki and Section Chief Akutsu.

No sooner had they parted their way through the crowd and spotted us than they began shouting to us—both sounding very in character. Though personally, I had been hoping for a slightly different greeting. A thank-you would have been nice.

But as for my senior, Hoshizaki... Her eyes were positively sparkling.

"I apologize for our late arrival, and I'd like to thank you for the helicopter."

Everyone else was looking on as well, so I gave a meek bow of appreciation. I had all sorts of things to ask the *second* person, but that could wait.

"Thank you for coming as well, Futarishizuka," said the chief. "We were able to keep casualties to a minimum, thanks to you. This will make it easy to spin for the media and the public. No casualties among the police, either. The worst was the damage to the bureau building."

"Is that so?" asked Futarishizuka. "Well, if I was able to help, that's wonderful."

"By the way, Chief," I said, "why *did* the magical girl attack the bureau?"

"She has approached employees in the past. Her exact motive is under investigation, but she had that other magical girl with her this time, right? I would guess she received assistance from somewhere and decided she had enough combined power to strike at our base."

"I see."

"Which calls into question the intentions of the newcomer's sponsors, but I digress."

The chief was thinking along the same lines as I was. No matter how talented he was, I doubted he had any connections to the magical girls' camp. What he'd just said was likely the truth. That meant I was actually a step ahead of him when it came to relations with magical girls.

Though if you were to ask "So what?" I wouldn't be able to answer.

"Still," mused Futarishizuka, gazing at the spot where the magical girls had disappeared, "by the looks of things, they may attempt another attack." Now it was time for her to make herself look good in the hopes of getting hired.

"The possibility is there," responded the chief.

"Then should you not bolster the bureau's combat forces to prevent that?"

"Right—about that. I'd like to officially accept you as an employee of the bureau."

"Truly?"

"Your letter of appointment will arrive at a later date, but you can take this as your unofficial notification."

"Gladdening news, indeed. Now I may finally call myself a proud public servant."

"I'll leave the more detailed explanations to Sasaki," said the chief.

Then, he turned to me. "Sasaki, if you could, I'd like you to look after her. She'll be going through the same training as you, fundamentally."

He turned back to Futarishizuka, continuing, "I'll give him a phone for you as well, so check that when you have the time."

"Understood," she replied.

No matter how I resisted, I had apparently been confirmed as Futarishizuka's chaperone. At this point, I didn't really mind, but still.

"Finally, I have something minor to discuss with you, Sasaki, so come with me."

"Understood, sir."

Whoa. The chief had just called me out. I rallied my nerves—I could only guess what kind of trouble I was in this time.

*

We moved from the building's entrance to a conference room in the bureau. I could hear everyone bustling around outside, trying to bring the situation under control. This distant noise continued in the background as our meeting began.

Section Chief Akutsu and I were alone in the room, facing each other across the conference table.

"Now then, Sasaki. First, there is something I'd like to confirm."

"What might that be?"

"Am I correct in understanding it was you who made the water that filled the magical girls' Magical Barrier? If memory serves, your power was creating icicles."

"Yes, that is correct. It was me."

If I made lame excuses here, things would probably get even worse. Instead, I'd do what I'd decided beforehand—explain that my power had leveled up. Now that I was supervising Futarishizuka, there shouldn't be much of a problem with that.

"As I learned during bureau training, by using a psychic power many times, it can sometimes change, broadening what the psychic can do. I was confused at first, but I believe that is what's happening."

"I see." The chief didn't openly doubt my words—he just nodded slightly. "According to Hoshizaki, you were in an odd place right before we called you here. Did some sort of issue occur related to Futarishizuka? I'd like you to write up a report about it, if so."

"We were in a fight with her old organization. I'll include the specifics in the report."

They'd already fished through footage from nearby surveillance cameras to track our movements, and yet he was still acting like this. He had an ax to grind—or two or three, most likely. Still, maybe he harbored a similar feeling about us.

Plus, he'd let Futarishizuka into the bureau despite us failing to neutralize the hurricane user. The anime fan had probably already caught him up. Which meant we were currently locked in a mental battle, trying to work out the other's intentions. I felt my stomach tighten.

"All right, I understand. Please submit it as soon as possible."

"Will do, sir. I'll e-mail it to you by the end of the day."

I still lacked experience, but it seemed best not to speak recklessly with Chief Akutsu. He was a smart guy, so if he spotted even the slightest inconsistency or contradiction, he'd pounce.

"And how is Futarishizuka? As I told you earlier, I'd like to keep you in charge of her supervision. Naturally, you'll have more chances to work with Hoshizaki as well. I'd like to hear your observations, including any thoughts on your compatibility."

"I've only been around her for a few days, but I believe her willingness to join the bureau, at least, is sincere. In terms of her psychic power, it's more than impressive, as I believe you know. In my opinion, her mental fortitude, in particular, makes her singularly suited to the role."

"...I see."

The words *But wouldn't you know more about it, Chief?* caught in my throat. Brazenly broaching that subject would only create suspicion. And if I *had* asked it, it wouldn't have benefited me. It would only invite unnecessary mistrust, so I'd be circumspect for now. I'd use my knowledge eventually—when I needed to. That said, by the time things progressed to that point, I had the feeling my own position as a bureau member would be in jeopardy.

"Anything you'd like to ask me, Sasaki?"

"Well..."

I now guessed the reason he'd been so flustered at Futarishizuka's heartfelt request had as much to do with his relationship to her former group as it did with the danger she personally posed as a psychic. And that implied that their representative, the anime fan, didn't have such a smooth relationship with the bureau.

Maybe that would be a good avenue to pursue later on. Depending on how I handled it, I might even be able to keep Chief Akutsu in check.

"Not at the moment, no."

"No? Well, then I have nothing else to ask, either."

"Regarding the future—can I have time to share information with her?"

"Yes. You can spend today and tomorrow on that. I don't know how it is the two of you came to be on such good terms, but if that relationship is to our benefit, I want to respect your privacy."

With that, I'd gotten the time I'd need for a short stay in the otherworld as well. With Mr. Marc's life currently in danger, I planned to go home on time even if I had to insist.

"Thank you for your consideration, Chief."

"I should be thanking you. I look forward to what you will do for us in the future, Sasaki."

It seemed fine to assume I'd survived our discussion. Though I hadn't intended to, it looked like I would get all the credit for solving something I'd stirred up myself. Considering my relationship to the magical girl, I wasn't just a double agent—I was a *triple* agent.

It was time to get back to the otherworld, clean up that mess, and practice my magic. I couldn't have Peeps help with my work for the bureau, so I would have to improve my own abilities.

\<Otherworld Business Negotiations, Part Two\>

Once my meeting with Section Chief Akutsu was over, I went to my desk to write my report and deal with all the other little details of the incident. Time passed quickly, and before I knew it, it was time to go home.

I felt bad about all the bureau staff who still seemed like they had a lot to do, but this field employee was heading straight home now that his job was done. On my way back, I stocked up on some things for the otherworld at the neighborhood supermarket, remembering to pick up a gift to take home to my pet bird.

I had just returned to my apartment when...

"Welcome back, mister."

...the next-door neighbor called out to me from in front of her apartment. She'd made the effort to stand up and greet me as I approached.

Thinking back, it had been quite a while since I'd last run into her. I realized several days had gone by without us even saying hello. It was probably because of how irregular my life schedule had become after changing jobs. Naturally, that also meant my handouts were delayed.

"I'm sorry for not being able to see you much lately," I said, using my free right hand to fish around in the plastic bag hanging from my left.

The first thing I spotted was the meat for Peeps—definitely couldn't give her that. Instead, I took out a blocky nutritional meal substitute. With how busy I'd been recently, I'd thrown quite a few in my cart in case I didn't have the time to eat, figuring I could give any extras to the neighbor.

I held this out to her along with a cool bottled drink. "If you'd like, you can have—"

"Excuse me, but can I ask you a question?" she interrupted. Her expression was more serious than usual.

Unconsciously, I braced myself. "What is it?"

"You said before you weren't going out with any women."

"Yeah, that's right. I've never really had much to do with that stuff..."

"Have you just recently started a relationship with someone?"

"Huh?" I said, surprised at the sudden question. What a weird thing to ask.

But as soon as I heard her next sentence, I understood why. "I heard a young person's voice coming from your room."

"Oh... I see..."

So that's what this was. A noise complaint.

Apparently, my conversations with Peeps had been drifting into the neighbor's apartment. The walls here were thin, and I often heard the sounds of other people's TVs. I thought I'd been careful enough, but it seemed we'd given ourselves away.

That's not good. I'll have to be a lot more careful in the future.

If her mother had gotten mad, and it had caused a family problem... It was well within the realm of possibility.

"I'm sorry. It sounds like we were being a little loud."

"W...w-wait, so you *did* start a relationship with someone?"

"No, I've just been having a friend over more often lately."

"A friend?"

I wasn't exactly lying. This friend just happened to look...unique. "We'll be sure to meet up outside the apartment from now on. I really am sorry."

"This might be rude to ask, but is your friend a woman?"

"No, he's a man."

"...Oh."

Peeps's voice *did* sound pretty androgynous.

She probably wanted to tell me to take it to a hotel if I was doing things with a woman. The girl was in middle school now and seemed to be rapidly becoming more sexually aware. She probably didn't want to hear any sort of sexual *anything* from the old guy living in the apartment next door.

That said, I was pretty far removed from anything like that to begin with.

"In any case, you can have these, if you want," I repeated, holding out the food and drink.

Her expression softened, and she took them. "Thanks. And sorry for asking something weird."

"No, don't worry about it. In fact, thank you for telling me about it so quickly. It really helps."

"...Huh?"

"I didn't realize how much our voices were carrying."

I wonder if there's some kind of soundproofing magic. I'll have to ask Peeps when we have a moment. I didn't know what population density was like in the otherworld, but it was pretty high in this one, so that would be a very useful spell to have. There were all sorts of potential uses—from regular everyday life to combating bosses who wanted to spy on their employees all the time.

"Huh...," she murmured.

"Something the matter?"

"No, it's nothing. Never mind."

Considering the future, though, it would be best if I moved. Not to quote Futarishizuka, but relocating somewhere with better security was a good idea. It didn't have to be a mansion—it could just be somewhere on the second floor or higher of an apartment complex with auto-locking doors and windows and walls made of reinforced concrete. Something along those lines.

And having a nice big living room would be amazing. I'd want a separate room for Peeps to have all to himself—private space was important, in my humble opinion.

Ah, now that it's on my mind, I'd like to take some time and seriously consider it. The financial problem was, after all, already resolved.

"All right, I'm off, then. Good-bye."

"Yes, and I'm sorry again for asking weird questions."

"No, I'm the one who should apologize. If anything else bothers you, feel free to tell me."

Bowing slightly, I parted ways with my neighbor. Then, with swift motions, I undid the lock, stepped in, and bid her a final farewell through the door.

*

After saying good-bye to the neighbor, I met up with Peeps, who had been waiting at home. Then, going through the base of operations we were borrowing from Futarishizuka, we entered the otherworld.

Along the way, we had grabbed the dozen or so tons of foodstuffs. These were the goods that required factory production, like superfine sugar. Our choices had broadened as well, thanks to Futarishizuka's cooperation. I'd asked her to stock some medicines previously, so now I was bringing as many as I could fit into my backpack.

These were medicines that normally required a prescription. To be specific, I had sexual dysfunction medication and birth control.

Like hunger and the need to sleep, sexual urges were a powerful desire that persisted for as long as you lived. Any medicine to support that would have a perpetual demand, even in the otherworld—plus, I was thinking I could trade them in for a lot of money.

Peeps had given his seal of approval to the idea as well.

Although the world was overrun by spells that could temporarily charm a person and unleash their lust, as far as the bird knew, magic to enhance sexual function or avoid unwanted pregnancies was extremely rare. And the medicine they had for it wasn't as good as the stuff we had here, apparently.

The way he'd explained it, medicine had stopped at the level of stuff like "boil ogre testicles and drink the broth to improve nighttime well-being." The effectiveness seemed to depend on the person, too. In other words, even a little modern medicine would give us the chance to do business with rich nobles.

That said, I was still uneasy about how effective they'd be on people from another world. Unforeseen side effects were another worry—there was a potential the drugs could act like poison.

So for now, we planned to recruit some volunteers and run something like a clinical trial. I wanted to ask the Kepler Trading Company for their support, including help with any necessary negotiations. I trusted Mr. Joseph not to do anything too crazy.

"I... I'm sorry, but Joseph is currently away..."

But though my spirits were high when we arrived, the one we were looking for was absent. Instead, we were speaking with someone who claimed to work under him.

We were in the Kepler Trading Company's storehouse. Behind us was a pile of bag-like bulk containers—the goods we'd brought in with Peeps's teleportation magic. We'd added another digit onto the quantity, so the sight of them all together had a lot more impact. Various even larger containers were piled up all around us, though, regrettably lessening the effect.

Why am I feeling this sense of defeat? I thought. *The Kepler Trading Company sure is something. Next time, I'll push just a little bit harder. Even though Futarishizuka is the one doing the actual work.*

"Oh. I apologize for coming when you're so busy."

"He did leave me with instructions to accept any and all products from you if you were to visit. I know I'm not Joseph, but would you mind terribly selling the wares you've brought—to me instead?"

The discussion about the medicines and manufactured goods would likely have been complicated for a number of reasons, so I decided to only sell him the foodstuffs for now. I had little enough of the rest that it fit into my backpack, so I could carry it around without issue. Entrusting them to Count Müller was also an option.

Thinking back, I had been very lucky in the past, visiting big trading companies without an appointment and being led straight into meetings with their top people over and over again. Not that I could help it, of course, given the time difference between the two worlds—I couldn't make precise plans.

"Oh, I don't mind at all."

"Thank you so much. Please, bring the wares out so I can see them."

Following the instructions of this extremely humble employee, the trading company members gathered and checked each of the products I'd brought in turn. So many of the ones who did the labor were *built*. They must hire employees for clerical work and those who carried and transported things separately.

I waited for a while as all this occurred.

Then the workers transporting the goods suddenly paled and went to whisper something into the clerical worker's ear. Upon hearing what was said, the humble employee dashed over to the goods. He talked with the others about this and that as they went around looking over everything I'd brought.

It took maybe a few minutes. Eventually, he turned back to face me.

"S-sorry for the wait. We'll purchase all of it. However, I fear I lack the discretion to value it on my own, especially with this much product. Would you mind waiting for a moment?"

"Not at all. I understand."

"Thank you so much for your understanding, and again, we apologize."

"No, I should be the one apologizing for visiting so suddenly."

"We will prepare the deposit with all haste. It shouldn't take long."

This was all because I'd increased the quantity without notifying them in advance. I had figured more was better, but now I felt bad about it.

*

I had sold all the products I'd brought to the Kepler Trading Company as is. After informing them that I'd be visiting again in the near future, we headed straight to see Count Müller. Incidentally, the deposit they'd proposed—when converted into Herzian currency—had been three hundred large gold coins. Another substantial sum.

We couldn't exactly walk around with that, so we put it in the bank in Baytrium. Our deposits thus far had decreased as a result of making the ingots; but now it seemed we had brought it right back up with this single deposit. I wondered how much it would be once we tallied up everything from the next deal, too.

As I thought this over, we entered Count Müller's estate for the first time in a few weeks.

"How good of you to come by, Sir Sasaki. Lord Starsage."

"I apologize for the delay in our visit, my lord."

"*Things have been keeping us rather busy in the otherworld, you see.*"

"Please, don't let it bother you. I only just returned from the royal capital the other day myself."

We were in the reception room, as usual. Another familiar face was present, too: the second prince of the Kingdom of Herz, Adonis.

"It's good to see you again, Your Royal Highness," I said.

"Good indeed, Sasaki. I am pleased to see you in good health as well, Lord Starsage."

"I'm truly obliged that you've come all this way from the capital, sir."

"What turn of events has brought you here in person?"

"When I received your request, I was simply unable to stay put."

As originally planned, it looked like Count Müller had spoken to His Royal Highness on our behalf. I hadn't expected the man himself to make the journey, however. And his arrival had come quite a bit earlier than I'd expected.

"I was considering paying Duke Dietrich a visit while waiting for your arrival, Sir Sasaki. I'd assumed you would be another few days; your timing is excellent. We can move into action at once."

"Ah. I see, sir."

With everything settled, we prepared to set off as soon as we were able.

In addition to me, our team members were Count Müller, the second prince Adonis, and Peeps—three men and one bird. Boarding a carriage the count had kindly prepared for us, we made our way to Count Dietrich's lodgings. Once again, we'd be charging in without an appointment.

When we arrived, we were shown to the reception room we'd met in last time. The man of the hour was already present.

"I hadn't expected the honor of laying eyes upon the second prince!" he exclaimed.

"You are with the first prince's faction, yes?" asked the prince. "No need to be so respectful."

"You are correct on the first point, Your Royal Highness, but my respect for the royal palace is sincere, I assure you."

"I hope so."

Right off the bat, the prince and Count Dietrich struck up a conversation. The three of us—the count, the prince, and I—were sitting abreast on the sofa. At first, I'd wondered if it would be better for me to stand behind them, but the prince had patted the empty seat next to his, so I had sat down without argument. Peeps was, as always, on my shoulder.

Across the low table directly in front of us sat Count Dietrich. He was the sole occupant of the other sofa, identical to ours—and he had plopped down right in the middle of it. The impression it gave was of a man who outranked us.

"I'd like to get right down to business, if you don't mind," said Prince Adonis as soon as the greetings were over. His eyes were locked on Count Dietrich's.

The man was younger than Count Müller—part of why he had seemed so unreliable during the war. At this moment, however, he looked quite dependable. His sharp, square expression plus the title of second prince gave him enough dignity to make me think this would work.

"I want you to release the merchant who has offended you, effective immediately."

"This is a very sudden request, sir."

"No need to beat around the bush. If you have incurred unlawful losses as a result of this offense, I shall have the men beside me give you compensation. I am sure they can manage that. Isn't that correct?" The prince's gaze shifted toward the two of us.

We'd discussed this part in advance, at my suggestion. Thankfully, Peeps and I had a good amount of surplus capital. It wouldn't amount to bail, but if a little flexibility was needed to release the prisoner into our custody, there was no need to make a big fuss over it.

"Yes, it is as His Royal Highness says."

"We would be glad to do so, my lord."

Count Müller nodded, agreeing without argument. I followed his example and kept my own agreement brief.

After confirming our assent, Prince Adonis quickly continued.

"I don't know what relationship you have to the head of the Hermann Trading Company," said the prince. "But is doing all this worth damaging your relationship with us? If you are dissatisfied with the vice manager's presence, then we shall convince him to move somewhere else."

This was another of my proposals we had discussed beforehand. At this point, Mr. Marc had already lost his place at the Hermann Trading Company. However, I explained to the other two men, I thought we might be able to use that as a bargaining chip. Count Müller had expressed concern for the man's future, but I'd assured him that I had something in mind.

"For you to go that far on his behalf, sir... Just who is that merchant?"

"If you're curious, then why not show him how open-minded you are, Count Dietrich?"

"Respectfully, sir, I've already offered the two other men here conditions. Should that knight agree to sell his many wares exclusively to me in the future, I would immediately release the merchant in question."

"I cannot accept that condition."

"Then I'm terribly sorry, sir, but I cannot acquiesce to your proposition, either."

Count Dietrich was remaining firm even against the words of the second prince. I had assumed that, when faced with royalty, he might yield a little more, but his attitude hadn't changed at all. The only thing different about him this time was how politely he was speaking.

At this point, maybe it would resolve things faster if we did something about the Hermann Trading Company's manager instead. Depending on the situation, there was a possibility he might even be calling the shots here.

That said, considering the trading company's scale, I couldn't imagine him having much sway with a noble outranking even Count Müller—I doubted the count would be able to do much with him. It was true that certain wealthy merchants wielded more power than the average noble. However, within the Kingdom of Herz, Hermann would be considered a small to medium enterprise.

All this I had heard from Peeps. Considering how they'd recently set up their main headquarters in the capital city, I could see them taking the handful of restaurants they successfully managed locally and launching a chain in the capital.

"By the way, sir, is your visit today at Count Müller's behest?" asked Count Dietrich, his eyes moving between the prince and the other count. He was probably trying to gauge the amount of influence his rival had within the court. Count Müller had only recently been promoted from viscount to count, and seeing the man now seated right next to the second prince had no doubt prompted him to err on the side of caution.

"No, it wasn't me."

"Then what is Prince Adonis doing all the way out here?"

"He is here as a result of the proposal of Sir Sasaki, the man seated over there."

"What? I had heard he was but a mere knight."

"Sir Sasaki is not a royal guard by title, but he is still a knight under Prince Adonis's exclusive service. Circumstances dictate that he be with me for the moment, but his position is completely different from other knights. Please consider it as equivalent to my own."

"Yes," the prince cut in. "Sasaki is a very dependable man."

"...I see, sir. Forgive my rudeness," said Count Dietrich, bowing slightly.

It felt good having them casually butter me up like that. Still, that didn't mean I was actually capable of anything. I didn't know the first thing about the court and had little experience as a nobleman. In fact, Count Müller had been the one to bring me to the prince to begin with.

That said, this was going fairly well for me. Since I was now the topic of conversation, it was my turn to speak up—and I'd be sticking with our original plan: leveraging my relationship with the prince to convince the count to yield.

"Excuse me, my lord, but may I make a few remarks?"

"I doubt your words will change my mind. If you are happy with that, then I will listen. Thinking back, it was your proposal that convinced me to give you a month before."

"Thank you very much, my lord."

"Now then, what plan does the prince-sponsored knight have for me?"

"It isn't really a plan, my lord. Prince Adonis has deigned to accompany us in order to explain to you, Count Dietrich, how the business I conduct and the products I sell are all carried out under the prince's permission."

"...What are you saying?"

This was where I needed to put my foot down for the sake of Mr. Marc.

Belatedly, I realized how incredibly convenient it was to accuse someone of disrespecting nobility. The accuser could roll up every little thing disadvantaging them into one neat package they could push with impunity. Which was why it seemed to me like such a cowardly move to bring that alone to the negotiating table.

"My lord, His Royal Highness has graciously given my products a high appraisal. I was instructed to sell them only to those I can truly trust, which is why, up until now, I have been selling to the Hermann

Trading Company under the auspices of Count Müller, who I trust even more than the prince."

It seemed to me that was why the prince had refrained from throwing around his authority and using terms like *disrespect* in front of us. For this particular case, however, maybe it would have been justified—after all, we were up against someone now who was attempting just that.

"Selfishly switching to another client," I said solemnly, "would be an act of rudeness toward Prince Adonis, my lord. I sincerely apologize, but I would like once again to discuss with you possible compensation for the crime of disrespect by the merchant in question."

"......"

Originally, my agreement had been with Count Müller, but Count Dietrich probably didn't know that. And though the latter was part of the first prince's faction, the former was in the second prince's—as well as being one of Prince Adonis's closest allies. Count Dietrich wouldn't be able to voice any objections in front of the man himself.

"...I see. I understand what you're saying."

"Thank you, my lord."

"As I mentioned earlier, my respect for the royal palace is sincere. Leaving aside noble ties, I find myself in awe of the prince's unsullied integrity and dauntless bravery on a daily basis. I was moved when I saw him eagerly depart for the front during our conflict with the Empire."

"Then you will consider it, my lord?"

"Taking into account all that has been said, yes, I shall."

"Thank you, my lord."

We did it! All thanks to Prince Adonis. Really brought home the value of having royalty behind you.

"However, the merchant in question has conspicuously scorned my noble respect. If I am to forgive him with no real punishment, I will require suitable compensation. I believe you must understand that, having received the title of knight from the prince."

"Yes, my lord. I understand perfectly."

"In terms of compensation, it need not be granted materially. Should you total up the profit on all sales, you, Knight Sasaki, have made to the merchant in question and pay me that sum, I would accept the proposal you have brought me."

"I see, my lord."

But he was still holding out. His plan was probably to take me for all I was worth.

"I've already confirmed the amount via the Hermann Trading Company's manager, as he handles the accounting for his company. You have been dealing in significant amounts of money, haven't you? Upon hearing you had close to one thousand Herzian large gold coins, even I was plainly shocked."

The count continued smoothly. He'd probably already predicted what objections we'd try to raise. It appeared he hadn't expected the prince himself to show up, but his current spiel seemed well thought out.

"One thousand large gold coins, and I shall acquit the merchant in question. How does that sound?"

Count Dietrich's lips curled in a grin—a *smug* grin. He was totally trying to rile me up.

Actually, I doubted even summing all my business profits thus far would yield *that* high an amount. It would be two hundred—three hundred at most. When exchanged for regular gold coins, it would be somewhere from twenty thousand to thirty thousand, and that included my dealings with Count Müller.

However, Count Dietrich had the evidence necessary to back up his claims. It must have been child's play to falsify the accounts.

Upon hearing this, Count Müller immediately raised his voice. "Count Dietrich, forgive me if this sounds rude, but do you honestly believe a single commoner is worth that much? One thousand large gold coins is far more than a mere merchant would ever be handling."

"You're right, the worth of a single commoner is considerably less."

"Then why have you proposed this?"

"I reasoned that is how much our noble *prestige* is worth. In fact, it is a low estimate. Normally, it would be intolerable to even attempt to set a monetary price on the honor and obligations of peerage bestowed by His Majesty."

"……"

Even Prince Adonis, beside me, took on a difficult expression at that.

I might have been a novice otherworlder, but even I could tell he was fleecing us. I was sure he didn't expect us to actually pay that amount.

The count's aim hadn't changed: He wanted a permanent supply of goods from yours truly.

Until a few days ago, a sum like that would have put me out on the streets. I would have said, "Well, this is quite the mess."

That, however, was in the past.

Now that I had Futarishizuka's assistance in the modern world, and I'd secured a major client in the Kepler Trading Company, one thousand large gold coins was no longer an unattainable amount of money. I'd probably have more than enough to pay it once I sold the rest of what I'd brought this time.

And I was more than willing to take this deal if it meant saving Mr. Marc's life.

"I understand, my lord. I will prepare one thousand gold coins."

"...What?"

As a result, Count Dietrich entertained us with some very amusing expressions.

His combed-back gray hair and his deep, pronounced features... Those blue eyes and that impressive mustache and beard... He was a very attractive middle-aged man. And now those features were twisted into a look of blank amazement as he stared at me. He'd lost his calm, sophisticated visage and actually looked kind of cute.

"W-wait. Are you serious?"

Until now, he'd kept a straight face. This change, however, comforted me—schadenfreude at its finest.

"Yes, my lord, I am quite serious."

"I'm talking *large* gold coins here, not just gold coins. One thousand of them. You can prepare that much?"

"I will prepare it down to the last coin, my lord."

"We will conduct the payment as swiftly as possible! I will not wait years for you to pay it all off. You will need to get the money by the end of the year. Are you saying you have that sort of financial power?"

"I do, my lord. I will pay the amount in full at the end of next month."

Count Dietrich nearly choked. His lips twitched, causing his well-kept mustache to tremble. This was no act—he was honestly shocked. And with good reason; this was no small amount of money.

Thinking back, when my business with Count Müller had concluded during the conflict with the Ohgen Empire, my total assets had

been about a thousand large gold coins. That included the restaurant Mr. French managed as well as my deals with the Hermann Trading Company.

Maybe that was why those nearby, hearing about the deals I was striking, started making a fuss.

"Sir Sasaki, you can't... That's too..."

"Asserting lies in situations like these is a criminal offense, Sasaki."

Count Müller and Prince Adonis watched me with worried expressions.

The former, especially, was one I'd made several deals with in the past. He probably knew what my financial situation was like. No doubt I looked like some crazy, olive-skinned foreigner spouting nonsense.

But the correct play here was to force my way forward. We'd finally put Count Dietrich on the defense. It was time to press even further, so he wouldn't be able to get another word in edgewise.

"If it's all the same to you, my lord, I will pay three hundred large gold coins by the end of the day as an advance payment. In exchange, I would like you to release Mr. Marc, even if it is only temporary. He is unused to living in a cell, and it has exhausted him greatly."

"Y-you talk very big in the presence of His Royal Highness. But if this should turn out to be a lie, you *will* lose your noble title. Knowing that, do you still insist that you will pay me? This is your only chance to retract your statement."

"Then as proof, my lord, I will now go to prepare the advance payment. It will take approximately one hour, and I will write a promissory note to you for the remaining seven hundred as well."

"......"

Count Dietrich was dumbfounded.

I did it, Peeps. It seems like I'll be able to get Mr. Marc out of there safely.

Casually, I glanced at the bird on my shoulder and saw him give me a subtle nod.

"I hope you are not thinking of running," said Count Dietrich, immediately getting up, eyes still on me. Since he was so tall, being looked down on like that was petrifying. His rank was much higher than mine, so it was possible he'd decide to just beat the snot out of

me. I could only hope he wouldn't do anything like that in front of
Prince Adonis.

"No, my lord. I would never dream of it."

"...What company are you spying for?"

"I don't work for anyone in particular, my lord. This is a private side
business of my own."

"Absurd! Even a knight in service to the prince could not pay
such an enormous amount! This isn't *your* idea, I trust, Count Müller? Have you brought the prince all the way here just to make a fool
of me?!"

Apparently, my proposition was even less realistic than I'd realized.
Count Dietrich had pretty much blown his top. And neither Count
Müller nor Prince Adonis could hide their confusion. They both
looked at me, clearly worried. We hadn't discussed this beforehand,
and I felt a little guilty; they were honestly concerned for me.

And therein lay my chance. This exact moment was my opportunity
to defeat Count Dietrich.

"Forgive me for repeating myself, but please release Mr. Marc. He is
worth at *least* one thousand large gold coins. His value will benefit not
only me, but Count Müller and Prince Adonis as well—and you yourself, my lord."

"What?"

"I know of the factional difficulties in the court. Before that, however, are we not all nobles of the Kingdom of Herz? Our neighbors are
sure to attack us again. It may be that once the succession has been
decided—no, even *before*—we will be entrusting our lives to each other
on the battlefield."

"......"

"Factions have no place when it comes to gathering the strength to
oppose them. This is our responsibility as Herzian nobles. And we
need Mr. Marc for that. Should we lose him now, our collective losses
will be *far* greater than one thousand large gold coins."

And that was certainly no lie. I'd already invested quite a lot in asking the Kepler Trading Company to establish the Marc Trading Company. Plus, all the deals we would be doing in this world in the future
would be managed through the company he would be representing—
an arrangement to which Mr. Joseph held the keys.

"I will pay the promised amount, my lord. So I ask you—won't you please lay down *your* arms?"

"...Are you referring to the relationship between Count Müller and me?"

"I am indeed, my lord."

I hadn't actually thought this far ahead. But in the moment, it seemed like this was the right way to go, so I went with it. The fewer enemies close at hand, the easier it would be for Count Müller to act. Count Dietrich was the kind of person who would plant spies in someone's home, after all—it would sure please Count Müller if he was to back off.

"......"

"What do you think, my lord?"

Unfortunately, judging by Count Dietrich's reaction, it still wasn't enough. He appeared to be thinking about it but didn't seem ready to make up his mind. That suggested the real problem was one of face, not finances. Both Count Müller and I were of lower rank. Even if the prince outranked us all, the thought of simply agreeing vexed him.

In which case, I had little choice but to take advantage of the prince's presence and start flinging criticisms.

"This may be rude of me to say in front of Prince Adonis, my lord, but to be perfectly honest, I would not mind either the first or the second prince succeeding the throne."

"Wh-what?!" exclaimed Count Dietrich, shocked again. His eyes darted back and forth between Prince Adonis and me.

The prince chuckled a little in response.

"That doesn't surprise me," he said with a sigh, his expression fond. This little cheat had only worked because the prince knew of my relationship with the Lord Starsage. Count Müller understood it as well, so neither of them criticized in turn.

"What's more important, my lord, is to strengthen the Kingdom of Herz so we are ready when the time comes. I'd like to assist Prince Adonis in that respect. Losing one's homeland must be very sad, indeed. I wouldn't want anyone to have to endure it."

I didn't say who, specifically. Despite my present company, it was a pretty cheesy line. *That'd be way too embarrassing.*

"You have quite the silver tongue, don't you, Sasaki?"

"Those are my true, unabashed feelings, sir."

"...I can tell why he puts so much stock in you," whispered the prince, eyes shifting to the sparrow on my shoulder.

The bird he was looking at showed no particular response. He simply gazed straight ahead, quiet as usual. I followed his gaze to some rice treats on the low table in front of us.

Wait, Peeps, are you hungry?

"...All right."

"Count Dietrich?"

"I will trust in your words this time," he said, looking me right in the eyes. Though his brow had remained stubbornly furrowed up to this point, that now changed. He seemed refreshed, and his voice calmed down as well. It was almost like we'd performed an exorcism. Almost. At the very least, I couldn't sense any more irritation or hostility from him.

"Truly, my lord?"

"You do indeed seem sincere."

"I deeply thank you for your understanding, my lord."

"I hadn't expected one from a foreign nation to sue for unity among Herzian nobles. But recently, it seems we have indeed sunk that far. If you've thought that far, I am left with nothing more to say."

"......"

So that was what got to you? I had to wonder.

Maybe the man had a more earnest personality than I gave him credit for. But anyway, all's well that ends well.

"You need not pay the thousand large gold coins, either. I will release the merchant in question by the end of the day."

"Are you sure, my lord?"

"If I don't show deference before His Royal Highness now, I wouldn't be able to call myself a Herzian noble."

"It would appear your respect for the court was genuine, after all, Count Dietrich," remarked the prince.

"The matter of factions and the succession dispute aside, sir, I do truly fear for the future of this kingdom. Thus, I do not want to deny the spirit this knight has shown when he spoke of becoming that foundation without heed to his own welfare."

"I see."

"And I admire your magnanimity, sir, for permitting such a relationship."

"My elder brother is different, then?"

"I said nothing of him, sir. But I believe you know the answer better than I."

"I suppose I do..."

The prince's gaze seemed to pass Count Dietrich, extending to some far-off place. Were he and his elder brother not on good terms? Prince Adonis was such an affable person that I couldn't imagine him getting into fights with his family.

"Knight Sasaki, the merchant in question is named Marc, correct?"

"Yes, my lord."

"If your earlier words were true, then I suspect the day is not far off when we may see those thousand large gold coins. Our factions may differ, but if, as you say, it is for the sake of the Kingdom of Herz, then I shall be looking forward to it."

"......"

Thanks to my embarrassing speech, we'd secured Count Dietrich's agreement. I'd been fully intending to pay the money, so now I felt a bit let down. Either way, everything had turned out fine.

At this rate, the relationship between the two counts might even stabilize. Now we just had to rush to Mr. Marc's prison cell and release him from confinement.

I breathed a sigh of relief—and clearly jinxed it. No sooner had I done so than the door to the reception room burst open.

"Excuse me, my lord!"

An exuberant greeting rang out, and all present turned their attention to the newcomer in the hallway. This was one I'd seen before—the manager of the Hermann Trading Company.

"Hermann! Don't you think it's rude to enter without knocking?"

Count Dietrich was the one to respond. He knit his brows, taking the man to task. His voice was fairly stern, too—he probably wanted to save face in front of the prince. Despite representing a trade company, the man was still a commoner, and the reception he received was exceedingly cold.

Even so, he continued to address Count Dietrich, his voice loud.

"My lord, someone has, without permission, transferred the bonds for our store, issued during the transfer to the capital! Not just the bonds, either, my lord—all the notes you paid during the previous conflict have disappeared from the central bank!"

"What?! Who *dares* do such a thing?!"

"I don't know, my lord. I tried asking the one in charge, but they insisted they knew nothing."

"That's not possible…"

Count Dietrich's calm had only lasted a few moments before his expression once again grew stern. *He's such an expressive person,* I thought in spite of myself. Also, was it all right for us to overhear what the manager had said just now?

"Count Dietrich, we'll show ourselves out…"

Reading the mood, Count Müller picked himself up off the sofa. The prince slid out of his seat as well. I followed their example, of course. I didn't want any more trouble here.

A moment later, the manager of the Hermann Trading Company shifted his attention to me. Apparently, he hadn't even realized we were here—probably because of the urgency of his news. Upon seeing our familiar faces, his eyes grew wide; Prince Adonis garnered an even greater reaction.

"Wh-what are Count Müller and that knight—? Y-Y-Y-Your Royal Highness?!"

"Is that the manager of the Hermann Trading Company you mentioned, Sasaki?"

"I—I—I… I'm terribly sorry for my rudeness!" the manager exclaimed, frantically kneeling and groveling on the spot.

His movements were excellent. Maybe he was used to this kind of thing.

"You seem busy with matters of your own, so we will excuse ourselves now."

"Y-yes, sir! I'm terribly sorry for…for interrupting your…"

The manager's whole body tensed up when Prince Adonis addressed him. It was so comically exaggerated, but it drove home the relationship between royalty and commoners.

Count Dietrich was the next to address him. "Hermann, I've decided to release the merchant as early as today."

"Huh…?"

The manager was struck silent by this unforeseen follow-up strike.

But that only lasted a moment.

Immediately, he began to complain. Loudly.

"B-but that isn't what we promised, my lord!"

"It has just been decided. I will not hear any objections."

"Wha...?"

Count Dietrich's tone was firm. Hermann fell silent once again. As a commoner, getting told off by a noble must be a painful experience. If I'd been in his shoes, it would have broken my spirit. This Herzian feudalism backed up by the aristocracy was truly terrifying.

"Hermann, I'd like to make something clear. Though I only have the word of these fine men, the employee you threw in prison is apparently a very shrewd businessman. If you desire great success as a merchant, you should use him to his full potential, not eliminate him."

"Please, wait, my lord. That means I will have to reevaluate my relationship with you as well."

"...What was that?"

"Regarding this matter, I have also received an opinion from Marquess Koch. If you would renege on our agreement and leave me no recourse, please understand it will also affect your relationship with the marquess. I am not operating at my sole discretion, my lord."

"......"

The manager of the Hermann Trading Company had just introduced a new character: Marquess Koch. It was getting more and more annoying to remember everyone's names. *Maybe I'll leave it to Peeps and just forget them all*, I thought. Still, judging from how this conversation was going, things wouldn't be so easily resolved.

It felt like we'd killed the final boss only to be greeted by a secret boss.

"N-no. I've already decided...," stammered Count Dietrich, his expression pained. His previously stern tone now grew labored. His expressions really did change by the second.

"Count Dietrich, please reconsider!"

"You say this, but have you truly earned an audience with the marquess?"

"Yes, my lord. I've had several opportunities to meet with him in the past. He helped immensely with our move to the capital. That relationship has given me the chance to help the marquess, however minor my help may be."

"Marquess Koch has connections to major trading companies in the Republic of Lunge. Pardon my words, but I doubt he would hand out any opportunities to a suburban trading company like yours. Can you explain this?"

This was getting complicated.

Considering my future, I should probably have tried to get as much information as I could, even if I had to interrupt. But in my mind, I'd finally done what I needed to do—I'd settled things. I wanted to go rescue Mr. Marc and have some food at Mr. French's place. Some of that meat with the rich seasoning.

The bird on my shoulder was probably hungry, too. And I was beside myself with worry—about when my stomach would start audibly rumbling. It would look *awful* if that was to happen here.

And then, as if summoned by my very thoughts, I caught sight of Mr. French out of the corner of my eye.

No, wait. That's not possible.

I did a double take.

But there he was—standing right there in his chef outfit.

Until now, he'd been beyond the door to the reception room that the Hermann Trading Company's manager had so rudely swung open. Now he was standing just outside the room's entrance, nervously peering inside. He looked helpless—a complete one-eighty from his bold, imposing countenance whenever he was working in the kitchen.

"E-excuse me…"

Eventually, he rallied himself and spoke up.

Everyone's attention shifted to Mr. French.

"What is it now?!" roared Count Dietrich.

Mr. French flinched, letting out a short yelp. It was kind of cute seeing such a big, stern-looking guy too frightened to say a word.

Nevertheless, he managed to respond. "I… I've brought someone who claims to be acquainted with you, sir…," he said, looking straight at me.

Unexpectedly made the topic of conversation, I automatically tensed up. "With me?"

"He came to the restaurant looking for you. We checked at Count Müller's estate and heard you were here, so I brought him along..."

As Mr. French finished speaking, there was movement next to him. Then another person poked his head out from behind the doorframe.

And just as Mr. French had said, this person was indeed someone I'd met before. The very one I'd gone to see even before Count Dietrich, whose absence on my visit had made me just a little lonely. I'd assumed I wouldn't see him until my next trip.

"Hello, Mr. Sasaki. It's been a while, hasn't it?"

"Oh? Mr. Joseph, I didn't expect to see you in a place like this."

Wait. What *was* he doing here anyway?

✳

For reasons unbeknownst to me, Mr. French had brought Mr. Joseph to us. Nobles used these accommodations, and the surrounding neighborhood was quite respectable. His store also catered to the upper echelons and was located in a similarly desirable area. In fact, it was not very far from our current location. Mr. French's response wasn't particularly strange in that sense.

However, that logic didn't extend to Mr. Joseph. Why was he in the Kingdom of Herz? The employee at the Kepler Trading Company had told me he was out. Finding him *here*, though, was the last thing I'd expected. The Republic of Lunge and the Kingdom of Herz were a fair distance apart. It would have taken something significant to cause him to make such a long journey.

"I don't want to sound rude," I began, "but what brings you here?"

"I had some minor business in Herz, and I figured I'd pay you a visit while I was here. I'd love to meet Mr. Marc as well, if you don't mind. I apologize for not contacting you in advance."

"No apologies necessary. Thank you for coming so far. I believe I can oblige you on that, but he is currently away. I would need a day or two."

"I understand perfectly."

I couldn't exactly bring him here straight from his prison cell. He'd been locked up for *months*. We'd need to get him a bath to wash off the dirt and grime and then spruce him up. He'd need food and rest, too. Sometime late the following day seemed a safe window to set up the meeting.

In the meantime, Mr. Joseph's attention had drifted elsewhere. He was now looking at the sofa opposite our own.

"Oh?" he said. "Is that you, Count Dietrich?"

"Lord Joseph! I, er, what are you doing here?"

"I wasn't aware you were acquainted with Mr. Sasaki."

Mr. Joseph's eyes flitted between Count Dietrich and me. Apparently, they knew each other. I supposed it made sense that any large trading company in the Republic of Lunge, which had agreements with all nearby nations, would have connections to one or two nobles from elsewhere.

"Acquainted? Actually, well..."

"Am I wrong? I do apologize."

The count was acting strange. He'd been on the offensive until just a few moments ago, but no sooner had he spotted Mr. Joseph than he'd suddenly grown meek. His back was hunched somewhat as he stood idly—a stark contrast with how he'd yelled at Mr. French.

Meanwhile, Count Müller and Prince Adonis were looking on in confusion. Neither of them seemed to have any idea who Mr. Joseph was. The Hermann Trading Company's manager had much the same reaction; he was currently glancing around the room, trying to grasp the situation.

"Mr. Joseph, are you familiar with Count Dietrich?"

"Yes, well, I've had several opportunities to speak with him in the past whenever I visited Marquess Koch. His good looks stuck out in my memory. I even considered growing a beard of my own."

"Ah, I see." Count Dietrich was certainly handsome. A real catch. His neatly trimmed mustache and beard, for example—really cool. *But you're quite the handsome middle-aged man yourself, aren't you?*

"As a handsome man yourself, I think a beard would suit you well."

"Is that right?"

"I could bring some useful items to help you take care of it in the near future."

"How intriguing. Please do."

He'd probably love a wireless, battery-operated trimmer, wouldn't he? In this world, where body hair was handled with a blade or a pair of scissors, beards and mustaches were considered a lot of trouble to maintain. Most people, I'd heard, just shaved it all off.

"Sasaki, would you mind introducing me to this esteemed personage as well?"

"My apologies, sir. Allow me." Just then, the prince interrupted. We'd accidentally become engrossed in our own private conversation. "This is the president of the Kepler Trading Company, from the Republic of Lunge—Mr. Joseph Kepler. We've recently had the chance to do some business together. I hope the relationship will be a long and fruitful one."

"Pleased to meet you. My name is Joseph."

Come to think of it, the Kepler Trading Company was another one Peeps had introduced me to. I wondered what sort of relationship they had.

However, I didn't have much time to ponder this question. My introduction had apparently gotten a strong reaction from those around us: complete and utter shock. It wasn't only the prince and Count Müller who raised their voices in surprise, but the Hermann Trading Company's manager and even Mr. French.

I wasn't sure what was going on, but I figured I may as well have finished the introductions.

"Mr. Joseph, sitting nearest to us on that sofa is the second prince of the Kingdom of Herz, Prince Adonis. Next to him is Count Müller, who rules over this town."

"What good fortune, to have the chance to meet royalty!" said Mr. Joseph with a smile.

He didn't seem the least bit nervous, even with a prince right in front of him. His behavior was gentle-mannered and proper, yet calm and composed—so impressive. I fervently wished I, too, could have that level of mental fortitude.

In response, the two men who had just been introduced tensed up. They hurried to straighten their postures, then bowed to Mr. Joseph.

"I am Adonis Herz. And may I say, the honor is all mine, to be able to meet the head of the Kepler Trading Company. I hear my father has never been granted a meeting with you, despite his requests, so allow me to offer my gratitude for our good fortune today."

"I am Müller, governor of these lands. I sincerely appreciate your visiting from so far away. Please allow me to apologize for not preparing a welcome, as I was unaware of your visit."

"No need to worry about that, my lord. It's my fault for having come here without sending word."

I was getting the distinct feeling that Mr. Joseph was a *lot* more important than I'd assumed. As I looked at the reception room now, he seemed to be standing at the very top of the hierarchy. Actually, I was certain of it.

He'd been so easy to talk to, so I'd interacted with him much the same way as I would the head of a smaller company I'd already had dealings with. Sure, he was the leader of a large trading company, but he was a commoner. It appeared I'd made a mistake and underestimated him.

As I looked at him now, I belatedly realized something else. Could the manager of the Hermann Trading Company have been so flustered because of this man's visit? The timing would line up perfectly, considering the request I'd made of him.

"By the way, Mr. Joseph," I said, "there's something I'd like to clear up."

"And what would that be, Mr. Sasaki?"

"I apologize for cutting right to the chase, but would you happen to know something about the recent confusion in Herz regarding bonds issued by the Hermann Trading Company and promissory notes with Count Dietrich's seal?"

After a pause, he glanced around the room and asked, "Shall I explain?"

Everyone here was a related party. Anything to do with the Hermann Trading Company would soon be known to all of them anyway. The manager had already brought it up. I doubted releasing the details here would cause any issues—in fact, it would make dealing with the matter more efficient.

"Things are already set in stone, right?" I asked.

"Oh, of course."

"Then please, go ahead." *Actually*, I thought, *I'm wondering what the heck is going on myself.*

As everyone looked on, he continued plainly, "As you have implied, Mr. Sasaki, I have taken the liberty of seizing it all."

His response had come without a scrap of hesitation, despite being right in front of the parties concerned.

As a result, everyone was staring at Mr. Joseph, more shocked than ever. The Hermann Trading Company manager—the main one involved and the principal victim—and Count Dietrich were stunned. They couldn't believe it.

"It would have taken too much time to negotiate, so I purchased it all from a qualified seller. Their price ran a bit steep, but when I think about my business with you, Mr. Sasaki, it wasn't even that large an investment."

"That certainly sounds promising for me, but…"

"As it's a rather small-scale trading company, if I were to let them send a bad check now, the Hermann Trading Company would then lawfully belong to you, Mr. Sasaki. If you were to choose a brute-force approach, things could be settled even sooner than that. As a result, the matter we discussed will be able to move forward next month."

This was even more of a power play than I'd expected.

I had indeed made a request on that scale. Like, in an M&A sort of way. I had been sincere about wanting to leave behind a place for Mr. Marc to return to. The Hermann Trading Company, subsidiary of the Marc Trading Company—something along those lines. I had *not* anticipated that he'd start using real-life yakuza strategies.

Thanks to him, the Hermann Trading Company's manager was now blue in the face. He stared at us, visibly shaking.

This was probably all because this world's ethical values were so much looser than Japan's. Slavery still had a lot of pull as a system here, after all. Compared to that, this was actually pretty tame. Similar things *did* happen in modern times.

"Then why the promissory notes with Count Dietrich's seal on them?"

"My information indicated the count held sway over the Hermann Trading Company. I couldn't be fully certain of the details, but if it was going to cause trouble in the future, then we didn't have any time to waste—and so we seized those as well."

Man, Mr. Joseph is a really thorough guy! Now I knew why Count Müller and the prince were in such a panic.

"But it seems," he continued, "you were a step ahead of us, Mr. Sasaki."

"Actually, I'm here for a different reason."

Saying he remembered Count Dietrich because of his cool beard? What a way to greet someone. Mr. Joseph was able to take part in such thrilling endeavors and yet still responded to everyone with such calm—terrifying. At this point, Count Dietrich seemed like nothing in comparison.

"In any case, all that remains is to meet Mr. Marc and run him through everything required to establish the trading company. He will need to visit the Republic of Lunge at some point. I would be very pleased if we could meet so I could explain in person."

"I see—so that's what this was about."

I couldn't allow him to learn that Mr. Marc was imprisoned. If he flip-flopped on the matter, we'd be in big trouble. Bringing along royalty from my own nation wouldn't have as much of an effect on him as it had with Count Dietrich. In fact, I'd really like to determine at least one of Mr. Joseph's weaknesses while I had the chance.

"Lord Joseph, there is one thing I would like to ask...," said Count Dietrich. No trace of his imposing dignity remained—it was clear he was nervous about this question.

"What is it, my lord?"

"What sort of relationship might you have with Marquess Koch?"

"My family has known him since my father's generation, and we still do business with him these days. I hear the deals of the past were impressive, but recently, they've only been buying sweeteners—sugar, honey—and only two or three times a year."

"Ah, I...I see."

"Oh, and regarding this matter, I had a proposition for you, Mr. Sasaki."

"What is it?"

"I would like to suggest you become their supplier. It will greatly decrease the cost of stocking their inventory, and your goods are of a higher quality than ours."

"Wouldn't that cause problems for the Kepler Trading Company?"

"I've personally been meaning to reduce how many small deals we make going forward. Since the year before last, we've been tailoring our clients with that purpose in mind. Most importantly, this proposition will benefit Marquess Koch as well."

"I see."

Compared to how Count Dietrich and the Hermann Trading Company manager had been talking about him, Marquess Koch seemed a little less significant to Mr. Joseph. When they mentioned he had acquaintances in the Republic of Lunge... Had that been referring to Mr. Joseph? I'd figured he was in better standing as a customer—and that they were more deeply involved.

Count Dietrich appeared to have had the same idea. He was watching our conversation with a blank, amazed look. Seeing him stare absentmindedly with that stern face of his, totally silent, actually made him look kind of cute.

"In that sense, too, I'm expecting a lot from the Marc Trading Company."

"I hope to be of service."

It looked like we didn't have to slay the secret boss, after all—we'd gotten the peaceful ending instead.

✳

The next day, it was time for the arranged meeting between Mr. Marc and Mr. Joseph. It was taking place in the reception room of Count Müller's estate, and aside from the two main actors, the lord of the house, Prince Adonis, and Count Dietrich were all in attendance. We hadn't seen the Hermann Trading Company's manager since he'd left right after the previous day's discussion.

"It's a pleasure to make your acquaintance. My name is Joseph."

"M-my name is Marc."

Two sofas, separated by a low table. Mr. Marc and Mr. Joseph sat facing each other. The rest of us stood behind Mr. Marc—it was a ploy to give him more of a sense of presence.

"Mr. Marc, I have received a strong recommendation from Mr. Sasaki that we, the Kepler Trading Company, enter into a partnership agreement with you. I heard you made quite a handsome sum during the incident with the Ohgen Empire. We would love for you to use that talent on our behalf."

"D-d-d-don't mention it! It's a pleasure to be working with you."

We'd informed Mr. Marc of the gist of what was happening last night. Accordingly, there was no need for a concrete discussion between them regarding the Marc Trading Company's establishment. This meeting was only to acquaint the two men, as Mr. Joseph had requested.

As the leader of a major trading company, he was a very busy man. After chatting for a little under an hour, we concluded our meeting.

Just before parting, as initially planned, it was decided that Mr. Marc would travel to the Republic of Lunge. Because of travel costs and possible safety issues, he would be accompanying Mr. Joseph on his return trip, to happen very soon. As he left, he said, "Let's meet again in Herz's capital."

Count Dietrich offered to supervise the Hermann Trading Company in the meantime, angrily saying he'd be keeping an eye on the manager to make sure he didn't make any strange moves. I wouldn't soon forget the sight of him desperately negotiating to have his promissory notes returned in exchange for the service.

Not long after seeing Mr. Joseph out of the count's estate, all parties returned to the reception room and, looking exhausted, began conversing among one another.

"Sir Sasaki, the breadth of your relationships astounds me."

"How on earth did you meet him?"

Both Count Müller and Prince Adonis looked at me as if they had more to say. For my part, the power of Mr. Joseph's influence still didn't feel real. But I couldn't exactly let that question go unanswered, so I took the opportunity to ask a question of my own.

"There's one thing I'd like to confirm first. What sort of position is the head of the Kepler Trading Company in, regarding the Kingdom of Herz? As a foreigner, there's a lot I don't know."

"It's not a particularly Herzian view. The Kepler Trading Company is one of the major businesses representing the Republic of Lunge. They don't have a long history, but other nations know it as a company that rose to great prominence in the last century due to the skill of its proprietors."

My explanation came from Prince Adonis. Essentially, they were like a general trading company operating internationally. Thinking about it like a major e-commerce website made the pieces fit together in my mind. My first impression had been of a very humble man, so I hadn't thought they were that big. He'd played dumb at first, too, claiming to be in charge of the foodstuffs department.

What interested me more, however, was the social standing of Lunge's merchants.

"But, sir, isn't Mr. Joseph a commoner?"

"Sasaki, especially when it comes to the Republic of Lunge, that way of thinking is dangerous. First of all, his nation doesn't have a system of aristocracy, nor do they have anything resembling a monarchy. National administration is carried out by a central council."

"I see, so that's the way it works."

"Lunge also has vastly more national power than Herz. In other words, they're much more affluent. The foundation of that affluence is their merchant class, which used major business ventures involving nearby nations to build a fortune."

This was speculation on my part, but maybe the difference between Herz's economy and Lunge's was like that of a developing nation versus a first-world nation. As I thought back, their city streets had been pretty sophisticated.

"In Lunge, social status is determined by how much wealth one amasses. In that sense, it would be safe to think of Lord Joseph as equivalent to a Herzian duke—or even royalty like me."

"They're that powerful, sir?"

"Without a doubt—especially when it comes to the influence they can exert."

"Thank you for informing me, sir. That was very helpful."

I'd have to go over several things with Peeps later. I'd be working with them for the time being, so I needed to get as much information as possible. Mr. Marc was probably reeling from the suddenness of it all, so if there was anything we could do in advance to help him prepare, I wanted to do it.

"Knight Sasaki, I have something to ask of you."

"What is it, Count Dietrich?"

Once the prince had finished talking, the count spoke up—he sounded timid, completely different from his attitude the day before. "When you said you were able to prepare one thousand large gold coins last time, did you mean...?"

"I did say that, my lord. I could have prepared it by the end of next month."

"...I, er, I see."

It sounded like Count Dietrich hadn't believed us. I had mixed feelings about seeing him so surprised this late in the game.

"Good for you, Count Dietrich. If you'd simply taken the money, or if you hadn't let the merchant in question go free, you would have had a major problem on your hands involving the Republic of Lunge. Your love for your country is what saved you."

"......"

Prince Adonis grinned as he spoke. Count Dietrich, in the meantime, had gone white in the face.

*

After many a twist and turn, the issues revolving around Mr. Marc's safety and security had been resolved, and calm returned to our lives.

I was sure Count Dietrich and the Hermann Trading Company manager were now extremely busy, but that wasn't the case for us. We excused ourselves from all the commotion early, deciding to enjoy our first rest in a while to the fullest.

Right now, we were in the living area in the high-class inn we used as our base of operations. There, I was enjoying a good chat with my beloved pet bird.

"It was a hard-fought win for you, wasn't it?"

"Thankfully, Mr. Joseph is a good person."

If he'd been the mischievous sort, like the Hermann Trading Company manager..., I thought, belatedly reflecting on how much I'd been playing the whole thing by ear. In the future, I'd have to plan things out a little more.

"I can't speak for his character, but as a merchant, he is trustworthy."

"Was he a friend of yours or something?"

"Not friends, no. We were merely acquainted."

"I see."

After spending so much time with Peeps, I found myself wondering again about his background. What sort of friendships had he had in life? How had he spent his days? Were there any close friends he wanted to visit?

"...You're having strange thoughts again, aren't you?"

"What?"

"I've quite enjoyed my life of late. There is nothing more I need."

Whoops, I thought. *Was it really that obvious?* As always, Peeps was one sharp Java sparrow.

"Really?"

"Really."

"Okay..."

Well, if he said everything was fine, then there was no need for me to force him into anything. For the time being, I'd give myself back over to our peaceful lifestyle and allow my weary mind some repose.

"By the way, I'd like to take this chance to return to the otherworld for a moment."

"Huh? Did you have something to do?"

"I've been measuring the difference in time flows between this world and the other using the device over there. I'd like to take the value I calculated last night and verify my findings based on the current time in that world—right away, if possible."

Peeps used his wing to point to the laptop computer we'd brought from modern Japan. Next to it was the golem he used for controlling the keyboard and mouse, hunched over like a marionette with its strings cut.

"...Peeps, you've been doing all that already?"

"Is there a problem?"

"No, not at all."

"You've also been hard at work in this world."

"......"

He'd just shown me the kind of work a real man can do. *So cool.*

"Also... Well, this MATLAB tool is excellent, but I feel NumPy makes it easier to specify conditions. This Python, or what have you, is a superb system. It seems to have some competition in R, but R's syntax is quite clumsy."

Suddenly, the bird perched on my shoulder felt very far away.

*

At Peeps's request, we left the otherworld and returned to modern Japan, coming out in the living room of my apartment. We'd been out so much recently that it felt like I hadn't seen it in forever.

As soon as we arrived, Peeps headed for the PC on the desk. Using his golem, he started hurriedly clacking away at the keys. I would have felt bad getting in the way, so I figured I'd watch TV for a bit. I went through the channels without any goal in mind, taking in the programs one by one.

A little while later, as I was vegging out, I heard the sparrow speak.

"It's as I thought. It's rapidly getting shorter..."

"Peeps?"

The fact that I was leaving all the mental labor to my pet made me feel a little guilty. Kind of like a man getting laid off, then doing nothing but eating and sleeping at home as he watches his wife diligently managing all the housework. Like a total failure of a husband watching his wife leave for her part-time job after she finishes cooking, cleaning, and doing the laundry, only to crack open a midday beer. I tried to conceal those feelings as I replied.

He turned back to me, sharply pointing a wing at the screen. *"Take a look at this graph."*

"O-okay."

The screen displayed a neatly constructed broken-line graph. The rows of characters had been set to a large font size, so that one could see them even if they weren't up close. Each of the lines was properly separated into its own color, making it very easy to understand. It was finally time for his superhuman—er, super-avian—presentation abilities.

You would never believe he'd only been using computers and the internet for a scant few weeks. Frankly, it was giving me an inferiority complex.

"This is the previous value, and this is the value now."

"You're right. The time periods are getting shorter."

At first, one day spent in the modern world caused one month to pass in the otherworld, but that number had been decreasing quickly. This, along with the passage of time, had been plotted on the graph in a more conspicuous way.

What I'd only had a rough handle on before based on my bodily perception was now being displayed in clear numerical values.

Plus, the graph showed the predicted gap in the future if the changes were to continue at the current rate. If it was correct, in about six months, one day here would just about equal one day there.

"Is it changing on a cycle, maybe?"

"I considered that as well. We just don't have enough data right now."

We traded opinions while looking at the screen. Incidentally, the golem looked so cute, awkwardly clicking the mouse buttons. I wondered if Peeps ever gave them names.

"I feel bad asking this, but I'd like to go back and forth a little more frequently to collect more data."

"That does seem like a good idea."

"Will you help me, then?"

"What? I'm the one who should be thanking you. You're thinking about all this stuff for me. If you need to measure the time more precisely, I can get the equipment you'll need. Just say the word. Thanks to you and Ms. Futarishizuka, our wallet is ready to burst."

"How dependable."

My distinguished sparrow was looking straight at me. His fluffy down chest was adorable. Combined with his pompous tone and history of accomplishments, he appeared extremely dignified.

I wondered if he'd get mad if I petted him with my finger. I *really* wanted to.

If there was one thing I was unhappy about in our relationship, it was the lack of that sort of intimacy. I couldn't help but be envious of all the other pet owners in the world who could always do that kind of thing with their birds.

"Peeps, I actually have a bunch of questions, if that's all right."

"What are they?"

I decided to use this chance to figure out several things about the otherworld. As a result of the matter with Mr. Joseph, I became aware of a number of things about which I had little information. I wanted to fill in those gaps before I saw him again. Once the Marc Trading Company was established, I could see competitions springing up between it and other trading companies headquartered in the Republic of Lunge. I couldn't afford to hold back its success.

"About the Republic of Lunge—"

Just then, a voice on the television suddenly rang out.

To quote: *"Whatever it is, it looks like a monster."*

To quote: *"Doesn't it look like a monster from another world?"*

The key words there were *another world.* Upon hearing it, we both naturally turned toward the TV.

There we saw something that did, indeed, resemble a monster.

As Peeps and I watched, the news broadcaster continued speaking excitedly. *"Please have a look at this video. This exclusive video appears to show the moments just before the monster that fell from the sky breathed its last."*

"*A reptilian*," murmured Peeps.

"...Huh?"

As Peeps had said, everything from the neck up on this "monster" was very lizard-like. On the other hand, its limbs were configured for bipedal locomotion, just like a human's. Scales covered its body.

We watched as the creature fell from the sky, landed flat on its face, and let out a groan. The video lasted about thirty seconds. At the end, the subject seemed to run out of energy and stopped moving entirely. Looking at its crushed limbs, I guessed it had died on impact.

The creature had slammed face-first into asphalt. According to the text on the screen, this was in a suburb relatively close to the city's center, apparently in the parking lot of a sprawling convenience store. You could clearly make out the blood spatter nearby.

"*If my eyes aren't deceiving me, that being is from the otherworld.*"

"...It seems so."

I mean, I had *heard* it. The reptilian's final words, over the TV speaker, came to me as clearly as if they were in Japanese. They included great confusion that must have stemmed from the sudden, unexpected event—as well as a cry of love for its family.

In other words, he, too, was a visitor from a world I knew.

"Can reptilians use the same magic as you, Peeps?"

"*Elites, maybe, but not in general.*"

"...I see."

I could think of several possibilities. Maybe someone had used world-crossing magic, like the spell Peeps knew, and sent the subject over as an experiment, or maybe it had been caught up in an accident. So many things could have happened.

But all of that was just in my head. We didn't have a way of proving anything.

"Peeps, if it's all right with you..."

I wanted to head to the bureau to confirm the situation—but before I could open my mouth, the phone I'd left on my desk started vibrating. The display said SECTION CHIEF AKUTSU.

"I'm sorry, Peeps. It sounds like I'm being called into work."

"*Then go. I, too, am curious about how this came to pass.*"

"I figured you would be. I'm sorry I have to head out."

Considering the timing of the call, there was no way it was unrelated.

My heart was racing just imagining what kind of conversation awaited me at the bureau.

\<The Death Game\>

(The Neighbor's POV)

Lately, I haven't had as many chances to talk to the man living next door.

It seems like his life schedule has changed. Ever since last week, he's been out of his apartment more and more. And I assume he goes to sleep as soon as he returns, because the lights are almost always off in his room. Even when I press my ear to the wall, I can't hear anything indicating he's there.

"......"

Is he busy with work?

It feels like he's staying out at night more often, too. As far as I've kept count, it used to be very rare for him to stay out overnight multiple times in one week. I've been watching his apartment from my front door for just about forever, so I figure my information is pretty accurate.

In these last several years, he's only stayed out for more than two nights in a week on three occasions.

"...Mister...," I murmur. I'm sitting in front of the door to my apartment again today, gazing at the identical door lined up beside it.

At about the same time, my stomach growls. Again, I think about how that man is the only one keeping me alive right now. At least half my body must exist thanks to him. Sometimes, I even start to feel like my own body doesn't belong to me.

When I speak to him, I feel fulfilled. That must be because half my body is overjoyed at returning to where it should be.

So today, once again, I wait in front of my apartment for him to return home.

But as I sit there, a different person appears before me.

"Huh? Wait, has your mom not gotten back yet?"

"……"

It's the man my mother has been seeing since last month.

There are other members of the opposite sex she seems to be close to, but this one has been coming over a lot recently. He is probably in his late twenties, and he is certainly not unattractive. I assume he falls into the "hot guys" category anyway, but something about him seems off to me.

His smile doesn't look natural.

To me, the man next door's smile and this man's smile are like completely different expressions.

"Well, okay. I'll just let myself in."

Apparently, he has a duplicate key.

He takes it out of his pocket, then sticks it in the doorknob above my head. Without much of a choice, I stand up and let him through. He can't open the door with me sitting there, after all.

"...Why don't you come in with me?"

"I'm fine, thanks."

He pulls open the door and takes half a step into the apartment when he asks the question. He turns back to me, still standing to the side, and stares into my eyes.

He's wearing a suit—maybe because he's just come from the office. A bag hangs from his hand.

"Isn't it cold out? Come inside and warm up."

"I'm fine. I'm used to it."

I won't be able to see the man next door when he gets home unless I'm outside. It doesn't feel right to go so far as to ring his doorbell in order to beg from him, so I'd held back from doing so. I'd drawn a sort of line there, not to be crossed.

I feel like if I was to do that, I'd stop being myself.

"Just come in already, dammit!"

"Ugh…!"

Just then, the man in the doorway's attitude takes a sudden turn for the worse. With an angry shout, he grabs my arm and pulls. His grip is so strong on my wrist that it hurts.

From his forceful behavior, I have a good idea of what he's thinking—I'd seen him glancing at my chest and thighs before. He's probably decided to catch me while my mom isn't home and take the next step. Maybe that's why he'd gotten a duplicate key from her.

No, I shouldn't flatter myself.

"Please, stop!"

"Just get in here!"

"Ugh…"

His build is just as formidable as his good looks. He probably works out on a regular basis. I try my best to struggle, but he pulls me inside the apartment before I can even cry out. I swing my leg up to try nailing him in the crotch, but he brings his knees together to stop me.

Then he pushes me down onto the floor of the hallway and straddles me.

He pins my arms and legs down.

Only a little girl, I can do very few things to resist at this point.

"I suggest you pipe down unless you want to get hurt."

"……"

He glares down at me, his face so close our noses almost touch. His eyes are bloodshot—I don't think I've ever seen eyes like that before. You could see all the individual blood vessels very clearly.

It doesn't seem like I'll be able to break free of the arms pinning my wrists or the shins pinning my thighs.

"What do you think I was fucking that old hag for? Figure it out."

"…Old hag?"

"Yeah, you heard me. What a loose pussy—and the *smell*. Worst bitch I've ever had."

I almost smile at how funny it is to hear someone treating my mother like an old hag. It seems like he'd used her to get to me. But I quickly grow angry when I realize my own chastity is in danger.

I had intended to let the man next door be my first.

He would lose himself in his excitement and forcefully violate me.

That's what I wanted.

I couldn't give myself to this bastard.

"You, on the other hand—now *you're* a cute little thing."

The man's tongue slides over my cheek. I feel goose bumps sprouting up all over my body. Out of reflex, I jerk my head, ramming it into him.

"Agh! ...You bitch!"

"Ngh..."

A moment later, the man bites my nose.

Seeing such a beastlike act up close makes me realize that no matter how much we try to pretend otherwise, humans are just animals, like dogs or cats. I also learn that being bitten in the nose makes you feel like someone just hit you in the head with a hammer.

I immediately squeeze my eyes shut, seeing stars.

"Just calm the fuck down. It'll be over soon."

The man's hand reaches for my lower abdomen.

His breathing is heavy, probably due to his state of excitement, and his tone is gleeful. His breath reeks of cigarettes, incredibly unpleasant as it strikes me in the face over and over. I can't help but scowl. I turn my head away, trying to get away from the stench.

Why couldn't it have been the man next door?

It would have been amazing, if it had been him.

To me, that is the ideal turn of events—I've been hoping for it every day.

Just then, I hear it.

"Do you want me to save you?"

Suddenly, I hear a voice.

I then lift my head reflexively.

And when I do, I see a boy.

He is standing behind the man straddling me as I am lying faceup on my apartment floor, and he is watching me closely. His feet would have been on the entrance tiles inside the closed front door.

When I turned my face away just a moment ago, there had been no one there.

He seems a little younger than I am—somewhere between elementary school and middle school. He is Caucasian, with striking golden eyes and light-brown hair in a bob cut. A pitch-black cape with epaulets sits across his shoulders. On his head is a king's crown of the same color.

He is dressed like someone straight out of a fairy tale—someone from the royal family or the nobility.

And he is asking me a question as I am lying there on the floor.

"Do you want me to save you?"

Apparently, the rapist couldn't hear the boy's voice. He is frantically trying to get his member out of his pants.

Only a few seconds remain before he'll violate me.

At first, I think I'm seeing things—that the horrible situation is creating images in my head.

But he is definitely there.

A boy wearing a crown and a cape.

Like some kind of ludicrous painting.

Maybe that is why I decide there's no harm in trying.

I look him in the eye and give him my honest answer.

"Please save me."

"Will you hear my request in exchange?"

What's the request? I have my doubts. But I don't have any time to think about it.

"...Yes."

"In that case, allow me," the boy responds with a pleasant smile.

Smoothly, he takes a step forward—and before I know it, his hand is reaching for the man pinning me down. His small fingers touch the man's shoulder. A moment later, the man's hands gripping my wrists suddenly go limp.

Then, with a thud, he collapses on top of me.

Out of reflex, I push his head away and find that his body moves without resistance.

"......"

I put a hand to his neck to check his pulse. I can feel it beating away with a regular rhythm.

"It's okay. He's not dead or anything. And anyway, if I killed a human in the Physical Realm, well, I'd be breaking a very important rule. I just knocked him out for a bit. You should hurry and gather yourself."

Maybe it's best not to assume this boy is as young as he looks. But whoever heard of something so ridiculous?

I change my mind when I see that his feet are hovering slightly above the floor.

"Who are you?"

"Isn't there something you'd like to say to me first?"

"...Thank you. You really saved me there."

"Yep! I love honest people like you." The boy crosses his arms, nodding several times.

At a glance, he just looks like a little kid. But the way he'd knocked out a grown man by simply tapping him makes him appear to be significantly more powerful. Not to mention how his body is still floating in midair.

"By the way, are you all right? Did he do anything to you?"

"No, he didn't get that far."

"Phew. That's good to hear."

I crawl out from underneath the man and stagger to my feet.

Once I'm standing next to the boy, I realize he's several centimeters shorter than I am. Now that I look at him again, I see that his hair is a little long for a boy's—and glossier. Plus, his eyes are big and round. All of that, combined with his lack of developed secondary sexual characteristics, make him seem rather androgynous.

"Anyway, you said something about a request..."

"Your adaptability surprises me. I didn't expect you to move the conversation along so quickly."

"Probably because I don't really care much about what's going on in the world."

"Ah. That's a fresh perspective for me."

My honest answer is met with a nod of admiration. The boy is very dramatic about everything he does. I wonder if everyone from overseas is like this.

"I'd like you to help me with something."

"...What exactly do you want me to do?"

"Well, aren't you in a hurry."

"......"

What? Am I going too fast for him? I really don't think I am.

But then I realize that the only person I talk to with any kind of regularity is the man next door. Not only do I have zero friends at school, I avoid speaking with teachers as much as possible. I talk to my mother even less.

"What's wrong? You went quiet on me."

"Nothing, I was just thinking maybe I'd talk a little more slowly from now on."

"Oh, that? Did you mean to accommodate me?"

"It wasn't about you. I just hadn't realized I was doing it."

My attention naturally drifts to the wall separating this apartment from the next. A few dozen centimeters past the kitchen is where he lives.

Yes, that's right. I have to finish this conversation and get back to the front door. His routine is so erratic lately, he always gets home at a different time. I've noticed a few times that he's come back while I was at school, so I want to be outside waiting as often as possible.

"Hmm? What's wrong?"

He must have seen my eyes shift, because he also looks over at the wall.

I continue talking to try throwing him off.

"Who are you, and what am I going to be doing?"

"I'm a demon. And from now on, you will be fighting angelic Disciples in my stead."

"......"

His answer is even crazier than I'd expected.

*

(The Neighbor's POV)

The boy proceeds to give me the details as we stand in my apartment hallway next to the fallen rapist.

Apparently, there are such things as angels and demons in this world.

They've been fighting each other in a conflict that has gone on for a very, very long time. However, each side is quite strong, and if they are all to battle it out personally in a fair fight, the world would likely be destroyed. So instead, they make use of humans to fight a proxy war.

His request is for me to participate as a proxy for the demons' side.

It is a questionable story, to say the least.

Had he not rescued me from danger, I never would have believed him. The ridiculousness of his story, however, makes me think back on a few things—like what he's done to the man still passed out on the floor, for example.

"This guy isn't with you, is he?"

"What makes you think that?"

"Hypothetically, if you knew you wanted to reach out to me... That would be pretty effective, wouldn't it? As you can see, I am actually starting to believe this ridiculous story about angels and demons, even though I've never seen one before in my life."

"*Ah, I see. You seem pretty clever for your age.*"

"*......*"

"*Oh, don't glare at me like that. It's true that I've been thinking of talking to you for a while. But the only reason you were attacked was because of that man's sexual urges. I played no part in it. It was a coincidence, and I only took advantage of it.*"

"Really?"

"*And if I were to give you a piece of advice, it would be... Yes, you should refrain from asking any more questions you have no way of independently verifying. Especially if you can't trust someone. You should break a problem down into things you* can *verify, then try to determine the overall credibility.*"

"...I agree with you there."

I didn't expect to get a patronizing lecture from someone I met less than an hour ago. It annoys me a little, mostly because the boy looks younger than I am. But I feel like what he is saying is correct.

He also said, before, that he likes honest people. Maybe he is just the sort who likes to lecture and explain.

In that case, I want to learn as much as I can from him.

"*Any other questions?*"

"I understand you're fighting a proxy war. But I don't understand what, exactly, you want me to do. As you can see, I'm a child. Any adult would be able to pin me to the ground," I say, my eyes moving to the man on the floor. My mom's boyfriend is still unconscious.

"*Okay, then I'll get into the nitty-gritty.*"

With a dramatic, self-important *ahem*, the boy begins to speak. The act suits his majestic stature oddly well.

"*The Disciples already participating refer to the mechanism of the proxy war as a 'death game.' It is my understanding that most humans these days have a good idea what that entails, but what about you?*"

This is another dangerous-sounding term. But what did I expect?

"I don't like the sound of that."

"*Yes, it seems the angels aren't very happy with it. Demons are generally quite accepting, however. What about you? I would appreciate it if you could read between the lines a little here.*"

"I think I know what you're trying to say."

"*Then I'll continue. We have our proxies house part of an angel's or a demon's spirit—a Division—within their body in order to act as their Disciple. You'll then use the spirit's power to do battle in a realm isolated from this world. The only real rule is that it continues until one camp or the other has zero Disciples remaining.*"

"Since you chose a child like me, does that mean you've seen cases where fights between angels and demons go on for several years—or even several decades? Or was it simply because you believe children are easier to control?"

"*Oh! You're right on both counts, actually. Pretty good!*"

"......"

The boy speaks very casually, but it seems that when he said *death game*, he really meant *death*. Whatever the direct cause, participants would be made to fight until they died.

And as of right now, there doesn't appear to be any benefit to being a Disciple—one of their proxies, that is. Are they forcing society's weaklings—like me—to do their bidding? If so, then how do they maintain the motivation of the people actually doing the fighting?

"*You don't seem satisfied with that.*"

"I don't, do I?"

"*No, you don't!*" The boy nods, a kindhearted grin on his face.

I start to feel like he's indirectly making fun of me. No, it's not just my imagination—I bet that's exactly what he's doing.

"*I can guess what you're thinking.*"

"Then please, explain."

"*Wow. I like you. You take what I say and learn from it.*"

The boy continues, his smile widening, though I can't guess what is making him so happy. I want him to hurry it up. I have to get this conversation over with so I can wait for my neighbor at the front door.

"*We make one promise to the proxies, our Disciples, before they participate in the death game. Should you kill an enemy Disciple as part of the proxy war, we will grant any one wish you have.*"

"Any one wish? That sounds pretty vague."

"*Oh, but it's quite significant, I assure you. Depending on the situation, you may even receive the help of angels or demons on your side. In the past, people have even brought corpses back to life—though, those instances tend to be reserved for Disciples whose performance is exceptional."*

"In other words, it all depends on how well you negotiate?"

"What? You're not surprised? People have come back from the dead."

"Not really."

Bringing someone back from the dead won't benefit me at all. More importantly, at the moment, I just want to get back to my front door.

"Huh. Well, anything goes, so give it some thought. It all depends on how well you negotiate."

"All right."

"About the game itself—well, maybe it's best if you learned by doing. Fortunately, your demon has quite a high rank, so you won't lose so easily. I believe humans would call it on-the-job training."

"......"

I've heard that term before from the man next door. I remember he didn't sound very happy about it.

"The previous death game began about a century ago, according to your human calendar, and took almost thirty years before it was finished. The quicker ones, however, wrap up in just two or three. It all depends on how talented the participants are."

"Thirty years..."

I can't begin to imagine what I'll be like at forty. I had assumed I'd die around twenty anyway. And after thirty years, the man next door would be all wrinkly. The next few years are going to be such an important, beautiful time for us.

"Why don't we move along to the contract?"

"Do you need my stamp or something?"

"Well, since you've already promised your assistance, I'll simply be unloading a part of my spirit into you. You may feel a bit of a physical shock, but please bear with it."

"Ugh..."

It happens as soon as the last words escape the boy's mouth. A terrible pain shoots through my entire body, from the crown of my head to the tips of my toes.

"Nghhhh...!"

It hurts so bad my eyes feel like they'll pop out. I grit my teeth and desperately try to hold on.

The walls in this apartment are thin and made of wood. If my neighbor gets home while I am talking to this boy, he'll hear my screaming. I want to avoid that, if nothing else, so I bite down on my lip as hard as I can.

Blood rushes into my mouth, its taste mocking my growling, empty stomach.

I get the feeling something bright and glittery is at my feet, but I can't concentrate enough to check.

After about ten seconds, the pain subsides.

"You're a trouper, you know that? Even I've never seen a Disciple who didn't cry out during a Descension."

"…I wish…you would have at least told me when you were going to do it."

"Sorry about that. But isn't it usually worse if you tense up?"

"……"

Belatedly, I begin to feel like the title of demon really fits this boy. He's been smiling the entire time—and behind his expression, I can sense a coldness, like he doesn't care about humans at all.

I only have a moment to be surprised about the pain. Almost instantly, our surroundings shift.

There is complete silence.

The noise of automobile engines drifting in from outside, the sound of the bathroom fan running—all the sounds I've been hearing up until now are simply gone, like someone has muted the volume on a stereo system. It is so startling I think maybe I've lost my hearing.

"Oh-ho. Looks like we've got some prey already."

"What is this?"

"It's the isolated space that appears whenever two Disciples get within a certain range of each other. What happens within this space will be negated as soon as you leave it. The only exception being the presence of the Disciples themselves, I suppose. The power to create and maintain these spaces comes from the demon or angel themselves."

"…I see."

This seems to be like a signal for the start of the game. Very easy to understand. With this, other than when I'm sleeping, I'd never be too late to react.

Right. So what about when I'm sleeping? I'll have to ask the boy about it later.

"Also, you look a little...not great at the moment, so let me fix you up."

"……"

With a smooth motion, the boy stretches out his arm toward me.

I tense out of reflex. As I do, the pain in my nose and lips recedes.

"How do you feel?"

"…Thank you."

I haven't checked myself in a mirror, so I don't know what my injuries look like. Still, the boy's action has made the stinging pain I'd felt disappear. I feel my few remaining doubts about all this wash away.

It doesn't look like he's cleaned up the mess, however. I lightly touch my lip and feel a slimy sensation. Redness stuck to my fingertip. Combined with my nose wound, I probably look pretty terrible at the moment.

"It's your first-ever battle. Why don't you wipe yourself off a bit before we go?"

"Could I maybe change my clothes, too?"

"I wouldn't mind. Why, do you not like the clothes you're currently wearing?"

"They're my best clothes, so I don't want them to get dirty or torn."

"Oh, no need to worry about that. Like I explained before, any physical losses you suffer will disappear once you leave this space, save for wounds inflicted on your soul. I'll be glad to go into more detail once your on-the-job training is finished."

"…All right."

"Now then, why don't we head off to the game?"

Following the boy's instructions, I leave the apartment.

I pray that the man next door won't come home while I'm out.

✳

(The Neighbor's POV)

We travel by foot from the apartment to our destination. The distance between Disciples required to produce the isolated space, as well as the size of the space created, seems to depend on the strength of the angel or demon attached to the Disciple. But no matter how powerful the

Division of any two Disciples is, it would never be more than a few kilometers at most.

I walk along, guided by the boy, as he explains all this to me.

There are no people in this soundless world. I am grateful, given how bad I am with crowds. It is refreshing to see places normally packed with people suddenly so empty.

Not long after we start walking, I begin to get the feeling I know where we are headed, though I'm not sure why. I intuitively sense the presence of the other person who has helped create this space—the other Disciple. It is kind of like hearing the ringing of a distant bell and judging the source of the sound.

"Can they tell where we are just like we can tell where they are?"

"We're not particularly trying to hide, so yes, they've probably located us."

Apparently, it is possible to purposely conceal yourself. Which also means you have the option of purposely revealing yourself.

I feel like I now understand why the current Disciples refer to this proxy war between angels and demons as a game. Strategizing and trickery probably have a significant impact on who wins and who loses.

The boy walking beside me seems very nonchalant about the whole thing.

"Are you really strong for a demon?"

"As I see it, we'll have an easy time against this foe, to put it conservatively."

"...I see."

The demon is brimming with confidence.

Has he already scouted out the opponent? I'd be extremely grateful if so, considering my life is currently in his hands. But if he is just spouting nonsense, I won't be able to rely on him at all. The fact that I can't gauge his words or actions makes me even more anxious.

"Once you see the enemy, say this to me: 'Reveal thyself!'"

"Will something happen?"

"They'll probably be so surprised they'll run away."

"Can I adjust...whatever it is we're using to sense each other?"

"You're really quick on the uptake, even though you're so young. I knew I chose the right Disciple."

By this time, I know it is very likely he's done his research in advance.

If that is true, as long as I act calmly here, I should be fine. Based on what he has explained so far, at the very least, our interests align.

Actually, it is more like he is getting me involved in *his* interests without giving me much choice in the matter.

"Oh, there they are!"

We are now in the middle of a shopping mall in the local shopping district. Two people are standing right in the center of it. They are the only people I've encountered in this world without sound, aside from the boy.

He comes to a stop ten or so meters away. I follow suit.

"Wait, a middle school kid? Seriously?" says one of the two upon seeing us.

The speaker has probably noticed my sailor uniform from school. If they were from around here, they'd know immediately what school I went to. Even if they didn't, a little research would do the trick.

Has the boy taken that into consideration?

The speaker is a man who looks to be around twenty years old and is wearing jeans and a collared shirt with a jacket. He's of average height and build, with short black hair—a typical university student. If there's anything about him that stands out, it's that he has something of a baby face.

Standing next to him stands a woman who also appears to be in her twenties. She is Caucasian—her pure-white skin and waist-length blond hair are striking. A pair of wings extend out of her back. She's about the same height as the man next to her.

The latter has to be the angel.

"Come on, give me the order," the boy says, without so much as greeting the others.

"Oh. Right."

I don't want them to act first and steal the advantage, so I follow his instructions.

"Reveal thyself."

"You got it! Just leave it to me!"

His energetic reply echoes through the shopping mall.

A moment later, his body transforms.

It collapses, almost like a water balloon popping. His loose entrails slop onto the ground. Soon, however, they begin to writhe and squirm.

I'm standing right beside them and have a hard time staying calm. I quickly back up a few paces.

"That's mean! I wish you wouldn't look so obviously disgusted."

"...Are you...all right?"

Before my eyes, the fleshy lump inflates.

It starts at about the size of a filled garbage bag, and in the blink of an eye, it has grown even larger, surpassing my height, swelling out to the size of a midsize car. The bloody flesh swallows up the clothing, crown, and cape the boy had been wearing.

The way it's covered in viscous fluid is incredibly gross. At the very least, I didn't pick up any smell.

That said, I can't handle the spatter of flesh and blood that hits my sailor uniform.

"Ugh... Masayuki, we're getting out of here!"

"Huh?! But we—"

"That's Abaddon. We don't stand a chance against him right now."

Just as he'd been bragging earlier, the demon boy seems to be pretty famous among angels. The expression of the woman I assumed to be an angel changes completely when she sees the fleshy lump he's become. Even from afar, I can tell she's panicked.

"Oh, you're not getting away."

By some strange logic, the hunk of flesh soars into the air.

It shoots up several meters all at once, then suddenly expands as if to cover the space above the two of them, like a net thrown to catch fish. But what expanded is not a net—it's a grotesque mass of meat—horrific, to say the least.

It must be unendurable for the people beneath it.

"Ugh..."

"Virtue?!"

The angel flies into the sky, holding the man in her arms, just barely avoiding the incoming fleshy mass.

The demon boy hits the ground, then shrivels back into his original form, the same as before. His shirt and pants, and even his crown and cape, are all intact. Perhaps he has preserved them inside the lump?

No, I should stop thinking about that right now.

It's not even clear whether matter is being conserved here.

"Aw. Too bad."

"What—?"

The boy's spiteful voice echoes around us.

Quick as lightning, the mass of flesh is behind the angel.

In no time at all, it puffs up, then engulfs the two as they fly. It seems he's gotten a piece of himself stuck to her wing. He'd let them flee, then caught them again—very unfair.

The pair is swallowed whole by the floating lump of meat.

A moment later, I hear cracking and crunching noises. Once I hear screams joining the other sounds, the words *death game* finally seem real to me. One wrong step, and I might have met a similar fate.

"What do you think? Went just like I said, right?"

"Why do I need to be with you? I didn't do anything."

"As a rule, we can't ignore our proxy's instructions and act on our own."

"I don't remember giving instructions."

"When we encountered the angel, you requested that I reveal myself. But I couldn't just stand around doing nothing, could I? We do have that much freedom, you understand. Otherwise, you'd have to give an order for every little thing."

"What I don't understand is what these 'instructions' are supposed to be."

"For example, I might want to walk straight, but if you tell me to walk right, my body will walk right. Does that make sense? I want you to be careful, because any casual instruction you give me could very literally affect my course of action."

Now that he's explained things, I finally understand our relationship.

I now know what he means by a "proxy war." The Divisions—portions of an angel's or a demon's spirit—are incredible weapons their Disciples can freely use. The limitations of each Disciple also have a considerable effect.

Which brings me to one fundamental question.

"Why me?"

"Hmm?"

"There are plenty of other adolescent girls to choose from, aren't there?"

"Oh, you want to know? Do you?"

"If it's better I not know, then don't tell me."

"You're really straightforward, aren't you? I appreciate that. Top of your generation, even, I'd say. But deep down, you hate the world. You

know hunger. And now you have a deeply warped passion lurking in your breast, too."

How much does this boy know about me? No doubt he'd seen me talking to the man next door. But would he know this much, even if he had?

"Demons love that kind of stuff. Well, more specifically, I like that kind of stuff."

"Have you been watching me?"

"The short answer is—yeah, pretty much."

"So you're not going to hide it."

"What's the point? I'm fairly honest for a demon, you know. I wouldn't lie about stupid stuff like that to a partner I might be with for several years—or several decades, even."

"......"

As we trade words, the mass of flesh hangs in the air next to us. *How surreal,* I think. Eventually, as the awful noises and screams from within subside, it darts back toward the boy. It struck his body with a sticky splashing sound before; like a clay model, it squirms back inside him.

Not a moment later, sound returns to the world.

All of a sudden, the empty shopping mall is swarming with pedestrians, as if they'd emerged out of thin air. The loud clamor of the crowds layers on top of the sound of their footfalls, reverberating all around us.

"When all Disciples of one camp, either angels or demons, are destroyed, or if they get a certain distance away, the isolated space collapses, like it did just now, and the world goes right back to normal. My bodily fluids stuck to your clothes have all disappeared, as you can see— you're nice and clean now."

"...I am," I say, looking down at myself. I can't see a single spot on me. "What happened to the man and the angel?"

"The angel's Division was obliterated, but she took no damage since her main body is in the Celestial Plane. As for the man—you can usually find their corpses lying around once the isolated space comes undone. Oh, but I ate him this time. I don't see him anywhere."

The boy glances around as he speaks. I follow suit, taking in our surroundings, but can't spot anything particularly noteworthy. All the people in the mall are walking around the same as always. Obviously,

I don't see any corpses. If one had been found, there would surely have been a few screams.

"*The extent to which the circumstances in the isolated space are reflected on the body depends on a few factors.*"

"...Reflected?"

"*In certain situations or as a result of certain abilities, a corpse's wounds might be reflected in the normal world in some detail. But in other cases, it will look more like a mysterious, sudden death where the soul leaves their body and nothing else. This time, it looks like there won't even be a corpse, since the entire body, and every drop of blood, was lost.*"

"I see."

The bizarre corpse I'd witnessed on my way back from school a few days ago—could that have been from this angels-versus-demons proxy war? I feel there's little doubt, given how the remains had suddenly appeared right before my eyes.

So that is what happens to those who lose this "death game" or whatever and get tossed out of the isolated space.

"*Anyway, I'm sure you have a bunch of questions, but we should head back first.*"

"All right." I nod to the boy, turning back toward the apartment.

If I don't get back soon, I think, *I might miss the man next door getting home.*

✳

(The Neighbor's POV)

It's true what they say—when it rains, it pours.

Once the boy and I get back to my apartment, my mother is waiting for us, and she's angry. Next to her I see the rapist, who has regained consciousness. My mother, standing outside the front door, grabs my arm and pulls me into the living room without giving me a chance to take off my shoes.

What she has to say is simple: The bruise on the man's forehead was an act of violence, perpetrated by me for no reason. My mother is infatuated with this younger man she'd literally just met. She had *already* hated me, her daughter—and now she's outright furious, her hate reaching even deeper than before.

"Just who the hell do you think has been keeping you alive all this time?!" she screams hysterically, slapping me in the face.

I almost say "the man living next door." That's what I really think. I stumble, but I dig in my heels and manage to keep myself from falling. Come to think of it, she'd sent me to the floor many a time when I was in elementary school.

"Hey, now, your daughter's probably sorry, so let's just leave it at that, all right? I really don't mind very much. Middle school is when kids enter the rebellious phase, you know? All kids her age want to lash out at adults."

Seeing this back-and-forth between mother and daughter, the man pipes up.

My mother's voice gets even louder. "She *hurt* you!"

"And I'm sure she's sorry. Aren't you?" the man asks, giving me a friendly smile. He is probably trying to win over my mother and lower my resistance at the same time. I wonder what he thinks about his sudden bout of unconsciousness.

"*Your mother really doesn't have an eye for people, huh?*" says the boy from right next to me, sounding amazed. Apparently, the two of them can't see him. Despite a boy they'd never met before coming straight in with his shoes on, neither my mother nor the man seem to react at all. It appears they can't hear him, either. Though, he had explained to me that he could make himself visible or audible if necessary.

"Mom, this man tried to rape me."

I know it's pointless, but I still try to appeal to my mother.

Out of the corner of my eye, I see the man's eyebrow twitch.

"What?! You're being ridiculous; you know that? Why are you constantly lying and making excuses?! If you don't get your act together, you'll be out on the street, you miserable failure!"

She whacks me in the cheek a second time.

And this time, I fall.

Now I'm kneeling on the floor.

"*Actually, there's something I still haven't told you.*"

"……"

The boy looks down at me and begins to speak.

"*By harboring the Division of a demon or angel, Disciples are able to use a portion of their power. It's a paltry strength, not even one-tenth of the power I can wield while in an isolated space. But it's more than enough to deal with regular people. This is another one of the rewards we grant our followers."*

Does he mean I can transform into that mass of flesh, too? Unlike isolated spaces, anything that happens here won't be reverted. Just thinking about having to clean all the flesh and blood out of the living room and off my clothes makes me a little dizzy. I have no intention of using such a power.

"Oh, and my original form has nothing to do with it. Basically, you become able to use...magic, as you call it. I healed your injuries and stuff, remember? Also, while demons and angels can't kill people outside of isolated spaces, Disciples aren't bound by the same rules."

It seems my apprehensions are unfounded. And now, like the vulgar, greedy person I am, I feel my curiosity grow.

"So what do you say?"

This must be what people mean when they talk about a demon on your shoulder.

But I have a life I need to protect, and that life is here.

When it comes down to it, I haven't even been in middle school a whole year yet. I need a guardian, even if it has to be someone like my mother. I won't be able to take back what I've done—and it could end with me getting myself locked away somewhere.

"If I do that, I won't be able to live next to *him* anymore."

"Man, I really like that about you!"

I don't know what he is so happy about, but his smile widens. How much does he know about my relationship with my neighbor? It's my treasure, and it's supposed to belong to us alone.

"...So what?"

"Since I like you so much, I'll tell you."

The boy's hand touches my shoulder.

Come to think of it, when he'd first spoken to me, he'd touched the rapist's shoulder in exactly the same way and caused him to lose consciousness. My sudden recollection and my guess as to what would happen next changes into certainty when I hear his next words.

"Try giving her a little tap."

"And what do *you* think you're mumbling about?! You're a creep! Ah, I should never have given birth to you at all! It's all your fault! When you were born, my life went straight down the gutter!"

My mother kicks out at me as I sit on the floor.

I stick the palm of my hand out toward the front of her leg.

A dull, thudding impact hits my wrist. Her leg had been traveling pretty fast, but since I'd been able to take the hit with my core, it didn't injure me. Her face, on the other hand, fills with pain.

Just then, it happens.

I feel something strange inside my body, flowing from the hand on my mother's leg up to my shoulder, where the boy was touching me. Like I'm getting a drip of something warm in my veins—I'd never felt a pulse like this before. It isn't quite pain, and it isn't quite discomfort.

A moment later, my mother sways and falls to the living room floor. Then she stops moving altogether.

It looks exactly the same as what the boy had done to the man earlier.

"What do you think? Have a good feel for it now?"

"...Yes."

"Then try it yourself this time."

I nod obediently, and the boy's gaze shifts—to the man who had just seen my mother collapse and is beginning to freak out. I know immediately what the boy is implying. His proposition doesn't even feel real. But considering all the things that have happened, I can't imagine he's putting on an act.

"All right."

I stand up, then reach for the man with my arm. As he bends down next to my mother, my fingers touch his head.

And then, the pulsation I'd felt moments ago comes back to me. The same feeling... That feeling of something flowing through my body. Something warm travels through my fingers, from the man's forehead and into me.

Honestly, it doesn't feel very good.

He is, after all, someone who had tried to rape me.

If it had been the man next door, it probably would have felt amazing...

"Take too much, and he'll die."

"Urgh..."

At the boy's warning, I immediately remove my fingers from the man's head. I'd been touching him for a few seconds, but the effect is striking. Just like my mother, the man collapses on the spot. They had both gone limp, one lying over the other. I take their arms to check for a pulse and get a steady beating rhythm from both of them. The strength and speed of the pulse I feel through their skin isn't much different from my own. It seems they've only passed out.

"Can you use this in such a way that it won't knock them out?"

"*If you're good at controlling it, sure.*"

"I see."

Apparently, this power is for weakening an opponent you touch, knocking them out, or killing them. I wonder what else it can be used for.

Oh, right. It can heal wounds, can't it?

"If you can do this, I don't see why you'd need to turn into a lump of flesh."

"*That was more like... Well, my self-introduction.*"

"You were introducing yourself?"

"*I wouldn't want to reveal that form suddenly in a desperate situation only to shock my partner out of her wits. Even a demon like me knows there's a time and a place. My appearance is nice and tidy at the moment, don't you think?*"

"Then where did you get that boy's body?"

"*This was my form before I fell from grace. It's pretty cool, don't you think?*"

"...I see."

Just how much evil has he done to go from that into a horrifying lump of flesh? Still, he looks exactly like how I might imagine a fallen angel.

At the same time, it gets me thinking. From what I now know, not everything about my meeting with this boy has been bad. Considering my current situation, it seems like the benefits outweigh the drawbacks. The power I've received as his is extremely useful.

"Can I ask you something?"

"*What is it?*"

"You mentioned I could get a reward for defeating an enemy Disciple."

According to his explanation earlier, if I defeat an enemy Disciple, I can have a variety of wishes granted, though it would depend on the strength of my achievements. The wish could even be something beyond human understanding. If that's true, then maybe I'll finally be able to realize my fondest wish.

"*That's true. What do you want to know about it?*"

"Does the incident at the shopping mall qualify?"

That's right—I could make my relationship with the man next door eternal. A world just for us, where we would remain beautiful and never grow old.

"Oh! That's the face of someone up to no good."

"That's not true."

"It's fine! I'll throw in a freebie. What would you like as a reward for your first battle?"

"Thank you. As a reward for my first battle, I wish for…"

I decide, in my heart of hearts, to give this "death game" or whatever my best shot.

Afterword

I'd like to thank everyone who purchased *Sasaki and Peeps*. I'd also like to apologize to those who have been waiting for so long for the web novel's continuation.

Well then, I'll get right down to it. Once again, Kantoku's illustrations in this volume are simply amazing. One look at the first volume's cover was enough to steal my heart—and the second cover has such a fantastical charm. I haven't been able to forget it since I first laid eyes on it. Kantoku, I know how busy you are, so thank you for creating so many beautiful illustrations. I am so obliged to you for all your help.

This work is also being serialized in comic form by *Shounen Ace Plus*, with artwork by Pureji Osho. His manga will give you an even more powerful sense of the wide world of the story—one that would have been impossible to portray with the original novels alone. Thank you from the bottom of my heart for such a wonderful adaptation.

I can't begin to express my thanks to everyone in the MF Bunko J's editing department, my editor O first and foremost, for doing the lion's share of the work getting this story published in print. I sincerely thank the sales team, the proofreaders, the designers, bookstores around the country, digital booksellers, and all the others who helped, for their incredible effort.

Please look forward to more *Sasaki and Peeps*, the new book series from Kakuyomu brought to you by MF Bunko J.

(Buncololi)

Sasaki and Peeps

3

Psychic Battles, Magical Girls, and

Death Games Are No Match

for Otherworldly Fantasy

~Or So I Thought, but Now Things

Are Taking a Turn for the Worse~

Buncololi

Illustration by Kantoku

Entirely new material!

Comic adaptation currently in serialization!!!

Sasaki and Peeps 2

*This material was originally included below the dust jacket in the Japanese version

While I Was Dominating Modern Psychic Battles with Spells from Another World, a Magical Girl Picked a Fight with Me

~You Mean I Have to Participate in a Death Game, Too?~

Buncololi   Illustration by **Kantoku**

Peeps, it looks like our story was able to get a second volume.

The sales are what's important. How are those doing?

Apparently, the author's previous works sold significantly more e-books than print copies.

Previous works? Can you be more specific regarding the numbers?

The editor tells me that for e-books at least, the sales are about the same as titles that have famous anime adaptations.

Well then, what about this work?

The digital copies seem to be selling very well, just like the previous works.

I wonder why that is.

Apparently, even the editing department doesn't know.

That is quite mysterious indeed…

All of us involved in the production of this book would like to thank everyone who purchased and read it, from the bottom of our hearts

HAVE YOU BEEN TURNED ON TO LIGHT NOVELS YET?

86—EIGHTY-SIX, VOL. 1–10

In truth, there is no such thing as a bloodless war. Beyond the fortified walls protecting the eighty-five Republic Sectors lies the "nonexistent" Eighty-Sixth Sector. The young men and women of this forsaken land are branded the Eighty-Six and, stripped of their humanity, pilot "unmanned" weapons into battle...

Manga adaptation available now!

WOLF & PARCHMENT, VOL. 1–6

The young man Col dreams of one day joining the holy clergy and departs on a journey from the bathhouse, Spice and Wolf. Winfiel Kingdom's prince has invited him to help correct the sins of the Church. But as his travels begin, Col discovers in his luggage a young girl with a wolf's ears and tail named Myuri who stowed away for the ride!

Manga adaptation available now!

SOLO LEVELING, VOL. 1–5

E-rank hunter Jinwoo Sung has no money, no talent, and no prospects to speak of—and apparently, no luck, either! When he enters a hidden double dungeon one fateful day, he's abandoned by his party and left to die at the hands of some of the most horrific monsters he's ever encountered.

Comic adaptation available now!

Can I talk a bit about the title?

 Is there some sort of story behind it?

 Apparently, they went through over twenty titles before arriving at this one.

 Oh my! It was that difficult to decide?

 The author is fond of short titles, but these days, long titles are more in vogue.

 I suppose one cannot ignore current trends. Books are products, after all.

 Exactly. And that's why they spent more than a year thinking it over.

 In that sense, the current title is truly choice—a mixture of both short and long.

 The one who proposed it was our series editor O. Thank you so much for your guidance. The author was really struggling.